MOONSTONE CONSPIRACY

A sequel to Moonstone Obsession

BY

ELIZABETH ELLEN CARTER

MOONSTONE CONSPIRACY
Elizabeth Ellen Carter
Copyright © 2018 Elizabeth Ellen Carter
All rights reserved.

First published 2015 by Etopia Press
Second publication 2018 by Business Communications Management
bcm-online.com.au

ISBN: 978-0-9874417-8-2

Printing/manufacturing information for this book may be found on the last page

Second Printing 2018
Cover Design by Dar Albert
Design for Print by
Business Communications Management bcm-online.com.au

VC:IS1906

Acknowledgements

A big thanks to my amazing husband who became
Abigail's champion before Daniel came along.
Without him, there would have been no happily ever after for her.

Also to the Baroness Orczy, whose timeless classic, The Scarlet
Pimpernel, continues to engage and inspire.

Titles by
Elizabeth Ellen Carter

The Moonstone Romances
Moonstone Obsession
Moonstone Conspiracy
Moonstone Promise

Warrior's Surrender

Dark Heart

Heart of the Corsairs Trilogy
Captive of the Corsairs
Revenge of the Corsairs
Shadow of the Corsairs

The King's Rogues Series
Live and Let Spy
Spyfall
Spy Another Day
Father's Day

Nocturne

The Thief of Hearts

The deWolfe of Wharf Street

The Promise of the Bells

Learn more at eecarter.com
or search 'Elizabeth Ellen Carter' on
Amazon

DEDICATION

To anyone who ever needed a second chance, or even a third one.

TABLE OF CONTENTS

PART TWO
TO FRANCE

* * *

PROLOGUE

July 24, 1790
The Pitt Family Masquerade Ball
Boconnoc House, Cornwall

One by one, the cards of ambition and hope, so carefully laid one on top of the other, fell in a graceless heap and Lady Abigail Houghall's future fell with them.

She had spent the evening of the masquerade ball dressed as a queen—Cleopatra, Queen of the Egyptians—waiting for the man she wanted above all others to announce their engagement. How dare he reject her now, after she had worked so hard to create a mutually profitable future for the both of them?

Marshalling the growing rage and seeking to arrest the falling sensation inside her, Abigail reached out and drew her exquisitely manicured finger nails lightly beneath his handsome chin, cupping it and forcing him to look at her.

Disinterest and, worse still, pity colored the rich brown eyes of James Mitchell, sixth baronet of Penventen.

"We have a *bargain*," she insisted, panic pushing the words out harshly.

James nodded. "An engagement, announced tonight," he answered absently, taking a step away from her. "There's something you ought to know. I'm already engaged."

The falling sensation stopped abruptly and her dreams exploded like a vase dropped from a great height to a tiled floor. It seemed millions of shards caused actual physical pain with her sharp intake of breath.

Abigail resorted to the only emotion left to her—anger.

"You *dog!*" She anticipated the corresponding flare of ire that would at least mean something still burned between them.

"Don't you mean 'you *bastard* dog'?" James asked mildly as he placed another step's distance between them.

Abigail blinked. He knew! How? How could he have learned the truth of his real father? "You weren't supposed to know. Not until…"

"Not interested."

The words were plain enough, but they made no sense to her. "What do you mean, 'not interested'? The chance to one day be an Earl means nothing to you?"

James gave a regretful shake of his head. "I no longer have my own name, Abigail. What good does a title do me?"

She was genuinely confounded. A title, connections, lands, and the fortune that goes with it…more than fifteen thousand pounds a year by her reckoning, all laid at his feet ready for the taking and he asked "what good"?

Her grasp was slipping, and she searched her mind quickly for another approach. The threat made against his business partner came to mind. Surely he wouldn't risk a scandal befalling William Rosewall, especially as James, for some unaccountable reason, seemed besotted by the Captain's mousey little sister Selina?

As though he read her thoughts, James offered a slight smile of condescension.

"Oh, and don't think about spreading rumors about Captain Rosewall or myself," he added, patting what appeared to be a wad of paper bulging in his coat pocket. "You're not likely to get a sympathetic hearing, that is, unless you fancy transportation to New South Wales for blackmail."

James glanced past her, up the small rise to the house, and nodded once. Abigail turned to see what had caught his attention. Two men dressed in masquerade costumes as Friar Tuck and Will Scarlett—a droll counterpoint to James's costume of Robin Hood—walked toward them in response to the signal.

"James?"

"I think these gentlemen want to have a word with you," he suggested.

"But…"

James regarded her with a sudden expression of compassion, the look extinguishing the last of her feelings toward him.

"I hope you find what you're looking for, Abigail."

PART ONE
England

CHAPTER ONE

The Home of Viscount Edgecombe
Bath
September 1792

Abigail placed a shiny copper penny on the six of spades card embroidered onto the rich green baize. She held her breath and trusted her "luck" would hold.

Don't let it be a six, she begged. *Do* not *let it be a six*. The silent instruction became a prayer she repeated over and over.

The banker, Admiral Cecil Worthington, flipped over the card.

The Jack of Diamonds.

She silently released the air in her lungs as Sir Reginald de Witt, seated to her left, let out a groan and watched his stake slide toward the Admiral. The squat-bodied fop, aged in his sixties, pulled himself up from the table, the jeweled rings on every finger glittering in the light of the overhead chandelier.

"Won't you play just one more game, Sir Reginald?" Abigail purred.

The man gave her a slight, lascivious smile, but shook his head. "I can't think of anything I would rather do than spend more time basking in your beauty, but I'm afraid my purse couldn't take the strain, my dear."

At the age of twenty-seven, Abigail knew she was past the first flush of youth, but her looks had not yet dimmed. Her lustrous platinum blonde hair was curled and pinned in the latest style, her complexion fresh and as yet unlined.

With no little pride, she still held a fashionable figure that attracted no shortage of male admirers and, in equal measure, envious looks from women a decade younger. Abigail's breeding and once close connection with the Princess Royal and also—as gossip mongers were wont to repeat—the Prince Regent himself made hers a sought after name to make up the numbers at well-to-do affairs in the bourgeois social circles of Bath.

For those who had already succumbed to the parson's mousetrap, a dash of glamour with the piquancy of *naughtiness* in hobnobbing with a successful demimondaine was just the spice needed to liven up evenings not otherwise spent dancing and drinking at The Assembly Rooms.

Abigail returned the compliment to her card playing companion with a coy smile of her own and gave her attention to the pile of coins sitting at the Admiral's elbow. Between the various players and the house, many guineas had changed hands during this evening's faro, but Abigail's initial stake was safely back in her purse. Now she played for profit.

The white-haired Admiral stroked his elaborate walrus moustache and waited for the other gambler, Lord Fforbes, to make his wager on the fall of a particular card.

Everything was sparse about Fforbes—his size, his thinning black hair, even the little moustache that clung tenaciously to his upper lip. After much prevarication, he slid his ten gold guineas onto the rectangular shape embroidered with the King of Spades.

As the card slid from the shoe Abigail hastily changed her bet, removing the copper coin and placing three pounds on the Ace. That was her card. The one she had waited all evening to see.

With a theatrical flick of his wrist, the Admiral revealed the Ace of Hearts.

Abigail allowed herself a broad smile. It had been a good evening. Sixty guineas richer, sixty guineas closer to her own independence. Far away from her meddling relatives who would have a fit if they knew how she was spending her evening while those desiccated prunes wasted their time discussing the mating habits of the Lesser Whitethroat with their equally dour cohort.

From somewhere within the fashionable new Landsdown Crescent townhouse, decorated in the modern neoclassical taste, a grandfather clock chimed the eleventh hour of the evening. It was ignored by the other participants in this private gambling affair until a small company of maids and footmen swept through the room, clearing away empty decanters and platters as well as the chamber pots and bourdaloues. Freshly filled decanters of wine, brandy, port, and other spirits on silver platters were installed, casting shadows like stained glass on the polished oak sideboard.

Abigail turned her attention back to the table, sweeping a large number of coins into her powder blue satin bag and listened to them tinkling, the sound of each one applause to her cleverness.

"Gentlemen, another hand?" she asked.

Fforbes shook his head adamantly. "I don't know what my wife would say if lost more." He mopped his receding hairline with a kerchief. "She will be most cross that I've lost this much."

The Admiral barked out a laugh and pushed himself back from the table. "Trapped under the cat's paw, that's always been your trouble, Roland. You don't know how to treat women. You're the man of the house. You just tell the little woman what's what. If you want to have a little flutter she has no right to tell you otherwise."

Lord Fforbes didn't seem to appreciate the unsolicited advice. Abigail dropped her head to avoid giving away a smile.

She schooled her expression to one of vapid disinterest and turned wide-open eyes to the Admiral. "What of yourself, Cecil? Surely you have nothing more pressing than to keep a poor lady company in a friendly game of cards."

With an avuncular pat on her hand, the older gentlemen shook his head with regret. "Not this time, my pet, I have some serious business to discuss with Colonel Campbell-Young before the end of this evening. The goings-on in France are a jolly nuisance and bound to get worse. It wouldn't surprise me if we were at war with the frog-eaters by the New Year." He paused, thoughtful for a moment. "Forgive me going on. This must be boring stuff for a young lady like you I'm sure."

Abigail's smile floundered for the barest moment before righting itself again. She would dearly love to tell him what a patronizing old fool he was, but she played politics of a different sort.

The Admiral stood, raising his hand to catch the Colonel's attention and, with a final polite bow to her, hurried to shepherd the man out of the room.

Abigail too rose from the table and brushed the wrinkles from her powder blue brocade dress embroidered with sprays of full bloom roses. Her jewelry was a simple single strand of pearls and pearl studs—a gift, a very expensive one—from a one time admirer. Years before, as a diamond of the first water, she would have been dripping with expensive baubles, but Abigail gave thanks for the emergence of the new minimally adorned fashion which had made its way over from France.

It was useful to disguise financial embarrassment.

Much of her fine clothing and jewels had been sold to pay debts and to furnish the modest home she was forced to share with distant relatives. Tonight, however, her purse weighed heavily on her arm, a promise that the tide of fortune might soon be changing. Adapting to the mood, Abigail judged it right to not press her luck any further. Instead she began to plan her strategic exit. She rose to mingle and give thanks again to Viscount Edgecombe and his wife for a perfectly profitable evening.

"Leaving so soon? I was so enjoying the entertainment."

A stranger stood in the spot vacated by Lord Reginald, a man aged in his mid-thirties by her judgment. He was tall, his body that of a sportsman. And although his hair appeared dark, the light thrown by the chandeliers picked out highlights of red-gold. He was dressed fashionably, but not elaborately; his dark green frockcoat was cut to fit broad shoulders and a tapered waist. Dark gray breeches fit snugly across muscular legs. He was handsome to be sure, but an arrogance in the set of his jaw put Abigail on her guard immediately.

"I don't believe we've been introduced," she said, turning away to search for Lady Edgecombe. "You'll excuse me I'm sure while I pay my respects to our hostess."

"The ace of hearts, the three of clubs, the seven of diamonds, the jack of clubs, and the four of spades. Shall I go on or do I have your complete attention?"

The stranger had named the marked cards in the deck. Suddenly the coins in Abigail's purse weighed more heavily on her wrist. Beneath the flounced ecru lace sleeves of her gown, she clutched her treasure in both hands and slowly sank to her chair.

The stranger also sat, unhurried and unconcerned by the slight flush she could feel rising across her cheeks.

Abigail straightened her back. Despite what the man thought he'd seen, she had earned every one of those coins, and the devil himself couldn't take them away from her.

"You have my attention for as long as it amuses me," she told him.

A slight smile, which might be equally taken for a sneer, crossed his face. "And you have my congratulations." He reached for one of the discarded cards on the table, the ace of hearts. The man placed it side-up on the table and a small tell-tale notch on its long edge became obvious against the baize.

"Your talents are legendary in some circles, but before I took the word of our mutual friend, I wanted to see for myself whether the reputation was deserved."

Abigail's eyes rose to meet his—a shade of blue that reminded her of a long past summer day. Her response was as icy as the upcoming winter.

"I find it exceedingly difficult to believe we have any acquaintance in common, let alone a *friend*." She waited for his expression to change. It did. The left corner of his mouth rose.

"Oh dear," said the man, condescension dripping from his words, "*Aunt Druscilla* will be most heartbroken."

At the name Abigail started. Two years of tightly contained anger ignited in her chest.

"More's the pity that one cannot choose one's relatives, *cousin*," she said, placing particular venom on the last word. "Do forgive me if I choose not to pursue our family connections." She rose again. "This interview is at an end."

"Not when I hold all the cards," replied the man, rising with her and glancing demonstratively at the ace in his hand before slipping it into his inside coat pocket.

"Well, one of them at any rate," he corrected himself with a smile.

Abigail's initial flush of fear and rush of anger slumped to dismal annoyance and, in doing so, exhibited a subtle change of stance that must have attracted the attention of their hostess some yards away. Although well into her middle age, Lady Jane Ashford, wife of the Viscount Edgecombe, was of the type that in youth were described as the perfect English rose. Age had not diminished her light brunette hair nor her peaches-and-cream complexion. She had thickened in the middle only a little over the years, her comfortable marriage and fortune enhancing rather than dimming her appeal. Now she approached, a vision in a primrose yellow gown designed to show off her fine bosom.

"My dear Daniel, you arrive and disappear so quickly at my events that I never get you alone," she exclaimed, threading her arm through the younger man's in a proprietary fashion.

"How could I risk the wrath of your husband should he learn my true feelings for you, sweetpea?" the man replied with a broad wink and a broader smile. "He would call me out in an instant, and you are too young and beautiful to be a widow."

"Naughty man!" The handsome matron giggled appreciatively before tapping his arm with her fan. She then bestowed a smile on Abigail.

"I see you have made the acquaintance of one of my favorite guests, Lady Abigail. May I introduce you to the Honorable Daniel Ridgeway; Daniel, Lady Abigail Houghall."

"Honorable?" Abigail raised an eyebrow and let sarcasm drip from her words.

The man responded with a full smile. "Purely an undeserved title, I can assure you."

"In your case, I'm sure I can believe it."

"Daniel is the youngest son of the Viscount Pemberley," interjected Lady Jane, looking from one to the other, aware of the tension between them, but no doubt uncertain as to its cause.

Abigail seized the opportunity. She clasped the hands of her hostess and offered a slightly pained expression. "This evening has been a delight, but I seem to have ended it with a niggling headache."

Lady Jane clucked her disappointment. "I shall send for your driver, darling. You must come with me to the morning room and you can rest quietly until he's ready to take you home."

Offering a vulnerable smile in a performance worthy of the stage, Abigail leaned heavily on her hostess's disengaged arm and, without a single glance back, left the damned *Honorable* Daniel Ridgeway standing alone.

The green morning room was blessedly empty, so Abigail walked its perimeter, around and around the small oval mahogany table set with six balloon-back chairs, past the fireplace where coals burned dully and the chaise longue in the bay window that, during daylight, offered a view of a picturesque formal garden.

The arrival of the *Honorable* Daniel Ridgeway was a damnable bit of luck. Why here? Why now? Was it blackmail? And what was he to *Aunt Druscilla?*

Think, Abigail!

She recalled the first time she heard the name, direct from the lips of Sir Percy Blakeney, private secretary to William Pitt, the Prime Minister of England. Sir Percy had been dressed at the Boconnoc House masquerade as the Sheriff of Nottingham. Despite the outlandish costume, the man was one not to be underestimated.

That night Abigail had been escorted back to the house by two men also dressed as characters from Sherwood Forest, to a private meeting in an oak-paneled study…

"I prefer not to insult your intelligence or mine with a pretty dance of accusations and denials, so I'll get right to the point," Blakeney had begun without preamble two years ago. "You're in my way and over your head in matters that are hazardous."

The man's supercilious tone bridled. She straightened in the chair and raised her head to stare daggers at him.

"Your concern is touching, Sir Percy, but I've achieved my majority and I'm of independent means. I don't answer to you or anyone else."

His answering smile was slow and dangerous. "That changes tonight, my dear. You *will* tell me what you know of the missing Exchequer gold *and* your knowledge of any conspirators, otherwise I'll hand you over to the authorities regardless of your position."

Abigail's eyes slowly lowered to the carpet at her feet and she unconsciously licked her lips. It would be a remarkably short story to tell.

A comment by the Prince of Wales on the night he ended their affair, that his allowance was insufficient to keep one mistress in the manner to which she was accustomed, let alone support two, led Abigail to a small flirtation with a very indiscreet treasury official who inferred, indeed, there *was* less gold in the treasury than was generally supposed to be.

Finally, a mention of the matter to a duplicitous family relation, Earl Canalissy, who was a member of Pitt's cabinet, resulted in broad hints from him that renewing her attention to Sir James Mitchell would be to their mutual benefit. With the Earl asking particular questions regarding James's coming and goings since his recent return from America, it hadn't taken Abigail long to deduce James had a secret to hide.

A short story it was indeed, but one she would not reveal the ending of, under her present circumstance, until she was assured of her future security.

Abigail had worn a sumptuous Egyptian costume. She adjusted her posture regally and pinned Blakeney with a direct look. "Should I furnish this information, can I trust your honor as a gentleman that investigations into my...*indiscretions* will go no further?"

The man folded his arms and leaned back into the studded leather chair, peering at her through his quizzing glass before breaking into a slow smile. "It would be a poor bargain for me to relinquish a winning hand on so small a bet, my dear."

Abigail raised her chin, her face hardening imperceptibly. She might have known this moment was to come. It would not be the first time she had leveraged sexual favors to elude punishment. Very well, if that's what it took, she would perform. At least Pitt's secretary, though tall and lean, was handsome in his own way. She leaned forward, bosom spilling a little further over the top of her gown.

Blakeney laughed heartily at the display. "Get those thoughts from your head. You're a fine actress and, believe me, I know actresses well. Your charms are wasted on me."

Wounded pride made Abigail angry. She stood and slapped her hands on the desk between them. "Then what *do* you want?"

Blakeney rose slowly, his eyes sparkling with clear amusement at her ire. Pride filled his voice. "My dear, I'm going to turn Jezebel into Rahab. One day, you are going to be one of my most accomplished spies."

Soon after that, Abigail had been ordered to live with her spinster aunt in Bath and write weekly letters of the gossip and goings-on in town. The letters, to be sent without fail, were addressed to "Aunt Druscilla."

It was hardly the stuff to determine the fate of the Empire. It was a school girl's punishment. Yet, so powerful was the threat Blakeney held over her head, Abigail became a most diligent correspondent.

She had not seen nor heard from Blakeney in two years.

Two long years with the threat of criminal charges—possibly even transportation to Sydney Town for blackmail—hanging over her head like the sword of Damocles and not a single word. It was torture of the acutest kind...

A brief knock on the door halted Abigail's reflection and her pacing. The butler entered and announced her carriage awaited.

Courtesy required she find and thank her hosts once again. As she did so, a quick glance around the private gaming room revealed no sign of Daniel Ridgeway.

One of the parlor maids helped her into a light silk rose jacket and a footman assisted her into the slightly worn and saggy interior of her carriage. No fashion trend could save her conveyance from revealing her genteel poverty.

Sitting back in the seat, Abigail opened her purse and felt the coins, cold and solid at her fingertips. Without the need to look, she found and withdrew two guineas, and slipped them into her glove. The gambling may have finished, but the true game was about to begin.

She slapped the leather seat harshly. Damn this Daniel Ridgeway. Why had this agent of Blakeney's shown up now? Abigail calculated she had enough already for passage and to last her several months abroad, but still not nearly enough to buy a villa outright, a property to secure her future far away from this wretched place.

If only, if only, if only...

The carriage slowed as it turned onto one of the lesser streets in Bath and rolled to a stop outside a modest townhouse. Alighting from the vehicle, Abigail smoothed her jacket and felt something unexpected in one of the pockets. She stood closer to the lamp light by the door and frowned as she fished it out.

It was a playing card.

The fine hairs on the back of her neck stood up as she turned it over.

"My Lady?"

Abigail blinked at Stanstead's inquiry from the open doorway.

"Is there anything amiss?"

She swallowed and shook her head, slipping the card back into her pocket. Stepping past the butler, she walked into the study to warm herself by the small fire recently lit in the hearth.

Stanstead followed and waited just inside the room. "Will there be anything more, my Lady?"

Abigail reached into her glove and deftly withdrew the guineas she had set aside for the purpose. "Just this," she said, holding out her hand.

The butler approached and accepted the gold coins. Half for him, half for her chambermaid and the groom. Such patronage assured their ongoing discretion.

"Thank you, my Lady," he murmured deferentially. "Good night."

Alone once again, Abigail retrieved the card.

It was the marked Ace of Hearts.

CHAPTER TWO

Abigail stared at the card for some seconds before the spell was broken by the sound of gravel shifting outside under the hooves of the horse being led to the stable.

She crossed the room and tried the handle of the door. To her satisfaction, it was firmly closed. Abigail smiled as her eye fell on her next task. An expensive drop front bureau, Aunt Philomena's desk, took pride of place in the room. Made of walnut with burr elm veneer drawers, its straight lines were relieved by ebony and boxwood stringing. The unlocked writing slope lowered like the drawbridge of a surrendering castle. Taking a letter opener from inside, Abigail reclosed the slope and ignored the disapproving look from the solid silver putto on the opener's handle.

There was a sliver of space between the desk top and the locked centre drawer below. Abigail gently inserted the blade into the gap and worked it above the bolt, creating some small amount of downward pressure. While her left hand held the opener steady, she retrieved a hair pin from her coiffure with the other, and eased it into the key hole, worrying the metal catch until, with a satisfying click, the lock returned home. Swiftly and silently, Abigail removed the drawer and felt for a recessed brass button in the back right corner. Another soft click, almost inaudible over the crackles and pops of the fire, signaled the desk's secret compartment opening in the upper section.

She replaced the centre drawer and it was the work of a moment to relock it. Lowering the writing slope once again, she saw the walnut panel right in the centre sitting proud of the rest of the finely fitted interior. Abigail eased the wood forward. The narrow, but deep, recess held a small black velvet bag.

Abruptly, she heard Stanstead cough loudly in the hall, then echoing footsteps descending the stairs. There followed quickly the voice of Aunt Philomena interrogating the butler as to Abigail's whereabouts. The butler coughed again, excused himself for doing so, then loudly announced the Lady Abigail had returned home and was in the study.

As he spoke, Abigail dropped ten guineas, plus two extra, into the velvet sack.

Aunt Philomena's steps tap-tap-tapped their way across the tiles toward the door.

The secret drawer slid back into place with a soft click as it locked home.

Abigail's breath quickened. She needed some pretense for being in the study, less her subterfuge be for naught. She drew up the chair, sat, and pulled a sheet of stationery paper from one of the desk pigeonholes. She had just flipped open the metal lid of the heavy glass inkwell and taken up a pen as the study's large brass doorknob shuddered and turned.

"Abigail! What are you doing at my desk at this ungodly hour?"

As the door opened, Abigail turned defiantly to confront her aunt, a tall and reed-like woman in her fifties. A single streak of gray started at Philomena's right temple and disappeared into the rest of the jet-black hair piled high on her head. Abigail noted that, despite protesting the lateness of the hour, the spinster was nonetheless fully dressed in a plain black gown unadorned by jewelry.

"What does it look like?" Abigail responded briskly. The lie came to her suddenly, but with ease. "I'm writing a note to the housekeeper."

"After midnight?"

"Of course after midnight. Last month The Lady's Magazine was not given to me until one week after it was delivered. I will not have it delayed to me this month."

Philomena's expression changed from anger to contempt as Abigail dashed off her note.

"You cannot imagine how embarrassed I was at the Assembly," Abigail pronounced, "when that silly little poppet Emily made an absolute peacock of herself attempting to wear a hat of the very latest style."

Abigail punctuated her complaint by banging her hand on the writing slope, causing it to jump slightly. "The very. Latest. Style!"

She gave Philomena a sideways glance. "I'm embarrassed to even acknowledge Emily as a relation," she sniffed. Then, sensing her aunt's continued low opinion of her was sufficiently reinforced, Abigail underscored her advantage by signing her name to the note with a flourish.

"That magazine is a perfectly good waste of sixpence, I'm sure!" the older woman grumbled.

Abigail stood and closed the desk, confident she had successfully distracted the old lady from speculating on what she was doing by her desk in the small hours of the morning. "Would you begrudge me a mere trifle to make my life just a little more bearable each month?"

And before Philomena could censure her further, Abigail raised her head and breezed past without another word in a performance worthy of the actress Fanny Abington herself.

Now safe in her bedroom, Abigail continued to methodically brush her long blonde hair, although she kept a sharp watch in her dressing table mirror on the departing reflection of Kathleen, her maid.

Once the door closed behind the girl, Abigail retrieved her purse. If Kathleen had felt it unusually heavy as she put away her mistress's things this evening, she had said nothing and indeed was paid well to do so. Abigail never questioned the worth of paying so much for the servants' silence and loyalty. Indeed, she had felt the investment vindicated by the revelation that Lady Sedley's recent public humiliation had been caused by not taking out similar "insurance."

Abigail's bedroom was not an overly large one. Two pieces of furniture dominated the room—a figured walnut bed with a large scroll-carved headboard, and a large French oak armoire. Abigail withdrew a key from one of the small drawers beside her modest dressing table mirror and turned to the armoire. She opened a lower drawer and rummaged behind some linens for a small strong box. To it she added the bulk of tonight's haul.

Over the past two years, she had watched the amount grow steadily. Nearly a thousand pounds had been amassed. Most now safely in the hands of her lawyers, who were under instructions to find her a suitable property in Naples and act as her agents.

Just one more year of her purgatory here in Bath fleecing wealthy and stupid old men a little of their coin, flattering their aged hides, pretending to enjoy the silly and pointless gossip, taking note of all the comings and goings for amusement of "Aunt Druscilla." Then she would slip out of the country quietly to where even the long arms of Sir Percy Blakeney could not reach her. Yes, even him. Dammit.

Damn *him*!

Abigail placed the lone lit candle on the bedside and slipped between the crisp linen sheets. Her body may be at rest, but her mind certainly was not. It had suited her purpose to think she had been forgotten by that scheming functionary, but tonight's arrival of the "Honorable" Daniel Ridgeway dredged up memories she thought buried of that summer evening two years ago in the grounds of Prime Minister Pitt's family home, Boconnoc House. She left the candle burning—Aunt Philomena would be scandalized by the waste—and watched the play of light across the ceiling, remembering…

It was the morning after the ball, another evening when she had not slept. Everything she had worked so hard to achieve was gone in a puff of smoke.

How different might things have been all those years ago had she not been found by James in the naked embrace of a wealthy man old enough to be her father. James was all of twenty-one then and she eighteen, well aware of his intent to propose to her. Foolish boy. Despite his love for her, she would never have accepted his proposal then.

Her affection for him was a half-formed thing. An exciting life at court—parties, jewels and intrigue, and the men who could bring it to her—were far more attractive than marriage and the prospect of decade after decade of boring domesticity, her figure forever ruined by year after year of child bearing. Yet those incomplete feelings still existed within her, lying dormant until James's return six years later, when they became a late summer bloom of nostalgia, warmed by his new-earned wealth and worldliness.

But her plans to engage him at last were dashed as disastrously as a ship drawn onto rocks by a wrecker's light.

Abigail had made her way to him in the banquet hall of the informal breakfast the next morning, but drawing nearer, he didn't see her. He was close enough to reach out to touch, but she did not.

Then James looked up at the sound of his name and at that moment Abigail knew he *did* see what the others did not. His face, which had never worn a dishonest countenance in its life, momentarily expressed its distaste of her, before adopting a mask of pleasant indifference.

She asked him to accompany her for a turn about the gardens, knowing the gentleman in him would not allow him to refuse.

"You will forgive me for not returning with you," she began formally as they had walked. "It seems I am to assist Sir Percy in some matter and I'd rather not talk to his men at Penventen. Anyway, I'm not sure I feel up to attending your wedding. I think a clean break would be best."

The sound of birds chattering in the trees on this glorious summer day seemed unnaturally joyful, so she concentrated on the sound of their steps on the gravel path, step after step, taking them away from the house and into the cooler, more private shadows of the arbor ahead.

James made no comment on her announcement and his silence was more oppressive than the growing morning heat.

"I did love you, you know," she offered after a long minute of silence. It was a confession that begged no forgiveness, but served as an explanation of sorts.

They stopped under the shade of a spreading tree and Abigail watched expressions of anger, contempt, perhaps even hatred color his face before his eyes would meet hers.

"I meant what I said last night," he said quietly. "I truly hope you find what you're looking for."

His warm brown eyes that once twinkled with passion and mischief were wary now. Abigail thought that might be the end of their conversation, but James continued with exasperation.

"I never could understand why you had to cheat and connive to get ahead. You have all of the advantages of beauty, wealth, and status. You're accomplished, intelligent, and witty. Men fall over themselves to be beside you."

"Not you."

"I did once," he replied.

There was a moment's silence.

"I ought to thank you," he continued at last, "for helping me see clearly all those years ago. Our marriage would have been as miserable as the one I grew up witnessing. I know I probably haven't treated you fairly over the past year either, but you are someone I once cared for. I hope you find the right man to love, one who understands you and treats you well."

Abigail hid twisting pain behind a mocking smile. "I thought I had found him."

She walked on, and James fell into step alongside her.

"It could never be," James said, shaking his head, "and you know it too, especially from the first night I met Selina."

Yes, Abigail did know. Selina Rosewall was a pretty young woman to be sure, but hardly a diamond of the first water. The beau monde would have tired of her within a week, yet she had verve and a sweetness which had been sufficient to win James's heart completely.

Last night and this morning seemed to be all about confessions, so Abigail spoke, "I think I did know even then. I hated her on sight, you know. But now I don't hate her at all. I haven't the energy. I hope she will love you in the way you deserve to be loved. And in a way that I simply don't know how."

Abigail's throat tightened with emotions she was still learning to identify—heartbreak, loss, regret…

"Perhaps you'll both give everyone hope that marriage is still an honorable institution."

James stopped and turned, looking back at the house. "I'm glad we've cleared the air," he said, "but let's not make any false promises of future friendship. If nothing else, you're not a hypocrite. And I don't bear you any ill will or malice, but I want to be perfectly clear. I don't want to see you again."

With that, James had walked away toward the house and did not glance back, and in doing so did not see the trail of tears Abigail allowed to fall unchecked down her face…

Although she would admit it to no one, she had shed further tears over James Mitchell and for herself too, but only in solitary moments of reflection. She knew of only one way to silence the ghosts of her past and that was to drown them with more society.

It worked for a short while until the emptiness—the empty words, the empty flirtations—became as dry and tasteless as two day old bread. Even the recounting of them to Aunt Druscilla became a ridiculous and tiresome process.

Life had lost its flavor and, as the days passed, Abigail could see her own future reflected in the dried husk of the woman that was Aunt Philomena. Still, despite their fractious relationship, she did have to thank the old woman for one thing.

About a year ago, Philomena dragged her along to one of her Blue Stocking events where the bespectacled Professor Edwin White shared his collection of souvenirs from his Grand Tour. He showed beautiful watercolors of azure blue skies, mellow green olive groves dotted in and among ruins of ancient Rome, gleaming glimpses of the Mediterranean past, and white-washed buildings clinging to the sharply rising cliffs of the Isle of Capri.

Among yet more small statues, Etruscan jewelry and artifacts offered for their appreciation, Abigail became captivated by a small snuff box depicting a young woman with softly curling blonde hair falling along the yellow and white draped robes. Her face was hidden and it seemed to Abigail she was mourning the death of her lover as she embraced a red urn upon a marble wall.

The image spoke to her; the loneliness of the young Roman woman could be her own.

It was even worth sitting next to the loquacious Professor to stare at it for the next half hour as he droned on and on in endless detail about how the lid was actually a micro mosaic, a painting made up of little chips of colored glass in every hue of the rainbow and more.

The idea of a fresh beginning in Italy germinated a seed of hope in Abigail. Suddenly, life had a purpose again and the idea of plotting right under Sir Percy Blakeney's nose held a certain piquancy.

The unexpected arrival of the *Honorable* Daniel Ridgeway simply added a little spice to the game.

With that, Abigail smiled and focused her attention on the candle as it flickered wildly, guttering in its holder, before she extinguished it with a puff of air from her lips.

CHAPTER THREE

Dear Aunty Dru,

    I've arrived safely in Bath. I must say what an interesting group of people dear cousin Abigail knows.

    I have given her my calling card, as you instructed, and hope to be invited to tea so I can share your news with her.

    Your description of my Lady's charms was disturbingly incomplete, although I'm sure that was simply an oversight on your part.

    On a more serious subject, however, there has been no word from Sawyer for over six months and my own inquiries have yielded nothing. His absence is causing a high degree of consternation for his wife.

    For anything you can do to give her solace, I'd be forever indebted.

    Your devoted nephew,

    Daniel

The wet indigo ink glistened briefly before sinking into the paper. Daniel gave the letter one last look over as it dried. Good ole Percy would have a fit over the flippant manner of address in the letter. He took his cloak and dagger stuff very seriously indeed.

As seriously as Daniel took his concern for Jonathan Sawyer, his closest friend.

The sound of the bell at the door downstairs roused Daniel from his thoughts. With more vigor, he addressed the letter and sealed it. He fished a couple of sixpences from his waistcoat pocket, as he bounded down the stairs of the boarding house and instructed the waiting footman to ensure the letter went by the first coach to London. The son of the housekeeper, a young lad aged no more than ten years Daniel guessed, had answered the door. Now, he hung around in the hope of an errand to take him out of the house. Daniel crouched down to eye level with the boy and leaned in, allowing a bright, newly minted silver coin to catch the light streaming through the morning room curtains and into the hallway.

"I have a shilling here for another job, just so long as you keep it between you and me."

The tow-headed boy's blue eyes widened, his attention torn between the shiny coin and the man who held it.

"Do I hafta rob a bank?"

"You'd like that and think it was a fine adventure, wouldn't you, little scamp!" Daniel laughed. "Well, it's not robbing banks, but something just as exciting. I want you to be a *spy!*"

At the conspiratorial sound of the last word, the boy's excitement grew.

"Who do I spy on, Mr. Daniel?"

"Do you know Lady Abigail Houghall?"

"Is she the beautiful lady what lives in James Street with that aunt of hers 'ats got a face to sour milk?" The boy stopped, openmouthed and aghast at allowing his words to run ahead of his better judgment. He waited for the punishment he would surely receive for speaking ill of his betters.

Instead, Daniel slapped him cheerfully on the back. "You have a talent for observation. That's a good trait for a spy. A second good skill is knowing when to keep quiet. Can you do that for me too?"

The boy nodded his head vigorously.

"I have it on good authority both ladies are planning to spend some time at the Assembly Rooms today. I want you to go to their house and wait. As soon as they leave, you race straight to the York Club and let me know. Can you do that for me?"

"It'll be a doddle, Mr. Daniel!"

"Well, do a good job and there might be another shilling in it for you."

The boy ran out of the study, through the entrance hall, and out the front door, nearly bowling his mother over in the process.

"Hoy!" she cried after him before shaking her head in dismay. "What's gotten into that boy, I'll never know. He's not been a bother has he, Mr. Daniel?"

Mrs. Tapper was a widow in only her late twenties, but whose ruddy complexion spoke of a hard life. She wrung her hands under her apron nervously, doubtful of her lodger's tolerance.

"Not at all, Mrs. Tapper," Daniel assured her. "Right now he's being of great service to me."

"Well…if you're sure then," she said, still uncertain.

"Indeed I am," he continued, "and the boy is being paid for his task, so don't be concerned about him earning his keep."

That mollified the woman somewhat and, as she left to continue the housework, Daniel watched after her for a moment, wondering what kind of life this woman had, raising a child on her own. He turned toward the stairs and his introspection faded as he considered his own obligations for the day. He took the steps up to his room two at a time.

Daniel removed his comfortable riding clothes to dress more in the manner befitting a son of a Viscount, in light gray breeches, a navy waistcoat, and a crisp white cravat.

He grimaced at his reflection in the mirror. Another costume, another little bit of play-acting; a bit of necessary deception perpetuated for a higher cause…or something like that. At least it kept the dogs of his past, the ones that nipped at his heels of his memory, quiet for a little while.

The Tapper lad reminded him so much of himself, before…

No! There was no going back, he reminded himself. Hadn't the past fifteen years taught him anything?

Daniel slammed the wardrobe door shut. A few deep breaths and he was master of his own mind once again.

* * *

"We have two perfectly good legs each. Why are we wasting unnecessary expense hiring sedan chairs?" Aunt Philomena snipped as she and Abigail waited on the porch.

Abigail spared her aunt a glance as she re-secured the ribbon of her pretty raspberry red bonnet. Going down to the Assembly Room was no difficulty, she thought darkly, but returning home after several glasses of sherry was a different matter, was it not, dear aunt? Rather than airing said grievances, she kept up her usual neutral façade.

Blakeney certainly had a talent for formulating the most unique tortures and his order that Abigail live with her spinster aunt was exquisitely devised. And now the claims of the dreadful Burchill family, related or not, was a further turn of the thumbscrew.

Abigail bit her lip to refrain from making comment as she watched the chair-men hurry up from the bottom of the street with their plainly painted rented conveyances, but another glance at the older woman in her simple, old-fashioned gray day dress told her that "dear aunt" expected a reply.

"Walk down? Like commoners? Isn't it bad enough our carriage is in need of repair that you would penny-pinch at our one outing of the week?"

Perhaps it was foolish to goad the woman, but Abigail could think of no better sport than to bait the bitter, sadistic Lady Philomena Fitzroy-deVries, first cousin of Randall Dobell, the disgraced Earl Canalissy. His reputation, even in death, had sunk so low that his name, and that of his insane son, was never to be uttered in polite society.

That side of the family was tainted—and Abigail with it—by association with the audacious scheme of using the threat of war with France and the agitation of English Radicals to disguise embezzlement from the Crown.

As the chair-men approached the house, Philomena's mouth thinned to a colorless line and she edged closer to her niece. "You're not a lady-in-waiting now, Abigail, all high and mighty," she hissed softly to avoid the ears of eavesdropping servants. "Such a wonderful lark I'm sure, to be a demirep when you were young, pretty, and well-connected. But where are your dear friends now? You have squandered every advantage given to you. You would do well to take a leaf from the Burchills. You may mock them, but they're respectable. Mark my words when they announce Emily's engagement to the son of Lord Templeton at the end of this year." A malevolent smile crossed the old lady's face as she prepared to deliver her coup-de-grace. "You, on the other hand, are nothing but a worthless whore."

A cold, dark anger fell over Abigail like a February frost. She surged forward the moment the chair-men arrived and muttered to the groomsman who assisted her into the vehicle, "Tell them, a sixpence each to get us there in the quickest time."

The young man grinned.

Abigail grinned too since the brisk pace resulted in the sedan chair violently bouncing its way across town to the Assembly Room. The cries of alarm from the chair behind hers was just the antidote she needed. At the end of the journey, Abigail considered the minor damage to the ostrich plume on her bonnet to be a very small price to pay to see Aunt Philomena looking pale and disheveled as she disembarked.

Not waiting for the woman to join her, Abigail strolled along the corridor. The Greek-inspired columns in white and painted walls in a pale blue gave the visitor a feeling they were walking through a giant-sized impression of one of Josiah Wedgewood's own jasperware confections. Chandeliers threw bejeweled pools of light on the elaborately tiled floors that beckoned Abigail forward through the spacious entrance corridor. Her spirits were buoyed by the lively musical sets she could hear echoing from the musicians' gallery above the tea room.

She nodded to acquaintances and stopped to speak to a few here and there. The same old faces here for the season, no one new to interest the socially insatiable Aunt Druscilla. Abigail recalled her last letter.

Dear Aunt,

Lady Violet Spearmont sprained her ankle riding the other week but did still insist on attending last week's ball, to prevent Miss

Tiffany Lake tipping her hat at Lord Beauvalet. Mrs. Lake, the debutant's mother, pretended to be most solicitous to Lady Spearmont but in her clumsiness ended up doing her an injury which necessitated a sedan chair to be brought into the ballroom itself to take the stricken lady back home.

The bluestockings of Bath are much a-twitter to learn that the Irish poet Eamon Dauncey has agreed to address them. I think it is more the man's good looks than his skill as a writer which has attracted such attention.

And you will recall that the younger son of Earl Ashburton had declared himself engaged to the daughter of Viscount Salisbury, much to the dismay of both families. We learned just yesterday the young couple are now wed after a journey north to Gretna Green…

Abigail shook her head. What interest could any of that be to the private secretary of the Prime Minister of England?

She stopped to speak with Sir George and Lady Templeton, here for the debut season of their youngest daughter Georgina. Their son and heir, William, greeted her politely before breaking ranks to join his good friend Viscount Richard Hamberley who was headed toward the Card Room.

"Abigail, darling! You're here. Thank goodness! I thought I should die of boredom otherwise."

She turned at the voice.

Lady Jane stood behind her in an orchid-pink day dress of the latest French style, cut wide and deep across the neck to short fitted sleeves trimmed in light cream lace. A darker pink ribbon was tied under the bust from which the skirts cascaded in long folds to the floor and the hem trimmed with dark yellow embroidered floral motifs.

Abigail forced herself to confess inwardly that, if it had been any other woman, she would be certain to hate her. But ever since arriving in Bath, Lady Jane and her husband had been nothing but kind. Jane's acceptance of her opened doors and opportunities for which she would be forever grateful. It had taken Abigail some getting used to—a friendship with another woman who was not a rival for the affections of a new beau. Jane was married, and quite happily so, to a man who doted on her and seemed to delight in indulging her every whim.

"Die of boredom?" Abigail responded. "And leave me all alone with the sharp-tongued mammas ready to snub me as a threat to their hen-witted chits? Don't you dare! I shall take my revenge and marry your Thomas before the last sod has fallen on your grave."

Jane laughed heartily and took her arm, leading her toward the tearoom. As they walked, Abigail considered her own plain day gown. She had been playing it safe for two years, trapped between the censure of Aunt Philomena and the threat implicit in Blakeney's instruction to "behave."

"You think I jest? I am in full earnest," Jane continued, ignorant of Abigail's musings. "I had to spend the entire morning with that dreadful mushroom Mrs. Eliot-Smythe who thinks just because her last husband left her with a decent income, we're now on equal station…"

Abigail offered her a sympathetic pout before being distracted by a glimpse of that upstart man, the *Honorable* Daniel Ridgeway, in the crowd.

"…utterly gauche, forcing that mousey little daughter of hers onto—Abigail, dear are you quite all right?"

A group of people crossed in front of them. Then he was gone.

Abigail turned a bright smile to her friend. "I thought I saw Lady Fforbes."

"Well, she would steal the smile off anybody's face." Jane grinned. "After Fforbes's losses last night, I expect to see him here with a black eye. It's clear who really wears the breeches in that household."

The Assembly tea room was filled with patrons taking advantage of the fine afternoon. Long reaches of late autumn sun streamed through the high windows, making the light from the elaborate chandeliers seem redundant. At one end of the room, a dozen tall columns supporting a gallery cast long diagonal shadows across the parquet floor.

A page escorted them to their seats and offered them a program. Venanzio Rauzzini was presenting a new series of musical concerts featuring some of his most gifted singing students.

Abigail turned to the matter which filled her thoughts this morning. She mustered a casual tone and spoke low to dissuade eavesdroppers and used the sound of the orchestra tuning up and the scrape of chairs as others sought their seats for cover. "Tell me, what do you know about Daniel Ridgeway?"

Jane gave her a sideways glance and a knowing smile.

"I *knew* you were interested in him last night," she said warmly, using the program as a fan close to her mouth. "I haven't seen you look like that at a man in all the time I've known you. I was beginning to think your reputation was wholly exaggerated."

Abigail's cheeks colored in anger. Doubtless Jane would think it was from another cause. She shifted in her seat and faced her friend.

"Let me assure you here and now, Jane Ashford, after his insulting behavior to me last night, Daniel Ridgeway is the last man I would have a tender thought about."

"He insulted you?" Jane's eyebrows rose high on her forehead. "What did he say?"

Abigail paused. What could she say? That he caught her cheating at faro and called her on it? The very fact that Jane and Thomas allowed private gambling in their home despite the King's *Proclamation Against Vice* opened them to fines, the pillory, and, worst of all, public condemnation.

She hastened to find another excuse. "It wasn't what he said. It was his manner. Very arrogant."

"I've only known him for a few weeks," admitted Jane. Infuriatingly, she paused at that point, offered only a knowing smile before continuing. "He's actually an acquaintance of Thomas's."

A hush settled over the room as the first singer stepped forward.

Jane leaned in closer and whispered, "They went to Cambridge together, Daniel and his two older brothers. They were all of a pretty fast set, as Thomas tells it."

The last of the audience took their seats, and the light scent of leather and sandalwood made Abigail conscious of a male presence to her right shoulder. It would be a social faux pas to acknowledge the presence without introduction, so she kept her eyes toward the stage.

As the first item began, Abigail lifted the program from her lap and dropped it to her feet. There it stayed untouched for the remainder of the first sonata, a fine performance from a young soprano, which was greeted with appreciative applause.

Still no reaction from the gent next to her, so Abigail risked a look sideways.

It was Ridgeway, who, should anyone be looking at him, might be considered an enthusiastic connoisseur of the arts. He did not acknowledge Abigail. His eyes remained fixed to the front as he applauded rapturously.

She took in his profile. A strong firm jaw, a nose that classicists might call patrician, a line running near his mouth. All further evidence of a ready smile. Or a knowing smirk.

Strangely, Abigail could hear her pulse beat in her ears. She looked away sharply to her left, fixing her gaze on the sun-filled windows.

Abigail had not allowed herself to become aware of a man since James Mitchell. Perhaps that was her problem.

As the second performance started, she relented and looked down for the program, only to find it sitting neatly on her lap. A glance to the right showed her Ridgeway was gone. Abigail opened the sheet to seek the name of next singer and a small slip of paper slid out onto her knee.

Discreetly hiding it with the program, she turned it over. The note read simply:

Meet me in the Octagonal Room at midnight.

– D

CHAPTER FOUR

*Y*ou are nothing but a worthless whore. Recalling the old witch's words stoked Abigail's anger as she pulled one garment, then another out of her wardrobe. She was more than ready to shuck off the bridle of propriety that kept her tied here to Bath, living a life of dull respectability shackled to an embittered old spinster whose venom was slowly poisoning her to death.

"My Lady! Please do let me help!" cried Abigail's maid Kathleen. She hastily placed her serving tray on the dresser, causing the tea cup to clatter in its saucer, and rushed to gather up the swathes of multicolored gowns strewn on the floor. "I put out the gray gown for you this morning."

Abigail chose to ignore the maid's slightly disapproving tone and swept up the offending garment in her hand.

"Get rid of it!" she ordered, throwing it at the maid's feet before picking up a deep mourning dress in black and shoving it at the girl. "This too."

That dragon had pushed her too far with her insult. Today was the final straw. Even now her plan was a half-formed thing, but Abigail was nothing if not a gambler.

If Percy had intended to release her from this tedious obligation, he could have done so quite easily in a letter. To send one of his men to see her meant something important. And something important meant money. Whether he knew it or not, the *Honorable* Daniel Ridgeway was going to be her ticket out of Bath, out of *England*.

"I will no longer wear black, or gray, or lavender or any other drab, dull, and lifeless color."

"But your aunt, my Lady…" Kathleen protested.

With a large sigh, Abigail calmed herself and turned to the maid. "Aunt Philomena be damned, Canalissy be damned. All of them be damned," she enunciated slowly. "I am going to live again."

The girl blinked owlishly before recovering. Her face reddened as though something large was stuck in her throat, then words tumbled out. "If you don't mind me sayin' so, m'Lady, but so you should!"

At the expression of support, Abigail felt her good humor start to return. "The question remains, what am I going to wear tonight?"

Kathleen answered with a sly grin. "I think I know which gentleman you want to catch, my Lady."

Abigail had no such "catch" in mind. Her attendance tonight was principally to see what Daniel Ridgeway had to say, and more importantly, how much he was prepared to pay, but the maid's remark ignited her interest.

"That poet fellow Mr. Dauncey is very handsome. I heard Lady Philomena's smart friends talking about him just the other day."

Dauncey. The Irish poet.

Abigail raised an eyebrow, intrigued. Her heart had been bruised when James left, but there was proof that time did heal wounds. What she needed was a conquest, something to have all of Bath talking... A charming and handsome Irish poet might be just the tonic.

"Then tell me, Kathleen, what shall I wear to catch the eye of an Irishman?"

"Ooh," said Kathleen, "that one?"

Abigail considered the emerald green gown Kathleen somewhat predictably favored, then discarded it for one in Persian blue. It was the perfect choice, and Abigail allowed Kathleen to help her put it and her dancing slippers on. Soon, she admired her reflection in the long looking glass.

The gown was fashioned in the latest style with fitted sleeves several inches above the elbow and a low-scooped neckline to show a tantalizing glimpse of creamy soft breasts, their shape captured from below by a satin band of purple under the bust from which matching ribbons draped beautifully to the floor. The hem, meanwhile, was elaborately embroidered in the form of peacock feathers in multihued silks.

Abigail sighed, not only at her reflection, but also contemplating her neglected dancing slippers on her feet which felt as welcome as long lost friends.

The maid fetched Abigail's jewel casket, a box of ebony, inlaid with mother of pearl, from the armoire. The casket had once been filled with a king's ransom in jewels—all gifts from lovers and admirers. Sadly, a great deal of them had been sold off. But the few items that remained were of the highest quality. It would be very grim day indeed if she was forced to part with *them*.

First she selected a necklace of fine gold links into which were set three large amethysts framed in a filigree border. Dangling beneath each stone, a smaller amethyst in a border of five brilliant-cut diamonds gave the impression of a flower.

A pair of simple square-cut Siberian amethyst earrings backed in gold were a perfect match.

Then, seated at the dressing table, Abigail directed as her lustrous blonde hair was curled and piled high by Kathleen, and held in place with a simple double gold band. Teasing little curls were permitted to flirt at her ears.

Abigail's mischievous gray-green eyes sparkled in the mirror's reflection; a tilt to her lips which had been missing for two summers had returned.

"My Lady," Kathleen breathed in awe, "you look beautiful! You'll outshine all the ladies and have your pick of every eligible gentleman."

Abigail dipped her head in acknowledgement of the compliment. "Go tell the footman to order the sedan chair," she said, and Kathleen ran to do her bidding still wearing a smile of pride in her mistress.

Turning back to the mirror, Abigail gave herself a final appraisal. The weakened, vaguely pathetic woman she had become since *that* night at Boconnoc House was vanquished at last. Rising phoenix-like from the ashes of her old life was the new Lady Abigail Houghall—reliant on no man to make her fortune, but strong and sufficient in herself. She would be mistress of her own destiny, not Canalissy, not James, not Aunt Philomena, and certainly not that damned Sir Percy Blakeney.

As she descended the stairs, Stanstead stopped to watch. He offered a low bow when she reached the final step.

"May I wish you a very pleasant evening, my Lady?"

"Indeed, you may, Stanstead. And you may also tell Lady Philomena not to wait up. I shall be out quite late this evening."

The butler allowed a slight twitch to the corner of his mouth, the smallest ghost of a smile crossing his face before answering, "Very good, my Lady."

Then a gasp of horror across the hall made both of them turn.

Philomena clutched a hand to her chest.

"Abigail Houghall! Isn't it enough to flaunt yourself at private gatherings without caring a jot for social propriety and my reputation that you now go out to a ball unchaperoned?" Philomena gasped again, as much to add emphasis as to summon the wind to add, "And with our family still in such disfavor?"

"Lady Edgecombe will be in attendance as you well know," Abigail responded sharply.

She accepted a wrapper from a nervously bystanding parlor maid and placed it around her shoulders, turning her back on her aunt as the steady crunch of gravel outside heralded the arrival of the chair-men.

"Thank you, Stanstead," said Abigail, and the butler stepped forward to open the door.

"You really are scheming little light skirt," hissed Philomena.

Abigail squared her shoulders in the doorway and slowly turned back to the room.

Stanstead stood to one side of the entrance, his eyes resolutely to the floor. The parlor maid had quietly fled, but Kathleen peered down from the top of the stairs, eyes wide and perhaps also her mouth, although that was covered by one hand.

Then Abigail's gaze fell on Philomena. The old woman's histrionics left her unmoved now, whereas only a few hours before they had driven her to anger. With a new plan about to unfold, a hundred-weight had been lifted and her response to the insult was delivered decisively.

"I think it is time we parted ways, dear aunt."

Abigail watched Philomena's face pale as the woman realized she had overplayed her hand.

"We shall discuss this tomorrow," Abigail announced.

Stepping out into the clear, star-filled night felt like stepping out into freedom.

"You did what?"

Jane hid the exclamation behind a rapidly fluttering fan and, with a firm grip to the arm, pulled Abigail into a recently deserted anteroom.

"Tell me everything, you little minx! You've been holding out on me. You have a new patron, haven't you?"

"A lady never tells." Abigail smiled.

That earned her a sharp rap on the arm from the now folded fan.

"And to think I call you a bosom friend," Jane sniffed theatrically before her good humor was restored. "Well, never mind, I have my own ways of finding out these things. Perhaps one of the new properties on the Crescent?"

"You will just have to wait and see."

The only way Jane could be dissuaded from pursuing the topic was to give her another one to talk about. "Tell me, has that fascinating Mr. Dauncey arrived?" she asked with deliberate emphasis on the name.

As expected Jane's eyebrow raised. "You do like to live dangerously, don't you darling?"

A sly smile crossed Abigail's face. "What is life for if not to live dangerously?"

Jane glanced about cautiously, then leaned in. "Rumor is he is a Radical with a great deal of sympathy for events happening across the channel."

"I'm not interested in the man for his mind, Jane," Abigail offered with a slight shrug.

The response was met with a shocked giggle that Jane was forced to continue behind her fan after several puzzled glances were thrown their way.

"Well, you can't be interested in him for his money," she hissed from behind the fluttering piece of hand painted silk and lace. "His sort *never* have any money of their own." Jane nodded in the direction of the refreshments table. "But you can test your theories on the subject over there."

Sure enough, there was Eamon Dauncey, a handsome man in his early thirties, tall and lean with a ready, rakish smile. His clothes were fashionably cut and expensive, and his dark hair flaunted convention in a thick, floppy fringe which occasionally fell across his eyes.

It was no surprise he was a magnet, though not for the marriage-minded mamas looking for wealthy matches for their daughters. Rather, he attracted bored, aristocratic wives titillated by the thrill of flirting with a man who, in other circumstances, would not be allowed to darken their parlor.

"You'll have an easy conquest indeed if you can free the poor wretch from the clutches of that dreary Baroness Vladinsky," Jane observed. "He'll be your slave out of sheer gratitude."

Abigail stood and gave a nod of acknowledgement to her friend and glanced back at her quarry.

Tonight, she felt it return, surging through her veins like life itself. It was the feeling she thought she would never experience again. The power of feminine allure, the confident knowledge anything was hers with a mere smile and the promise of sex.

She knew her worth; she was a woman beautiful enough to be desired by the Prince Regent and welcomed into the finest salons as a lady-in-waiting to the Princess Royal. Indeed, as mistress to some of England's most powerful men, her good opinion was once considered vital for those who wished to influence or curry favor with her patrons.

She remembered listening to a botanist at one of those bluestocking evenings. He told of a species of spider that would wrap its prey in yards and yards of silken thread until it was immobile, suffocating to death.

Today she would break free of the thread and no one would ever imprison her again, nor—

"Do you dance this evening, Lady Abigail?"

Standing before her, blocking her way forward was the Honorable Daniel Ridgeway, impeccably dressed in black. Abigail looked beyond him to where Dauncey remained in conversation with the Baroness.

Ridgeway lifted a corner of his mouth. "One dance," he cajoled, holding out his hand. "Your Irishman will still be there when we return."

Abigail caught Jane's encouraging nod and, with the most condescending smile she possessed, extended her own hand.

It rested lightly on top of his as she allowed him to lead her to the dance floor, joining the end of the line—the ladies to the right and the gentlemen to the left—just as the orchestra started the first few notes of the minuet.

With sure and practiced grace, Abigail curtsied and Ridgeway bowed, stepping forward lightly to take her hand.

Step forward, step back, a slow turn out, a step forward. All the while his soft blue eyes never left hers.

Step forward, step back, a slow turn in. His gloved hand at her waist was warm and firm even through the fabric of her gown as he led her through the procession down the centre.

Abigail waited for him to begin a conversation, to finally tell her why he sought her out and for what purpose he was in Bath.

They parted. A step, pause, a step past the other dancers to return to the beginning and yet, although separated by a dozen others, she remained the sole object of his attention. An unexpected thrill of desire ran through her as he took her hand once again.

Step forward, step back, a slow turn out, another step forward. His hands tightened on hers ever so slightly.

Step forward, step back, a slow turn in. This time it seemed that hand on her waist held her more closely to him. He smelled of lime, cinnamon, and clove. Abigail became conscious of her own hand at his waist, even through her gloves, and feeling the crisp silk of his jacket where it fit perfectly just above his hip.

And when they parted again, she was surprised to feel the loss.

However, she was not an inexperienced ingénue. Abigail knew what the sensations were and why she was feeling them. Yet, after lying so long dormant, they surprised her with their intensity.

For the entire duration of the dance, the man did not utter a word, but his focus on her never wavered. It only served to heighten her awareness of him.

A polite applause greeted the dancers when the minuet ended. Couples gathered at the edge of the dance floor waiting to take their places.

He escorted her back to where Jane sat in conversation with Lady Pearl Bradstoke.

"I thank you for your company, Lady Abigail. Perhaps you will allow me the pleasure again," he said with a short formal bow before disappearing into the crowd.

"You made a fine-looking couple on the floor," Jane observed lightly, then concern colored her voice. "Oh! Come sit down, before you fall down. Are you feeling quite all right?"

Flushing, Abigail did as her friend bid and, once seated, gave a quick shake of her head. The amethyst earrings tickled her lobes as they swung about. The strange sensation left her.

"Yes, quite well," she answered at last to Jane.

"Well, I'm glad of that because you've certainly made your relative Miss Emily there jealous. What is she again? I keep forgetting, a second cousin thrice removed or something?"

"Or something," Abigail agreed.

She followed the direction of Jane's nod, and sure enough Abigail saw the young woman's pointed look before she turned her head and pretended to engage in amused conversation with a group of other debutants.

"Jealous?" Abigail scoffed. "Mr. Ridgeway is nearly old enough to be her father."

"He's hardly that and well you know it." Jane laughed. "And don't pretend you don't know what I'm talking about either."

Abigail recalled being pressed on the family connection when she was introduced to the girl during her coming out last year. Her manners were very pretty, but her attitude was not.

She glanced back at the girl. This evening, Emily Burchill was dressed in a fetching apricot gown. With her lovely blonde hair, a fine figure and face, she was undoubtedly a popular guest at the sought-after events of the season. Abigail had enjoyed letting Philomena believe she considered the girl a rival, mainly to irritate the sour old prune who was keen to rehabilitate the Canalissy side of the family by grafting it back onto a more reputable branch of the family tree.

And yet there was also much in Emily's manner which reminded Abigail of herself. It was the look Emily would favor young men with when her chaperone was insufficiently attentive—a worldly gaze, a *knowing*. Whether from experience or affectation, Abigail wouldn't hazard to guess.

"I thought William Templeton was her beau?" Abigail accepted a glass of champagne from a passing footman and continued. "I know he's a little slow by not offering for her last season, but I know he's keen."

Jane shrugged as she sipped from her flute. "Who knows? One thing I do know is her mother and father are anxious to secure a match this season. Don't they have another daughter they want to bring out?"

"Well, if Emily is wise, she'll accept young Templeton before Christmas," Abigail said firmly.

"She still young yet," Jane countered with a shrug. "She can afford to keep several young men on a string until nearer the close of the season."

"That strategy doesn't always end well," Abigail observed dryly.

Memories of James came back to her, although without the same pang of loss they once held. Now his memory evoked a shadow of regret. Her actions had been dreadful; she could see that now. She didn't like the woman she had become.

And if their conversation in the morning after the Boconnoc House Ball was not exactly an absolution, it was at least the start of self-reflection.

She watched the dewy-faced girls make their debut and felt old enough to be their mothers. The young men who would have once danced attendance with the hope of a smile or some other little notice from her, now focused their attentions on the debutants.

As eligible gentlemen, they were in hunt for *good* wives to breed them good children, and only those without scandal attached qualified for consideration. Abigail knew she could offer neither goodness nor respectability. That left only lecherous married men seeking a mistress to enhance their standing and ego.

However, her Blakeney-enforced exile to Bath had given Abigail ample time to think…and determine a future on her own terms.

Just one more year to accumulate the funds she needed to escape completely, she reminded herself—less if Ridgeway could be persuaded to be co-operative. A villa in Naples where the renowned hostess Lady Hamilton lived. If any society would accept her, it would be that of Lady Hamilton and the English émigrés who called Italy home.

"I should hardly think someone like Ridgeway would catch the eye of that little social climber," Abigail responded at last.

"Perhaps," conceded Jane, unaware of the direction of her friend's thoughts. "But the fact you've shown an interest by dancing with him is enough to pique her curiosity. I've seen her keeping an eye on us ever since the concert this afternoon."

"Yes, well…let her watch, she may learn something."

CHAPTER FIVE

Mindful of the gimlet-eyed mothers and the sharp-tongued dowagers, Abigail had ensured her dance card and behavior were works of art. No one man was favored over another; suggestions of a private moonlit stroll were politely refused. She had wondered if her skill at charming men and disarming women—an ability abandoned two years ago—might have deserted her, until she caught the eye of Emily Burchill sitting beside a handsome young man, Viscount Richard Hamberley.

Abigail found herself laughing on cue to a half-attended tale being related by Jane's husband, Sir Thomas Ashford, but her main attention was on Emily's closed fan. It slid through her gloved fingers once, twice, a third time. The message was clear. *I. Hate. You.*

A raised eyebrow would be Abigail's only response, but, as she turned away, she noticed a grim face staring intently at Emily and Viscount Hamberley. She placed the face and name, William Templeton, Emily's beau.

Interesting. Young Emily was playing a risky game. She would need to mind her manners if she was to land her suitor.

Another gale of laughter broke Abigail's concentration and she turned her attention to the circle of friends and acquaintances of which she was part, gathered to one side of the ballroom.

Sir Thomas, sporting a neatly trimmed moustache and smartly dressed in emerald green watered silk, was still holding court. Jane, dressed in periwinkle blue and a little tipsy from champagne, looked rapturously at her husband as he regaled Lord and Lady Spearmont and Viscount Salsbury with another story.

It was just too, too adorable.

Abigail hid a smile, but apparently not well enough. She caught the eye of Eamon Dauncey who had been standing in the periphery of the conversation.

"So you think all of this a little ridiculous too," he stated, his face revealing a faint look of disdain toward the Ashfords before easing back into something more benign.

Abigail could see why the bluestockings considered their newfound pet so intriguing. A handsome man who wore contempt of them openly? If only they were aware how much of it was for show and how much was real.

"A rather cynical posture for such as yourself to take, Mr. Dauncey," she replied. "I thought all poets were romantics—particularly the Irish ones."

Dauncey took two or three steps back, putting a small measure of distance from the group and forcing Abigail to take a step forward in order to continue the conversation.

"You're confusing the romantic with the sentimental."

"And are they not the same thing?"

"Mawkish sentimentality is a tool of oppression and no more evidenced than by the construct of marriage, as you must certainly agree."

"Must I?" Abigail smiled. "I've heard marriage called many things, Mr. Dauncey, but a 'tool of oppression' will be a new one that I shall add to my lexicon."

"You're mocking me," he observed without rancor.

"How should I not? I know of many fine marriages and I would count the Ashfords' among them. A cynical observation such as yours points not to the faults of matrimony, but of its participants." She raised an eyebrow the merest fraction. "And its observers."

"Yet you yourself remain outside the bonds of matrimony though you possess all the charms of any one of these debutants."

Dauncey did not wait for a response. "Look at them," he continued, casting his eye across the room. "Little more than sheep herded together for the auction block:

'Wife and servant are the same,
But only differ in the name

When she the word 'obey' has said,
And man by law supreme has made,

Fierce as an Eastern Prince he grows
And all his innate rigour shows.

Then shun, oh shun that wretched state
And all the fawning flatterers hate.

Value yourselves and men despise:
You must be proud if you'll be wise.'"

"A very original observation, Mr. Dauncey," said Abigail dryly.

"Not so original," he said, turning back to her. "It was written by Lady Mary Chudleigh in 1703. And you're not so much different to her are you, *Lady* Abigail?" he suggested, his emphasis on the word "lady" conveying his disrespect. "Your power comes from your ability to decide how much and with whom you share your charms. Were you wed, all of who you are would belong to *him.*"

The comment was pointed and personal.

Dauncey was becoming tedious.

Abigail decided to disengage herself and, with a practiced smile, took a step back. Dauncey immediately drew close again, taking hold of her hand and bringing it to his lips.

"So, who has caught your eye tonight?" he whispered. "A rich mark, no doubt."

Low, simmering anger rose in Abigail. Dauncey was not merely tedious, he was over-familiar, offensive, and partially correct.

She looked around to see if anyone had observed his manner. It seemed no one had, but then her eyes fell on Ridgeway in conversation with Admiral Cecil Worthington on the far side of the ballroom. As though he felt her look, Ridgeway raised his head and met her gaze. Abigail wasn't sure what her expression had conveyed, but she felt relief as he appeared to excuse himself to the Admiral and start toward her.

"I wish you a good evening, sir," said Abigail, attempting to tug her hand away from Dauncey.

Plainly feigning disappointment, Dauncey released her hand and stepped back. "Now don't be like that Lady Abigail. We're not so different, you and I. We both need patrons and, from everything I hear, you are very well connected."

Abigail's anger flared, but, before she could respond, Dauncey turned to a passing footman and took a tumbler of spirits from his tray. Abigail sent the servant on his way with a quick shake of her head.

"We shall continue this conversation at some other time, Milady," Dauncey said with a smirk, before saluting her with his glass and walking away.

Vile creature, Abigail thought. Astute to be sure, but distasteful. His manner might well appeal to bored society wives—she imagined they were perversely titillated by his mockery—but his keenness of observation cut too close to the bone for Abigail's taste. He was more of her past than the future she desired.

She shook her head and focused her attention to the dance floor. Ridgeway was making his way across the room with unhurried grace, yet there seemed purpose in his stride. As she watched him approach, it occurred to Abigail that the only person with whom she could discuss what just happened was a man whom she was not sure she could trust.

He drew closer, then stopped as a handkerchief fluttered at his feet. Miss Emily Burchill, from her seat near the dance floor, offered a sly smile Abigail's way before raising her eyes to the man gallantly returning the silk.

Although too far away to hear the words, Abigail nonetheless knew this play well.

Indeed, Emily rose and Ridgeway straightened with her on his arm. Though polite, he was no fool however, and he threw Abigail a glance that might have hinted at panic.

Abigail merely offered a smile and tiny shake of her head. No, she would not rescue him. The panicked glance narrowed sharply, and Abigail laughed as he reluctantly led Emily to the dance floor.

At that moment, William Templeton returned with two lemonades, beads of condensation falling from each one. He stood bemused at the empty seat which Emily had only just vacated. Abigail couldn't bear his crestfallen face and crossed to him.

"Very kind of you to think of an old maid like me." She smiled, indicating the tall glass in his right hand with a nod of her head.

William started, then ingrained manners took over where conscious thought left off. He gave a small bow and presented her with the glass. "With my compliments, Lady Abigail," he replied dully.

Abigail sat on one of the abandoned chairs and another inclination of her head invited the young man to sit beside her. William craned his neck to peer at the dancers on the floor for a moment before he accepted her silent invitation.

He was a pleasant young man and, with sandy blond hair and soft gray eyes, he was also agreeable to look upon. Even without those attributes, being heir to the Templeton fortune made him most eligible indeed. So far as Abigail could tell, if William had any faults, it would be his youthful inexperience and infatuation with Emily.

After watching William drain his glass in one long swallow, she was glad for his sake there was no alcohol in it.

"Would you permit me the observation that you don't look happy this evening?" Abigail began.

"I'm sorry, Lady Abigail, I didn't mean to appear rude, it's just that…"

She hushed him with a gentle tap of her fan on his arm. "No need to apologize, but I shall say one thing, if I may, and then we'll pretend there is no unpleasantness in the world which cannot be fixed by convivial conversation."

William nodded his assent with a vague frown.

"There may be questions," said Abigail cautiously, "about the nature of women that a young man may not feel comfortable discussing with his father or be confident of obtaining wise advice from his peers. Should you wish a mature female confidante, then you have one in me."

She observed a hitch in the lad's throat as he considered her offer. After a moment, he spoke. "Your offer is gracious and kind, Lady Abigail…it's just that, ah…"

He paused, and Abigail could see he was marshalling thoughts into a sentence he could articulate. With a final sigh, he blurted it out and, when it did, it came out in a half sob. "I love her! So why does she do this to me?"

Abigail experienced a pang of sympathy for the young man, the depth of which surprised her, but to spare him embarrassment, she didn't allow the emotion to show. There was no need to ask who "she" was.

"Father says Emily's too young to marry, but I can't get her out of my head. She torments me," William continued, slumping a little lower in his chair. "She says she has feelings for me, but she flirts outrageously, even with old men like the one she's dancing with now."

The description of Ridgeway as elderly, and the fact she herself had nearly said the same thing to Jane, tempted Abigail to laugh out loud. However, the seriousness of the young man's heartache erased her amusement immediately.

Abigail took a sip of her drink and examined William's profile— the shape of his downcast mouth, the unlined softness of a young man's face unfamiliar with true sorrow.

Dear God, he was so young.

"Love is not in flowery words or impassioned speeches," she said. "Words can be cheap and manipulative. Love is not what a person says, it is what they do."

Memories of the many times she had played men off against one another cascaded in her mind and flooded her with shame. Had she put James through this much torment? Yes, she supposed she had.

The heart is deceitful above all things, and desperately wicked. Who can know it?

"I love her," he began weakly. "What I feel for her is…"

His words trailed away and, after a long silence, Abigail spoke.

"I will not tell you what to do. You're a fine young man; an honorable one. But you can profit from my experience. Do not listen to your heart when it comes to your feelings for this young woman. Use your head instead. Be sure the one you choose to be your wife respects you for the man you are. And, if she does not, and you love her as much as you say, then let her go to find her happiness and you yours."

William nodded slowly, and Abigail could see him thinking about her words, although he kept his face in profile.

After a moment, it seemed a thought occurred to him and he turned to Abigail. "You mentioned your personal experience. Is that why you never married?"

His artless words hit a nerve, and Abigail took a deep breath in careful consideration before answering.

"I was once a foolish young woman who didn't recognize the gift of love when it was presented to me and I wounded the heart of a fine man as a result," she said so softly that she wondered whether William could hear her over the music. "It took many years before I experienced the full consequences of my actions."

Abigail closed her eyes and listened to the music, a sweet melody with a hint of melancholy which tugged at her. She hated self-reflection; it revealed a hard and care-worn soul. It was an image of herself she kept under lock and key.

"What happened to him?" William asked.

Abigail finished the rest of her lemonade, grateful for its coolness against the lump in her throat. "His broken heart mended and he's now married to a very nice girl who loves him truly."

"Oh," he responded and looked away.

"William?" Abigail paused and waited for the young man to face her. "Make sure you find such a girl."

He nodded his response just as the tune came to an end and the dancers left the floor. Now would be a good time to leave, Abigail told herself.

She stood and stretched out her hand. William clasped it and placed a soft kiss to the back of her gloved wrist. "Thank you, my Lady," he told her.

Abigail gave a small smile and a squeeze to his hand, then slipped away. It would be as well to not be there when Emily returned. She skirted the edges of the brightly lit ballroom, avoiding acquaintances, to slip through one of the side doors into the grand hallway.

A few couples strolled its length; the sound of the music from the ballroom was muted. Abigail walked past the entrance to the tea room, now set with tables and chairs as a quiet place for refreshments, and into the Octagonal Room.

Painted in orange, the room was more than a thoroughfare into the card room at the back of the Assembly Hall. Several small fireplaces were set into the angled walls, screened off by oriental-inspired black lacquer screens, offering semi-private places for informal gatherings and assignations by the light of a single multi-tiered chandelier suspended over the centre of the room.

On other nights, she would not have lingered long here—not when there was a purse to win at cards—but tonight Abigail chose a quiet alcove to sit in. She closed her eyes.

Poor William. She wasn't sure what right she had to offer anyone advice on finding and keeping true love, especially when she couldn't be sure she had ever experienced it herself. Affection, passion, lust… they were all were familiar to her, but love?

Abigail wasn't even sure she knew what it was.

"I'm glad you remembered our appointment."

She recognized the droll tone and did not even bother opening her eyes.

"It's not yet midnight," she replied and felt the couch shift as Ridgeway's weight settled down into it.

"In our business, we take our opportunities whenever they occur."

Abigail opened her eyes and her fan to hide a yawn. He did not look fatigued. If one was to assign his expression right now, Abigail would have described him as being studiously nonchalant.

"And what business are we in, Mr. Ridgeway?"

"A very dangerous one."

"I don't recall signing up for a *dangerous business*," she retorted, keeping her voice low to prevent anyone overhearing. "If my experience of *your* business over the past two years is any guide, stultifying boredom would be a better description. You can tell *Aunt Druscilla* that my obligation to her is complete. I'm going abroad at the end of this season."

A slow feline grin spread across his face. "Are you now?"

Fatigue fled and Abigail straightened in her seat, ready to rise to the challenge. "Are you going to stop me?"

"I don't particularly care what you do after this season," he said brusquely. "If you can't give me what I want by the end of June, then you're not half the woman Blakeney thinks you are."

CHAPTER SIX

Daniel knew he had been deliberately provocative and he paused to measure Abigail's reaction. "And what type of woman does Blakeney think I am?" Abigail fanned herself languidly, her gray-green eyes sparkling with equal parts anger and challenge.

Daniel wasn't fooled by the beguiling note of her voice, nor the soft scent of her perfume which tumbled in gentle waves with each movement of her wrist. Abigail was angry, and he knew the right answer meant the difference between her willing co-operation and the need to add some…coercion.

"Blakeney thinks you're a very clever woman; one who knows how to play the long game for her own interests," he said.

As an experienced card player, Daniel waited and watched carefully for the "tell," a raise of an eyebrow, a flare of nostrils, a tap of a finger, a tic to betray what was going on in that mind of hers. His heart beat away several seconds, but she refused to break eye contact or the silence. But there it was—a slight lift of a stubborn chin which told him he had mollified Abigail enough to make her listen to him.

"Tell me about the game."

An odd feeling of relief filled him at her acquiescence, and a grin escaped him unbidden, broadening further when it was returned. There was something in that moment, a connection he felt as a swell in his chest, and the conviction it was not one-sided.

The moment disappeared as a group of men walked out of the card room, among them Sir Reginald and Lord Fforbes. Fforbes nudged his friend and shot a knowing look Abigail's way.

Sir Reginald leered.

Daniel was irritated, but he waited until the gentlemen disappeared into the tea room. He stood and extended his hand to Abigail. "Come on, we're taking a stroll."

A slight frown marred her face, but she made no comment as she placed her white gloved hand in his.

He helped her rise and, tucking her arm through his, they looked for all the world like a courting couple as they strolled outdoors and up the rain-washed street. Although the scent of rain lingered, the shower itself had passed, and pinpricks of stars ventured out from behind scudding clouds, backlit by a nearly full moon.

The evening was chilly, and Daniel was keen to get out of the freshening breeze for Abigail's sake. She wore no coat. He made a fair clip up the street and, despite wearing dancing slippers, Abigail kept pace without complaint. The warm yellow glow of lamplight spilled out of an open inn door, and Daniel took advantage of it to shepherd Abigail through.

Daniel surveyed the room with a practiced eye used to quickly identify threats. It was late and all of the guests had already retired. He caught the attention of the innkeeper, a portly, balding man who had been polishing glasses and goblets. A neatly ordered pyramid of them stood on the bar at his elbow. The man offered them a speculative look, so Daniel decided to command the narrative.

"My wife isn't feeling well. Is there somewhere private where she can recover?" He flipped a coin in the man's direction, causing him to stir into action.

"What are you doing?" Abigail hissed.

"Go with it," he whispered in her ear before he addressed the man again. "And a cup of sweet tea for my wife too."

With a swiftness that belied his bulk, the innkeeper reached out to catch a second tossed coin, then opened a door to the right of the bar.

"Follow me," the innkeeper said. He led them past the dining room and indicated another doorway. "You can use the snug. I'll get the tea."

The man disappeared into what Daniel supposed was the kitchen while he ushered Abigail into the snug. It was a small room, little bigger than a dressing room, but it did have a tiny stove burning on one wall and a respectable-looking over-stuffed sofa opposite.

Daniel shut the door behind him and positioned himself to guard for the innkeeper's return.

Abigail seated herself and made a great display of spreading out her skirts to take most of the sofa. The look she offered him was a challenge.

What the hell was Blakeney thinking, he pondered. Lady Abigail Houghall was too clever and too sure of herself to be a reliable partner in this enterprise.

Oh well…

"Eamon Dauncey."

Abigail blinked and her brows furrowed slightly.

Daniel smiled to himself; it was right to keep her off-balance until he fully knew her measure. "You seemed to be getting on with him quite well."

The frown disappeared and a feline smile emerged. "Jealous?" she drawled.

"Not at all. I want to you to get to know him better. That's the game."

Abigail returned a disbelieving look. "You jest."

Daniel put a finger to his lips and Abigail lowered her voice. "What possible interest could Blakeney have in a penniless Irish poet?"

"Dauncey has interesting friends he wants to know," he replied, "but the type of friends our poet has aren't likely to accept an invitation from Aunty or me. However, they will accept an invitation from Dauncey, but he's clever. He's not going to let his guard down unless he feels safe and at home. You are going to make him feel safe…and at home."

Abigail lowered her head, and Daniel waited for the outburst of affronted anger, outrage at the slur on her character.

The rattle of a tray in the narrow hallway beyond announced the arrival of the innkeeper's wife with the tea. The woman was as round as her husband and, as she placed a trivet and tray on top of the stove, she glanced sidelong at the lady on the settee. On cue, Abigail provided a tremulous smile.

"Thank you for your kindness," she said softly. "I'm sure I shall be quite recovered shortly."

The woman curtsied and left the room.

Daniel watched her go until he was certain she didn't linger within earshot, then he closed the door and moved to the stove. He poured the steaming brown liquid into cups and liberally added honey to one. An unsweetened tea he took for himself and joined Abigail on the settee.

To his surprise, her hand was steady when she took her cup from him. She took a sip, wrinkling her nose slightly, and spoke. "You said you wanted this by the end of June?"

He nodded.

"Then I'll need a well-furnished house with staff I can trust," she told him briskly. "In addition, I want a wardrobe suitable for entertaining and an allowance to run the house and for my personal expenses. My commitment ends on June thirtieth, after which time the furniture, fittings, and any personal items I acquire will be signed over to me along with a sum of three thousand pounds in gold."

Very business-like, very pragmatic. Daniel wasn't sure whether he should be appalled or impressed. "You set a very high price on your services, my Lady," he told her drily.

"Blakeney does not strike me as a man who wastes his time," she answered after another sip of tea. "To require me to prostitute myself to that obnoxious Radical means the stakes in this game are very high— high enough to demand a king's ransom. Whichever way the cards fall at the end of the day, my worth as a spy to Blakeney and the Crown will be completely valueless, so I expect to be suitably compensated.

"Those are my terms, Mr. Ridgeway. Take them or leave them."

* * *

Abigail drank the stewed tea silently, watching him absorb her demands.

Her bald description of what she was being asked to do seemed to surprise him. It made her wonder how much Blakeney's man had been told about her.

The tight lines around Ridgeway's mouth and eyes eased as he seemed to reach some conclusion. His eyes flickered into awareness and met hers. His expression became dark.

"I think we can come to terms," he said, and his deep, dangerous voice sent an involuntary shiver through her.

He agreed? Abigail felt a moment of panic which expressed itself as a slight shake of her hand as she set the cup on arm of the settee. She had been out-maneuvered. For him to have agreed so readily to her not insubstantial demands told her it really *was* a serious game she was being asked to play.

"It's only fair to warn you I have some conditions of my own," Ridgeway continued.

"And what might they be?" she countered, adding a measure of imperiousness to her tone.

Abigail knew her every expression was being carefully watched and catalogued, so she fought to keep her face neutral. She was planning to place much in the hands of a man who was a virtual stranger to her. Her reputation, her future, perhaps even her very life. It was a risk, but with the funds to start her new life in Naples at her fingertips, she calculated it would be foolish not to take it.

"Since you're not one for beating about the bush, I'll be blunt," he said. "This is the way it works: from this moment on, should anyone see us together, you are my mistress. That gives me the right to be at your new townhouse any time of the day or night. I will tell you what you need to know when you need to know it, and that is for your protection as it is mine. You will tell no one about this arrangement, not even your friend Lady Jane. Is that understood?"

Abigail nodded silently.

Ridgeway's expression remained thunderous, although she couldn't understand why it might be. Hadn't she just agreed to go along with everything without question?

He stood, taking her empty cup and saucer and putting it along with his on the tray on top of the stove. He remained with his back to her. The uncomfortable silence stretched out and tension filled the small room until it was claustrophobic. Ridgeway half glanced back at her. The fire threw deep shadows across his face. Abigail felt self-conscious, as though she had failed a test.

"Is that all?" Abigail snapped. She watched Ridgeway slowly turn to her, his face now a neutral mask of disinterest.

"One final point. Whether or not you *actually* take Dauncey to your bed is your business. I don't care what you do as long as he feels at ease in your company and we get what we want."

Abigail stood and mustered as much pride as she possessed. "Now that's agreed, Mr. Ridgeway, we'd best make our way to the Assembly before we're missed."

She had intended to dismiss him, treat him as coldly as he did her, but as she edged past, he grabbed both hands firmly.

"You'll be spending a lot of time in my company," he said, leaning in to whisper in her ear. "Call me Daniel."

Despite the heat in the tiny snug, a delicious shiver ran through her—a reflexive reaction to being in such close quarters with not only a handsome man, but also one who intrigued her.

Abigail pulled back slightly so she could see his face. There was more to the *Honorable* Daniel Ridgeway than met the eye. It seemed he was not above playing games. Just as well she could wear down more than cards.

She allowed her hands to remain in his and leaned forward, standing on tiptoes, her breasts pressed against his chest as she whispered back to him, "Then you'd best call me Abigail."

Dropping back to the floor, Abigail watched the blue of his eyes darken, then drop lower. Her lips parted in silent appeal and her tongue emerged to wet them in anticipation.

Reckless desire, submerged for two long years, resurfaced stronger and she willed him closer. And he did. Ridgeway leaned forward to whisper again in her ear.

"Save the performance for an audience."

Though frustrated, Abigail grinned triumphantly at him, and preceded him from the snug.

CHAPTER SEVEN

1 October

Dear Daniel, I'm delighted you have renewed acquaintance with your cousin Abigail and I'm not surprised to learn she has expensive tastes. Still, family has never been more important as it is in these uncertain times, so I'm willing to accede to her request.

Ask her to continue to write. I do enjoy reading her news.

Assure her that Aunt Philomena enjoys her new residence in Truro. I'm sure this will be a great comfort to her.

Regarding your last enquiry, I passed on your warmest solicitude to Mrs. Sawyer, although to my regret I have nothing further to tell her.

But some news which may interest you. A celebration, complete with fireworks is rumored to be planned for London early in the New Year, although the date is as yet uncertain, as is the identity of the organizers.

It's causing a great deal of interest here as you might imagine, and guests are expected from both France and Ireland. Isn't that exciting?

Perhaps your poet friend knows something of this? If so, we'd be delighted to make him and his friends most comfortable should they ever find themselves in London.

Best wishes for the season ahead,
Aunt Druscilla

* * *

With the practiced eye of an experienced society hostess, Abigail choreographed her staff. Footmen rearranged the furniture, housemaids set the linens ready for the little delicacies that would be served on dainty silver trays. The bright and airy parlor was the venue for this morning's poetry recital on behalf of the Ladies' Education and Benefit Club of Bath.

Satisfied with the progress, Abigail was content to leave the supervision in Stanstead's hands while she readied herself for the guests arriving in a little more than an hour. Despite three weeks of non-stop activity setting up residence in the townhouse on The Crescent and re-establishing her credentials as a fashionable hostess of renown, she was too excited to be tired.

She was born for this.

Her bedroom bustled with activity too. The housemaid finished her duties, dipped a curtsey, and exited, leaving Kathleen, who was now elevated to the role of lady's maid.

"My Lady, I've laid out the new floral cotton outfit for you," she informed Abigail before stepping behind her to assist with removing her morning dress. "Your new gowns are expected to arrive today including the rose-pink satin which will be pressed and ready for this evening."

"Did the matching slippers arrive yesterday along with the riding boots?"

"They did, ma'am."

Abigail braced herself as the stays were fastened. She glanced over at her day dress, made from imported Indian cotton in white. The fabric was patterned all over in floral sprigs of purple, red, and blue and the design boasted long sleeves, de rigueur for daytime events.

This was her first occasion hosting since becoming mistress here. To this point, it had not been necessary to explain whose "mistress" she purported to be. The *Honorable* Daniel Ridgeway had been most obliging in staying out of her way.

All but one of the times she had seen him since that night at the ball—cards at the Assembly Rooms, dinner parties with Jane and Thomas, crossing paths riding in the extensive park just across the road—he was in the company of other people. Only a politely formal nod of acknowledgement had passed between them.

As Kathleen finished dressing her, Abigail expected to be a flutter of nerves, but she felt none. Instead, strength and power ran through her veins fuelled by confidence in her own abilities as well as the unquestioning non-interference of her new benefactor.

Her maid directed her to the dressing table where her hair was to be a simple upsweep, held in place with a white bandeau as light curls framed her cheeks. Abigail closed her eyes as her long blonde hair was brushed and thought back to the occasion she had exchanged more than a nod with Ridgeway. It had been two weeks ago at the Tea Room:

He had placed a thick envelope on the table.

"A gift for me?" she replied sardonically. "You shouldn't have."

Ridgeway returned a dry smile. "It's a gift from Aunt Druscilla. The keys to the town house, a letter of credit, and an address of a solicitor. Anything related to our quarry should be sent directly there. Your bills and a weekly accounting of expenses too. Don't forget."

Abigail ignored his admonishment and slid the parcel to the hatbox, surrounded by the bounty of a morning's shopping, beside her.

"The furniture has been delivered," he continued, raising his coffee cup and taking a sip while glancing casually about. "There's some unpacking to do. You'd better get a move on."

"I already am." Abigail smiled. "There's to be a ladies' poetry morning with our Irish friend in a fortnight's time. In the afternoon, I plan to hold an at-home. I trust you'll be there?"

He gave a non-committal shrug of his shoulders. "Don't count on it."

She straightened. "And what exactly do you intend to do while I spy on the beau monde of Bath?"

Revealing nothing more than a wink would convey, he sipped his coffee again. He seemed amused at her pique and it irritated her all the more.

Abigail could feel the lingering annoyance with him leaching into her good mood, so she opened her eyes just as Kathleen finished with her hair.

"The coral cameo choker and earrings, my Lady?" she asked.

Abigail nodded. Her humor was restored by the time the guests began arriving.

Jane was the first. She was an unfashionable fifteen minutes early.

"You've been so mysterious over the past few weeks, I just had to come ahead of time," she exclaimed as she stepped into the parlor. Her kiss of greeting missed Abigail's cheek by some inches as she was distracted in admiration of a console table.

Jane followed Abigail into the first floor drawing room and gasped. The sumptuously decorated room with its brightly colored Turkish carpets and cut crystal vases and decanters gleamed in the morning light.

"Where have you been hiding all of this?"

"It belonged to someone in the family," she told Jane blandly.

"Wonderful!" her friend exclaimed. "It's marvelous when you're left something nice. Even better when it's someone you don't know, then the whole thing comes a great surprise."

"A great surprise indeed." The irony in the reply was lost on Jane. Abigail too had been stunned by the furniture when she first stepped into the townhouse.

The finest quality furnishings in oak, mahogany, and walnut, all magnificently finished and fit for a first rate stately home.

All of this was to be hers, thanks to an agreement in writing, yet she was askance that Blakeney would lavish such finery for a charade. Then she witnessed the opening of the barrels containing the dinner services and the silver.

Piece after piece bore a monogram of the Canalissy coat of arms.

Blakeney really did have an exquisite sense of humor, Abigail reflected bitterly.

* * *

Daniel gave his bay stallion its head as it galloped along the road west of Bath.

The Somerset countryside was alive with autumnal color. Rich gold and red elm leaves held on tenaciously in the face of a stiff breeze that buffeted Daniel's back, pushing him onward to Pensford, eight miles west of the city. Wildflowers in pinks and purples waved encouragement as he raced by. He acknowledged their best wishes with a smile, his mood buoyed by the letter he had received this morning promising more than just a little hope that Jonathan Sawyer was still alive.

He counted Sawyer as his only friend—a rarity in a profession where, after a while, one couldn't be sure of one's own name. Sawyer had covered his back more times than Daniel cared to count, and it was no small bone of contention between him and Sir Percy that the baronet had ordered him to stay out of France.

Dammit, it should have been Jonathan here in England instead. It just wasn't right, not when Rachel and the children needed a husband and father at home.

He reined the horse back to a canter as they reached the outskirts of Pensford. The historic village teetered on the brink of extinction. The wool industry it had been famous for a century earlier had all but vanished, although rumors of rich coal seams buoyed entrepreneurial spirits. Still, the sleepy village did play its part as a staging post for coaches enroute to and from Bristol, another seven miles away to the west.

Past St Thomas's church stood The Rising Sun. Daniel hoped the answers he was looking for would be found there. The coaching inn was nearly deserted, but the rich aroma of freshly baked game pies drew him in along with his mission, and he ordered one along with a pint of ale.

"There's a package waiting for Simon Thorpe," he told the barmaid who eyed him appreciatively.

On her return with the package, he winked and slid an extra coin across the bar, not only ensuring the food would be hot and the ale cool, but also his privacy as he sat in the back corner of the inn's dining room. The rectangular package was a wrapper of rough paper tied with string around its contents. It had been sealed with unadorned wax across the knot. One sharp stroke of a penknife and the taut fastening gave way.

Inside the brown paper were two envelopes. The larger, fatter one was blank; the other was addressed to "Simon."

To Daniel's relief, a hand-drawn motif of a primrose lay in the bottom right-hand corner of the addressed envelope. To the casual observer it would seem to be a simple doodle, an idle decoration without purpose, but its presence was a reassurance Jonathan wasn't communicating under duress.

It was this envelope he opened first and withdrew a single sheet.

Long time since I wrote, but these are perilous times and I'll keep this message brief. I have tracked Roux to Paris, but he's gone to ground. I curse the man every day. No matter how hard I press our contacts, no one has heard a thing. Mark my words, that means trouble for us.

The second envelope will tell you everything I have learned that I dare entrust to a messenger.

Paris has descended to madness. Last night was the worst violence I have witnessed and pray God I will not see the like of again. Women, even nuns, were raped, then run through, left to die in the streets. Men strung up on lampposts, families dragged into the street, fathers executed while their children are forced to watch on.

I've moved to where it is safer just outside of the city. There are very few I trust, although one family in Bicetre has been kind. For their sake I shall not identify them. I don't know if I'm being watched, but assume it is safer to believe I am.

This also means you cannot write and tell me how Rachel fares. How I miss her. Tell her I wear her miniature close to my heart.

You said when I wed her that the better man had won. Now I wonder if that was truly the case. Look after her, should anything happen. I know you love her almost as much as I do.

Forgive me, friend. I'm tired, maudlin, and too far from home.

-J

"You fancy some comp'ny then?"

Daniel looked up at the voice. The barmaid, a blowsy young woman with dirty blonde hair and a figure bordering on voluptuous, set his pie and ale in front of him and pushed her shoulders back slowly, drawing attention to her bosom.

Seeing she had his attention, the young woman smiled seductively. "When you're finished, you might want something for afters."

It wouldn't have been so long ago he might have accepted the offer without hesitation or regret, but Jonathan's letter pining for Rachel filled his thoughts. His beautiful English rose, light brown hair, peaches and cream skin, lovely dark eyes, and the sweetest disposition.

Tumbling this girl would be like cheating on Rachel.

He acknowledged the absurdity of being faithful to another man's wife the moment the thought entered his head. Still, Daniel gave her a regretful smile and shake of his head. The barmaid moved on.

He returned to his meal, his mood darker than it had been when he'd arrived at Pensford. As good pub fare filled his belly, he thought how Abigail's first event as one of Sir Percy's league of spies this morning would by now have given way to her "at home." It would have been amusing to attend the affair and see Houghall in full bloom with men buzzing like bees for her attention, especially Eamon Dauncey.

The poet's slightly risqué and subversive doggerel might titillate the bored matrons and his Irish brogue might make their calf-eyed daughters swoon, but the man himself was dangerous. He was clever, but not clever enough for Abigail, Daniel hoped.

Perhaps, he *would* go along to the Thomas's soiree tonight to see if she was still mad at him for snubbing her "at-home."

The second envelope waited for him. He opened it and peered inside without removing the contents. A quick leaf through them revealed copies of ship manifests among other things. They'd require careful study and this was not the place for it.

The long case clock opposite the door chimed a quarter past two o'clock, and Daniel drained the last of his beer. There were two more people to see before returning to Bath.

With the plain envelope now hidden in a coat pocket, Daniel stood, crumpling the accompanying letter and paper wrapping, then lobbing them into the large fireplace that warmed the inn's dining room. Slipping on his coat, he watched carefully as the paper curled and browned, then ignited in a momentary burst of brilliant yellow and orange before becoming indistinguishable from the rest of the fuel the fire feasted upon.

He watched the flames a moment more and reflected on how events were unfolding.

Officially, Abigail may be shackled to him until the end of June but, in light of Jonathan's letter, Daniel intended to give her an early parole.

He was going back to France, the sooner the better.

CHAPTER EIGHT

Daniel dismounted in a field just outside Bath where a group of brawny men were setting up bleachers in a large pavilion about the size of a circus tent. The tent was bigger and newer than he remembered. Business must be looking up.

He left his horse to graze and called out to a man hefting a crate across broad shoulders. "Where's George?"

The man nodded across to the far corner of the field where a group of wagons stood like sheep at pasture. Standing proud of the group was a gaudily painted gypsy wagon emblazoned with the slogan *Jamaica George's Prestigious Pugilists & World Renowned Wrestlers.*

Daniel skirted the edge of the tent, but turned at the sound of thundering hooves. A group of six young bucks from town had evidently learned of the arrival of the traveling show and were there to sign on for the amateur bouts that preceded the professional shows.

There were some faces he recognized, the young Viscount Richard Hamberley and his friend William Templeton among them, but he didn't acknowledge the acquaintance. He rounded the back of the marquee and, from a distance away, heard raised voices. The substance of the dispute became clearer as he approached.

"No more, George! Mick was so drunk last night, he couldn't even beat that mawga boy."

Daniel smiled; Bossy and George hadn't changed, not for one minute, and for that he was glad. A rush of bitter nostalgia came over him at the term they'd used. All of a sudden *he* was that "mawga"—skinny-boy—running desperately short of blunt and without a friend in the world.

"Bossy, everyone deserves another chance," the man implored.

"Naht when they taking my money they not!"

Daniel wondered whether George and Bossy had ever argued over him like that. As he rounded the back of the caravan, he could see Bossy seated at her desk, a fine-looking mahogany ship's campaign table with bobbin-turned legs. She had an open ledger in front of her. Bossy was the one who made sure the show was profitable every night.

Although head and shoulders taller than his wife, George sat hunched on a nearby stool weathering the tempest of her fury.

Daniel rapped the side of the caravan to announce his presence, and it was Bossy who recognized him first.

"Oh my word, Dapper Dan, ah you!" And with surprising speed, the little middle-aged Jamaican woman rushed past her husband and threw her arms around him and squeezed asking, "Where did you come from?"

Bossy gripped his arms and held him back to take a good look. Daniel accepted her scrutiny with a familial affection.

"I've missed you too, Bossy," he said, hugging the woman to his side with one arm while reaching forward with the other to shake the hand of Jamaica George, the boxing and wrestling impresario known the length and breadth of England.

Despite being in his mid-fifties, gray, and a little thicker in the middle than when Daniel last saw him, George nonetheless still looked strong and fit, though, as Daniel later learned from Bossy, he no longer boxed. These days, George performed only in the choreographed exhibition wrestling with other members of the troupe and not against those men who paid good money to try their luck and fists against the professionals.

"Well, it's a fine day to see you again, boy," said George, his Jamaican patois shifting to a soft clear English.

"You too, George."

"Tell me," Bossy asked. "What about that nice girl you was so keen on? You go make her your wifc?"

"No, she found a better man," he replied and felt his smile falter before he breathed life back into it by sheer force of will. "But I didn't come here to talk about the past. I need your help."

The big black man stood back and gave him a thorough appraisal. "Your clothes are very fine and if that's your horse over there, so it is too. I guess you do not want your old job back."

Daniel laughed. "Despite the worst expectations of my family, I'm doing all right for myself." He plunged on, determined to change the subject. "I'm looking for a man—a man who doesn't want to be found—and I need someone to be my eyes and ears."

Bossy crossed her arms over her ample bosom. "Daniel Fitzgerald Ridgeway, don't be askin' us to do somethin' bring us to the attention of the law. We leave them alone and them leave us alone and that's the way I like it. I don't want to be in the hands of them deceivin' slavers."

George swiftly overruled his wife.

"Hush, Bossy, there be no risk of that. We're baptized Christian and we're lawful English. We make good money from people who want to see the black folk while we look at the white folk for free. Daniel wouldn't ask us to do something outside the law."

The last statement was delivered with an edge, as if daring Daniel to contradict him.

Daniel hastened to reassure George. "No, nothing like that. The man I'm looking for is a bad man, a criminal. If you see him, do nothing except send me a messenger, that's all."

"You be a thief-taker?" demanded Bossy.

Daniel shook his head.

"You be a spy!" she breathed.

Daniel dared a quick look in her direction and the expression that greeted him was one of disapproval. He could never stand Bossy's censure so he kept his eyes on George, who returned his gaze steadily. Perhaps he could silently will George into helping with the strength of sincerity. In any event, Daniel remained focused on the man in front of him—a man who had been more than employer. He was a friend, and at one time, the only friend Daniel had.

"What is it you'll have us do?" George asked after a time.

Bossy threw up her hands and let out a cry of exasperation before stalking off, muttering something about getting her boys ready for tonight's performance.

"I would never do anything to put you and Bossy at risk, George," Daniel told him. "You know that and you know me."

George slumped down in his seat and indicated with a gesture that Daniel do the same. He sat in the chair Bossy had vacated.

"England is on the brink of war with France and there are men who want to bring revolution to our shores. I'm trying to stop them."

George straightened, but said nothing. Daniel pressed on.

"There's an Irishman by the name of Eamon Dauncey. I believe he is part of a group of Radicals who plan to set off a bomb in London early in the New Year. I can't wait that long. We don't know who his associates are, and I'm beginning to run out of options. But I have an idea to draw them out."

* * *

The last of the guests who attended her "at-home" said their farewells just as the clock struck three in the afternoon. When Abigail returned to the drawing room, only Dauncey remained. He stood by the fire, staring at the flames, swirling a glass of whiskey in his hand. The time had come to earn her keep.

Her eyes were drawn to the decanter which now sat a quarter full. It had been much fuller than that earlier in the day.

Abigail smiled at her guest as though thrilled to have him all to herself. Eamon Dauncey was the most pompous, self-important, obnoxious *ass* of a man she had ever met. And that was saying something, considering the debauchery of her past.

And yet the silly women flocked around him as he spouted nonsensical philosophy dressed in a pretty accent and fine-sounding words. Abigail may not have had a broad education, but she did pride herself on having a great deal of common sense.

To fortify herself for the rest of the afternoon with this man, she poured a measure of brandy and took a healthy draught before she faced him. And there was the Ashford's party tonight…

Abigail took another sip.

"You've done very well for yourself, darlin', and in such a short time too," he offered with a sly smile. "No wonder you didn't want to play a few weeks ago. Your pigeon really was ripe for the plucking, was he? Tell me, is he that walrus-faced fustiluggs you play cards with?"

Abigail glowered at him contemptuously.

"Ah, I see, perhaps it's the cork-brained Lord…Fforbes, is it?"

"Perhaps you've outstayed your welcome, Mr. Dauncey."

He placed the glass on the mantle and raised his hands in mock surrender. "I sorry if I'm insulting your friends, darlin', but someone has got to call these lazy parasites out for what they are—annoying biting fleas carrying the pestilence of their aristocratic entitlement on society's body corporate," he said, watching closely for her reaction.

Abigail hid it behind another swallow of the liquor while she considered her next move. The man was utterly insufferable and yet he was happy to play court jester. There was only one reason why someone with such obvious self-regard would debase himself.

She smiled seductively at him and sashayed closer.

"You're going to have learn some manners if you want me to provide you with invitations."

"Is that *all* you want, milady?" he asked silkily in the soft brogue that so captivated Bath's matrons and bluestockings.

She stepped close, close enough to smell the fresh tobacco in the pouch in his jacket pocket and the smell of whiskey on his breath.

"You fascinate me, Mr. Dauncey. I want to know what makes you tick. You hate the moneyed, yet you crave their wealth. You hold the aristocrats in contempt, but you are drawn to them. You go to great lengths to charm the ladies yet, if the gossip I hear is true, you've spurned the invitations of every one."

"Not everyone," he said, sweeping up her hand in his and kissing it fully.

"I should be flattered, if I didn't suspect your motives to be entirely self-serving," she said, withdrawing her hand.

Dauncey laughed, delighted as a child with a new toy. He claimed his whiskey glass once more before collapsing indolently on a nearby sofa.

"Well, I can say the feeling is mutual," he said, toasting her. "Among the silly, trite and pampered canaries in this gilded cage, you're a true breath of fresh air—cleverer than most. I think we can help one another."

"Pray enlighten me as to what aid you can offer me?" She spread her arms wide to draw attention to the expensive finery in the room. "As you can see, I do very well on my own."

"Ah, but it's not enough, is it, darling Abigail? You want more than that, don't you?"

She straightened, feeling the prickling of awareness crawling up her back. Abigail lowered herself on the sofa.

"You want freedom," Dauncey continued, "the ability to decide to live and love on your own terms without the bourgeois shackles and expectations of social norms."

He grinned at seeing her reaction.

"Don't worry, you're not alone," he assured her. "There are many of us who feel the same way. As my friend William Godwin says, 'the dissolution of political government, of that brute engine which has been the perennial cause of the vices of mankind, is not otherwise removable than by its utter annihilation.'"

"Talk like that will get you arrested," Abigail said lightly as she mentally urged him on.

"Now don't you be fretting," he said and winked. "It's only talk. Once people know the truth for themselves, they'll gladly take the weighted bonds from their own feet. Our friends across the channel know this. They yearn for enlightenment and a rational world that requires no laws, no government, and no religion. And they'll do it too. Mark my words, this is the beginning of France's golden age—a model society for the world to emulate."

Dauncey was just warming up. He left his place and joined Abigail on the settee. When he took her hand, she moved to protest, but he placed a finger on her lips.

"Shh, little lamb, close your eyes a moment while I describe a world just within our grasp. Go on," he cajoled, "just for moment."

She felt his other arm snake around her shoulder and against her better nature she closed her eyes, but not before she had worked out how many steps it would take reach the bell pull by the fireplace.

Or the poker in it.

Just in case.

"Imagine it, Abigail," he whispered close to her ear. "The only law being one of your own making. Free to live, to dance, to love exactly how, and whom, and when you please. No judge to sentence you, no priest to shame you. It'll be grand, dear girl."

Dauncey shifted closer. She could feel the press of his body by her side and the long gentle strokes of his fingers on the side of her cheek.

"Are you imagining it? Walking down the street in fear of no one and nothing, free to do whatever you please, whenever you please, however you please. Imagine a world where all men are ruled only by rational thought, where every man is his own religion."

Abigail did imagine, walking down the sun-dappled streets of Naples with no shame following her, the baggage of her past jettisoned behind, no censure from anyone.

Like a dream, it was lovely.

It was also a lie.

Abigail sat stock-still, counting each heart beat, not aroused—her attention was too focused to entertain such a thing even if she were disposed. Instead, she waited for Dauncey to act, willing him to tell her something of use.

"There's a new future, Abigail, one for people like you and me who are smart enough to take it," he continued, his lips now so close to her that his warm breath eddied in her ears. 'Nature has placed mankind under the governance of two sovereign masters, pain and pleasure.' What choice are you going to make?"

She opened her eyes to see Dauncey studying her intently. Not with passion or lust, but with a strange kind of detached curiosity that made her feel as though she were a butterfly pinned for his inspection.

Dauncey could reveal something important, she was sure of it, but what? Abigail couldn't be certain.

She brought her breathing back under control and, after a hesitant start, said, "I don't believe you." She offered a coy glance to soften her words. "You're all talk. Pretty words are not going to change the world. I need something to believe in."

"What if I tell you there are men who are willing to do more than just talk about it?"

Abigail straightened up on the couch and put a more respectable distance between herself and Dauncey. He took that as a cue to stand up and refill his whiskey glass.

"Really?" she said. "Like what?"

To her disappointment Dauncey put a finger to his nose in a gesture of secrecy before pointing it at her and giving an accompanying wink. "That's enough questions on that topic, darlin'."

Abigail pouted. "Well, since it's not feminine company you want, I have to say I'm quite at a loss as to what you *do* want."

"This is the thing…" he began, and Abigail knew she was in for a treat of masterful story telling. She gave him her full attention and he acknowledged it with a knowing half-smile.

"It's hard for a prideful man to admit he has needs—and believe me, I have *many* needs—but the most pressing one for me and my friends is money and I think you can help us."

CHAPTER NINE

One by one, the oil lamps were lit, flaring into life as they hung from various points on the tent—like constellations in the now darkening night sky. They bobbed and swayed in a cold breeze that marked the transition from afternoon to early evening. Snatches of instructions by George to his men as they prepared their show were carried on the breeze to Daniel as he strode away from the camp. The voice and its commands were as welcome and familiar as the curried goat dish Bossy insisted he eat before leaving.

He made his way toward his horse in the dimming light, grinning at Bossy's grumbled complaints about his plans.

"You are a 'fool fool', you know?" she'd scolded him.

Yes, he did know. And should his scheme go wrong, he could end up with something far more serious than a broken nose and few bruised ribs, but he didn't have the luxury of time or options. Not with three months before the threatened "fireworks" in London.

At least Abigail might be able to keep Dauncey occupied for the next few weeks while he investigated the man's connections. She seemed capable enough.

The face of his partner in this enterprise swam into view. Gray-green eyes deep enough for a man to lose himself in, the shape of her mouth full and generous and so often quirked "just so" in knowing amusement.

He needn't have taken Blakeney's word for it; he saw for himself how capable she was of captivating a man's attention and holding it. But drawing room flirtations were one thing, taking the man to bed was another.

Images suddenly filled his head of her and the Irishman together. He shook his head violently against the thought. Yet it nagged at him.

Lady Abigail was not like Rachel, and the idea of comparing the two of them was ludicrous on its face. Rachel was pretty, sweet, and amenable. Abigail on the other hand was breathtakingly beautiful, headstrong, and dangerous.

Despite her apparent abilities, however, Abigail's welfare was *his* responsibility. He'd rather put *his* body on the line than hers. His black thoughts stayed with him as he crossed the meadow. Jamaica George's troupe would stay here until after Guy Fawkes Night, the busiest night of the year when most of Bath from its highest citizenry to the lowest would gather for the lighting of the bonfire and burning of the effigy.

Daniel needed answers by then if he were to slip across the Channel into France before the crossing was made hazardous by winter storms and fog. Now standing beside his mount, Daniel toed a stone, then, with a swift kick, punted it into the darkness, irritated with himself.

He cocked an ear, waiting for the satisfying thud of the rock landing somewhere, when a brief respite in the breeze on his back permitted sharp, angry words to carry to him. With the raised voices came the whinnying of alarmed horses.

Daniel ran toward the noise. Two men were brawling and one appeared to be getting the better of it.

In the gloom, it was impossible to identify the participants, but Daniel weighed in for the losing protagonist, giving the other an unexpected and mighty boot up the backside. It sent him sprawling before the second fighter who, alarmed at the intervention, rewarded Daniel for his troubles with a panicked swing of his fist. It connected with air, and Daniel responded by stepping forward to sweep the man's legs from under him.

Daniel hauled the first to his feet by the collar and turned his attention to the second as the moon emerged from behind a cloud.

"Templeton and Hamberley!" he growled as he identified them. He let go of Hamberley's collar, and the two young men had the good grace to look shame-faced. "I'm not going to ask what all of this was about, but get out of here before I tell your parents you've been brawling like schoolboys."

"Thank you, sir," they answered breathlessly in unison and, with tension still thick between them, ran to their horses. William Templeton mounted his first and took off at a gallop; Richard Hamberley mounted more gingerly and turned toward Bath at a more sedate pace.

Daniel walked back over to his own mount. The horse nudged him on the shoulder as he adjusted its bridle, and he responded with a reassuring pat.

"Our day's not over yet," he said, "let's go see how our *espionne* fared."

The townhouse on The Crescent was minimally lit, and the window of the ground floor drawing room was in darkness. In the first floor window Daniel knew was Abigail's bedroom, the curtains were open slightly and a lamp burned on the sill.

A wide red satin sash hung down one edge of the curtain. That meant the Irishman was in her company, most likely at the Ashford's soiree this evening.

Daniel shook his head in amusement and turned his mount toward town. At least Blakeney was consistent in his avowal to turn Abigail into a Rahab, and he chuckled at Percy's sense of humor. By Daniel's reckoning, he had three hours to uncover some of Dauncey's secrets.

The first hour was lost to stabling his horse and to dressing suitably for a less salubrious part of town. By the time the tenth hour chimed, Daniel returned to Dauncey's lodgings, a hostelry respectable enough in its own way, but certain not to lighten the purse too much.

A week ago, Daniel had sent young Master Tapper to deliver a week-old edition of *Freeman's Journal* to the Irishman's door and, in return for a shilling, the lad had identified the location of his room— first floor, right at the back of the inn. Just across the passage there was a narrow service staircase to a back entrance. Convenient for clandestine comings and goings.

However, Daniel started his investigation via the front door. Now clothed as a nondescript working man, he kept his red hair covered with a gray cloth cap, purchased an ale with coppers, and slouched into a shadowed corner.

The dining room was busy, so no one paid the solo drinker any mind. He had been here every night for the past week, but, frustratingly, each and every time Dauncey had dined alone.

Tonight, once again, he watched the comings and goings of the patrons for a good hour, noting a couple of young harlots plying their trade, disappearing with their clients through the curtains and up the stairs to the rooms beyond. Two men sat at a small square table, playing draughts; two more quietly talked by the fireplace while a companion nodded off, making only the occasional asthmatic snore as his contribution to the conversation.

These five would stay until the innkeeper announced time at the bar.

Daniel kept his eyes on four tulips, a group of rather well-to-do young men who were well foxed by the look of them. Their conversation had grown louder and more incoherent in the hour he'd been watching. Now they were singing:

"I've traveled all over this world
And now to another I go
And I know that good quarters are waiting
To welcome old Rosin the Beau"

Men that drunk were unpredictable, but potentially useful. Daniel watched as they launched into another verse:

"When I'm dead and laid out on the counter
A voice you will hear from below
Saying "Send down a hogshead of whiskey
To drink with old Rosin the Beau"

Then, noticing their glasses empty, they called for the serving girl. The young woman's approach drew additional whoops and yells from the group, but it was the innkeeper behind the bar that Daniel observed. The man was now focused, along with several of the other drinkers in the room, on the rowdy group as one or two of their number grabbed at the girl.

It was the distraction Daniel had been waiting for.

On each previous night, he had sat and drank until closing time. Tonight, with what he had in mind, he didn't want to attract attention leaving early. As the innkeeper craned his neck and yelled a brusque "keep it down there!" at the carousers, Daniel eased inconspicuously to his feet and slipped quietly out of the premises.

He walked unhurriedly down a street alongside the inn, then paused at an alley which ran behind the building and made a point of putting his hands down and fiddling with the buttons of his breeches. He glanced left and right, then slipped into the alley. Anyone seeing him would assume he was caught short, but it gave him time to survey his way ahead.

Weak moonlight barely touched the objects along the passage, proving just sufficient illumination to make his way, but in deep enough shadow to go without detection. The alley led to a small courtyard. Daniel ducked behind a stack of crates and watched the half-open rear door of the inn. Sounds from the kitchen, along with an orange glow from the coals of the fireplace inside, told him the room was still in use, yet no one had crossed the passage to go up the stairs in some time.

Using the shadows to his advantage, he stalked part way across the courtyard, staying close to the wall. Then the two harlots from the dining room threw open an upstairs door and banged their way down the steps, giggling and swearing like sailors.

Damn!

The cook emerged from the kitchen and an argument ensued in the courtyard just feet away from Daniel. He silently huffed his frustration and edged along the wall, shrinking against it, his dark cloak helping him merge into the blackness. He held his breath as he passed the corner of the building. The argument showed no sign of abating, its participants too well involved in their own strife.

Good fortune favored Daniel again. Dauncey's first floor room on the corner had just one window and it had been left slightly ajar. The ground floor was a blank wall; the back of a storeroom, he guessed.

A lead downpipe dropped to a half-full rainwater barrel just to the right beneath Dauncey's window. Daniel drew himself lithely up onto the edge of the barrel. The additional thirty-eight inches of height gave him just enough reach to grab the sandstone sill of Dauncey's window with his left hand.

He shimmed across the ledge, easing his right arm beneath the window, raising the sash enough to scramble in, avoiding a small table and chair placed under it.

Dauncey may have been out all day, but a maid had banked the fire, and it burned low in the grate. Daniel lit a taper, then the lamp, although he kept its light low. He walked to the door and turned the lock. The sound of the argument below in the courtyard was muffled, but still audible.

Daniel quickly surveyed the room. It was nothing especially grand—whitewashed walls, an oak wardrobe, and a dressing table set opposite the window. The bed was against the end wall, the nightstand and pot cupboard to one side.

The table by the window was clear. Dauncey appeared to be a cautious man.

A brisk, but methodical examination of his baggage stored under the bed revealed no papers. Too obvious a hiding place. The drawers and even the pot cupboard yielded no clue. The dressing table had an inkwell and some stationery on it. Daniel took the first two sheets of paper and placed them in his coat pocket.

The clock struck eleven. He picked up his pace.

He glanced at the wardrobe. It was unremarkable on its face apart from a decorative carved crown. Daniel drew over the chair and stood on it to peer over the top. A folded blanket covered something. He rummaged beneath and found what he sought—a leather satchel.

A thick wad of papers was inside, but too large a bundle to remove and not be immediately missed.

Daniel cast about for a replacement. There, lying in the hearth beside the coal scuttle was a discarded copy of the *Freeman's Journal,* the very one young Tapper delivered. Daniel folded and stuffed the newspaper inside the satchel and slipped it back beneath the blanket atop the wardrobe.

To an extent, the substitution was quite pointless. It would be discovered the moment Dauncey opened the satchel. However, if he did nothing more than step on the chair and check to see the satchel was still there without opening it, it might purchase at least until tomorrow morning, maybe even longer.

Daniel glanced about the room, checking to see everything was as he'd found it. The missing newspaper in the hearth might be thought used by the maid to light the fire.

He extinguished the lamp.

As though a curtain had fallen, silence too had settled on the inn. The row in the courtyard was long over and lodgers had settled themselves in for the night. Daniel listened, carefully alert to any sound that would determine his plans for leaving undetected. He cracked open the door and a cautious peek down the quiet hallway made the decision for him. He would exit down the stairs and leave no one the wiser to his visit.

* * *

Through the partly open window of the landau, the smell of late autumn, the scent of damp and decay, suited Abigail's mood. It had been a long day in the company of the Irishman and not even the conviviality of the Ashfords and the Templetons were enough to fully lift her spirits.

As the evening had worn on, the more certain she'd been that Dauncey would try to insinuate himself into her bed and she dreaded the very thought of it. Were she responsible only to herself, she would send him away with a flea in his ear. Arrogant upstart!

But her life was not her own. A refusal might send the man away permanently, and she would have failed in her task for Blakeney. And Blakeney was the key to her future. At this juncture, Abigail feared *him* more than she detested Dauncey.

Fortunately, Dauncey did not importune, and she was more than happy for her carriage to drop him at his lodgings just after one o'clock. The landau rolled to a stop at the front door and it was opened immediately by Stanstead. The weight of her coat removed from her shoulders by the butler and the warmth of the townhouse lifted her spirits momentarily.

Seeing Stanstead suppress a yawn, she bade him a good night and told him to dismiss her maid, assuring him she could find her own way to bed. The man accepted the instruction with gratitude.

Abigail couldn't blame him. She attended lunches, concerts, and at-homes every day, and soirees and card parties every night. In two weeks time, she was to hold a Guy Fawkes party from which her guests would be driven out in carriages to see the big bonfire in a field just out of town. If she was exhausted, then her servants must be also, their days beginning before hers and ending after.

It was certainly time for bed.

First though, she would deposit her winnings from playing faro tonight and warm by the fire in the study. She smiled at the thought of her more secure location for her savings. She had purchased Aunt Philomena's desk, though the old lady demanded an extortionate sum. Now she did not need to force locks to access the secret drawer.

She crossed to the desk, but stopped before it. Although the room was shrouded in semi-darkness, lit only by embers that glowed invitingly in the fireplace and a couple of lamps dimmed about the room, a prickling awareness worked its way across her spine.

She was not alone.

CHAPTER TEN

Abigail considered leaving the study and calling for Stanstead, but what kind of fool would she look like if there was no one there at all? Skills honed at court, where gossipmongers and backstabbers thrived, had served her well, but since being paired with Ridgeway, it felt as though her senses had been heightened all the more. Over the past few weeks particularly, she had honed a talent for participating in a conversation fully alert to other activity around her while her companions remained unaware her true attention was devoted elsewhere.

Unexpectedly, other senses and skills had sharpened also. Her hearing seemed at times more acute, small sounds taking on greater significance. Even her sense of smell seemed heightened. And now she realized she could smell brandy and the ashy residue of a spent cigar and there, very faintly, the sound of another person breathing.

There *was* someone else in the room. A man.

Abigail edged around the perimeter of the study to the fireplace and felt for the poker at her hand, then cast a glance at the places where an intruder might hide.

A cluster of furniture—a tan Chesterfield sofa and two matching wing back chairs—huddled around an occasional table facing the French doors, which was closed, as were the curtains. It afforded the most likely place for someone to hide.

She approached it cautiously, yet a quick rake of the poker across the fabric revealed no one hiding behind it.

Abigail turned back to the room and started. A man lay stretched out on the sofa.

"You're back late."

Her alarm ebbed away as she recognized the voice. She ought to be angry at the intrusion, but such effort was more than she could face at this late hour.

Abigail approached and sharply rapped the side of Ridgeway's booted foot with her hand, giving him a look of irritation. He offered a tired half smile of apology before swinging his legs off the sofa and sitting up.

"I didn't expect to see you tonight after you didn't show at the Ashfords," she said, sitting beside him.

On the low table in front of the sofa, a cigar, half consumed, sat on an ashtray and a full finger of whiskey remained in a tumbler. There were papers strewn on the table. She fingered one, but the light was too dim to make anything of it.

She sat back and turned to Ridgeway. He disguised a large yawn with one hand while stretching with feline grace. He looked exhausted; his hair spiked from frequently running his hands through it. Dark circles surrounded his eyes.

Abigail wondered how she must look to him. Probably not much better. Her weariness was now bone deep.

"You should be home in bed," she suggested softly.

"Not before I saw you tucked in safe and sound."

"I can take care of myself." Abigail smiled to soften the words, but his smile in return seemed somewhat wistful.

"I have no doubt about that at all," he whispered.

After a moment's silence, she nodded at the haul on the table. "Profitable day?"

"I don't know yet," he admitted through another yawn. "And you? You'd better put your winnings away."

Abigail glanced at her purse before rising slowly. Rather than unlatching the secret drawer in front of him, she made do for the moment by slipping her purse into the centre drawer and locking it.

Even with her back turned, she could feel his eyes on her, but he didn't speak until she rejoined him on the couch.

"How is your friend Dauncey?"

Abigail sighed dramatically. "He's no friend of *mine*."

"Pity," he responded mildly. "You seemed keen on him at first."

"Yes, well," she snipped, "that was before I got to know him."

Ridgeway turned and seemed to consider her carefully, supporting his head on a crooked arm resting on the back of the Chesterfield.

"You don't have to do anything, you know," he said. His eyes, warm and blue, met Abigail's own. "I mean, anything you're not comfortable with. That you're keeping Dauncey occupied is more valuable than you know."

He said nothing further, but his words thawed some of the chill around Abigail's heart and she appreciated his kindness for a moment before reminding herself his concern was purely professional. She felt a frisson of disappointment before the emotion was locked away, unexplored.

"Something about the Irishman is wrong," she said. "I wish I could explain it better."

At Ridgeway's murmured encouragement, she took a deep breath and marshaled her thoughts.

"He is not what he pretends to be. What he does is mimicry, almost as though he is play acting. There's another face he mostly hides, a laughing face…contemptuous of everybody."

There was no reply so Abigail allowed her eyes to close. The study was warm and the silence companionable. She let her mind drift through the events of the past few days to see if there was anything further she could add. Abigail had observed Dauncey's manner toward women in general was courtly, perhaps even flamboyantly so, yet he openly insulted them and their station with his witty words and wry observations.

Only with her had he shown himself to be a Janus.

This afternoon Stanstead alerted her to potential correspondence in Dauncey's coat pocket. While he dressed for the evening with the Ashfords, she copied their contents. Nothing but inane chatter involving someone called Molly H.

Was any of this of use? Did it mean anything?

A gentle brush on her cheek returned her to the present. Abigail opened her eyes to find the study bathed in mellow lamplight. The papers which had been strewn haphazardly on the table before had now disappeared. She looked at him and it was with the same thoughtful expression as before.

"You fell asleep," he offered by way of explanation. "You should go to bed, get some real sleep. Shall I call your maid?"

Abigail shook her head and started to rise. "I don't want to wake the household."

He rose with her.

"Well, before you go, point me in the direction of the kitchen."

"You're hungry?" she asked. It hadn't occurred to her to ask when he had last eaten. "Perhaps I should ring for Cook."

He halted her movement toward the bell pull with his hand covering hers. Her offer was rejected with a shake of the head.

"I can make my own supper, no need to wake anyone." He paused and cocked his head, thoughtful for a moment. "Do you want to join me?"

The invitation was made with an appealing smile and her tiredness was replaced by curiosity.

"You can cook?"

He tugged her hand and led the way to the door. "I'm a man of many talents."

Abigail laughed, but lowered her voice as they passed through the threshold of the study into the hall.

"I have no doubt you are," she replied and led on to the kitchen.

Soon they were sitting at the plain pine table in the centre of the room, and Abigail watched him make his way around the range and utensils confidently. Before long, a sizzling omelet slid off the cast iron skillet onto a plate and within a few minutes a second one onto another.

"This is first time I've been in a kitchen since I was a little girl," she confessed as he sat to join her.

"You're jesting, surely," he asked around a forkful of food.

Abigail shrugged and took a sip of tea. She had made short work picking the locked tea caddy—her skill, while noticed, went unremarked upon by Ridgeway—and he had prepared the large pot which sat on the table.

"No, why should I be?" she replied. "When I want to consult on a menu I call the cook to the drawing room."

An amused snort of laughter and an indulgent shake of the head was his response.

Odd.

If it were anyone else at any other time, Abigail would have responded cuttingly to such effrontery, but there was something about being a pair of co-conspirators together in the semi-darkness of a kitchen in the early hours of the morning that made it different. It felt as though their entire world began and ended within these four walls.

It felt intimate.

And the thought didn't scare her at all.

* * *

The sounds of the advancing morning could be ignored no further, but it was with great reluctance that Abigail opened her eyes to the grandfather clock chiming the eleventh hour. She stretched beneath the covers and reached out to ring the bell.

Mornings had never been her favorite part of the day, yet, despite the late night and the unexpected company on her return home, Abigail was surprised to find her mood was bright.

By the time Kathleen entered with her breakfast, Abigail was nearly dressed in a pale green morning gown and was brushing out her hair.

"My Lady doesn't have any engagements today, that's why I thought it best to leave you to sleep."

The statement held the mildest of admonishments. Abigail smiled and allowed Kathleen to take the brush.

"For some reason, I feel quite invigorated," she said and closed her eyes, allowing Kathleen to continue. The long brush strokes out from her crown left her scalp tingling. Again, she wondered about the increased awareness of sensation. "Did Mr. Ridgeway say anything before he left?"

In the reflection of the mirror, Abigail watched Kathleen frown.

"There have been no callers this morning, my Lady."

Ah, so he must have departed as stealthily as he'd entered.

Kathleen paused, the brush hovering a few inches from Abigail's head, apparently waiting for an explanation, but knowing, as a servant, she was not entitled to one.

Abigail gestured with a lift of the head that the girl should continue brushing and, under the rhythmic strokes, she returned to her private thoughts. All of a sudden, last night took on a new significance.

For a few short hours the world had been theirs alone and being alone with him was…nice.

She glanced out of the window, down to the meadow opposite the crescent where sheep grazed peacefully on one side of the green. Riders on horseback and drivers in gigs reveled in a sunny, autumn day. Beyond, the wide expanse of parkland opened out to the treeline, the branches swaying in the breeze as though beckoning her.

The thought of being indoors was suddenly unappealing.

"Is there mail this morning?"

"I believe so, my Lady. If so, it will be waiting in the study."

And indeed, a pile of correspondence lay waiting there.

Before addressing it, Abigail unlocked the centre drawer of the writing bureau and transferred last night's faro winnings from her purse to the secret drawer. Then she turned her attention to the mail.

Acceptances to the Guy Fawkes party accounted for most of the correspondence. Due accounts were bundled and addressed to the solicitors in town for payment. Buried at the bottom of the pile, in an unaddressed envelope Abigail recognized as her own monogrammed stationery, was a single piece of paper.

She unfolded it and frowned at the unfamiliar handwriting before a heartfelt grin drew across her features like the sun from behind clouds.

It was a recipe for omelets.

* * *

"You have well and truly launched yourself back into society! Isn't it all too delicious? Getting Dauncey as your favorite this season has been quite the coup."

Abigail slowed her horse—the bay mare was a new acquisition thanks to the seemingly bottomless pockets of *Aunt Druscilla*—and allowed Jane's cabriolet to catch up with her, nodding to a few acquaintances along the way as she did so.

"I've had the most unexpected people asking *me* to curry favor with *you* to get an invitation to your next event."

"Like who?"

Disregarding her control of the reins and the gasp of alarm from the groom behind her, Jane leaned dangerously from the vehicle to answer *sotto voce*, "The Burchills."

"Oh, that's just too rich!" Abigail erupted angrily, lowering her voice again as the groom hunched down on the back platform of the cabriolet, trying to make himself less conspicuous. "Not only have the family cut me dead, their spiteful little hoyden Emily has made her dislike quite personal. Just the other day at the Pump Room she stared daggers at me because Templeton came up to greet me and speak a few words."

"Speak of the Devil…"

Jane nodded up the hill to the road bordering the park. Viscount Richard Hamberley was driving a splendid curricle and pair of matching grays. Even at that distance, Abigail recognized the passenger as pale blue-bonneted Emily Burchill.

"Well, well, well," Abigail observed, straightening in her saddle. "Wednesday's musical recital at The Tea Room should be interesting; William Templeton is scheduled to be singing a series of duets with Emily. I think I might get there early, I would hate to miss out on a good seat."

"Perhaps you can invite the Burchills to tea afterwards," Jane chuckled. "Or perhaps not when you learn Miss Emily has started a rumor that you're Lord Fforbes's mistress."

Abigail returned a withering look. "*Please*. That milk sop? He wouldn't dare sneeze without his wife's permission."

"Perhaps it wasn't him she said. Perhaps it was Reginald or maybe the Admiral, I can't remember now." Jane shrugged.

Abigail caught the glint of merriment in her friend's eyes and narrowed her own warningly. "Now you're just fishing."

Jane shrugged again, nonchalant. "Well, I have to get some answers from somewhere. The story about inheriting your fabulous townhouse and all its furniture only goes so far. Thomas tells me the death duties would have taken a large portion of any unencumbered cash, so someone has to be paying the bills."

"Well," said Abigail, "if the truth be known…"

Jane rubbed her gloved hands and nearly bounced up and down on her seat with excitement. Abigail leaned across from her horse and Jane leaned toward her also, almost precipitously from the carriage.

"I have a wealthy aunt," said Abigail, allowing a chuckle at Jane's instantly crestfallen face.

"You and Daniel seem to have all the luck when it comes to mysterious rich aunties," she sniffed. "Next you'll be telling me her name is Druscilla!"

Abigail was unable to hide a momentary change of expression and her friend seized on it, exclaiming, "Ah-ha!"

"I'm sorry, did you sneeze?" Abigail enquired, brushing the sleeves of her new hunter green riding outfit and picking up the reins. "Perhaps you've been out in the fresh air for too long."

"Don't go!" Jane begged. "Don't you dare deprive me of the most interesting bit of news all season!"

"I'm sorry to disappoint you, Jane," offered Abigail in her most haughty tone of voice while allowing her horse to edge ahead of the cabriolet, "but there is no news, interesting or otherwise."

"Wait! I'll tell you everything Thomas has told me about Daniel!"

Abigail reined her mount to a stop as Jane did likewise with the cabriolet.

Jane turned to the groomsman. "Get down and take Lady Abigail's horse home. She'll be riding with me."

The young man came around the side of the vehicle and gave her a dubious look. "Go on, go on!" ordered Jane. "I can manage one of these things on my own, you know."

He looked up to Abigail as if for her approval. She acknowledged the silent, but pleading look with a shake of the head and dismounted, handing him the reins. The groomsman looked uncertainly at the mare's sidesaddle, then similarly at Abigail.

"I suggest you walk it back," she said.

"Yes, my Lady," he replied and began leading the animal back in the direction of the Crescent.

"I swear, if you breathe a word of this to another living soul, I shall never speak to you again," Abigail warned as she stepped up into the vehicle. She sat beside Jane as they carried on for another turn about the park.

"There's not much to tell," Abigail hedged. "We met a month ago at one of your faro nights and one thing led to another—"

"So your public flirtation with the Irishman is a sleight of hand!" interjected Jane. She gaped admiringly at her friend. "Of all the delicious frauds! Too bad I'm happily wed to Thomas, otherwise I'd be envious. I'll expect more details about your *affair de coeur* when I come to tea on Thursday."

At a look of alarm from Abigail, Jane swiftly glanced back to the path ahead and steered the cabriolet around a large fallen branch before it went under the nearside wheel.

"That is if I live long enough," Abigail commented ruefully on her near miss.

Now on a straighter path that required little more than the horse to follow its nose, Abigail cooled in her desire to snatch the reins and turned her attention back to Jane.

"On second thought," Jane was adding slyly, "as you and Daniel are now *intimate* acquaintances, I'm not sure there is much I can tell that you wouldn't already know."

"Darling, we're not together for polite conversation." Abigail smiled.

Jane laughed, completely unaware the double entendre was actually a statement of fact.

Daniel was still an enigma to Abigail, as much as he had been when she'd first seen him. She knew little more than he danced well, and was quick-witted and shrewd.

Yet in that strange place where night had not yet yielded to morning, she had caught a glimpse of someone else. The man behind the spy. She knew with certainty there was a richness of character to him, a complexity only hinted at in those shadow hours that drew her.

"…and no one really knows why Daniel dropped out of Cambridge, he was said to be a gifted mathematician," said Jane, unaware of Abigail's momentary inattention. "Everyone expected him to be awarded his first class honors as well as become…now what did Thomas say the university calls it? Ah yes, a 'wrangler.' Dear Thomas, he's a man who wouldn't dream of betraying a confidence, so he won't tell me why, but I suspect a scandal of some sort because a friend of Daniel's had been found drowned just a few days earlier."

"What happened?" asked Abigail.

"Well, no one really knows with these things. The inquest said it was an accident," Jane said and shrugged, "so accident it was. Viscount Pemberley was furious when Daniel disappeared, he—"

"Daniel disappeared?" Abigail asked with surprise.

"Oh, didn't I mention that bit?"

Abigail shook her head and Jane cautiously turned the cabriolet in a wide circle and slapped the reins to encourage the horse to head back to the park.

"Well, after the death of his friend he dropped out of sight completely," she continued. "Some people said he fled to Europe or went to fight in the American Revolutionary war. No one—at least Thomas, at any rate—is sure what happened. According to his brothers, Daniel showed up briefly for his mother's funeral to claim a small bequest left to him. But they just treat him as the proverbial black sheep now. Thomas wasn't sure whether he should acknowledge him when he arrived in Bath a couple of months ago, but I rather have a fondness for black sheep as you well know. They make evening entertainments far more piquant."

But for Jane's revelations, she wouldn't have guessed at any of the specifics of Daniel's life, yet its shadow remained over him, revealing itself ever so briefly last night.

Abigail mulled over what she had learned. Could we ever truly escape our past? Reject it utterly as Daniel had done?

That was what Abigail longed for herself. A new start in a new country where she could be known for the woman she was, not the one she had been, tainted by the scandal associated with the Canalissy name.

As Jane drove the carriage back to rejoin the residents of Bath soaking in the autumn afternoon sunshine, Abigail wondered what Daniel thought of her.

Blakeney would have no doubt informed him of her infamous past and what use she could be while earning atonement for her sins against the Crown. Yet last night he'd treated her with kindness without demanding anything in return. For the first time she felt an interest toward another person beyond opportunism, beyond Professor White's detached scientific curiosity. It felt odd.

Daniel interested her for himself alone.

Who was this man, really?

CHAPTER ELEVEN

Abigail cast a last glance at her reflection in the mirror at the top of the stairs. Like an actress examining her costume, she considered the view returned to her. It did not disappoint.

The ballgown was a tribute to the dressmaker's art.

The white silk shot with silver, blue, and pink thread created an iridescent glow in the lamplight and its effect would be manifold in the light of chandeliers. The gown featured beautifully embroidered ribbon of silver, pale pink, and blue that gathered under the bust. The ribbon also gathered under the small puffed sleeves at the arms.

Furthermore, the gown was au monde, designed to entice the male gaze and to make other women jealous.

Around her neck, Abigail wore a choker of graduated moonstones set in yellow gold. When she swallowed, the stones shifted and it seemed lightning erupted from them with the movement. Her hair was similarly featured to attract with movement, dressed in soft curls around a powder blue ribbon from which a white ostrich feather shivered flirtatiously.

She reflected on the hasty nature of preparations for this evening's excursion to The Assembly Rooms. They followed receipt of a note delivered by messenger.

Daniel's instructions were brief and to the point:

Aunty speaks, we obey. Tonight we move forward. Attend the Assembly this evening with Dauncey. If he is reluctant, tell him you will introduce him to someone who can get the blunt he needs. Essential that he remains in Bath until after Bonfire Night. I'll meet you there.

Downstairs, Abigail heard a footman open the door to an inquiring knock, and the sound of Dauncey's brogue echoed its way up the staircase. From her vantage point, she watched unseen as the footman directed him to the drawing room.

Taking a steadying breath, she waited for her cue. It appeared in the form of Stanstead climbing the stairs to tell her Mr. Eamon Dauncey awaited her pleasure in the drawing room.

With an incline of her head in acknowledgement, Abigail descended, her beaded and embroidered dancing slippers tapping softly against the white marble tread, and she watched the footman open the drawing room door in anticipation of her passage.

She quieted her performance butterflies with an intake of breath, an arch of an eyebrow, and a wide smile as if to take on her character for the evening, and entered the room.

"My dear Dauncey, so accommodating that you would escort me to The Assembly tonight," she began. She observed his reaction closely. He took in her dress and skirted her figure. The butterflies re-emerged.

A wolfish grin spread across the Irishman's face as he took note of her jewelry. It was as though he could completely ignore its aesthetic beauty and merely calculate its monetary worth. Abigail waited for him to speak on this, perhaps tell her in that mocking tone of his her patron had once again been very generous.

Most of all she waited for him to see her as the fraud she felt.

Instead, he came out with a poem:

> *While gazing on the moon's light,*
> *A moment from her smile I turn'd,*
> *To look at orbs that, more bright,*
> *In lone and distant glory burn'd.*

"One of your efforts?" Abigail asked, grateful her voice hadn't deserted her.

Dauncey shook his head. "Alas not. A young man I know, a protégé you might say, a Dubliner. I think he has the makings of a fine poet."

He stepped forward after a moment and took her hand. Abigail forced a shiver back down to the pit of her stomach as he kissed his way along the inside of her white long satin gloves, his breath hot on her skin where it eddied between the mother-of-pearl buttons.

She could feel her smile become brittle as he stepped closer, sliding his hand across her upper arm and bare shoulders where his fingers strayed beneath the satin before trailing across to her neck. There, like a spider, his fingers uncurled and wrapped themselves around her neck with the barest squeeze.

"You're not afraid of me, are you darlin'?" he whispered in her ear.

Abigail forced herself not to react in revulsion. Instead, she kept her answering voice low and husky. She turned her head so she could see his profile. "Should I be?"

"Oh yes. I think you should."

Forcing disquiet into anger, Abigail shrugged him off with little effort and glared at him.

"Don't be such a bore," she warned, icily.

Dauncey stepped back, his hands clasped over his heart. "I'll take many insults but that one! You've wounded me to the quick, dear girl."

"Then stop being ridiculous, Mr. Dauncey. You're as dangerous as blancmange," she replied, her heart pounding less. "Come along, the coach is waiting outside."

She set off toward the door with purpose, but Dauncey's hand shot out and gripped her left arm. He cruelly dragged her to him and turned her to face him.

"Don't mock me either," he ground out as his hand squeezed hard into her arm. "I'm happy to play the clown for you and your vapid aristocratic friends, but never, *ever* underestimate the depth of my commitment to the cause."

Abigail staggered as he pushed her away from him. She rubbed her arm against the bruises she suspected would appear by morning and watched his lip curl and nose wrinkle in an open expression of utter contempt.

"You disappoint me," he told her. "I thought you of all people would have a better understanding of our goals and ideals. Liberation and equality, freed from the shackles of societal conventions, freed from shame. I thought you were a true believer."

Now, like an actor on the stage, Dauncey paced the length of the drawing room, then turned, throwing his arms open and bracing his legs apart, seeming to Abigail that he might actually sing his next words.

"'Terror is only justice: prompt, severe and inflexible,'" he quoted. "'It is then an emanation of virtue; it is less a distinct principle than a natural consequence of the general principle of democracy, applied to the most pressing wants of the country.'"

"Revolution," Abigail answered.

"But of course! Revolutions are the produce of passion, not of sober and tranquil reason. Have you not being paying attention? America… France… England will be next, mark my words, darlin' Abigail, and we're going to make it happen."

Abigail interjected with a quote of her own, "'Revolution is engendered by an indignation with tyranny, yet is itself pregnant with tyranny.'" She pressed on at his changing expression. "Oh, I've certainly being paying attention to the writings of your friend William Godwin. He also says, 'Tyranny and anarchy are never far apart.' Is that what you have planned for England?"

Dauncey deflated like the sails of a ship becalmed. His head was bowed, but his arms remained outstretched as though he was waiting for his final curtain.

"…it is a tale

"Told by an idiot, full of sound and fury,

"*Signifying nothing*."

Abigail recalled the fragment from Macbeth and she waited for his next line. When he raised his head, slowly and dramatically, his expression was odd, and for a moment she was mesmerized. His dark eyes glittered like obsidian and the tightness around his mouth softened.

In any other man, Abigail would consider the look to be lustful, a countenance she had never seen him give to any woman, and yet some instinct told Abigail what aroused him was not her.

"The things we have planned for New Year..." he cooed. "If you deliver what you promise, I will guarantee you a front row seat."

She swallowed her bile and beckoned him closer with her fan before unfurling and wafting it slowly, as though the heat in the room stifled her. "Then let us not tarry," she said. "I'm sure you and my friend will have plenty to discuss."

She offered him a seductive grin—whether Dauncey saw it to be false or not, she neither knew nor cared—and turned to walk to the door. Dauncey stepped forward anyway to hold her shoulders and press his lips once again to the back of her neck.

She was grateful he could not see her face.

Once, Abigail thought she had a limitless capacity for such intrigues but, now, what used to be spice was a flavorless as sawdust.

The thought of vineyards and olive groves, and warm endless sunshine softened by the Mediterranean's etesian breeze tugged at her. She held firm to her dream even as Dauncey held her firmly to aid her into the carriage.

As they departed the Crescent, Abigail glanced back and saw Kathleen had draped the scarlet satin sash down her bedroom curtain as per her instruction to do so immediately once they had left.

She wondered how long she could continue the charade.

CHAPTER TWELVE

The entrance to The Assembly Rooms shone as a beacon in the drizzling rain, drawing the city's well-heeled into its brightness and warmth.

As Abigail's carriage rolled to a stop, footmen opened the door and damp air eddied around her. She drew her peacock-blue wrap close around her shoulders before accepting assistance down onto a wooden board placed to protect shoes from water gathering on the uneven cobble stones.

Without waiting for permission, Dauncey placed her hand in the crook of his arm and urged her toward the columned portico, out of the weather.

"Well, Abigail, darlin', you do have me intrigued, I can tell you that with no word of a lie." He grinned, nodding in acknowledgement to a group of young bucks making their way through the corridor, lured by the card room beyond.

"Patience, my dear Dauncey, is one of the chief virtues," she answered lightly, surveying the crowd that accompanied them out of the rain. Familiar faces, unusual pairings, notable absences would provide the substance of her latest correspondence with Aunt Druscilla, and she hoped too that Daniel would make an appearance sooner rather than later.

Augusta Burchill tried to catch her eye. After being the subject of the woman's snide asides for nearly two seasons, the temptation to cut her was too much. Abigail deliberately gave her the shoulder, choosing instead to speak to Lady Cecil Worthington and sympathize with her various ailments.

Gout? No, that was last week. This week it was lumbago, and the doctor told her it was the very worst case he had ever seen.

Dauncey gallantly offered his free arm for Lady Worthington's support, his underlying tone of mockery going unnoticed by the round-faced matron as he turned his charm on her. Her gray curls trembled as she giggled girlishly at one of his lavish compliments. The three of them sailed past Mrs. Burchill without a single glance.

"Do you feel well enough for a turn about the room?" Dauncey continued in his solicitous attention to the older woman. "With two lovelies on my arms, I'll be the envy of every man here."

It was surprising, Abigail mused, how quickly the effects of lumbago could disappear when a lady had the attention of the celebrated coxcomb of season. Nonetheless, she was glad to be free of Dauncey at least for the moment as she watched him and Lady Worthington make their way about the room.

Then, as though it were a physical touch, awareness of another person bloomed through her, manifesting itself in small gooseflesh on her arm. A casual glance to her right revealed the cause, another Burchill female, young Emily, charmingly dressed in a spotted voile gown in rose pink. Emily's distaste was apparent by the curl of her lips before she turned her head. There was a flick of a painted silk fan to shield her mouth as the chit offered commentary, no doubt unflattering, to her friends.

At the sound of their titters of amusement, Abigail held her temper and forced herself to relax the grip on her own fan. The little sow wasn't worth a moment of her time—not any more. The secret little pleasure of needling the girl after being snubbed by her family seemed hollow and childish now.

And yet the odd sensation of being watched, no, *studied* wouldn't be shaken.

"Would the lady care to dance?"

Abigail pulled her attention to the speaker, the warmth of his voice settling her nerves like a balm.

This was her cue.

Daniel's hair shone like brass under the light of the chandeliers. Its warmth was matched by his expression—a smile that held a touch of mischief and a light in his eyes suggesting humor. Dressed in matching breeches and cutaway coat in rich corbeau green, he extended his hand to her.

She stepped forward about to accept it as Dauncey's arm swept in unexpectedly and tightened on hers.

"The lady is otherwise engaged."

Abigail shook off his arm and glared at him irritably. "The lady can speak for herself!"

Beside Dauncey, Lady Worthington watched the byplay and quickly excused herself to claim a seat—close enough to see and hear, but far enough away not to be caught in the storm she could see brewing.

Abigail held her breath. An unwitting Dauncey was playing his part in this improvised charade to perfection!

Daniel spared the Irishman the merest glance and extended his hand to Abigail once more.

"Would the lady care to dance?" he repeated, slightly louder now, for the benefit of other guests who now paused in their chatter to watch a more exciting entertainment. The fascinating Irish dandy who had been the talk of Bath all Season and who had convinced the most notorious demi-monde of London out of retirement was being challenged by a *nobody*.

Abigail raised her head and her voice to match his. "Indeed I would, Mr. Ridgeway."

She was drawn closer by the hand that enclosed hers and, with it, felt steadied. Abigail tossed her head back and gave Dauncey a flirtatious smile.

"Fret not, Dauncey, the night is still young," she teased and nodded over his shoulder to draw his attention to Mrs. Burchill making a beeline toward him. "You never know what interesting people you might meet."

Without a further glance to him or the small audience they had attracted, Abigail accompanied Daniel to the edge of the dance floor where they waited a full minute for the start of the next dance. When it began, it was an allemande. Abigail breathed a sigh of relief. In this they would have time to talk.

At the sound of the orchestra striking up, Daniel squeezed her hand lightly. Strange, she hadn't been aware he still held it. That will certainly add to the talk of the Subscription.

She saw a slight frown now etch his features.

"Are you well? We don't have to dance if you don't wish, but I do need to speak with you."

His solicitude was disarming and Abigail smiled.

"It will be a very sad day indeed when the thought of dancing begins to pall," she told him with genuine levity as the opening strains of one of Bach's Cello Suites began to play.

"Then let's ensure that day never happens," he whispered into her ear before leading her to the floor.

They lined up at the back of the dance floor. The ladies curtsied, then men bowed before they stepped and hopped to the triple meter. With the grace that belied his muscular build, Daniel pivoted and turned adroitly, first turning Abigail under his arm and following in turn under hers in well-practiced steps.

The thought of Daniel as a school boy, drilled time and again by a dance master, brought a wide smile to her face.

"Did I say something amusing?"

"When you do, I'll be sure to let you know," she said, turning "allemande left" to the sound of his laughter, but the smile had left him by the time she faced him again.

"Bring Dauncey to the Card Room after eleven," he instructed softly. "I will be meeting him there with an offer he won't be able to resist."

Their hands met as they stepped together, stepped apart.

"I don't know if I can," Abigail confessed, finally giving voice to her disquiet.

Both turned in a complete circle before their eyes met again.

"He's losing interest in me," she rushed before the next turn. "There's something strange about that man. I can't keep his attention, he disappears for the day and…"

"You're doing just fine," Daniel assured her with squeeze of her hand as she turned under his arm. "I just need two more weeks and we'll both be free."

The dance ended. Daniel took Abigail's hand once more and kissed it warmly.

Even through her gloved hands, a sensation ran up her arm and cascaded throughout her entire body with an emotion she was hard pressed to name.

"Trust me," he whispered, escorting her from the floor.

"Abigail!" Jane called to them.

Daniel smiled. "I'll leave you in some friendlier company and I'll see you in the Card Room after eleven. And don't worry about Dauncey, just remind him he stands damned low in the water and the man he is to meet will refloat his boat."

They approached Jane and Thomas.

"Ah Thomas," Daniel said. "I've come to defend my honor, sir!"

Thomas frowned. "What are you prattling on about, old boy?"

"I've been struck, right to the core. My very heart has been pierced by the beauty that is your wife and my only recourse to mend it is to soundly beat you in a game of cards."

"I'd be a poor husband indeed if I didn't defend my own honor and that of my wife. Are you up for a hand of Speculation, dear chap?"

Daniel broadly winked to the ladies. "I'm always up for speculation."

Thomas kissed his wife's hand and Daniel took hold of Abigail's once more. "Remember, after eleven," he whispered.

"For someone who swore me secrecy only a few days ago, you're doing a very poor job of hiding your affections from everyone else," Jane scolded the moment both men bowed and left the ballroom.

She took a seat and Abigail followed suit.

"You're the talk of evening," her friend continued. "Everyone could feel the tension in the air when Daniel claimed you for a dance right in front of Dauncey. And that Allemande—pure desire! All the ladies were fanning themselves. It would not surprise me in the least if some of the husbands are to be offered some convivial society tonight."

"Jane!" said Abigail, appalled.

"Oh, don't you get missish on me," Jane sniffed, dismissing her with a downward wave of her hand. "It's there for the whole world to see. You were a triumph, so much so I have it in me to feel sorry for this year's debutants." Jane gestured theatrically. "Lady Abigail Houghall has come out of retirement. You know you've become the envy of every woman and object of desire by every man?"

Abigail smiled wanly. Once the attention would have thrilled her endlessly. She had lived for courting praise and admiration, but something changed just over two years ago at Boconnoc House, and it wasn't just the threat of prison for blackmailing Blakeney held over her head.

Indeed, she could play the courtesan and was very good at it, and once it had seemed her whole life. But now… Now it was a performance. The thing she feared the most was that Dauncey might see through her before the final act was played.

She scanned the crowd and found the Irishman holding court surrounded by a coterie of women—Mrs. Burchill, Baroness Vladinsky, and Lady fforbes among them.

Thankfully, she was not required to comment due to the arrival of William Templeton.

He bowed politely to Jane and then to her. "Lady Abigail, would you care to dance?"

"Are you sure?" she smiled indulgently at him. "There must be plenty of lovely young debutants you'd prefer to dance with?"

With a look of assurance Abigail would bet good money was merely a sham, William thrust his chin forward.

"Silly little girls who can't make up their vacant little minds?" he avowed. "No ma'am, I prefer ladies who know exactly what they're about."

"I'm not sure that I…" Abigail glanced about, looking quickly for Emily Burchill. She was already on the dance floor with Richard Hamberley. "Perhaps Lady Edgecombe might oblige you."

Jane shook her head rapidly. "No, don't look to me, dear, I'm quite done in. New slippers. Not broken in yet. Feet are very sore. Besides, you're younger than me."

Abigail responded to Jane with the most contemptuous glare she could muster and received only a sly grin in return for the effort.

When she turned back to young Templeton, his facade of self-confidence was slipping. She truly felt sorry for the young man, so, against her better judgment, Abigail found herself being led to the dance floor once more.

To her chagrin, the dance was a cotillion and now she found herself face to face with Emily and young Hamberley as the part of the set of four couples per group.

The musical introduction swelled. Abigail took a deep breath and, from somewhere within herself, mustered a polite smile. It was returned by one from Emily so brittle it threatened to splinter the girl's features.

A glance at her own dance partner showed him with a pointed, semi-triumphant expression. It was a message clearly for the young woman opposite them. Abigail's suppressed irritation was now unchecked.

As Templeton glanced down to her, he had the good grace to look shamefaced.

"Lady Abigail, there was a reason why I sought you out for a dance tonight," he began as he took her hand.

"Was it to teach Emily a lesson? Because I don't appreciate being treated as a bargaining chip in your courtship," she spat before turning her head to take the hand of the male dancer next to her.

The dance continued and, after a whirl of male faces—Raleigh, Hamberley, Wannacott—Abigail found herself back with Templeton. He tried to muster a sheepish apology.

"I don't know what else to do other than make her jealous. I know she doesn't love Hamberley."

She held her tongue as Templeton turned her under his arm. Then the steps changed and all the ladies skip-stepped into the centre with right hands joined.

"Beware of this one, girls, not only does she set a cap for your beaux, not even your fathers are safe from her claws," announced Emily to the amusement of the other two girls. Before any response was possible, the men had reclaimed their partners for a swing to the count of four.

The damned cheek!

Abigail forced her anger into check until the dance ended. At its conclusion, she briskly curtsied to Templeton before giving him a restrained measure of her fury. "Next time, sir, be as good as to leave me out of your pathetic calf-love tragedy."

She did not wait for him to escort her from the dance floor, instead catching the eye of a footman who held a tray of drinks and crossing to him as he approached her. The footman rotated the tray to proffer a champagne. She took a tumbler of spirits instead and downed a healthy quantity.

Then she refused other invitations to dance and took Jane's seat, vacated while she took to the floor with her husband. There she waited. And watched. And observed.

Emily finally danced with Templeton. Hamberley was enjoying a conversation with a mixed group of young people. Even Dauncey had been persuaded to dance with the youngsters, and Abigail noted that despite his pronouncements of disdain for these gatherings, he seemed to be quite a home at them.

The dance ended, but Abigail kept her attention on Emily. A few kind words and a smile for Templeton and the lad looked like he had been gifted the moon and the stars. Abigail took another sip of the dark amber liquid and watched the play unfold in front of her.

Emily shook her head. *"Oh, I'm all done in,"* her mannerisms expressed. *"But do ask me later on"* was implicit in the shy glance she threw his way. Templeton retreated, his ardor momentarily sated. Now arm in arm with Miss Tiffany Lake, Emily threaded her way through the crowd toward the ladies' retiring room.

Abigail gently tapped her fan to catch the attention of a gentleman passing by.

"Could I trouble you for the time?" she inquired. The man turned and Abigail started. There seemed something familiar about the fashionable dandy. He stood tall and lean; his light brown hair was curled and coiffed just so, the cut of his navy blue coat was as sharp as a knife-edge and, oh my word! His buff indescribables clung to every muscle in his legs.

"Sink me! I always have *time* for a lady."

Abigail laughed lightly at the jest and waited for him to withdraw a gold hunter from his yellow and gold embroidered waistcoat pocket. He released the spring-loaded lid and peered at the face.

"It is a quarter to eleven o'clock. Do you have somewhere special you must be?"

She offered him a slightly flirtatious smile as she stood, brushing down her gown. "A lady never reveals her assignations, but now I know I have time to repair myself before it's time."

The man bowed. "Then I wish you bon chance, mademoiselle, on all your endeavors."

She strolled nonchalantly toward the ladies' anteroom. "Revenge is a dish best served cold" a little voice within reminded her. Abigail acknowledged it. Indeed, revenge could wait, but lighting a little fire under Emily Burchill was well overdue.

The anteroom was abuzz with feminine voices. Groups of older women chatted, seated on the overstuffed brocade divans. By the mirrors, debutants gossiped away from protective mamas and companions, sharing confidences about prospective beaux, while a tired-looking middle-aged attendant stood in a corner, surreptitiously yawning behind her hand.

Re-entering the room through a discreetly placed service door, two maids brought freshly rinsed bourdaloues to replace the ones in use behind the tapestry screens along one wall.

Emily emerged from behind one of the screens and started on seeing her. Abigail had to give the girl credit, she regained her poise quickly.

"It's time we had a word," Abigail told her.

"I don't think I have anything to say to the likes of you."

"I'm so glad, because I have plenty to say to you," Abigail volleyed, "and I'm happy to say it in front of the whole room."

The space fell into a slight hush, the ladies sensing the tension between the pair.

"You don't like what you see in me?" said Abigail. "Before you judge me, my actions, or my ways, just be sure to make full use of the mirror over there. You have become the very thing you claim to detest."

Emily gasped, seeming unable to speak.

Abigail glanced at the mirror and primped her hair, then walked to the door before pausing to turn back. She held the room theatrically. By God, she *was* a good actress.

"A piece of advice from a woman of the world to…" Abigail paused on the word, filling it with as much condescension as she possessed, "…a child. If you're going to take part in the game, never bet more than you're willing to lose. You're playing two good young men against one another and one of them is prepared to play for keeps. You're not clever enough to deal with the consequences, Miss Burchill."

At that, Abigail turned and sailed from the room without acknowledging the presence of anyone else, but she did allow herself a satisfied smile to see she left Emily pale and openmouthed.

CHAPTER THIRTEEN

Daniel shuffled the deck absently, enjoying the feel of the sharp edge of the gloss card scraping along the ridges of his fingertips. The action was comforting. The cards themselves were solid and predictable; the action he could control. It focused him.

Tonight he would play his trump card, making the bet that Dauncey's pride equaled his greed. However, Abigail's reservations concerned him, and the letter he'd received from Rachel Sawyer this afternoon worried him more.

"You seem preoccupied, dear chap," observed his companion. "I shouldn't worry, Abigail knows her duty, she won't let us down."

Daniel looked up at the man who sat opposite and took in his dandyish attire including a lurid yellow satin waistcoat that shone, even in the muted light of the card room.

"You must give me the name of your tailor," Daniel said dryly.

"He does good work doesn't he?" his companion preened. "Levi Goldwell is the chap's name. He's a theatrical costumier my wife introduced me to; moonlights as a tailor."

"And that's when he does most of his sewing?"

Sir Percy Blakeney looked at him blankly, eyebrows raised in an expression of bemusement.

Daniel knew full well his jibe was understood. Tonight, Blakeney was playing the dim-witted fop, tomorrow he might be the rag-and-bone man, able to pass by the very same people each day utterly unrecognized.

"You've changed the subject," said Percy softly with no affectation in his voice. "There is more than just tonight on your mind, isn't there?"

The man was like a dog at a bone; he wouldn't leave the matter alone. Daniel reflected that, when Blakeney owned you, it was "one to command, and all to obey."

"Rachel wrote to me today asking for news of Jonathan." Daniel placed the well shuffled deck onto the green baize. "She hasn't heard from him in months, which means he hasn't sent money in months, though she would never say as much."

"Mrs. Sawyer is a remarkable young woman," said Percy. "I'll ensure she's taken care of. Anonymously, you understand. London has more spies than Paris at the moment."

"For the love of God, Percy, pull him out," Daniel pleaded urgently. "Send me back to France instead."

"And waste six months of his good work and yours? Would never countenance the idea. He knew what he signed on for, and so do you."

"But Rachel didn't."

The man was unmoved.

"It would be different if it were your wife," Daniel retorted.

The briefest flash of anguish exposed itself in Sir Percy's eyes before the mask was replaced.

"We all have to make sacrifices in the cause of liberty and justice," he told Daniel tightly.

The clock in the Card Room struck eleven o'clock and, in the time the sound of the chimes had decayed, Sir Percy Blakeney, the care-free coxcomb had returned. With great exaggeration, he stood and bowed with a flourish.

"Gad, what a game you play, sir! Thanks to you, I'm quite light in the pocket, but no ill feelings. I will best you next time."

Daniel stood also, offering a wry smile. "Never underestimate a determined player, Sir Percy."

"Be sure that I never will!"

Percy's grin turned secretive, his voice low. "I believe I spy your next mark."

Daniel turned toward the door to see Abigail and Dauncey walk through. He took advantage of being unobserved to watch them. Abigail looked like an angel, an ethereal being who didn't belong in this world.

He watched Blakeney exit the room, giving a theatrical bow as he walked by Abigail. She smiled and dropped a curtsey in reply. Dauncey, however, eyed the man with contempt.

Daniel considered how Blakeney had been right to have warned him all those months ago. Abigail was a breathtakingly beautiful woman—a man would be a fool to resist her charm—but what the spymaster had failed to alert him to was her intelligence and determination. She was no empty-headed siren; Lady Abigail Houghall was a force to be reckoned with in her own right.

He recalled the late night visit that had offered him a glimpse of the real woman behind the jewels and beautiful clothes. Desiring an attractive woman was easy; there were such women aplenty; more difficult a proposition was becoming attached to a woman he *liked,* and that was bad.

Very bad.

The sight of her on the arm of the Irishman stirred a concoction of emotion in him he was unsure he could identify. Jealousy? Protectiveness? Anger? Lust?

Abigail spotted him and gave a smile that seemed to express relief as well as genuine pleasure at seeing him. The churn of emotions settled and disappeared.

Daniel cursed himself a fool because resisting that charm was something he was compelled to do, was convinced he *could* do while, at the very same time, he lifted her hand to his lips in greeting. A slight squeeze of her hand in his reassured him that whatever disquiet she had felt earlier in the evening had been assuaged.

"Dauncey, you remember my friend, the Honourable Daniel Ridgeway?" she asked, taking the opportunity to disengage her arm from her companion's.

Daniel forced himself to look at the man. Eamon Dauncey stood an inch or two shorter, with shaggy black hair brushing his collar. He was dressed fashionably, but plainly, in black and white but for a maroon and silver embroidered waistcoat that accentuated the crispness of his white shirt and frothy white cravat. The Irishman's expression was unbearably smug. Daniel forced the hand by his side to not curl into a fist.

"Is this some sort of joke, Abbie darlin'?"

"Indeed not," she answered. "You've been so vocal about the need for *change* in our society—and the necessity of funds for your plans— that when I learned Daniel here was a kindred spirit, as it were, and a man of some means, I thought an introduction was appropriate."

Dauncey's eyes narrowed. "I know who he is. I know exactly who he is."

Out of the corner of his eye, Daniel saw a glimmer of apprehension spread over Abigail's face and a hint of thunder on Dauncey's. He disarmed them both by laughing.

"Of course you do! I'd be disappointed if you didn't know all of the Season's Subscribers." With a flourish borrowed from Percy, Daniel gestured to the chairs to indicate they should sit and flagged a footman to bring a tray of drinks to the table.

Dauncey took his seat before speaking. "You're the son of Viscount Pemberley, one of the unrepresentative swill who sits in the House of Lords."

"I see you know my father well." Daniel grinned as he swept the playing cards across the baise. "Then you must also know that, despite my red hair, I am what they call the 'black sheep' of the family and now completely cut off."

Using the card on his right, Daniel tipped the displayed deck over and the cards traveled like a wave to the opposite shore. The action revealed the suits momentarily before he used the end card on the left to flip them back.

"Surely you know I was cast out of the family without a penny more than fifteen years ago," he stated. "Reason would tell you I have no love of privilege and unearned wealth."

Dauncey watched closely as Daniel swept the cards into a neat single pile. "Rag-wearing radicals we have aplenty, Ridgeway. What we don't have is malcontents with money."

Certain of his audience, Daniel cut the deck into two even piles. "I can get you money. Two hundred pounds at least."

"That's a fine trick if you can do it."

Daniel raised the half decks, one in each hand, and executed a perfect faro shuffle, neatly interleaving each half deck. It was an old magician's trick he had perfected and it never failed to impress an audience.

"I know many fine tricks, including how to fly a kite without dipping a hand into one's own pockets." He smiled slyly and performed the split and shuffle action again before fanning out the deck, suits down. "But I have a condition."

"Of course you do," Dauncey responded sarcastically.

"I want in. I want you to introduce me to your society."

The Irishman sat back and folded his arms. "That's going to cost you more than three hundred pounds, and I want surety. The English Prime Minister has spies everywhere and I think you may be one of them." Dauncey made a point of glancing at Abigail. "Her too."

Out of the corner of his eye, Daniel watched Abigail for any change of expression. He willed her to be silent, but she surprised him with a bright laugh.

"Oh, my dear Dauncey, what a vivid imagination you have!" she said. "Next you'll be claiming my maid is a soothsayer and my butler a necromancer!"

"Spies," Daniel commented mildly. "Now that's an interesting notion. And a slur on a lady's character."

Dauncey curled his lip in scorn. "I'm sure she's been called worse."

Abigail shook her head. "No, I think a spy is the very worst thing I've ever been called."

"Let me make it easy for you, Dauncey," Daniel said, drawing attention back to himself. He swept the cards into his hand and intricately shuffled them once more. "I'll tell you my proposition to buy my way into your cause for three hundred pounds, then we'll let the cards decide—high card wins." He placed the deck face down on the table. "You first."

Dauncey wore a look of reluctance, but then relented, taking the top card and giving it a quick glance before placing it aside, face down.

Daniel picked up the deck and shuffled once more.

"Lady Abigail," he invited, placing the deck before her. Abigail retrieved her card and, on inspecting it, gave a brief smile and lay it down, suit hidden.

For a third time, the cards were shuffled and, with all the stage business of an illusionist, Daniel slid the top card off the deck toward himself without looking at it.

"My proposal is this: a boxing match hosted by Jamaica George out on the commons on Bonfire Night. The best of ten rounds."

Dauncey was clearly unimpressed. "How many times do you propose to do this *trick?* Fighters get five quid a match at best."

"Just the once," Daniel replied. "We each nominate seconds to run a book on our bout. Consider it a test of the new order against the old. Egalitarianism at its best, the working man and the toff support their favorite. If I win, I'll have earned my buy in. If I lose, you have your money and no obligation."

The real bet was on Dauncey's ego. Daniel knew taking Abigail out from under his nose tonight stung and his hatred of the aristocracy only stoked the fire. However, Blakeney had shown him Dauncey's dossier. The Irishman had been a back alley scrapper in Dublin. Despite his airs as a poet, he was very familiar with the "noble art" and Daniel wagered he would assume himself the better man and not be able to resist the temptation to get his money while giving a few lumps to the upstart whelp of a Viscount.

He waited for a response. A second felt like decades.

Dauncey looked thoughtful and then shrewd before answering silkily. "We should let the cards decide, you say?"

With an incline of his head, Daniel indicated his rival should go first. Dauncey obliged. He turned over his card, revealing the nine of diamonds.

Now it was Daniel's turn. His card was the Jack of Clubs, and he looked up at Dauncey in triumph.

"Then we have an agreement?"

"I believe there is one more card to see," the Irishman said, turning to Abigail. "Will the lady oblige?"

She didn't immediately.

"It's an intriguing proposal to be sure," she said, toying with card between her fingers.

Little minx, Daniel thought with fond amusement. She was enjoying this.

"It will be the man of the people against the aristocracy," she continued. "The ladies' favorite versus the man their jealous husbands would back. It will be the highlight of the season."

She flipped over her card with her fingernail. It was the Queen of Hearts.

CHAPTER FOURTEEN

Dauncey rose from his chair. "Well, that is certainly some proposition, Ridgeway, but you'll be forgiving me if I don't accept straight away. Would my answer tomorrow be good enough for you?"

Daniel stood with him, pocketing the deck of cards. "I don't usually extend credit to those I've just met," he said, "but tomorrow's good enough. Where?"

"The Lady's townhouse." After a deliberate and provocative look at Abigail, Dauncey turned back to Daniel. "But not too early, you understand."

Abigail struggled not to blanch. She stood and allowed her hand to be taken in his once more. This time however, the press of his lips was quick and perfunctory.

"Darlin' Abigail, I won't be seeing you home. My scattered brain has reminded me of an urgent appointment."

"Now?" she responded incredulously, in spite of the relief she felt at her reprieve.

Dauncey shrugged and left the Card Room.

Abigail turned to Daniel whose attention remained fixed on the withdrawing Irishman. She leaned in closer to avoid being overheard.

"Should we follow him or whatever it is that spies do now?"

The smile she received was filled with amusement. "No, I think Sir Percy and his men have that covered."

"He's here?" she gasped. Surely she would have recognized the man who upended her life, even if the only time they had spoken was two years ago and he'd been dressed in the costume of the Sheriff of Nottingham.

"He didn't stand out to you?" Daniel queried. "His waistcoat was bright enough to substitute for the Eddystone Rocks lighthouse."

Abigail knew a look of incredulity was apparent on her face by the expression of great amusement on Daniel's own.

"*That's* the great spy master of England?" she hissed.

Daniel put a finger to his lips in warning, and Abigail was struck by how handsome he was with his light blue eyes twinkling in merriment. He reached across the table, inviting Abigail to place her hand in his. She did so and was surprised by the warm glow suffusing her being as she stood and waited for him at her side of the table. It would be easy to read more in his attention than just a collegial regard, but there was something in the way he made her feel, as though he could see more than simply her past as a notorious demirep.

Abigail rebuked herself. She was no naïf filled with a schoolgirl's illusion of love and romance. She recognized in herself the feelings of desire, but there was a yearning for something more. Abigail indulged herself by keeping hold of his hand. Strange, there was no hurry on his part to remove it either.

She edged closer.

"And where on earth did you learn to faro shuffle, you dirty dog?" she asked softly.

"I had a very misspent youth," he said, grinning conspiratorially.

Abigail shook her head and laughed. "I was afraid Dauncey was going to twig when you gave him the 'Scottish Curse' card."

Daniel glanced around, and Abigail too noticed several people pointedly eyeing their obviously disused gaming table.

"Come with me, we'll find somewhere quiet to talk."

She felt the warmth of his other hand as he placed it at her waist, urging her through the press of bodies until they reached the entrance of the Assembly. A maid quickly returned with their cloaks, a modicum of protection against the chill and the rain that thrummed relentlessly on the portico roof.

At Daniel's direction, a footman sent a page to call for Abigail's carriage. They huddled together in the lee of the Corinthian columns, Daniel's body blocking the worst of the frigid wind.

"I take it our cards weren't an accident either?" she asked. "That was a French deck you were using. The court cards have meaning, you know."

If Abigail looked hard she might convince herself there was meaning in the slight shift of expression on his face too. Indeed his eyes met hers steadily, and she was drawn to them. She was almost overwhelmed by the need to stroke his cheek, to feel the hint of late-evening stubble graze her fingers, to recall the memory of his touch in that quiet moment just a few nights before.

It awakened in her a feeling that was new, precious, and unsullied by her past.

She dropped her head, now unable to look at him in case her feelings were so plainly etched on her face.

"Abigail." She heard her name as a whisper and wondered whether she had imagined the longing in it. Then there was just the sound of the rain, over which could be heard the clatter of hooves on cobble stones as the carriage approached.

"Sir? M'lady?" The discreet interjection of the footman broke the reverie, and when Abigail looked up, the door to the carriage was open. At Daniel's urging they made a dash, avoiding the water that dripped from the portico overhang. He gave the instruction to head to the Red Lion Inn, located a few miles out of town. It wasn't a place Abigail knew, but a curt nod from the oil skin-clad head of the driver confirmed he did.

Once the carriage started rolling, Daniel stretched, his long, booted legs banging against the underside of the seat opposite, both arms raised in victory for a moment before he angled himself toward her, one arm resting against the back of the seat. Still disquieted by the recognition of mutual desire which flared between them, Abigail turned her attention to what—to her mind—was a far less dangerous business.

"A boxing match? Really?" she asked, keeping her voice faintly amused, rather than breathless. "That is your grand plan, the one that is going to save England from revolution?"

Daniel offered a nonchalant shrug. His cavalier attitude goaded her. She had seen men come to blows and leave bruised and bloodied.

"Do you know *how* to fight? I don't think you really know what kind of man you're up against. Dauncey is underhanded and ruthless."

"I do believe the little woman cares," Daniel teased.

"You're very much mistaken," she announced, shifting her body away from him. "If you have no care for your physical safety, then I have none either."

Daniel laughed heartily, and the rest of the trip went on in silence.

The Red Lion Inn, built during the reign of the Tudors, was a single story stone and thatch building hunkered low and squat in the hills just outside Bath. The rain that accompanied them up from the town had eased to a drizzle by the time they stopped.

The coachman dropped nimbly from his seat and knocked on the closed door of the inn. A panel opened in the door, spilling yellow light through the aperture. Abigail shifted to see if she could glimpse the figure inside, but could not. Daniel slid along the bench beside her and brushed his hand against her arm as he looked over her shoulder to the scene outside.

"We'll wait until we're called," he instructed softly. She nodded absently, but did not move her hand away and watched. The inn door opened a sliver and the driver sidled his way through it before it slammed closed behind him.

With no more to see, Abigail straightened. She felt the firmness of Daniel's thigh against hers and the solid warmth of his body against her back as they looked out the window. She could smell his cologne, a mix of cinnamon, clove, and lime, as it mingled with her own rose and jasmine scent.

"Why are we here?" Abigail whispered, although she supposed there was no need for it. They were alone in the middle of nowhere.

"Sir Percy has news about the Radical plot to set off a bomb in London," Daniel answered, his voice close to her ear. "I don't know any more."

They waited.

Despite the fact no lightning split the night sky, a charge filled the carriage. A persistent thrum of arousal settled low in her, and Abigail savored the sensation. It had been such a long time since she had been in any man's arms, let alone one she was beginning to care about.

Just as she wondered if she had misread Daniel's feelings for her, his arm moved from the back of the seat to encircle her. She could feel raised gooseflesh with the warmth of his breath as he leaned forward to drop a light kiss on the back of her neck.

Her sigh was accepted as encouragement, and Daniel drew her closer to him with both arms. His kisses deepened where her flesh was bared, on her neck and shoulders; his fingers slightly caressed the curve of her waist and teased the undersides of her breasts.

Abigail's own hands stroked the soft wool of the jacket that covered his arms. She was restless for more…restless for him.

"Daniel…"

She whispered his name with longing and started to turn so her lips could claim the kisses he was lavishing elsewhere.

Bang!

The inn door slammed shut against the rising wind that had driven away the rain. The sound of booted feet crunching on the gravel heralded the approach of an occupant from the inn.

Abigail turned completely to look at Daniel. In the dimness of the carriage, his face was edged in shadow. Even so, she could see the stiffness of his posture, the tension in the line of his jaw. His nostrils flared as though he had just run a mile and the brightness of his eyes attested to the desire now being restrained.

"Abigail."

Her name sounded like agony on his lips as he reached out to stroke her cheek tenderly.

She breathed in deeply, then offered a rueful smile and turned to look out the window as their driver approached and opened the door. The raw wind removed any last vestige of heat from the carriage.

"They're ready for you inside now," said the man in a thick Somerset accent. He offered his hand to aid her from the vehicle.

As soon as she alighted, Daniel was right behind her, placing his cloak about her shoulders, and Abigail drew the scent of him in deeply as he settled it on her.

"Let's go see what Aunty wants," he said.

* * *

The sound of their rapid footfalls toward the inn remonstrated with Daniel in every step. Fool, fool, fool! he admonished himself.

Succumbing to temptation like that was an idiot's mistake, and he cursed himself heartily for it even as the sweet floral scent reached him, heated by the warmth of Abigail's body as she strode beside him. He couldn't deny it now. He wanted the woman with an ache that was damn near painful.

Fleetingly, he could see in his mind's eye the face of Rachel Sawyer, the sweet young woman who was his first love. It reminded him bitterly there was only room for one on this journey. Anger rose violently in his chest.

Dammit! Jonathan was responsible for her. How could Percy keep him in godforsaken France?

The maelstrom of emotions blurred his feelings for Abigail and Rachel until he was unsure what place each held in his heart.

A lungful of cold night air was enough to clear his head as they reached the door. He rapped the timber hard, and the door opened to reveal a well-lit room. In the wall opposite, a large fire burned.

Six other people were in the room, and Daniel nodded to them. He recognized them all by face and even knew the names of some, although he was sure they were aliases.

Behind them, a voice called the room to order. Daniel escorted Abigail to a table where they watched the bedraggled "Somerset" coachman take off his rain-slicked coat and broad-brimmed hat and transform himself into a leader of men.

Daniel suppressed a smile as he felt Abigail stiffen; a quick glance revealed the surprise rising on her face. Yes, Blakeney could have that effect on people.

"Gentlemen," he began, and, with a nod and smile to Abigail, continued, "and Lady. We don't have time for socializing tonight, so we'll save the introductions for another time. According to my sources, it's believed our Radicals have one of two dates in mind for the attack on London. It will be either January the thirtieth—the anniversary of the execution of Charles the First—or January the thirty-first for the execution of Guy Fawkes.

"In any event, it has left us with precious little time to identify all the major players, though, thanks to our light-fingered new recruit," he continued, acknowledging Abigail yet again, "we have some new addresses to try on our return to London and a lead to run down, one Molly H.

"On the assumption the two dates are significant, they may be sentimental enough to gather together on Bonfire Night itself. We've given them just the incentive, an opportunity to raise cash and settle some scores. It takes the form of a boxing match on November the fifth with Dauncey in one corner and, in the other corner…"

Blakeney paused and the character of Sir Percy, the garrulous fop, made a momentary appearance as he presented Daniel to the gathering.

"It's my pleasure to announce the coming out of retirement of Dapper Dan, the Gentleman Boxer, terror of four counties!"

Daniel stood with a grin and bowed, acknowledging the applause and laughter of every man in the room. As he retook his seat however, he took note of Abigail. Her mouth, which he knew to be full and sensual, was now in a tight, straight line as Blakeney continued speaking.

"Dauncey is a poseur who cannot resist self-aggrandizement. Dapper Dan gave him a metaphorical slapping tonight, so there will be little love lost. Watch the Irishman closely. I expect this will be a honeypot affair with a few hitherto unknowns buzzing about. I'm banking they will not be able to resist the money or the theatre. "Now, Dan will need a second. Who volunteers?"

"I do."

Daniel turned to the voice and gave a nod of acknowledgement to Sir Phillip Glynde.

"Good. Meet tomorrow to sort out the particulars," instructed Blakeney. "If there is no further business, then our meeting is adjourned. You all know your parts. Be good, be safe, be victorious!"

The scrape of chairs on the flagstone floor filled the room as the gathering rose and Sir Percy approached Daniel. "Before you see the lady safely home, I need to have a word."

Glynde joined them with four mugs of cider and took one for himself. He slapped Daniel on the shoulder. "York Club tomorrow afternoon?" he said and Daniel nodded his ascent.

Blakeney took a large draught of the spiced apple beverage. "My dear Lady Abigail," he greeted her in his normal voice. "My apologies for the subterfuge earlier this evening, but if my appearance can exceed even your keen eye, then it will certainly continue to confound the Frenchies and their confederates."

"Your apology is accepted, Sir Percy," she replied, soberly.

"And am I finally forgiven for press-ganging you into my group?" he asked with more emphasis. Abigail cocked her head, seeming to consider her answer, when he raised his hand.

"No. Don't tell me, my heart would break if you had only censorious words for me," he told her, the fop stealing momentarily back into his tone before receding, "but I can promise your full release from your obligation at the end of this year and I know that will win your favor. You'll be free to travel to Naples, and I will even furnish you with an introduction to the new Lady Hamilton, if you wish."

Abigail's features brightened. "Your kindness would most certainly go a long way in restoring my good opinion of you," she said, toasting the proposal.

Daniel watched the exchange with feigned disinterest. The measure of cider he drank soured in his stomach and he pushed the mug away, relieved that his disquietude went unnoticed.

CHAPTER FIFTEEN

Daniel's jaw clenched as he anticipated the impact. His right hand, strapped with linen and then with leather, struck the stuffed leather punching bag with a force that sent pain running up to his shoulder.

It felt good.

Moisture ran down a lock of hair and dropped onto his nose. He shook his head furiously and the sweat scattered about, just as he landed another blow to the bag with his left hand.

"Faster, Dan," George urged. "You go faster than that, mon! Go on, pummel him!"

He didn't need any urging. Anger and disappointment fuelled his aggression and, here at the camp, he could allow it full rein as the recollection of last night's parting from Abigail ran through his mind…

Abigail had been silent the entire ride home. Even after the footman opened the door outside her townhouse, she sat with a faraway expression on her face.

"A penny for your thoughts," he said, nudging her shoulder.

Abigail gave him a wan smile. "I was thinking of Italy," she confessed. "Lady Hamilton has become the most sought-after hostess in Europe, and her husband as England's envoy in Naples would ease my way into society there. A sunny clime, plenty of exciting people…" Her voice grew softer on that last part. "Have you spent much time on the continent?"

He shook his head. "A little. Not as far as Italy. Austria, some of France. Not Paris though."

"Oh? Paris is lovely," she said, distractedly, then shrugged and looked wistful. "At least it was when I was last there with Princess Charlotte, but that was before the revolution."

The footman discreetly gave up waiting for them. He closed the carriage door quietly and retreated inside the house.

Daniel swallowed and asked the question that had been burning him up since they had left the inn. "Are you really going to do it?"

Abigail cocked her head and looked at him quizzically. "Move to Naples you mean?"

He didn't trust himself to speak, so he nodded.

"Of course!" she replied. "What is there for me here? Thanks to that tart-faced Maria Fitzherbert, George won't see me. And that puts Charlotte in a pickle because she doesn't want to upset her brother.

"I've become nothing more than a social curio because of the Canalissy scandal; I'm just a piece of silver to bring out at parties, something to be pointed and stared at because it's *de rigueur* to have someone *naughty* at fashionable events. Well, I'm tired of being an exhibit."

Abigail paused and bowed her head slightly. She took a slight, shuddering breath.

"I have no family. If I stay here the best I can hope for is to be some man's mistress." She shook her head. "I've already trod that path. I don't know if I can do as Lady Hamilton did and marry a man thirty-four years my senior. But in Naples I can live as an independent woman—on my own—to do as I truly please. I'll be free at last."

Abigail's face glowed and Daniel could see she was already far away from England in her mind's eye. Far away from him.

"And that means a lot to you?" he asked.

Abigail gifted him with a radiant smile. "It means *everything*."

With a series of left-right combinations, Daniel pounded the bag. Muscles screamed out for surcease, his legs ached from the stance. Only when they felt as much pain as he did in his heart did he stop and stagger a few steps back.

His chest tightened, making it difficult to breathe. Black spots danced merrily before his eyes. He lurched toward the suspended bag and hugged it drunkenly, gasping in great lungfuls of air, and waited for his head to clear.

When it did, he saw George, his expressive brown eyes revealing concern for his well-being.

"Perhaps this fight is too much for you, eh? You no longer a young man."

"Younger than you," Daniel gasped, grateful that enough air filled his lungs to be able to talk.

"He has something else 'pon his mind. That's why he cannot fight."

They turned and Bossy stood behind them, her arms folded in an expression of displeasure. She was dressed in her show costume—a white blouse and a skirt which was a multicolored riot of yellow, green, and black. She wore a headscarf of the same material as the skirt, and big gold hoops dangled from her ears. To Daniel she looked for all the world like an angry sunflower and he burst out laughing at the thought.

"You be laughin' 'pon the other side of your face when that Dauncey man hits you," she sniffed.

"You be all right. You've been trained by the best," countered George, giving Daniel a wide grin and slapping him on the shoulder. "You might be slower than you were at twenty-one but yuh technique is better. Bossy's right though. You're distracted today."

Daniel shook his head as much to clear it as to deny the observation.

Bossy came forward. "You go get our boys ready for da show," she told George. "I want to have a word with the champion here."

Her husband grinned and dropped a towel onto Daniel's shoulders. "And everyone wants to know where she got her name from," he laughed, walking away.

Daniel felt like a schoolboy once again, called out for punishment by the master. He toweled himself perfunctorily and put on a shirt, ignoring the sweat that still clung to him. Bossy looked on, arms folded as he added a coat to ward off the chill, then she turned and strode back to her caravan, leaving Daniel to follow.

Inside, the smell of aromatic spices filled the air, and Bossy ladled stew from a vessel atop the pot-bellied stove into a bowl. She passed it to Daniel.

The flavor of the tender goat went a great deal to restoring his humor. He ate slowly, hoping Bossy would just give him a lecture and not start asking questions. But for a woman who could be quick to temper, she was also surprisingly patient and she waited without speaking until he finished the bowl.

Daniel wondered if she would catch on to his delaying if he asked for a second helping. One look into her eyes told him the ruse would not work.

"'Ave known you for a very long time," she began. "Back when you were just a scared boy wi' no home and us took you in."

"I'm grateful, Bossy," he said. "You and George did more than take me in, you made me feel like I was part of a family. I've never forgotten."

"I know you 'aven't," she said, refilling the empty bowl he now offered her. "Even when you left us you wrote, and every few months a new letter was waiting for us in the next town."

Daniel nodded, but Bossy shook her head.

"Don't you see?" she implored with all the tenderness of a mother. "I don't want your gratitude, I want you to be happy."

"Can't you just settle for me being safe and well?"

The joke fell flat.

"Who is she?"

Perhaps obfuscation would work.

"Who's who?"

Bossy glowered. Perhaps not.

"The woman you pining over."

Daniel stiffened; the observation was a little too close to home, but he didn't answer.

"You behaved like this when you were lovesick for…what was her name…Rebecca?"

"Rachel," Daniel managed to speak her name without the stabbing pain that usually accompanied it.

"You ought have married that girl and you didn't. You let your friend get ahead of you. Are you going let it happen again?"

"Bossy, this is different…" said Daniel, a warning tone clear in his voice. For whatever reason, Bossy chose to ignore it.

"Suit yourself, make your life a torment, eh? And for what?"

"Enough!"

He stood and placed the bowl of uneaten food on the table, his appetite all but vanished. "Thank George for me," Daniel said quietly. "I'll be back to train again tomorrow."

* * *

Ever since Daniel had embarrassed Dauncey at The Assembly, each day had been a procession of personal visits from people Abigail hardly knew and cared even less for. They were angling for an invitation to the Bonfire Night Party—and some none too subtly either.

And through it all, Abigail smiled politely and entertained impeccably. While these tedious people prattled on endlessly, she imagined herself walking down a piazza, perhaps in the learned company of Lord Hamilton who would point out some interesting, but arcane facts about the fountains and statues they'd pass.

While such fantasies got her through the day, here in the study, lit only by firelight with the sound of an autumn wind gusting outside, the sundrenched climes of Italy seemed more remote and unattainable, despite Blakeney's promise.

Abigail took another sip of the dark fruity claret, savoring its feel around her tongue and on the back of her palette as she swallowed.

She thought of Daniel and wondered where he was tonight.

It had never occurred to her to ask where he had been living. How did he spend his days? Did spies have hobbies? Surely one can't make a career of being a spy? What if there was no war with France? What does an out-of-work spy do?

Guilt, a relatively unfamiliar and new emotion, gripped her. Was she always so self-absorbed?

The thoughts drifted on, some nonsensical, as her mind warred with her body over the need for sleep. The thought of Daniel's touch kept her awake and made her so much more aware of him, even when he wasn't there. So too did the conversation they'd had in the carriage.

It only occurred to her this evening that the questions Daniel had asked were more than they'd appeared to be. However, she had been so excited by Blakeney's promise to release her and his offer to help ease her into Italian society, she had missed the point behind Daniel's inquiries.

Was it too late to recapture that moment in time? Was it destined to be blown away, to be forever out of reach? What could she do? She had no playbook for what she was beginning to feel for Daniel. What if it was love? How would she know? What should she do if it was and she missed the opportunity?

For a moment, panic gripped her, and the hand that brought the glass to her mouth trembled slightly. Perhaps she should ask Jane; she had been happily married for more than twenty years now. Surely she would know what love was?

As soon as the thought appeared, she dismissed it. As much as she liked the woman, she had not more than an ounce of self-reflection in her entire body. No, Jane would be a useless person to ask.

"As if you're so experienced in introspection yourself," she chided herself mentally.

Click.

The sound of the door could be heard over the steady tick of the mantle clock above the fireplace. She sat up and placed her glass on the side table.

"Can I join you in one of those?"

Abigail turned to see Daniel standing in the study doorway. He smiled tiredly at her, his expression darkened with fatigue and stubble. She rose to fill him a glass, handing it to him just as he dropped onto the couch.

"What is it that you do all day?" she asked, the words rushing out.

Daniel sniggered. "It's very nice to see you too, *dear.*"

Abigail scowled at him. "That's not what I meant."

"Forgive me if I seem obtuse, but I'm exhausted," he offered by way of an olive branch.

Abigail accepted it. "I'm sorry too. I've been sitting here thinking that I know next to nothing about you."

"Occupational hazard." He shrugged before downing half the glass in one mouthful. "Spies are supposed to drift in and out of others' lives like ghosts. Give it a few years and you'll not even remember my name."

"I'm not sure I can do that."

"Then that's too bad. I learned the hard way this business is no place to form attachments, let alone to fall in love."

Abigail's heart beat faster wondering whether he could see her feelings for him despite the long practice she had in masking her emotions.

"I did it once," he added softly, and Abigail shook her thoughts aside so she would not miss his words.

There was a long silence, and Abigail began to think he would not continue with his revelation. Then, "I fell in love with a beautiful girl. Even my father would have approved of her.

"I wanted to ask her to marry me; I know she was expecting a proposal, but I was called to the continent with no idea when or even if I would return. I loved her so much I couldn't even ask her to wait for me, not if she could find love and security elsewhere.

"In the end I was gone twelve months and by the grace of God even managed to survive unscathed. I returned just in time for the last reading of the banns. She married my best friend that autumn."

Daniel let out a soft, derisive snort.

"Jonathan's in the business too, but he saw things differently to me."

"I'm very sorry," said Abigail.

"Don't be." He downed the last of the claret. "He's the type of husband she deserves to have."

Abigail studied the flickering flames of the fire, pondering how to phrase her next question. As the moment lingered on, she decided bluntness served her just as well. Better that she know now than wonder needlessly.

"You still love her, don't you?"

She ventured a look at him and in profile she could see him shrug.

"Yes. Maybe… I don't know. Does it matter? She's married to someone as close to me as a brother. I'd never disrespect her. Or him."

"You said Jonathan was 'in the business.' Why isn't he here? Or is he, and you're too ashamed of me to let us meet?"

It was intended as a joke, a little self-deprecating humor Abigail hoped would alleviate the tension. Instead, Daniel pivoted sharply and grabbed her shoulders.

"Don't let me hear you say that again!" he growled.

Abigail was taken aback by his reaction. She was well familiar with the gossip about her, and the jealousy and mean-spirited envy in the tittle-tattle that masqueraded as propriety. She dealt with it and mostly ignored it, although she could not say it entirely ceased to bother her. However, it did seem to anger Daniel.

"You are a woman of rare quality," he insisted. "I hear the gossip, I know the things people say, but you outshine them all. You are beautiful, smart, and courageous. Never be ashamed to let the world see the Abigail that I know."

One by one the walls of Jericho fell. The impregnable citadel of her heart crumbled. She was free, yet vulnerable. Her heart raced as it had done the very first time she'd coaxed her horse to jump over a hedge. Abigail blinked away tears, demanding from herself the mastery of emotions she knew she possessed. But here in the sanctuary of the library, cloaked by the privacy of the night, she let them fall.

Daniel regarded her tenderly and reached forward to brush the rivulets away from her cheeks. His hand brushed the nape of her neck and drew her to him.

The touch of his lips on hers was soft, almost tentative as they waited for a response. Abigail parted her lips, and the kiss went deeper, achingly tender, and it touched and warmed parts of her soul that had long been scarred and hidden.

His other hand ran itself though her loosely bound hair. The ribbon that tied it fell away, and soft waves of icy white cascaded past her shoulders.

His lips left hers and offered openmouthed kisses from her eyelids and down her cheeks. Daniel's tongue darted out to taste the salt of her now-drying tears. Desire and need bloomed through her with an intensity that ached before settling with a throb between her legs.

Abigail held his shoulders and whispered his name as his touch brought heat to her neck. Her nipples puckered, blossomed, and ached.

Daniel's lips kissed their way back up the column of her neck. His lips and tongue played with her earlobe. "I've tried my damndest to resist," he breathed, low and husky, "but I want you, Abigail."

She pushed herself away just far enough to turn her head and offer an answering nod before she parted her lips and kissed him. Questing tongues explored and savored. Their bodies were so close she could feel the evidence of his desire for her. Using his superior strength and leverage, Daniel pressed Abigail back on to the settee. She pulled at his elbows in a silent demand to join her, but he resisted, pausing as though to drink the sight of her in.

Bang! Bang! Bang!

Furious pounding at the front door of the townhouse made them start and shattered the erotic tension between them. A look of disappointment crossed Daniel's face, a mirror of her own regret. He helped her to her feet as another series of rapid knocks beat upon the door.

"I'll go," said Daniel firmly. Abigail followed as far as the study door, remaining out of sight, but still with a view of the hallway, and watched.

Daniel opened the door and Abigail heard hysterical sobbing from on the step. She surged forward just as Emily Burchill crossed the threshold. The girl glanced at her and then back to Daniel.

"Please, you have to help us! William has been shot!"

CHAPTER SIXTEEN

Richard Hamberley stumbled across the threshold with William Templeton in his arms and sank to the tiled floor. As they went down, Templeton's coat, which was wrapped around him, fell away and revealed the entire left arm of his shirt soaked in blood from the shoulder down.

"Abigail! We need hot water!" Daniel's voice carried an urgent note. "Now!"

She ran back to the study to fetch an oil lamp and with the other hand gathered Emily by the shoulders and bustled her down the hall, calling out to Daniel behind her. "Bring him to the kitchen!"

"I didn't mean for it to happen…there's so much blood…I didn't think he'd do it… I didn't mean for it to happen…" Emily repeated herself over and over, all the way to the kitchen. Abigail itched to slap the hysteria out of her. And then slap her again just for the sheer pleasure of it.

She had warned Emily, told her she was too immature to understand the stakes, and now a young man's life was jeopardized.

On second thought, it would be better getting the girl to do something useful. Abigail urged her toward the butler's pantry, taking one of the white table linens and shoving another into her hands. "There are shears on the second shelf. Cut bandages," she ordered.

Abigail laid out the other tablecloth on the scrubbed kitchen table, then turned to the fireplace where she used the bellows to breathe life back into the glowing embers before shoveling on a fresh scoop of coal from the scuttle. A kettle, already filled, thank God, hung on a hinged arm. She swung it over the fire to heat as Daniel and Hamberley carried the wounded young man into the room between them.

Templeton moaned in pain as he was laid on the table. Daniel tore away the bloodied shirt and quickly surveyed the gunshot wound to his left upper arm.

"Abigail, do you have vodka?"

"In the study," she replied and noticed Viscount Hamberley, his face pallid, swaying on his feet as he looked at his injured friend. "Hamberley," Abigail called and he looked at her uncertainly. "Richard! Vodka decanter. In the study. White spirit. Name on a silver plaque. Bring it now!"

Her words seemed to bring him out of a stupor. He stumbled away into the hall just as Stanstead appeared around the corner, having made his way from the top floor dressed in his nightshirt and robe.

"Is there anything amiss, my Lady?" he asked, but immediately comprehended the scene and addressed Daniel. "What do you need me to do, sir?"

"Just keep the servants away, Stanstead," he answered. "We don't need gossip. And go make sure Hamberley hasn't fainted somewhere."

"Very good, sir," he nodded and left. For a moment, he could be heard just outside the door telling Cook, who had emerged from the basement quarters, to return below stairs and instruct any other staff awakened by the noise to go back to sleep. Their voices faded as they moved further away.

Abigail stood at Daniel's side and looked down at Templeton's injury, a ragged round hole in his bicep. The young man's left arm was limp, but he gripped the edge of the table with his right in betrayal of his pain.

"Pistol ball," said Daniel aside to her.

When he lifted the arm and palped the area, Templeton cried out, but Daniel ignored his distress.

"It could have been worse," Daniel told the young man, "but I think it's all meat and no bone. It might feel like it, but you're not going to die, though before I'm finished you're going to wish you had. It's still in there. If you think it hurts now, just wait until I prod around to get the bugger out."

"Oh…" moaned Templeton.

"What do you need?" Abigail asked Daniel softly. He gave her a look of gratitude.

"A short, sharp skewer, a pair of sugar nips, and a couple of teaspoons. Place them in the spirits. I can't tell how far the ball's penetrated, but I want to try to get it out without doing any more damage."

She nodded and went to fetch the utensils, placing them in a bowl just as Stanstead returned with Hamberley and the vodka. A glance at the young man suggested he was about to lose the contents of his stomach.

"Shall I assist, sir?"

Daniel swiftly accepted Stanstead's offer before turning to Abigail and nodding at Hamberley and Emily.

"Get these two out of here, they don't need to see this."

"Agreed," she said. "You two, come with me."

The two young people followed meekly as Abigail returned to the study. They stood by the fireplace, soaking in its warmth against the chill of the new autumn morning and the shock.

Abigail observed the pair. Hamberley had his head bowed and his hands stuffed into the pockets of his gray greatcoat. It was smeared in rust-red blood. Emily had her arms wrapped around herself. They did not look at each other or at her.

Abigail suppressed a sigh and poured a large measure of brandy for each of them.

"But I don't drink strong liquor," Emily protested weakly.

"Sip it slowly," Abigail instructed.

Hamberley needed no lesson. He downed the brandy in one gulp, then coughed wetly as the alcohol burned its way down his throat. He turned and set the glass on the mantle with a thud. A cry of pain from the kitchen reached them, and Emily started sobbing. Hamberley paled, but did nothing to comfort her. If anything he turned away even more.

A knock on the study door interrupted Abigail's reflection.

Hell's bells, she cursed, Stanstead was told to keep the servants away! Who else was going to come traipsing in? Rufus the Groom?

It was Kathleen at the threshold, looking hurriedly dressed and exceedingly uncertain.

"Cook said Mr. Stanstead said to come," she explained as though she could observe her mistress's ill-temper at her being there. Her next statement was directed to Hamberley. "If young sir would be pleased to follow me, I have a washstand and clothes for you to borrow."

Abigail had to concede Stanstead was right. "You'd best go with Kathleen."

Hamberley walked like a somnambulist, slow and heavy. He stopped half way to the door and half turned back to Emily.

"I'll never forgive you for this. William is my friend and I nearly killed him because of you."

Kathleen's eyes were big and round at the vehemence of the words as well as the revelation. Abigail cleared her throat to catch the maid's attention.

"Discretion, Kathleen," she warned her. "Do not breathe a word to another living soul. Any questions, talk to no one except Stanstead. Do you understand me?"

Kathleen nodded vigorously and dipped a curtsey. Hamberley preceded her from the room, and Kathleen pulled the door shut behind her.

The sound of the fire crackling in the grate competed with the rhythmic tick of the mantle clock. Stripped of her naive self-assurance, Emily Burchill cast a pathetic figure trapped in paroxysms of body-shaking sobs now that Hamberley had left the room.

Abigail found herself torn between compassion and contempt. She stood apart from Emily, warring with herself whether to offer her comfort or let the stupid little girl wallow in her own grief.

Considering how Emily and her family claimed kinship, then spread gossip about her, it would serve her right to suffer. It would serve the whole family right to suffer.

One word and she could destroy her parasitic relations. It would be fitting revenge. A dish served cold indeed. Let them suffer the disgrace and humiliation as she had been made to suffer. In her mind's eye she could see it and it gave her perverse and spiteful satisfaction.

Just as quickly the thought soured…hadn't she tried to warn Emily about the dangerous game she played?

"Don't be afraid to show the world the Abigail I know."

Surely it was better to salvage lives than destroy them. Better to be mocked for pointing out the danger, than saying nothing and watching others fall.

If someone had cared enough to warn *her* all those years ago, perhaps she might have listened and saved herself along the way.

Abigail made her decision. She would be the Rahab that Sir Percy had promised she would be.

"Emily," she began softly. The young woman raised her eyes, swollen and bloodshot. "Come. Take a seat."

Emily sat on the settee, and Abigail joined her. She took the still half-full brandy glass from her hands and placed it on the side table next to her own abandoned glass of claret.

"Would you like to tell me what happened tonight?" she asked gently.

A shuddering breath was the only response, and Abigail wondered whether the girl would answer. When the words came they were whisper-soft.

"No, I don't think I would."

Abigail shrugged, then reclaimed her glass and sipped the wine. "The choice is yours. But you *will* have to talk about it—to your father, to Templeton's, to Hamberley's—perhaps to the authorities should the Templetons wish to press charges against Richard."

Emily swallowed and bowed her head. Abigail could see she was trying to muster what little bravado she had left. Then the girl fell silent, and Abigail wondered if she had fallen into tears once again.

Abigail rose and for a moment considered the bell pull. She had no idea where Kathleen had taken Hamberley and dismissed the idea of using the bell to summon her. Instead, she left the room, went to the kitchen, and tapped on the door before opening it slightly. Daniel and Stanstead were tidying up; Templeton lay still on the table, barely conscious, his upper arm and shoulder bound.

"Stanstead," she said, "when you're finished, find Kathleen and send her to me in the study."

Abigail returned to the room. Emily had not moved, but looked up at last.

"I didn't mean it to happen," she said haltingly. "I didn't want Thomas or Richard to be hurt, I just…"

After a long pause, it was clear no additional words would be forthcoming.

"Emily," said Abigail. The young woman raised her eyes. "I won't give you a lecture. I'm sure that is to come from elsewhere, save for this: everything you do and everything you say has consequences. Be sure you can live with them beforehand."

There was a soft knock and Kathleen entered.

"See that Miss Burchill is settled in my room. She will need her rest."

Through a slit where the curtains met, the black of night was ebbing to a gray pre-dawn light. What had already been a long night looked to be shaping up into a longer day.

* * *

"Did you get much sleep?"

Abigail hid her smile. Daniel's question over the breakfast table was rather domestic, strangely at odds with the events of the hours before. "A couple of hours…about as much as you I suspect."

He acknowledged the truth of her words by lifting his teacup in salute.

"Well, at least our two duelists are sleeping," he said. "The patient will live if his wound isn't fatally purulent, though he'll be feeling sorry for himself for some time. And Hamberley is sleeping like the dead."

At Abigail's grimace, he grinned.

"Poor choice of words," he conceded. "What of Miss Burchill?"

"She's sleeping too. I've sent Stanstead out with a groom and notes for their parents," Abigail told him. "I'm expecting a delegation here within the hour. I don't know what your plans are, but if you need to leave—"

"Why would I be going anywhere?"

"Because it might be awkward, and you know what a real stick Mrs. Burchill is—propriety over commonsense."

Daniel helped himself to a roll and buttered it, then reached for the preserves. He seemed to be so engrossed with his task Abigail wondered whether she had offended him in some way.

But when he raised his head, mirth was written all over his face. "It's sweet you care for my reputation, but we started this together and we'll finish it together. Besides, I think you'll find Mrs. Burchill will be grateful if this matter should be quietly forgotten. I think all three families will find excuses to end their Season early."

Silence descended once more, and Abigail popped a portion of fresh sweet roll into her mouth, savoring the soft texture of the bread. Suddenly, there was a renewed tension in the air, akin to the one that had enveloped them in the study before last night's emergency.

It was expectant, powerful.

Suddenly, it was difficult to swallow and Abigail reached for her cup, hoping to wet the lump that had formed in her throat.

"Abigail…" Her name from his lips was faint, as though he called her from far-off. "I meant what I said last night."

He didn't have to tell her what he meant, even the little bit of sleep she'd managed had been filled with those words.

"And if I or anyone needed further proof," he continued, "there was everything you did to help those three upstairs. No one could have done more. If you want others to see that, you have to believe it yourself."

Abigail wanted to believe. Desperately. She tried to hang onto the words as a drowning man onto flotsam, only to see it pushed farther out of reach.

"How you see me and how others see me are worlds apart," she said. "Until I'm released by Sir Percy, I have to live in this one."

Daniel pulled his chair away from the table and dropped the snowy linen napkin on the table.

"I'll leave then."

Abigail broke out of her self-pitying stupor. "Where will you go? You've barely slept in a day."

He shrugged. "The chairs in the York Club are comfortable enough."

"You have a fight tomorrow. You can't enter the ring with Dauncey in that state."

"Stay or go, Abigail? I'm too tired to argue."

Something within urged her to once again reach out. She expressed all her yearning in one word.

"Stay."

CHAPTER SEVENTEEN

The grandfather clock in the hall struck ten, the earliest civilized hour one could expect callers, and by the time the last of the hour had been struck, three sets of visitors were on the doorstep of The Crescent townhouse.

Stanstead, who'd had just as little sleep as Abigail and Daniel themselves, was nonetheless immaculately turned out and invited Sir George Templeton, Earl Hamberley, and Mr. and Mrs. Burchill into the drawing room. From across the hall in the study, Abigail waited with Daniel. Sharp voices could be heard from her visitors.

Stanstead opened the door a crack. "My Lady, Sir? The young persons' parents have arrived. Shall I have Kathleen show them in?"

"Give us ten minutes, old man," Daniel instructed. Stanstead nodded his understanding and departed.

Abigail rose and examined her reflection in the mirror. She looked tired and drawn, but determined that the most sought-after hostess of Bath could not leave the room looking anywhere less than her best, so she pinched her cheeks hard. In the mirror's reflection, she saw Daniel rise and smooth the sleeve of his jacket which had only just arrived from the club.

"Do you want me to go in first?" he offered. "As I recall, my namesake did rather well dealing with ravenous lions."

The fact he jested lifted her spirits. Abigail shook her head. "I will remind you of your words at breakfast. We started this together and we will finish this together."

Daniel swooped in for a quick peck on the cheek, and Abigail felt a flush of color surge through her face. "That's better," he assured her.

* * *

"Ridgeway! What the hell is going on? Where's my son?" thundered Sir George Templeton, his face already an alarming shade of puce.

Daniel kept his voice calmly modulated. "Calm yourself, sir. William will be with us shortly. He has a wound caused by a pistol ball. If he takes care, he will be sore for some weeks, then have a heroic scar to show off."

"How the deuce did he get shot?" the young man's father demanded. "Who shot him?"

"Young Hamberley. They were dueling over Miss Burchill. Your pistols are in their case on the mantle, by the way."

Sir George turned and, identifying the weapons in the case as his own matched pair, became silent.

"Mrs. Burchill, gentlemen, please do take a seat," Abigail said, drawing the focus away from Daniel and moving toward the sideboard where a silver kettle sat, kept warm on its burner and stand. "I think I can speak for everyone when I say the last thing we want is a scandal that may harm the future prospects of William, Richard, or Emily."

She poured the steaming water into a porcelain tea pot and swirled it gently.

"I recommend we all keep our tempers and discuss this civilly, over tea."

She added several scoops of black leaf into the pot and added more hot water. The aromatic smell of pekoe filled the air.

"It's a fine thing for you to be talking about protecting reputations," sniffed Mrs. Burchill, ignoring her husband's attempts to shush her. "I'm sure my daughter would never have dreamed of participating in such a thing if she didn't have your poor example."

Abigail's expression did not falter as she picked up a pair of sugar nips.

"Would you like one lump or two?" she inquired pointedly.

Daniel cleared his throat.

"You have my word, as well as that of Lady Abigail, there will be no gossip from this house, so rest assured on that account," he said. "Our hostess is correct, as she so frequently is. Our concern should be for the welfare and reputations of your children. Are you prepared to discuss this calmly with their future in mind?"

There was silence from those assembled in the room, which Daniel allowed to carry for several moments; long enough for the silence to become strained. To break the tension he opened the door and called for Stanstead. Daniel issued a discreet instruction and the butler left.

Shortly after, the three young people entered the room looking extremely sheepish.

Emily was freshly attired in one of Abigail's more conservative day dresses. Richard and William wore plain shirts borrowed from one of the grooms. William's shirt remained largely unbuttoned to accommodate the sling on his left arm.

As they entered, the two young men made a point of distancing themselves from their one-time sweetheart. The girl shuffled to her father's side and said nothing. Richard and William looked at one another, clearly recalling a rehearsed speech.

William, clearly in pain, supported his injured shoulder, and addressed his father in the first instance. "Sir, I've let you down. I let my temper rule my head and for that I apologize to you, Earl Hamberley, and to Richard who I placed in an invidious position that forced him to defend his person. He has been good enough to not end our friendship over this."

He paused as though determining whether he should end his speech here, but he pressed on reluctantly.

"As a gentleman, I want to say I attach no blame to Miss Emily. As a man, it is my obligation to make allowances for the frailties of the feminine sex, but then to do the right thing regardless. I beg your forgiveness and ask that this matter be allowed to go unspoken from this moment."

Emily's father, plainly uncomfortable, cleared his throat. "I'm not unaware of the responsibility my daughter shares in this misadventure,

William. I am glad your wound is no worse. For the sake of all concerned, I believe a withdrawal from the Season would be advisable."

Beside him, Emily burst into tears, and Mrs. Burchill squeaked in alarm.

"We've only just started with this one!" protested the woman. "Emily has not yet accepted an offer, and what about Caroline? She is supposed to follow her sister next year."

Burchill turned to his wife with impatience writ large across his features. "Quiet, Augusta! This is not a conversation to be had here and now. I've thrown away several hundred pounds on a second season and I have nothing to show for it except trouble. I suggest you and your daughter consider the best way to recompense my loss."

Mrs. Burchill opened her mouth as if to reply, then, thinking better, closed it. She turned to her daughter instead. "Oh, shut up!" she snapped, and Emily swallowed her sobs, blinking.

Sir George and Viscount Hamberley looked briefly at one another, just as their sons had done earlier, and it seemed the Viscount would speak for them both.

"Yes. Indeed. There doesn't seem to be anything gained by pursuing this matter any further. Agreed, George?"

Sir George nodded stiffly and tucked his leather-bound pistol case under his arm.

Hamberley glared at his son. "What about you, sir? Have you anything to say for yourself?"

"Yes, sir. I'm very sorry, sir," said Richard, downcast.

"So you should be, young fool."

William held out his good hand to Daniel. "Thank you, sir. I owe you a great debt and Lady Abigail as well."

Daniel shook the young man's hand and accepted his thanks with a slight nod of his head.

The guests left and did not hesitate, retreating to their carriages with discreet haste.

Abigail sat down. The climax of the morning of unexpected drama had left her drained. Seated on the study settee, she closed her eyes and listened to the sound of Daniel pouring himself a drink.

"One for you?" he offered.

Abigail's eyes remained closed as she declined with a hum and a shake of her head.

Daniel chuckled, and Abigail found enough energy to open one eye.

"Just recalling what you said to Mrs. Burchill. One lump or two… for a moment I was afraid you were going to administer those lumps personally."

"Ooh, that woman gets on my nerves," said Abigail. "This madness was coming for weeks. She's a fool for not keeping a tighter rein on her daughter."

There was silence once more—just the crackling of the fireplace and, faintly, the sounds of servants at work around the house.

"Abigail?"

The question in Daniel's voice prompted her to open her eyes. There was a level of tension in his voice she had not heard before. Her tiredness fled. He had her full attention. He stood with his arm resting across the mantle, his head cast down staring into the drink in his other hand.

"I don't know what the future holds for us."

"I wasn't aware there was a future for us."

As the words left her mouth, she was pained and pressed the palms of her hands to her eyes. She couldn't look at him, not at that moment; not when she had so inelegantly expressed what was so close to the surface.

"That's not what I meant to say…"

"Abigail." His voice was much closer, now seated beside her. "Please, look at me."

"Daniel, what I…"

"Shhhh."

Daniel took both of her hands, his thumbs slowly, rubbing her fingers and knuckles, before raising both hands to his lips to kiss them. Warmth trickled along her nerve endings.

"This is important, I need you to listen to me. Will you?" he asked.

Abigail drew in a breath and nodded. One of his hands left hers and with it he caressed her cheek tenderly, as a lover might. The thought aroused her, but she wanted more than that. Daniel's touch alone wouldn't be enough, not if he didn't care, because the truth was beginning to dawn on her. She was falling in love with him.

The very thought was a revelation. Here she was, at one time a lover to the Prince Regent, once one of the most desired women in London, for whom sex was a currency to be traded for wealth, position, and self-gratification. Abigail had laughed and mocked silly little chits and their calf-eyed beaux as they experienced the first rush of passion and called it love.

Men who promised to forsake all others at their wedding day had proved to be only too willing to make exceptions, and women who promised to love, honor, and obey broke those vows just as frequently. Courtiers and those in the orbit of the Beau Monde treated marriage with a benign contempt. Little wonder, Abigail considered, that her views on love and marriage were skewed. That was why James Mitchell's rejection of her for that captain's daughter—*Selina,* her memory supplied—had been so shocking.

James loved Selina; he actually loved her, and that night at Pitt's masquerade Abigail had known it too. She had watched it bloom over three months that summer, but like viewing exotic flowers under glass, she could only look, not experience the depth of its beauty for herself.

Now, it seemed she had begun to understand, just as the opportunity had already slipped away.

"It's too late for us, isn't it?" she whispered.

Daniel pressed a finger to her lips, his brow furrowed. The lines around his mouth tightened. He was warring with himself, Abigail knew.

"I'm swearing you to the greatest secrecy. Only those within the League know of this."

"League?"

"No questions." He shook his head. "Just listen.

"The man Jonathan and I were shadowing in France for months is called Alexis Roux. He is part of a secret committee of the French National Assembly tasked with exporting revolution.

"We have information he is behind an English Radicals' plot to blow up the merchant fleet anchored in the London Pool and block the Thames. Not only will that strike terror in the city, it will cripple trade for months.

"The Radicals are also planning a coordinating series of violent riots in the major cities, organized through the political correspondence societies. If they're successful, England will most certainly be plunged into civil war. After the fight tomorrow night, Percy will send me to London to join his other agents there."

"I never underestimated what it is you do," she said.

"And you shouldn't underestimate your role in it," he told her warmly. "Thanks to you I have a new lead to pursue—finding Molly H. The name has come up again and again. The addresses from Dauncey's correspondence you lifted from his coat, matched with documents I found in his room, point to the fact their meeting places, although varied, all center around the docks.

"As soon as this affair is dealt with and the ringleaders are in custody, it will be safe for you to leave. Percy will release your three thousand pounds, and you can go wherever and be whoever you wish."

Abigail had not forgotten Blakeney's promise of releasing her at the end of the year—less than two months' time. "What will you do then?"

"I'm going to France."

"What on earth for?" Abigail exclaimed. "Tensions are worse than ever, there's rioting on the streets almost every evening I hear."

"Jonathan is there."

At the mention of the name, Abigail paused. "You're going to try to talk him into coming home."

Daniel dipped his head in mute assent.

"Surely Sir Percy can order him home," Abigail suggested.

"I'm not sure even Percy knows where he is. Jonathan needs to be home with his wife. She needs him. I would have been in Paris months ago if I hadn't been ordered here."

"And if Jonathan is already dead?"

"Then someone needs to break the news to Rachel."

At that moment, Daniel raised his face. His eyes met hers, and Abigail could see the truth in them. It was same truth that had confronted her at Boconnoc House.

"And that's why you said there couldn't be a future for us," concluded Abigail. She pulled herself upright off the couch, trying to wrap dignity as close to her as possible. "All things considered, that's very wise decision. I'll be enjoying spring in Naples, and hopefully you will have kept England safe from anarchists while dodging revolutionaries around Paris. I see how emotions can become entangled in this type of enterprise and, as you once told me, it is not a business in which it is wise to form attachments. I must say, this intrigue has given me some personal insight. It would seem I am not as sophisticated as I thought."

Now she was keen to put physical distance between them, a prelude to the long journey to the emotional distance she would need if she were to survive with any shred of self-respect.

Abigail would not fight for Daniel; the cost was more than she could bear. She would let him go. She extended her hand, pleased to see it did not shake. "I wish you all the best, Mr. Ridgeway…for tomorrow's fight and for your future."

He took it and held it firmly.

"You are the most beautiful woman I have ever met," he said, his voice low and harsh, and the emotion behind it raw.

Abigail smiled. She took the compliment without conceit; many men had told her this, and she took it each time with a casual indifference. However, from Daniel…

"But you're more than that," he continued. "You are a woman filled with life and passion. You are brave and have more wits about you than most. You are intelligent and formidable."

His words, deep and dangerous, rang alarm bells within her. She tried to retrieve her hand, but he held it securely even as she tried to tug it away. Slowly he drew her toward him. Steady breaths became shallow as she looked deep into his eyes. They promised her so much and her body responded. Long forgotten sensations nipped and pricked across her breasts and beat lower between her legs, in time with her heart.

"I want no regrets before I leave," he said, moving his lips closer to hers. "And if I never do this, I'll regret it for the rest of my life."

Chapter Eighteen

Daniel scowled at his reflection in the mirror as he tied his cravat. The stinging red mark left by Abigail's hand on his left cheek may have disappeared, but shock remained, a cold dousing that brought him to his senses.

He should thank her for that—if she'd ever speak to him again. How close he had come to making a mistake, the very same mistake that he had made about Rachel. It was wiser for him to leave without attachment.

He could hear his curricle being brought to the door. Daniel had time to shrug on his jacket and don his gloves and hat for the Gunpowder Plot thanksgiving day service when Sir Phillip Glynde bounded into the room.

"So how are you faring, old man?" he said with his ever-constant cheerfulness. At any other time it was amusing, but today his joviality grated. Daniel tamped his irritation down.

"Do you want the good news or the bad news?" his friend inquired.

"The bad news. Is there any other kind?"

Glynde shrugged and gave himself a once-over in the mirror. He too was dressed formally for the church service that would precede the rest of the holiday.

"It seems the bookmakers of Bath have you at slightly long odds, dear chap." He turned back from the mirror. "I say, that Lady Abigail Houghall is a crafty one. After talking you up for the past fortnight, she's now made it known she's now picking Dauncey as her favorite. It seems one word from her sweet lips have the smart set all backing the Irishman."

Daniel watched his second give him an assessing gaze.

"I hope you're up for it, old man."

"I thought you were giving me the bad news first," bit Daniel as he tossed over a valise containing his fighting togs. Glynde caught it adeptly. "Lady Abigail is doing her job. The bigger a spectacle this fight becomes, the more likely Dauncey's compatriots are to stick their necks out in promise of a windfall."

Discussing her brought a knot to his stomach. He had to change the subject. "You said there was good news?"

"Ah, *now* you want to hear the good news." Glynde responded to Daniel's glower with a grin. "We've already identified two plotters who have arrived from London. They've connected with a group of five who've spread themselves across three inns in the city. They're being secretive but they won't want to miss the show, so you'd better make a good sport of it."

"Oh, don't worry," said Daniel, opening the door. "I'm just in the mood to pound something, and Dauncey will do fine."

* * *

The field just outside the city had benefited from several days of sunshine and slightly warmer weather, becoming firmer under foot. The day had taken on a festive atmosphere.

Daniel steered the curricle off the road and into the field, following the heavily worn tracks where revelers were staking their vantage points. For the past week, children around the city had been knocking on doors begging for scrap timber and "a penny for the Guy."

The results of their efforts could be seen in the center of the field. A pyramid of timber stood fifteen feet tall. At the end of the day as the sun went down, an effigy of the traitor would be paraded through the crowd, then affixed to the top of the pyre. In effigy, there would be no "escape" from punishment such as the real Fawkes had achieved. The fire would be lit, and the evening's celebrations would begin as the Guy was consumed in the flames.

Daniel directed his horse toward the boxing troupe's brightly painted wagons and their tent, over which a large banner proclaiming *Jamaica George's Prestigious Pugilists & World Renowned Wrestlers* had been set up.

Strung on poles between two of the caravans was more hastily painted canvas:

See the fight of honor

Dapper Dan v the Irish Mauler

Before the tent, at eye level, a typeset poster glued to a board on a pole displayed the admission prices. Daniel shook his head as he entered with Glynde. George was charging nearly twice as much as he usually did for his shows, and Daniel suspected the hand of Bossy behind the profiteering.

Good for her.

He grinned to himself as they were directed by one of George's men to the ring. They walked around the men setting up tiered seating.

Dauncey and his second, a man Daniel did not recognize, were already making their inspection of the ring. Having spotted him, Dauncey called across the canvas. "I'm looking forward to teaching you a lesson in front of an audience."

The workers laughed and called on Daniel to respond.

"You spend a lot of time with the ladies, Dauncey," he called back. "I imagine they've taught you some useful skills—like lace making and gossip."

"You've made another mistake, Ridgeway. It's not what they can teach me, but what I can teach them!"

Bawdy laughter erupted.

"Well, I'll be back later to prove I'm a lover *and* a fighter."

At the sound of cheers, Daniel found himself satisfied with the look of scorn Dauncey threw his way. Glynde and the man who was Dauncey's second were called by George, presumably to discuss his rules, so Daniel headed out of the boxing compound and into the field.

The midday sun had brought out the picnickers while touts in colorful jackets and eye-catching hats wandered around the groups collecting bets on the afternoon's sport. The largest party was by far the one hosted by Lady Abigail Houghall.

Daniel knew she had not spared any expense; at least, that's what the solicitor had ruefully told him.

A low white picket fence surrounded a large marquee where a string quartet was playing. Inside the enclosure was a like a mini fair. Footmen and serving girls stood beside tables offering food and drink, while invited guests, identified by bright rosette ribbons, stopped to applaud jugglers, laugh at the Punch and Judy show, or to try their luck at a coconut shy.

Daniel took a drink—a lemonade—and from his vantage point watched Abigail, the center of attention. She was dressed in a jade green dress, and he fancied that even from this distance the color matched her eyes. Her scent of rose and jasmine came to him, as well as the feeling of holding her in his arms while they danced.

Go ahead, he cursed himself, torture yourself further and think of how she responded to you. In his minds' eye, he could see her in the throes of passion under his hand. Desire, and jealousy, thrummed through him as she tossed her head in laughter and placed a hand flirtatiously on some man's chest.

"Well, well, well, for all your big talk, she still eludes you."

Daniel barely had to turn to see that Dauncey had sidled up. He ignored him.

"You want her, that much is clear. You and every other man," the Irishman observed. "You fools treat her like a goddess, as though she inhabits a rarified plane far above your own, but you have no idea what kind of woman she is."

"From what she's told me, you don't have much idea what kind of woman she is either." Daniel gave him a sidelong glance to see if the barb hit.

Dauncey shrugged, nonchalant. "Despite what you think of my… predilections, a man like me knows women. If I wanted, I could have the lady warming my bed tonight, perhaps with a friend. In fact, I could have any woman." Dauncey made a show of casting his eyes around the marquee. "From bored matrons to eager virgins, but alas there is nothing here to my taste. But do you know why I do really like our spoiled little princess?"

Dauncey turned to face him fully. "It's because she thinks and acts like a man."

Any response Daniel might have offered evaporated, interrupted by the approach of William Templeton and Richard Hamberley, the former with his left arm in a sling beneath his coat.

"Mr. Ridgeway," said Templeton. "Richard and I wanted to wish you the very best of luck this afternoon. We each have a guinea on you to win."

Hamberley, having just recognized Dauncey, nudged his friend and said belatedly, "All the best to you too, sir."

Dauncey smiled, slow and reptilian as he turned his attention to one then the other of the two young men, looking them up and down. "Thank you for your wishes. Perhaps you can offer your personal congratulations to me in a few hours time."

Hamberley stepped on his back foot, frowning slightly, and his well-mannered smile faltered momentarily. Dauncey bowed slightly to the three of them and walked away.

If Daniel hadn't been paying attention, he might have missed the undercurrent in the byplay with Templeton and Hamberley. Now, he watched Dauncey move across the field, chatting to his mostly female admirers, and a nagging thought, little more than a buzz in a distant part of Daniel's mind, demanded attention.

Predilections?

* * *

"D'you really think so? I mean, all the ladies throw themselves at him," said Glynde.

"But he's bedded none of them," Daniel insisted. "He must have imagined I knew already."

"It makes sense, I suppose," admitted Glynde, watching distractedly through the window of one of the caravans as Jamaica George tossed his wrestling opponent onto the canvas.

Glynde dropped the curtain and absent-mindedly recited:

"…Should any youth (worth being drunk) prove nice,
And from his fair inviter meanly shrink,
'Twill please the ghost of my departed vice
If, at my counsel, he repent and drink…"

"What are you prattling on about?"

Glynde shrugged. "It's a poem. By the Earl of Rochester."

"That's it!" Daniel answered urgently as he stripped off his formal clothes. "We're not looking for a woman called Molly; we're looking for a *molly house*." He emerged from behind the screen dressed in rough linen breeches, his chest bare. "Of all people, they know how to keep secrets and they aren't going to question men coming and going."

His friend blinked once, and Daniel watched the pieces fall into place for him.

"Now we have to talk Percy into sending men to every seedy gin house around the Docks to find backgammon players willing to talk to us for the sake of King and Country." Glynde smirked at another thought. "If you win today, I don't envy you your next job."

"Believe me, I'll personally request Sir Percy sends you in with me," Daniel replied sardonically. "But first things first, let's get this fight won."

From outside the caravan, the crowd suddenly roared.

Daniel paused. "Wait."

Glynde halted by the closed door. "But they've called your name."

"Let them wait a minute."

He closed his eyes and was twenty again, going out for his first bout as one of Jamaica George's fighters…

Daniel had watched from the sidelines, his nails gouging furrows into his hands, as his first opponent, one of George's more experienced men, ginned up the crowd with a display of aggression, growling at the hecklers and vowing to take them on after he'd mopped the canvas with his challenger.

"What's a matter boy? You nuh be 'fraid of Big Bailey, eh?"

Daniel turned to Bossy, eyes wide. "He'll kill me."

Bossy smiled. "You know your Bible, Dapper Dan?"

"Some, I guess."

"An' the story of David an' Goliath?"

From that night on, before every fight, Daniel would breathe in deeply and exhale slowly, once, then twice, then say the Lord's Prayer aloud.

"Ready now?" asked Glynde.

At Daniel's sharp nod, Glynde opened the door.

The roar of the crowd was a force that gusted like a hot August wind. The habits drilled into him for eight years as one of Jamaica George's band of players served him well. He thrust both fists into the air as if he already had been declared the winner.

Daniel accepted the slaps on his back from pressing well-wishers as he passed. Even so, Abigail stood out among the crowd, her blonde hair shining like a beacon in the late afternoon sun. He was drawn to her.

He veered away from the timber risers that would take him into the ring where Dauncey already waited. A confused frown briefly marred the man's face. Daniel gave his opponent a mocking salute. Like the Red Sea parting for Moses, the crowd in front of him melted to the sides to allow a clear passage to where Abigail stood.

"My Lady."

Abigail gave a slight tilt of her chin. "Are you supposed to be my champion, Mr. Ridgeway?" she asked in the honeyed voice that stirred him.

"A champion requires a token from the lady."

Abigail met his look without reservation. Daniel drank in her features—the soft arch of her brow, her gray-green eyes, feline-like in their regard of him, the soft fullness of her lips. Regardless of the outcome tonight, he would remember this moment and treasure it. In this moment, surrounded by a crowd baying for the spectacle to come, she was his alone.

It would never be again, so he savored it.

Her eyes swept across his body, from his breeches up his bared chest, and he wondered whether he imagined the look of longing in it.

"I don't see any place where I might bestow a favor," she answered.

The crowd near enough to hear laughed out loud and a few ribald suggestions were called out.

"Then give me just one kiss to sustain me for the hour at hand."

A moment's hesitation flitted across her face, and Daniel wondered whether his public gamble would be a losing bet.

Then she raised her hand as regally as a queen and presented it to Daniel.

He took and held it briefly, then kissed the back of it and the crowd cheered once more.

He might have left it at that, but his heart cried out at the unfairness of it all and he swooped in for the kiss she had denied him the day before.

In her surprise, Abigail's lips were parted and did not resist the entry of his tongue. He kissed her thoroughly and with as much passion that a few seconds allowed. He felt her answering passion just as he broke away.

The roar of the crowd could be the roar of blood rushing in his ears. Daniel couldn't tell, but to his great satisfaction Abigail's lips were swollen and her face flushed red, although her expression was unreadable.

That was the woman he would remember for the rest of his days.

CHAPTER NINETEEN

The taste of him lingered on her lips long after Daniel entered the ring. Abigail tried to remind herself it was theatre, a moment of playacting with which to whet the appetite of the crowd and increase the bets. After all, it was for a good cause. A public kiss to help protect England's security, what was that? She had done a whole lot more for a whole lot less.

And yet...

Abigail was nudged on her arm. She opened her eyes without having recalled closing them.

"Are you all right, dear? You do look rather pale," said Jane with concern. "You must be exhausted. Come take a seat."

Abigail sat on the cushioned seat beside her. Her friend patted her arm and looked about. "Perhaps it was foolish to come here after all. Thomas didn't want *me* to come, but I told him if you went then it was *de rigueur*.

"Did you want to leave? I can ask...well, someone, to bring the gig around."

The crowd stood to its feet and roared. Abigail rose with them and peered around those who blocked her view. Daniel had just fended a swinging blow from Dauncey. Sweat poured from both men despite the rapidly cooling autumn afternoon.

"No. I can't."

"Well, suit yourself, dear, you *are* the reason why most everyone is here. It's too late for second thoughts. If it's of any comfort, Thomas says these things don't go on for very long, especially among the amateurs.

Although I do recall him telling me that after Daniel left Cambridge there was a rumor he spent a little time as a touring professional…"

"For God's sake, Jane, shut up!"

Jane halted suddenly and slapped a hand across her mouth. She looked about, but everyone was too engrossed by the pugilists on stage to take notice of her.

At Abigail's thunderous expression, she shrugged. "I know, I shouldn't have said anything. You know me, I just say whatever pops into my head, that's what Thomas always says."

Too late for second thoughts, too late for regrets, too late for Daniel if Jane's indiscreet chatter reached the wrong ears. Dammit, Abigail cursed silently, must everything she touched be cause for regret in one form or other?

She swallowed sourly and forced herself to watch the fight. It wasn't the first match she had seen. Once, she had been squired to a boxing tournament at Covent Garden with a young lieutenant who had taken her fancy.

She watched Daniel move, fascinated. Unlike the match she had seen where it was all raw strength and power, he moved with the agility of a dancer. Strikes were just glancing blows as he floated at the extent of Dauncey's reach before leaning in to place a stinging jab, then away to avoid a clinch.

Dauncey was becoming angry and he threw an aggressive pot shot at Daniel's middle. It connected, and Abigail felt sickened.

Daniel appeared unfazed however. In retaliation, he responded with another jab, a short sharp strike at his opponent's face, and when Dauncey stepped back to avoid the blow, Daniel stepped forward with a right cross that connected strongly.

Sensing blood, the crowd roared and were rewarded with a glancing left hook follow-up by Daniel and another solid right cross. Dauncey would not be fooled a second time. He intercepted another follow-up jab with his right hand and added an inside left hook. They fell into a momentary clinch and tension filled the arena.

The pair stood toe to toe, arms locked around each other and trading insults with the same ferocity they had just traded blows. George and his wrestling opponent from earlier in the afternoon stepped forward and pulled the fighters apart. On being released, Daniel and Dauncey crashed together again with clashing right jabs.

On a viewing stand about twenty feet away, a woman fainted. Other women nearby, apparently unused to such displays of masculine violence, swooned in sympathetic response.

Abigail found herself staring at Daniel's right hand. Knuckles clenched tight were bloodied.

"How long can they keep this up for?" Jane asked softly.

Abigail asked herself the same question. "It's supposed be ten rounds of three minutes each, I can't remember what round we're in," she replied.

"Fret not, dear ladies."

Abigail did not fail to identify Sir Percy Blakeney at first glance this time. He stepped forward, his gold watch in hand, and considered the dial carefully. "It is the fourth round and, if my time piece is accurate—and I shall be having words with my jeweler, if it is not—we near its end."

Abigail offered a wan smile and her thanks.

"Lady Jane," he said, "may I leave you here with your companions? I need to have a word with Lady Abigail."

Jane acquiesced with a gracious smile, and Abigail found her arm in Sir Percy's as they walked away from the stands.

Another roar from the crowd erupted, and Abigail stopped and looked back, straining to see through the standing crowd.

"I should go back," she said.

He gave her an avuncular smile and patted her hand indulgently. "I don't think you should."

Abigail turned on him swiftly, nostrils flaring. "Is that a suggestion or an order, Sir Percy?"

His pleasant, almost vapid expression hardened momentarily. Abigail could see the shrewd intelligence behind his eyes, but she refused to be intimidated by it. She disengaged her arm from his and folded hers across her chest.

With his hands now free, Sir Percy withdrew a silver engraved snuffbox from his coat pocket and deposited a small amount of the tobacco on the back on his hand, surreptitiously watching the crowd, glancing left and right as he sniffed.

"You're still mine until the end of the year, my dear," he said with a quiet menace as he swept his hand with a lace-trimmed kerchief. "You've been an admirable asset, but never forget—I can have you in irons and bound for New South Wales before the day is out. Now," he said, reclaiming her arm once more. "Come with me and trust that our friend Daniel knows what he's doing."

Sir Percy escorted her to one of the outer ring of caravans. Inside the largest of these was like a drawing room in miniature. Fitted oak cupboards and drawers were trimmed and decorated to look like furniture, sprigged red and yellow floral wallpaper was bright and cheery while, in the center of the longest wall, sat a cast iron wood burning stove to diminish the chill. Three-quarters of the way down the caravan's length, a heavy maroon velvet curtain screened what Abigail presumed was the sleeping quarters.

She spotted a place to sit—one of two low-backed club chairs in olive green leather—and found it surprisingly comfortable. Sir Percy sat in the adjacent chair and pulled a sheet of paper from an inside coat pocket.

With great deliberation, he unfolded the paper. "I want you to take a look at these names and see if there are any you recognize."

Abigail took the sheet and scanned it. There were a dozen names written neatly as though an accountant were keeping a ledger. She weighed each name carefully. She saw a name Daniel had mentioned, Alexis Roux, and passed it by. Midway through the list, Abigail spotted another.

"I recognize one name," she told him as she handed the paper back. "Sir Henry Witheren was a friend of my cousin, Viscount Canalissy—Geoffrey Dobell."

"How well does he know you?"

"Well enough," Abigail gave a delicate little shrug. "As you know, in our circles everyone knows everyone else."

"Or at least they *think* they do," Sir Percy offered with a wry grin.

"The truth of the matter is I haven't seen Henry in over a decade," Abigail continued. "He's spent most of his time abroad."

"Do you know where?"

She answered with a shake of her head, and Sir Percy exhaled and settled back into his chair, looking thoughtful. Abigail closed her eyes for a moment and reopened them. It would seem even after all this time there was no escaping the Canalissy curse.

Dear cousin Geoffrey, now dead, lay most likely in an unmarked grave in France, unmourned in a foreign country. There were times over the past year and a half, in the darkest nights when sleep would not claim her, that she considered whether the blame for Geoffrey's death lay with her. She knew full well the antipathy her cousin had for James. Just a whispered word here and a flattering of his ego there; it hadn't taken much to direct his jealousy toward the young woman to whom James had formed an attachment.

It had all seemed so simple in her mind. Geoffrey would sweep Selina Rosewall off her feet, and Abigail would reclaim James's affection. She'd had only an inkling that her cousin's desire for the girl had become a dangerous obsession when she'd happened upon Selina running for her life with Geoffrey in pursuit at the Boconnoc House masquerade. Abigail had saved the girl's life that night, although she doubted Selina would recognize the fact.

By the time Abigail learned Geoffrey had gone to France in pursuit of James and his bride it was too late.

Abigail watched the small fire flicker behind the slotted grate of the cast iron stove and considered the names on the list. In her minds' eye, she read them over again. Most appeared to be English names, but others were more obviously French, and she wondered what connected these men.

When she looked back at Sir Percy, his head was tilted back as though he were dozing, although she suspected this was far from the case.

"Can I ask how you came by these names?"

Percy lowered his head slightly to regard her for a moment. "No," he replied.

Thanks to the late unlamented Geoffrey, Witheren's name on that list meant she was involved whether Blakeney liked it or not. But hadn't she proven her discretion and value to this man yet?

Abigail tried hard to swallow her irritation, but it seemed her struggle had not gone unnoticed.

"Calm yourself, my dear. It's nothing personal. Perhaps after—"

The caravan door opened and a dark-skinned, well-dressed lady bustled through, then halted at seeing she was not alone when she was clearly expecting to be.

Sir Percy rose to his feet.

"Forgive the intrusion, my dear, I needed somewhere private to talk with Lady Abigail," he said. "Permit me to introduce you. Esther, may I present Lady Abigail; Lady Abigail, it's my pleasure to introduce you to Mrs. George Clarke."

The woman stood almost half a head shorter than Abigail, but seemed to fill the space with her presence. She swept her hand to indicate Abigail should sit and she took the chair vacated by Sir Percy.

"Call me Bossy, everyone does," she said, before gracing Blakeney with a look which could be regarded as saucy. "Except for him."

"Everyone calls me bossy too, but not always to my face," Abigail quipped, then waited for the other woman's reaction.

Bossy seemed to approve of the jest and perhaps was about to laugh when her expression suddenly changed from amusement to one of revelation. "You! You're the one our Daniel is mooning over!"

Abigail straightened in her seat. "I beg your pardon?"

For the second time, an important discussion was interrupted by someone at the door. There was a sharp rap and, almost immediately, without waiting for a response, a mustached man, broadly shouldered and muscled, opened the door and poked his head in.

He glanced about a moment, appearing surprised at the number of people inside, then spoke. "Bossy, George asked me to get you. The match is over."

Abigail rose to her feet instantly, as did Bossy. The latter crossed to a cupboard, unlocked the door, and pulled out a medicine chest which she unlocked in turn with a key that hung around her neck.

"Get Andy to boil up some water," she called out.

The big wrestler nodded sharply and was beginning to turn away when Abigail called out, "Wait!"

The man stopped, looking at her quizzically.

"Daniel Ridgeway, is he hurt?" She corrected, a bit too quickly, "I mean, who won?"

Behind her, Abigail could hear the clink of glasses followed by the familiar aroma of crushed cloves.

"As if there be any doubt, miss," said the wrestler, a satisfied grin splitting his face. "Experience tells. It may have looked an even match for those who don't know, but experience tells, even if Dapper Dan has been out of the ring for nearly seven year. Even those on the losing side of the wagers' ledger recount the bout as an enjoyable one."

Night fell on the green, and with a roar of approval from the crowd, the effigy of Guy Fawkes was hoisted onto his funeral pyre. Very quickly, the bonfire caught alight as torches were applied to the lower regions. Large tongues of orange and yellow flame tasted the offering and devoured it, forcing revelers back from the heat.

Abigail remained well away from the crowd and the flames. She stood at the edge of the dim half-light from half a dozen lamps that lit her marquee. She wanted solitude and found it.

She had rushed from the caravan to see Daniel hoisted on the shoulders of two of George's burly wrestlers and carried through the crowd.

Dauncey too had his fair share of admirers who were content to commiserate with him. She watched him, a whiskey bottle in hand, being escorted away in the company of a dozen men and a number of hangers on.

A message had arrived later saying the Irishman would pay his respects in the morning, after which he was leaving for London. That meant Daniel would be too. And of him she had had no word.

He was hardly the type to be "mooning," she considered, let alone over her, despite what the Jamaican woman said.

Abigail looked across to the ring of caravans that marked the Jamaica George's compound. Perhaps she should talk to Bossy again and find out what she meant by her remark. Not that it would matter. Abigail had heard the truth as good as from Daniel's lips himself; he was still in love with another—married state notwithstanding. She wondered about her too. Was Rachel another coquette? Perhaps she was a sweet girl, completely unaware of her own charms, like the one James had wed?

"A penny for your thoughts."

Abigail looked up. Daniel stood silhouetted in the lamplight.

"I thought you had gone," she confessed.

"The day after tomorrow," he replied. "Percy has allowed me a day of rest. I think he believes that I'll scare the horses in my current state."

He dropped into a chair beside her and his injuries became obvious—a cut above the left brow, a dark swelling over one cheekbone, grazes by his nose and cheeks, and a split and swollen lip. His hands were bound in fresh white linen bandages that smelled of liniment.

How many times had Bossy done that for him? Had Rachel?

"Does it hurt?"

Daniel shrugged stiffly. "Not now."

Silence that had sat comfortably between them on previous evenings, tonight pressed down like a weight. What could they possibly talk about that wouldn't bring up unpleasant reminders of the past or plans for futures that would pull them ever further apart?

"Abigail..." Her name on his lips seemed filled with longing and loss. "I'll never forget you."

Pinpricks of moisture beaded behind closed eyelids. Then she felt the warmth of his bandage-covered hand in hers, familiar and strange at the same time.

"Nor I you," she replied.

END OF PART I

PART TWO

TO FRANCE

CHAPTER TWENTY

"What do you mean, you don't know where he is?" Jane nudged her horse to keep up with Abigail. "First Dauncey and now Ridgeway?"

Abigail refused to answer, or even acknowledge the question.

She had hoped going for a ride would put her in a better mood. All morning she had been signing contract after contract. The remains of the Canalissy's unencumbered estate, the release of her savings, the payment of three thousand pounds in gold—each one increased her wealth substantially; each one made her feel more miserable and alone.

Abigail nodded to a set of acquaintances in the park and urged her horse into a trot to put some distance between her and Jane with her troublesome questions.

Sadly, the woman would not be put off.

"I have it!" she gasped, catching up. "You have *another* lover!"

"Oh, stop being a perfect ninny!" snapped Abigail, heaping scorn. "What do you think I am? Some kind of satyress with a new lover every week?"

Perhaps she should count to ten? Abigail tried the trick and found it mildly diverting. At least she could talk to Jane afterwards without losing her temper.

"But you two seemed so well suited," Jane complained. "Now you say it's been more than a month without a word from him? Would you like Thomas to write to Daniel's brother?"

"No, I would not!"

Abigail wouldn't tell Jane she had already written to Sir Percy, politely seeking an address for Daniel or, failing that, if he would be so kind as to forward on her best regards.

For someone who was once so assiduous about writing, *Aunt Druscilla* was being rather elusive, so Abigail told her oft-rehearsed story, hoping she would be the one convinced by it.

"Not that is any of your business," she went on, "but it is hardly worth continuing an affair with someone only to break it off when I leave for Naples in the New Year."

"Oh." Jane's expression was downcast. "I didn't think of that...but still, imagine the legacy of leaving a lot of heartbroken swains in your wake."

Enough was enough! Abigail pulled her horse to a stop.

"Don't you have something better to do?"

Jane looked perplexed. "Do?"

Abigail let out a frustrated scream and slapped the reins twice. Her horse responded immediately with a canter. Abigail was a much better horsewoman than her friend and outpaced her easily, ignoring the fading cries to slow down.

Soon, Abigail was out of the park and its well-kept gardens and into the meadows beyond. She allowed the mare its head and it galloped freely, approaching a low stone wall at speed. The horse cleared it beautifully and continued to gallop without missing a stride. The exhilaration of it was wonderful. Abigail laughed for the first time in weeks. Gales of laughter convulsed through her before ending in hiccoughing sobs.

She recalled Daniel's words. "*I want our parting to be without regret.*"

She reined in her horse to a walk just outside the field where the Bonfire Night revelry had taken place. A large scorched circle dominated the field. In one corner, a cluster of men had largely dismantled the tent. Jamaica George's traveling fighters were moving on and, in a few weeks time, snow would cover the field, completely obliterating all evidence of their presence.

Abigail urged her horse on. She skirted the edges, trying to keep out of the way of the men lugging heavy ropes and pegs. She couldn't see Bossy, so she looked across the sea of faces for George. She caught his eye, and he marched over with a frown of disapproval.

"Can I help you, miss?" he asked from some distance off. "I trust you haven't come to accuse my men of causing trouble."

Before Abigail could answer, another voice called out, "You becoming blind as a bat, George!" Bossy appeared from behind one of the wagons. "This be Dapper Dan's lady friend."

"Ah, so it is," he said as he drew closer. "Forgive me, but we were never introduced. I shall leave you with Bossy if that's suitable, miss. We promised the landowner we'd be away by the end of the day."

George moved off, but not before yelling at two of his young men who, it would seem, were not pulling their weight.

"Don't worry about him," said Bossy. "Moving day is always a bad day."

"I'm the one who should be sorry," Abigail began, dismounting as she spoke. "I arrive unannounced and…"

Bossy took her by the elbow. "You come with me—let the men do some work for once; we'll sit down and have a cup of tea."

Soon thereafter, they were seated in Bossy's caravan with the woman serving tea in dainty china cups. The genteel surroundings inside seemed out of place with the banging and the occasional yells from the activity outside.

"You want to know about Daniel," prompted Bossy after a few moments of silence.

"He's gone."

"And he's left something behind?" she asked, pointedly looking at Abigail's stomach.

The action caused an unexpected pang of regret.

Abigail squeezed her eyes shut and then opened them. "Quite the contrary," she eventually answered, keeping her voice as matter-of-fact as possible. "Apart from Sir Percy, who is also gone, you're the only person who knows him from…before."

"Well, I don't know where he's gone."

"It's not that," said Abigail. "I need to know who Daniel *is*."

"Why?"

The question took her by surprise.

"What business it is of yours to ask why?" she demanded. "You're part of Sir Percy Blakeney's circle. You know what he is and what we've done."

Bossy put down her teacup forcefully and folded her arms, which stood out darkly against the light-covered traveling dress she wore.

"I've known that young man since before he were a man," she said firmly. "He was nearly destroyed two times over, and I won't let his heart be broken again. You tell me why I should tell you anything 'bout him? I asked Percy about *you,* and I know your big plans to run away across the sea. Daniel is a good man and he deserves a good woman who loves him. Are you that woman?"

Abigail looked down at the teacup in her hands.

She thought about her assiduously laid plans. Ahead lay Naples and the warm Mediterranean Sea. She could book her passage tomorrow and leave the baggage of her past behind.

Abigail took a deep breath and looked back up to Bossy with a surge of passion that would brook no second guessing.

"That's what I need to find out."

Abigail watched the older woman closely. She seemed to come to a decision about something, glancing away deep in thought and then looking back. With a single nod she indicated that Abigail should continue.

"Why is Daniel estranged from his family and why did he drop out of Cambridge?"

"You'll have to ask him those questions." Bossy shrugged, taking up her cup again. "He never talked about his past. We have many men through here over the years who don't want to talk about the past. And we don't talk to them about it either.

"But I'll tell you what I *do* know. One night, one of the men caught Daniel trying to steal food from us. He was hungry, you see. George took pity on him and took him in. We knew he was a gentleman because of the way he talked. That's why we gave him the name Dapper Dan, but we didn't know who he was until Sir Percy told us."

Abigail nodded. Sir Percy seemed to have a habit of keeping an eye on aristocratic strays. It wouldn't surprise her if Daniel's father had sent him to find his son.

"Did you know his friend Jonathan?"

Bossy shook her head.

"What do you know about a young woman by the name of Rachel?"

"Ah," said Bossy, with a knowing glint in her eye, "now we're getting to the real question. After eight years with us Daniel left to work for Sir Percy. I saw him about a year later with a lovely young lady. Her name was Rachel. He was squiring her around Brighton one summer. He introduced us. They looked so much in love, but that was seven years ago."

Abigail wasn't sure whether she wanted to hear this. She swallowed a lump of air and pressed on. "Do you think he still loves her?"

Bossy set down her tea once more and paused. Abigail fought her impatience and remained silent, waiting for the answer.

"I think he *believes* he still loves her because she had his heart once. Then I think he met you and now he's not so sure."

Abigail sat back. It was the answer she had been hoping for, that Daniel had more of a regard for her than merely a colleague thrown together by the machinations of the Prime Minister's spy master.

Still, the answer gave her no peace.

Bossy again remained silent, and when Abigail returned her attention to her, she found herself being subject to the Jamaican woman's silent, but thorough observation. At last, she spoke. "I know what it is like to have shackles on my feet. I was a maroon slave in

Jamaica. I ran away to find George. But I was caught and my master, he put the iron shackles, the *l'empêtre*, around my ankles for six months as punishment.

"For the first month it was hard. I could walk, but not easy. But you get used to these things. Sometimes I could go for hours and forget, then you stumble and it is harder to get back up or you try to run, and you are slow."

Abigail nodded, remembering how she'd only just escaped her own pair.

"George, he found me and spirited me away from the plantation. We hid in the mountains for weeks until a ship, The Liberator, arrived in Kingston. He bartered passage with a sailor he knew on the ship. The captain did not like the slave trade and would turn a blind eye to passengers with no papers."

Abigail smiled politely, wondering why this woman would want to share her life story with her. Bossy smiled too and it seemed as if she'd read Abigail's mind as she continued.

"I'm telling you this because you and Daniel have a lot in common with George and me. When George took the shackles off my feet, I thought I would just float away. I was free and we came to England. Thanks to Lord Mansfield, we can never, ever be made slaves again.

"George and I haven't been slaves in twenty years, but you are. So is Daniel. You may not see the shackles on your dainty, stockinged feet, but they are there. You know they are.

"We had to fight for our freedom. But all you have to do is choose to be free."

It was another hour before Abigail left, and by then the camp party was ready to leave for Glastonbury.

"…and also, you mind what the Good Book says," Bossy told her as they stood in the doorway to the caravan. "'Stand fast therefore in the liberty wherewith Christ hath made us free. Be not entangled again with the yoke of bondage.'"

Then Bossy gave her a hug so tight it nearly squeezed the air from Abigail's lungs.

"God bless you both," said the woman, wiping a stray tear from each eye. "May He give you every happiness. And don't you be forgetting old George and Bossy."

The grandfather clock had just chimed midnight. Once again, Abigail had retreated to the study and hoped, not first the first time, that Daniel would walk unannounced through the doors.

The only person treading unannounced tonight, however, was the ghost of Rachel Sawyer. Her presence was palpable.

Abigail sipped a glass of sherry and watched the fire, bright and lively, consume the small log in the grate.

Bossy had given her such a vivid picture of Rachel that Abigail felt she would know her on sight. She would be the very model of the perfect English woman—creamy white skin with a tint of color to her cheeks, doe brown eyes, and soft nut brown hair. The type of woman who would make a good wife and never give her husband a moment's grief.

What a fine pair she and Daniel would have made.

Abigail imagined Daniel as he may have been seven years younger. The lines around his eyes that appeared when he smiled would be less pronounced. The furrow between his brows would have been completely absent, along with his scars. Not the visible ones that crisscrossed his knuckles, all ghostly white, but the others carved deeply into his soul.

As Bossy told it, it seemed Daniel regretted his past as much as Abigail regretted hers. Surely it must be possible to remove the weighted shackles of the past.

It was a choice to do so, Bossy said.

Abigail made a choice.

CHAPTER TWENTY-ONE

*E*very bosom burns with indignation in this kingdom, against the ferocious savages of Paris, insomuch that the very name of Frenchman is become odious. A Republic founded on the blood of an innocent victim must have but a short duration… LOUIS XVI of France was murdered for the same crime for which Agis, the Macedonian, was put to death by his ignorant rebel subjects; in fine, for wishing to revive the reign of Liberty and Justice, among People, incapable of knowing the intrinsic value of either.

—*The Times, London, 25 January 1793*

The mood of London changed as the news spread. King Louis XVI of France was dead, executed by his own people. Now there were riots in the streets and more people dead. Suddenly, the small strip of water separating the two countries seemed so insignificant, and the threat of war so real.

The first of the winter snow fell during the last week of January, turning the streets of the city into a cold, wet slurry, and the populace with a bitter mood to match.

And buried in the newssheets under an avalanche of thunderous denunciations of the French Revolutionary Government was a small story, just a few column inches, missed by all but the most avid readers: *Irish Poet Arrested in London after Foiled Bomb Plot*. Even those readers would miss the connection to the story on a series of raids on certain taverns along the docks. Abigail smiled. That treasonous Molly H.

Abigail's coach pulled up a block away from her destination and could go no further. A collision between a fruiterer's cart and a wagon carrying furniture had blocked both sides of Marlborough Street. She rapped the ceiling of the carriage and opened the door. Frigid air swirled through the coach, and Abigail hunched under her fur-lined cloak, alighting unaided. Despite the heavy gray clouds, all swollen and expectant with the promise of more snow, a weak midday sun fought the battle to keep the day dry.

She fingered a half Crown warmed by her fingers and handed it to the coachman.

"I'll walk from here," she told the driver above the yells of impatient and irritated road users whose way had been impeded by the accident. Odd, none appeared willing to go the aid of the two unfortunate drivers who yelled at one another and threatened to come to blows.

"Suit yourself," the hired coachman grumbled from behind the scarf wrapped around the lower half of his face. "Not my business if ye get ye death of chill."

Abigail returned her hands to her fur muff and took a few tentative steps along the street, saying a silent prayer that her boots were up to the task. She cut across the street and made her way against the flow of traffic past King Street toward White's on King James Street.

After several minutes of determined walking, she arrived at the gentlemen's club. The footman who opened the door stared at her, blinking several times as if he had never before seen a woman.

Inside these hallowed halls, Abigail supposed he hadn't. That made her all the more determined to hold her ground.

Any comment the footman was of a mind to make was quashed by the butler who appeared behind him and, after taking in Abigail's appearance, apparently decided she was mistress to one of the members and stepped forward.

"I'm afraid you've arrived at the wrong destination, madam," he said politely, but purposefully steering her away from the windows. "The modiste is at number fifty-eight."

From her carved ivory case, Abigail handed him a calling card, her title featured in copper plate script on the expensive heavy paper stock.

"I was informed by Sir Phillip Glynde's secretary that he would be here," she said as the butler peered uncertainly at the card. "Be a good man and give him my card and tell him—"

"Lady Abigail?"

Abigail looked over the butler's shoulder to see Phillip emerging from the hall. He left his two companions and hurried toward her.

"What are you doing here?"

The butler raised an eyebrow.

"How silly of you, Phillip!" Abigail called out, side-stepping the butler and extending her hand, forcing Phillip to accept it. "I told aunty only last night you were bound to forget our appointment today. You do remember? You were going to help me with that little real estate matter."

Sir Phillip's brow puckered in a severe frown, and the butler was alerted to something amiss between the honorable member and the young woman who claimed familiarity.

Abigail ignored the servant, looking unflinchingly at Glynde for a moment, then beamed him a generous smile, one she employed frequently to get her own way. It didn't fail this time.

With a slight, put-upon sigh, he turned to his friends and promised to catch up, then asked the butler to fetch his hat and gloves.

"Come on, then, Lady Abigail," he grumbled as he turned back to her. "Since I promised aunty to look out for you, we had better go somewhere to talk."

Phillip hustled her down the street and picked a quiet coffee house with a table toward the back of the room, positioning himself to observe any comings and goings.

"You couldn't have come at the worse time…" he muttered, shaking his head, more to himself than his companion.

Abigail leaned forward. "Why?"

"Oh no, you don't," he said with dark humor. "The less you know the better, for all our sakes."

They sat silently as a discreet waiter brought coffee for two. Even after the man left, Abigail remained silently watching Phillip.

Eventually it was too much for him.

"I must be mad," he said with a rueful shake of his head. "If Percy knew I was talking to you he'd have my guts for garters."

She could feel the tension emanating from Phillip. He was on edge and his head was slightly bowed. If she was to get her way, she would have to box clever.

"Well, I certainly won't tell him if you won't," Abigail said huskily, placing a hand on top of Phillip's, giving it a gentle squeeze. "You can rely on me to be the very soul of discretion."

He looked up, resigned. "So tell me, what the hell *are* you doing here? If you're going to sweat me for information about Daniel, then stop right there. I won't tell you."

"I've read the papers, I know about the arrest," she said softly before looking at him directly. "I want to pay my regards to Mrs. Rachel Sawyer, but I don't know how to contact her."

At the name, Phillip stiffened. "You know Jonathan?" he asked in an incredulous whisper.

"Indirectly," she shrugged. "But I've learned I have much in common with his wife and, moreover, that his long absence has been strenuous for her. I would like to do her a good turn."

She could see him waver, rocking back slightly in his chair, weighing her words carefully. He then came to a decision, but judging by the line of his mouth, it was not an easy one.

"I have a thousand misgivings, largely because I don't believe you're telling me the complete truth," he began. "It's true that Rachel has found life difficult, and if any woman can understand it would be you. Swear to me that if I give you her address, you will say absolutely nothing about our business? She knows nothing of it. Not a thing. She believes Jonathan and Daniel to be trade attachés. Rachel is a lovely woman, but she's not strong like you."

"I swear, Phillip. I promise—not a word. Upon my life."

He looked at her long and hard as though the answers he sought could be read on her face. Abigail kept her expression earnest.

Phillip extracted a pencil from the spine of his silver card case and wrote an address in Soho on one of his calling cards.

* * *

The next day dawned, cold but clear. "Bracing," as Stanstead enthusiastically described it as he opened the front door.

In the privacy of the carriage, Abigail glanced at the address written on Phillip's card and back up to the genteel, but down-at-heel townhouse just off Soho Square. The once fashionable part of town had suffered from a benign neglect over three generations. She had already instructed the driver to circle the square, using the time to pluck up her courage.

Abigail disembarked and told the driver to wait. She dropped the brass knocker with three hard raps and waited beneath the porch.

Over the street traffic, she could hear snatches of a Scottish brogue booming.

"Be not deceived; God is not mocked: for whatsoever a man soweth, that shall he also reap. For he that soweth to his flesh shall of the flesh reap corruption; but he that soweth to the Spirit shall of the Spirit reap life everlasting. And let us not be weary in well doing: for in due season we shall reap, if we faint not."

Abigail turned to look at the big man, dressed head to toe in black, standing on a wooden crate in the Square with a Bible in his hand. He had attracted a crowd of about a dozen. A couple of people listened intently; others chatted in twos and threes. Beyond the gathered audience, others merely spared the man a glance as they hurried by.

She had seen more and more of these unconventional preachers who eschewed the pulpit for the street in the three years since the rumble of Revolution was heard in France.

The notorious White's House was in view across the corner of the square. Abigail reflected on the irony of difference between *this* White's and the gentleman's club of the same name she had visited the day before. A pair of well-to-do young men emerged from the brothel in high spirits from having their every vice indulged even at this early hour. They drunkenly mocked the Scot who studiously ignored them before the hecklers were distracted by better attractions, leering and cat calling to the young maids who scurried about their errands with their eyes fixed to the ground.

Behind her, the door opened at last, and Abigail turned to a rotund housekeeper who eyed her head to foot. "Can I help ye, my Lady?"

Abigail handed the woman her card. "My name is Lady Abigail Houghall and I hope to have an audience with your mistress."

The woman hesitated, forcing Abigail to improvise. "We have a mutual friend, Mr. Daniel Ridgeway."

The name seemed to unlock a door of another kind. The housekeeper nodded and bid Abigail go through to a small, but neat and tidy drawing room. The furnishings were old but well kept. There was no obvious display of wealth, no paintings on display, and no liquor on the sideboard offering hospitality. The only thing out of place was a small well-thumbed red leather-bound book which sat on a diminutive upholstered chair by the window. What there was of the winter's sunlight streamed through the panes.

Abigail was drawn to the book. She picked it up and read the spine; it was a volume of Shakespeare's sonnets. She opened the cover and read the inscription.

My dearest Rachel,

"My bounty is as boundless as the sea,
My love as deep; the more I give to thee,
The more I have, for both are infinite."

Yours always,
Daniel

Abigail's heart plummeted like a stone. There it was. Evidence in Daniel's own hand.

"May I help you?" a soft voice inquired.

Abigail turned quickly, discreetly dropping the book back on the chair. She looked at the woman in front of her and was conscious of being over-dressed.

Her own fur-trimmed cloak in deep emerald green was of the latest style and exuded wealth. By contrast, the woman in front of her wore a modest woolen dress that might once have been blue, but had faded to a mid-gray. A black knitted shawl rested neatly across her shoulders.

"I'm sorry," the woman said, a little uncertainly. "My housekeeper said you were a friend of Daniel's?"

"My name is Lady Abigail Houghall—"

"Oh, forgive me my manners! May I offer you tea?"

Abigail assented, and Rachel turned to the housekeeper hovering by the door.

"Tea for two, Mrs. Padget." She turned back to Abigail. "I'm afraid I wasn't expecting visitors. I can offer bread and jam?"

"No. Thank you," Abigail said quickly. "Just tea would be fine."

After the door was closed, Rachel spoke more candidly. "You're a friend of Daniel's? I'm sorry, but he's never spoken of you, although I have to say it has been quite a few months since I've seen him. Is he well?"

Abigail felt ill. Rachel was as lovely and as sweet as she had feared and exactly as she imagined, right down to the large soft brown eyes she knew would turn just about every man into a gallant. She had sincerely hoped Rachel was a sophisticate. She would feel so many fewer qualms in pumping her for information. Regrettably, Mrs. Sawyer appeared to be a very nice woman; worse, she reminded her so much of James Mitchell's wife.

Rachel tipped her head at an angle in mute inquiry, and Abigail remembered she hadn't given the woman anything but her name. "I haven't known Daniel very long, only since August, but I understand you and your husband have been friends with him for quite some time."

"Yes," Rachel offered cautiously. "Our friendship extends over ten years."

An awkward silence descended over the room, fortunately broken some moments later when Mrs. Padget returned with the tea. As the door swung open, two young children, a boy and a younger girl, bounded into the room with the enthusiasm of young puppies.

They spoke to their mother over one another in a jumble of words until the boy—aged about five, Abigail guessed—said, "We heard the door! Did Uncle Dan come back with the presents he promised?"

Three faces turned to Abigail. Two were written with disappointment and one with a small expression of watchful pride.

"My husband and I have been wed for seven years. We have two children." Her words were weighted, even provocative.

Abigail was prepared to rise to the challenge. "I'm sure they are a great comfort to you."

Rachel stood and nodded to Mrs. Padget who shooed the children in front of her, then watched her leave the room, keeping her attention on the door until it closed. She turned back to her guest with a vigilant expression, ignoring the tray of tea on the side table.

"I'm afraid I'm entertaining you under false pretences, Lady Abigail."

Abigail felt the prickles of awareness run up her spine and she stood also. "Oh? How so?"

"You see, I know who you *really* are."

"Pray tell," Abigail asked. "Who am I?"

Rachel strolled across to the chair by the window and picked up the discarded book from the chair. "Daniel has never mentioned you by name, but I could tell there was someone when he was last here. That was nearly two months ago, and I wondered who it was," she said, stroking the spine of the book tenderly as she moved again to the fireplace and placed the book on the mantle. "But now we have met, I find you are more typical than I dared hope. The scandalous Lady Abigail Houghall, a woman who uses her…*advantages* to enrich herself and who thinks nothing of discarding those who have ceased to be of use to her.

"Daniel's head may have been momentarily turned by a woman like you, but you will never hold a man like him. Men have their needs, of course, but you're nothing more than a bit o'muslin no matter how well born you are."

She was jealous! The revelation took the sting out of the insults, allowing Abigail to smile knowingly. "I shouldn't play the high and mighty if I were you, *Mrs.* Sawyer. Does your husband know you still retain a *fondness* for a former beau, one who is his closest friend?"

Through the first floor window, she looked down into Soho Square at the street preacher.

"I'm prepared to own my sins," continued Abigail. "You cannot even acknowledge yours."

She turned back and took satisfaction in seeing the woman shift uncomfortably on her feet.

"True, my motives have not been completely unselfish, Mrs. Sawyer, but I came prepared today to do you a good turn. I imagine your husband's long absence has been hard."

"No harder than any woman whose husband is frequently away on business," Rachel said with spirit. "My children and I will do well enough without your charity…or pity."

"I offer you neither, only the hope we might eventually be friends—for Daniel's sake."

Abigail picked up her cloak and slipped it about her shoulders.

"I bid you farewell, Mrs. Sawyer. When I next see Daniel I will offer him your *warmest* regards."

* * *

"Sir Percy Blakeney awaits you in the drawing room, my Lady," said Stanstead in low, urgent tones.

"Does he know where I was?" Abigail asked *sotto voce*, turning to allow her butler to remove her cloak.

"I cannot say, though I did tell him you were at the modiste's this morning."

Abigail nodded and watched as a young footman brought in parcels. "At least I can corroborate that story."

In a louder voice, one designed to carry across the hall, Abigail spoke again. "Thank you, Stanstead, have my purchases brought straight upstairs for Kathleen to put away."

"Very good, my Lady," he answered in a volume to match her own and walked ahead of her to open the drawing room door.

"My dear Percy!" she exclaimed, making her way to the unlocked tantalus atop the side table. "I do hope I haven't kept you waiting too long. A drink?"

Percy, looking something like an exotic bird, shook his head. He wore a yellow striped frockcoat beneath which a frothy white neckerchief spilled over a vivid turquoise blue waistcoat. Abigail poured herself a small glass of sherry, just enough to ward off the chill from outside.

"I had no idea you'd be calling. What brings you to see me in the middle of a busy Parliamentary session?"

The drink gave her something to do with her hands and, with each warming sip, also provided cover for her expression. Flushed. Guilty. She waited for Percy to call her out on her clandestine activities.

"I'm little surprised to see you still here in London, my dear. When last we met you seemed dreadfully anxious to get to Naples," he said before shuddering theatrically. "It certainly would be a damned sight warmer."

"I made the decision to stay when I heard the news of Louis's arrest last month," Abigail said truthfully. "Then to learn that he had been executed without due process of law…"

"Believe me when I say that his demise won't be the last," Sir Percy responded, then nodded at the decanter. "Perhaps I will join you in that drink, after all."

Abigail obliged. "Does this mean this call is not a social one?" she said, passing his glass.

"Ah ha! You adjudge correctly. It would appear circumstances have conspired against me, and I need your particular talents for another enterprise."

"Will it be as profitable as the last?" she asked.

"Zounds woman! Your last invoice just about broke the Exchequer!" he exclaimed. "No, this escapade is one you will just have to do for love."

Pleasure at the thought of possibly seeing Daniel again surged through her, although his name remained unspoken. She marshaled her self-discipline.

With a twinkle in his eye, Sir Percy continued, "By that I mean a love for England and for liberty."

CHAPTER TWENTY-TWO

"**A** doubtful friend is worse than a certain enemy. Let a man be one thing or the other, and we then know how to meet him." The words of Aesop came half-remembered from a schoolboy copybook exercise, but they suited Daniel now.

He took a glass of champagne from a passing footman and, from his vantage point at entrance to the ballroom, he could discreetly watch each new arrival as they were announced. Vigilance had always been the watchword for those in Sir Percy's employ. London had always been awash with spies.

Daniel nodded to one he recognized. Sir Andrew Ffoulkes escorted Margeurite St Just, Sir Percy's wife, through to the dance floor.

Phillip Glynde too strolled by, talking with a pretty young woman and completely ignoring their acquaintance.

He smiled briefly into his champagne. Turnabout was fair play.

Just a couple of weeks ago he'd had to walk past Glynde without a glimmer of acknowledgement. It had been the final night before the promised "fireworks." All the key players had been there, including Dauncey himself. A lamp moved by the window was the signal for the raid.

Their occupation came with certain risks, and these he accepted, but to learn this week the entire League was imperiled by a traitor was a betrayal that cut deep.

Their excursions into France had been running like clockwork for three years, but now trusted contacts had disappeared. Worse, two of their number had only just escaped France with their lives after a tavern raid carried out by soldiers looking for the "Scarlet Pimpernel." What had begun as code to provide subterfuge for certain clandestine activities had taken on a life of its own. These days there were few victories in service of the Crown not attributed to the mysterious Pimpernel.

"There is a new envoy from France, Citizen Armand Chauvelin, who has been none-too-subtle about asking after the identity of the Scarlet Pimpernel," Sir Percy had informed them earlier this week.

"Egad, I plan to have a good time leading this man in a merry dance. The dour old fish is of the opinion the Pimpernel is but one man."

The men had laughed and one called out, "No wonder they can never find him!"

Sir Percy continued his theatrics, holding one hand, then the other across his brow. "They seek him here! They seek him there!"

As though a candle had been extinguished, Sir Percy's dandyish performance ended. "That all your lives are in danger should come as no great surprise. The only men to be trusted are the ones in this room," he said.

To Daniel's dismay, it amounted to no more than twenty—worse still, Jonathan Sawyer wasn't counted among them.

Sir Percy continued, "Under the napkins by your drinks, each of you will find an envelope with an assignment. Read it, learn it, destroy it."

Daniel's assignment was to attend tonight's ball at the home of Sir Henry Witheren. There he would be contacted with further instructions.

He crossed the floor to the bottom of the stairs, stopping once as he did so to renew acquaintance with some old family friends. His story of starting a new enterprise abroad was sufficient to satisfy their curiosity. Their interest in him was merely perfunctory and polite.

From his new position, Daniel could see Sir Percy entertaining a group of ladies with his latest doggerel and came close enough to hear the final lines:

…Or is he in hell?
That damned elusive Pimpernel!

The women giggled and gave enthusiastic applause. Sir Percy glanced up and peered across at Daniel through his quizzing glass. Daniel offered a roll of the eyes, and the expression was met with a grin by the fop.

"Lady Abigail Houghall."

Daniel started at the name called by the major-domo. He turned to watch Abigail descend the stairs.

She wore a gown of midnight blue, a dangerously low décolleté revealing the tops of her soft creamy breasts. Around her neck was a glittering diamond choker. Her platinum blonde hair was upswept to reveal drop earrings with pear-shaped sapphires perfectly matching the shade of blue in the gown.

She was bewitching.

Daniel shot a look back to Sir Percy. Did *he* know she was going to be here tonight?

Dammit, the man was still grinning.

Abigail was only four steps from the bottom and appeared to have not seen him. He was tempted to step back and let her pass him by. Then the scent of her perfume, rose and jasmine, reached him. Memories of Bath had fuelled his dreams of her over these past three months and desire hit him full force. As Abigail descended down the last riser, he stepped forward and swept her hand in his.

He watched hungrily as her eyes widened in surprise and her lips parted. Daniel pressed his lips to her gloved wrist urgently.

"Dear Mister Ridgeway," she said huskily. "I was hoping we might be reacquainted this evening."

"I should ask what the hell you're doing here," he hissed as loudly as he dared, "but I suspect I know the answer to that already."

Abigail raised her head and with it her eyebrow.

"Abigail, what the hell has Percy got you into now?"

"Shhh," she cautioned as she glanced about. "Let me do the rounds of the ballroom, then claim a dance with me in half an hour."

With a final squeeze of his hand in hers, she let him go and walked toward the ballroom as though she were once again one of Princess Charlotte's ladies in waiting. His heart swelled with an undeserved pride as he watched heads turn to look at her.

It also made him sick.

Daniel turned back to Sir Percy, intent on demanding answers, only to find him caught in an animated conversation with that Frenchman *Citoyen* Chauvelin.

He huffed and thought of the assignment Percy had pressed upon him earlier—keep a watchful eye on Sir Henry Witheren who had recently returned from several years abroad in France and Austria. If possible, discreetly scout for locations where secrets of interest might dwell. Well, there was nothing stopping him doing that while also keeping an eye on Abigail Houghall.

He wandered to the ballroom entrance and watched the dancers. Abigail was easy to pick out in the crowd, beautiful and graceful, so very at home among the Beau Monde.

But Eamon Dauncey had been wrong about how Daniel, at least, saw her.

He knew full well she was no goddess, no celestial being. Abigail was a woman, a remarkable, beautiful, infuriatingly strong-willed woman, as fallible as he. Daniel saw her faults, but he also saw her strengths.

Daniel flexed a stiff right hand a couple of times. In the ensuing melee on the night of the arrest, getting a few "accidental" hits on Dauncey was a particular pleasure.

He mentally shook himself. It was time to get to work. Daniel decided to make himself familiar with the house. From the hallway, down a corridor, was a smoking room set with cards. It had already attracted a good number of men who would rather dice than dance. Down another corridor was a drawing room for the ladies.

The home was a rabbit warren, an ill-considered jumble of rooms where one might be lost for hours. Perhaps there was a study on one of the upper floors, but there was very little chance of doing a systematic search for it without attracting attention. He tried, but several turnings led to dead ends and he decided to head back to the ballroom after some of the household servants started to eye him suspiciously. He was on his way back down one hallway when a door caught his eye. A surreptitious jiggle of the handle told him it was locked, but it might hold some promise.

He re-entered the ballroom just as the musicians had finished playing a reel. Daniel watched the dancers leave the floor and didn't see Abigail among them. He stepped forward and, glancing about, spotted her in apparently genial conversation with a group of young men to the side.

Making his way over, he held his hand out to her. "I believe this dance is mine," he said for the benefit of the young men who lingered, hopeful of securing the upcoming waltz.

Abigail placed her hand in Daniel's and, smiling apologetically to those whose hopes were now dashed, allowed him to lead her to the floor.

"Your timing was superb," she said under her breath. "I didn't think it possible to die of boredom."

"Only you could make dying of boredom look so entertaining," he teased.

"Flatterer." She smiled as they took their places. Daniel slid his arm around her waist, took her right hand in his, and breathed in the warm scent of her.

"It's wasn't all for naught," she conceded. "I did learn that Henry has a map room on the ground floor in addition to his study on the first."

"Shhh."

Abigail frowned at him.

"Dance first."

He felt her relax as the first notes sounded. They moved about the room, skirting the edges of the crowd. His eyes never left hers, their gray-green shade hypnotizing him as she watched him with equal intent.

She felt good in his arms and he savored every moment of it. Leaving her in Bath was difficult, but manageable. The dull ache that sat on the edge of his consciousness disappeared during the day when he needed his wits about him. But at night when his body was exhausted, the tight rein he kept on his mind was loosened and it was then he thought of her. He ached to touch, and her absence sat hollow in his chest.

He returned his focus to the reality of the woman in his arms. Her eyes were closed momentarily as she allowed him to guide her, and her lips once again were slightly parted. He wanted to taste them. Now. The strength of the need shocked him and became a near physical ache. It was a bodily discomfort not helped in the least by the sight of her bosom displayed in front of him.

He had heard of opiate addicts who went back to their drug again and again even while knowing it was killing them. Now he was beginning to understand the appeal.

Just this one moment, he bargained with himself, and then he would let her go. Part of his mind mocked him. It was already too late.

When the dance ended, they were both breathless. At least Abigail had the excuse of her pale skin to excuse the blush that colored her face. Daniel wondered if all of her skin flushed so becomingly and he squashed the thought ruthlessly. He needed air now, and she needed to tell him what she'd learned.

He escorted her upstairs to where a wide balcony overlooked the dance floor. Standing shoulder to shoulder, his arm around her waist, they might have been mistaken for lovers. It had worked for them in Bath, he thought bitterly.

"A new career as a decorator?" he asked. Abigail frowned, obviously not comprehending the remark. He began again. "So tell me why Percy has you determining the use of our esteemed host's rooms?"

"It seems Henry has something Percy wants, and I'm the only person he knows who is familiar with the house. Henry's been away for years, and I had to determine whether he's renovated."

"Has he?"

Abigail shook her head.

"So what is it we're looking for?"

"We?" Abigail was her imperious best with a raise of an arched eyebrow.

"You don't imagine I'm going to let you run through this house on your own, do you?"

Abigail tried to push him away, but his arm around her waist tightened, keeping her close to him. She also blushed when she was angry. He filed that observation away for future reference too.

"Together or not at all, Abigail," he told her in a tone of voice that would brook no argument.

He watched as she considered his demands. The anger and annoyance shading her expression turned thoughtful and, with a single slow blink of her eyes, Daniel knew he had won. He fought another sudden urge to kiss her.

"You said the study is on this floor?"

"Mmm, far end of the hall, last door on the right."

* * *

Abigail followed Daniel's lead. They maintained an animated conversation as they promenaded up and down the passage, closer and closer to the study. At first Daniel acknowledged those they encountered—guests and servants alike—either with a nod of the head or a greeting.

He made no attempt to hide their presence and, on the third journey, the servants who passed paid them no mind as they went about their duties. They reached the study door once more.

"Drop your fan," he instructed, and she did so, positioning herself between Daniel and the passageway. Daniel stooped to pick up the fan and peered quickly through the keyhole before rising.

They strolled back and forth twice more until they reached the study door once again.

"Keep watch," he whispered urgently, and Abigail did, while pretending to make a study of the portraits lining the walls.

Long seconds ticked by, and Abigail resisted the urge to ask what was taking so long. After a single frustrated huff from Daniel, the crisp click of the bolt returning home seemed unnaturally loud to her heightened senses.

"Clear," she whispered as Daniel rose to his full height.

Out of the corner of her eye, she saw him glance about. Together they slipped into the dimly-lit study.

A banked fire burned low in the grate behind a four-fold brass fire guard. Daniel crossed to it and took a spill of paper from the jar on the mantle to carry a flame across to an oil lamp on the desk. Daniel lit it, and the room was bathed in heavy shadows.

Abigail turned on the spot, getting her bearings, then held her breath as she heard approaching voices outside. She exhaled in relief as they passed.

A mahogany breakfront bookcase nearly eleven foot long dominated one end of the room. Abigail examined it. Books, journals, ledgers, and assorted papers were protected behind the glass, along with various curios of brass and porcelain miniatures and finely painted plates from China.

Four brass escutcheons, one for each set of doors, glowed in the low lamplight.

"The desk is locked," Daniel whispered.

"So is the book case," she replied, pulling out a hairpin. The book case locks were rudimentary and in an easy movement she opened the first.

"Should I ask where you learned how to pick locks?" Daniel asked as he busied himself with examining the desk.

Abigail flashed him a grin. "It's a trick every schoolgirl knows. How else are we to read a rival's diary?"

Daniel gave her an answering grin of his own and went back to examining the locked desk drawers.

The smell of leather-bound volumes was a testament to the fact that the bookcase seemed very rarely opened. Quickly and methodically,

Abigail examined the printed volumes and leafed through them. They revealed nothing but Sir Henry Witheren's taste in literature.

Behind her, she could hear Daniel had successfully unlocked the desk and was leafing through papers.

There were upper shelves of the bookcase to examine. A chair placed in front was, in fact, metamorphic library stairs. Abigail unhinged the panel and mounted the revealed steps.

She reached up to the archived ledgers from the house, some so old that the stitching binding the pages had rotted and the books were falling apart.

Without an expression of discovery from Daniel at the desk, Abigail was beginning to wonder if their search was a futile one. Where would one hide such a thing? If not locked desk drawers and secret compartments, then it must be hidden in plain view.

Abigail looked again at the old ledgers. It should be hiding in the place where no person would have an interest in searching, and displayed so baldly those interested would leave it overlooked. There! A long envelope fell into her hands from between the pages of one of the rotting ledgers. It was marked "Accounts" and dated "1792." The year seemed suspiciously out of place among documents that were at least a half-century older.

"Daniel?" she said in a low voice. "I think I have something."

Abigail stepped down from the library steps and drew closer to the lamp to open the envelope. Daniel stood at her shoulder as she unfolded the first loose paper. Densely written text in French dominated the first half of the page. She would need more time and better light to translate it. What was more alarming was a list of names filling the second half of the paper, the names of at least thirty people. And a dozen had been crossed out in red ink and a date written next to them, all within the past six months.

Among the remaining names was one that stood out to her.

Jonathan Sawyer.

CHAPTER TWENTY-THREE

Abigail wasn't aware her hand was shaking until Daniel took the sheet and envelope from her. Without examining the rest of the contents, he reinserted the single page and slipped the envelope into an inside jacket pocket.

"Let's go," he whispered urgently.

They hastily erased any sign of being there. The bookcase and study were locked once more, the oil lamp extinguished. Daniel held Abigail's hand tightly in his left while opening the door slightly with his right. The way was clear.

With a tug, he pulled her out into the well-lit passage and closed the door behind him. She stood to shield him from view as he hastily relocked the door, then, with a firm hand at her waist, he urged her along the passageway until they had reached the top of the stairs again.

Abigail opened her fan and wafted it beside her face, willing her pulse to steady as they descended step by step.

"Find Sir Henry. Keep an eye on him and whoever he speaks to," Daniel told her as they reached the bottom on the stairs. He took up her hand in a courtly gesture and kissed it. "I'm going to give the envelope to Percy and, if time permits, search the map room."

Abigail nodded briefly and, with a quick squeeze of her hand, Daniel was gone, absorbed into the crowd of partygoers. A moment later, the crowd cleared a little, and Abigail observed the new French envoy standing at the entrance to the ballroom.

He was tall and lean, his thin face unremarkable except for dark eyes, almost black like the clothes he wore. To Abigail he seemed like a crow in an aviary of smaller, more exotic birds.

Apparently, the avian analogy had also occurred to Armand Chauvelin too.

"Ah, the blue bird of happiness I have been longing to meet all evening! Enchante, mademoiselle," he said as he approached.

"Your flattery does you credit, sir," she said. "I was just thinking myself how few could wear black so effectively as you do."

"And I was wondering why such a charming young lady had been so long absent from the dance floor," responded Chauvelin.

With pounding fists, panic clamored for release inside Abigail's rib cage. Their absence had been noticed! May as well as be hung for a sheep as a lamb, she thought, and, with more bravado than she felt, leaned forward conspiratorially.

"May I confess something to you?"

Chauvelin frowned, long black brows furrowed as Abigail placed a hand on his arm.

"You see, my friend is married and his wife is the old-fashioned type. Unfortunately for her, he would rather me to have and to hold instead of her. You won't tell anyone, will you?"

A twisted smile crossed his face and in it Abigail read equal amounts of cynical amusement and contempt.

"That's a very bold confession of a very bourgeois sin," he said. "Perhaps you would find France more to your liking. The state has divorced marriage from the church and given divorce as a right to the people."

"For any reason?"

"Any reason or none—does it make a difference?" Chauvelin shrugged, then turned away, clearly wishing to end their conversation.

Abigail felt her smile falter for the moment. She thought of all the married men who had flirted with her and given expensive gifts in expectation of purchasing a mistress and reminded herself that her jaded experience was not the only one. She thought of Thomas and Jane, George and Bossy, even James and Selina—in them there was hope, at least, that some marriages lived up the ideal.

Abigail attracted the attention of a footman and, with a fresh glass of champagne in hand, re-entered the ballroom and espied the host of the evening. Witheren was in animated conversation with a young woman in a gown of daffodil yellow—a difficult color to wear well—but Margeurite, Lady Blakeney did so admirably.

She thought of Daniel furtively making his way through the halls and a half-formed prayer went up for his safety.

Abigail wondered whether Daniel had found Sir Percy, whose absence from the ballroom she noted. Did Lady Blakeney take part in her husband's clandestine activities? She was French and perhaps her loyalties lay with the dispossessed aristocrats, and yet…she was French. Her loyalties may lie with the revolutionaries. Either way, the two surely possessed a more inspiring partnership than most.

She watched the woman, who was about her own age and said to be a legend on the French stage, accept an invitation to dance. Margeurite St Just, to refer to her by her stage name, was indeed striking. Her beauty, dark brunette hair, and vivid blue eyes had portrait painters Joshua Reynolds and George Romney, already great rivals, desiring her as their muse.

When the set ended, her companion escorted her from the dance floor. With a flash of a smile, the woman curtsied to her partner and sat. Abigail decided to take advantage of the vacant seat beside her.

"Good evening, Lady Blakeney, is this seat taken?"

The woman smiled politely and indicated Abigail should sit.

"I do not believe we have been introduced, but I think I do know you," she began in softly accented English. "Lady Abigail Houghall, I presume?"

Abigail acknowledged it with a nod. "Delighted to make your acquaintance at last, I've met your husband on a number of social occasions."

There, that was a nice, safe, non-committal opening gambit that was all the more plausible because it was, mostly, the truth.

"You have?" she said with surprise. "Then I pity you. What a dull time of it you must have had."

Abigail's eyes widened in surprise; she fumbled with her fan in an attempt to mask the bewilderment she was sure showed plainly on her face. Dull would be the very last word she would use to describe Sir Percy—arrogant, supercilious, manipulative—but dull he certainly was not!

Abigail's reaction was closely observed. "Eh," Margeurite shrugged. "Perhaps it is you English I don't understand."

As though he had been conjured up, Sir Percy appeared before them and offered them an elaborate bow. Dressed in a vivid red striped frock coat embellished with row upon row of little five-petaled flowers embroidered in gold thread, the fabric was flamboyant enough to be found on any woman's gown.

"Sink me, if I haven't been dazzled by the two finest creatures the good Lord has put upon the Earth," he said, observing them both through his elaborately fashioned silver quizzer. "The dressmakers of London deserve the praise of every man here tonight. Goddesses descended from the heights to bestow the favor of a smile or a kind word to us mere mortals."

Abigail laughed appreciatively at the hyperbole. Margeurite simply rolled her eyes and greeted her husband coolly.

"Can't you rise above trivialities for once?"

"Can't rise above anything more than three syllables, my dear—never could." Percy shrugged. He glanced at the musicians returning to their instruments and addressed his wife. "I see the orchestra is ready to perform. Would you make me the most envied man by dancing with me?"

"Oh Percy, you exhaust me even when I'm sitting still. Perhaps Lady Abigail will oblige you."

A flash of disappointment crossed his face before his expression rebounded to the familiar bon vivant. "If you'd do me the honor, Lady Abigail, it might go some small degree to mend my wounded heart," he said, offering his hand to her instead.

Abigail accepted it and rose to her feet. "I trust the wound is not too deep, Sir Percy. I'd be delighted to perform this small service for Lady Blakeney."

The dance was an allemande, giving them time to talk.

"Oh Percy, she doesn't know?" Abigail asked as she turned under his arm. Her tone, rather than her words, belied her true question.

"The art of love can be more dangerous than the art of espionage, my dear," he said, smiling broadly as he turned out and bobbed. "I'm sure I'm not telling you anything you don't already know."

Abigail was not fooled by the expression he displayed in public. He was hurt and Percy was a good man deserving of a wife who loved him as dearly as he loved her. Success in marriage would seem to be as arbitrary as the turn of a lucky card, Abigail reflected.

It was clear he would not be drawn any further on the state of his marriage, so she changed subjects as they circled one another once more. "Did you see Daniel? The names…"

"I have his message," he answered abruptly. "And that's all you need to know."

Abigail swallowed her disappointment, but allowed it to show on her face. As the steps brought them back together again, Percy looked at her countenance and sighed.

"'Od's fish, I seem to be out of luck with all the ladies tonight!"

As the dance came to an end, a man approached Sir Percy, tapping him on the shoulder and asking him discreetly to follow. Abigail watched him join a group of men to one side of the floor. The group, including Sir Henry Witheren, were mostly titled, but Citizen Chauvelin was also among them.

The other guests seemed oblivious to this tightly organized tete-a-tete. The musicians played on for another dance.

The meeting was out of the ordinary. Perhaps Henry had discovered the documents missing. Champagne soured on her stomach.

She looked about the room for Daniel. He was nowhere to be seen. She edged her way to the back as Sir Henry approached the orchestra leader. Citizen Chauvelin, escorted by two Englishmen, brushed past her hurriedly and called for a footman to bring his carriage to the door.

The liveried musician raised his baton and the trumpets blared to call the room to attention, then he stepped aside for Sir Henry Witheren to take his place on the dais. Abigail glanced around once again—still no sign of Daniel!—before giving her full attention to the front.

"News has reached London," said Sir Henry, "and the Prime Minister's office has now confirmed, that the Republic of France has declared war on England."

Murmurs of surprise filled the ballroom. Witheren glanced down at a sheet of paper he held in his hand.

"According to the special envoy to France, who this evening also confirmed the news, the declaration is as follows: *In the name of the French nation, that the French Republic is at war with the King of England and the Stadtholder of the United Provinces.*

* * *

Daniel picked his moment carefully. He watched Sir Percy's wife leave with another group soon after the announcement was made. And although he made no especial effort to hide, he nonetheless remained in the shadows. He pulled out a cigar and lit it on a nearby taper.

As soon as he heard the footman call for Sir Percy's carriage, he stepped forward into the carriage and waited for Blakeney to join him.

"Send me to France, Percy," he said as soon as the carriage jolted into motion.

"I'm not going to do that," Blakeney replied.

"You can't just leave Jonathan there!"

"He signed on knowing the same risks as you."

"He has a wife and children!"

"And you seem inordinately fond of them," Sir Percy snapped back. "You saw the list you gave me tonight. A dozen good men and women dead because of the Jacobins. I'm not prepared to risk more. Not until we know what we're up against."

"It could be too late!"

"You took an oath when you joined the League, Ridgeway. One to command, all to obey. Bear that in mind."

Daniel leaned forward and rested his arms on his knees and exhaled long and sharp. He felt Percy slap him on the back.

"Just wait a week until we know the lay of the land. I haven't studied the documents you gave me, and Parliament hasn't even prepared a response to the National Committee's declaration of war."

"A week is a long time, Percy," Daniel warned.

"So is eternity, dear chap. Don't lose your head. As you well know, those Frenchies have a devilish way of parting you from it."

Daniel suppressed a shudder. He had seen Madame Guillotine's handiwork for himself—efficient, impersonal, deadly. The head tumbling like an overripe melon into a basket to the fanatical cheers of the crowd.

"Besides, you have more to consider than just yourself," Sir Percy added silkily.

Daniel looked at him warily.

"You seem very close to the Lady Abigail Houghall; you work well together. I suspect she would be somewhat heartbroken should you disappear."

Sir Percy's observation caught him off guard. On seeing his hesitancy, Sir Percy examined the back of his immaculate kid gloves, wearing a smug expression Daniel would only be too happy to help him lose.

"That was a low blow, even for you," he growled.

"Needs must, old boy." Sir Percy shrugged. "This is only the beginning, and I'd rather have you working for us than against us."

The ride was silent, save for the sound of the carriage making its way through the rain-soaked streets of London. Daniel had endless respect for Sir Percy, but his conscience bothered him.

"Let me out here," he asked softly.

"Are you sure? It's a long walk to anywhere."

Daniel gave a single emphatic nod. "I need time to clear my thoughts."

Understanding and acceptance crossed Sir Percy's face as he rapped sharply on the carriage roof. The conveyance rolled to a stop beside Kensington Gardens.

Daniel stood on the pavement as the carriage pulled away and turned up the collar of his coat against the cold. He strode along the deserted streets and thought about Sir Percy's words.

Yes, he was "inordinately fond" of Rachel. His mission to find Jonathan was to reunite him with his wife and finally drive temptation away. At least, that's what he told himself, and thus what he chose to believe. He loved her once and, for a long time, even recently, thought perhaps he still did. The way she looked at him when he called on her, the longing that filled those warm brown eyes, and her hints of loneliness. To explore a past that might have turned out differently had another choice been made all those years ago…

It played on his heart like the memory of a much beloved tune, a sentimental and wistful ache. It would be so easy to accept the invitation she now made. Jonathan would never know. Yet to do so would be the ruin of them all.

And then there was Abigail. Vivacious, beautiful, and with an intellect and a mind of her own. He was conscious of how his body reacted to hers—even more potent when he felt her body respond to his.

Yet there was more than simple physical attraction. If it had been just that he could have ignored it, or found relief elsewhere. But by God, she was a fascinating woman, a priceless treasure for the right man to explore and value. It's a pity, he considered, so many men were imbeciles who couldn't see beyond her beauty to appreciate the worth of the woman beneath.

The thought of their escapade tonight warmed him, and he grinned in spite of himself. How many women did he know who would throw themselves so fully into breaking into rooms and prizing secrets from locked cabinets?

One. There was only one.

The early morning air, cold and wet, filled his nostrils, and he breathed in large lungfuls of it. He stopped at the edge of Mayfair, where Park Lane met Oxford Street. He could turn here and arrive at Abigail's townhouse in just a few minutes—he'd learned that information before leaving tonight—or he could walk less than a mile and be at Rachel's home.

Both women would welcome him.

Daniel made his decision.

Chapter Twenty-Four

The pounding on Abigail's bedroom door grew insistent. She opened her eyes reluctantly. Kathleen, with hair unbound and dressed in her nightshift, opened the door. She partly drew open the heavy drapes. It was barely dawn outside, and soft gray light seeped into the room.

"My lady, Sir Percy Blakeney is downstairs. He insists he see you immediately," the girl said as she lit the bedroom lamps.

Less than three hours sleep by her estimation and she suspected Sir Percy had had even less. Abigail arose.

"I will dress myself," she told Kathleen. "Go and make sure Stanstead offers our guest full hospitality."

A few minutes later, Abigail entered the study dressed in a riding habit, her long blonde hair tied in a simple chignon. "Daniel, is he…?"

A half-drunk cup of sweetened tea sat beside Sir Percy on the side table. He stood as she entered the room. He was immaculately, but casually, dressed, and faint stubble on his cheeks hinted at the haste in which he'd prepared.

He gave a bitter smile. "I was hoping he would be here with you."

Abigail swallowed her disquiet. "I haven't seen him since last night when he went to find you and search the map room."

He sighed wearily. "Daniel came to see me after the ball. He wanted my backing to go into France to find Jonathan Sawyer. I refused."

Abigail's consternation expressed itself as anger. "Why? Jonathan is a friend, he has a wife and young children!"

"He may be a traitor!"

217

The harsh words were a splash of cold water. Abigail inhaled sharply and steadied herself on the back of a chair.

"Then, sir, you'd better sit and tell me all of it."

"Not here." He shook his head and picked up his hat. "In my carriage outside, we have a call to make."

"At this hour of morning? To whom? To where?"

He took a hold of her elbow and drew her from the room.

"To the only other place I can think of where Daniel might be."

* * *

If it were possible, Soho was louder in the early morning than it was when all of its denizens were fully awake. Abigail accepted Sir Percy's hand to alight from the carriage and stand in front of the Sawyer residence. Street hawkers called out their wares, kitchen maids and cooks haggled over prices of fish and other produce. Carts two and three abreast tried to navigate the street, their drivers swearing vociferously and gesticulating rudely.

Over the top of them, the same big, rough-looking Scottish evangelist could be heard.

...Hear, O Israel, ye approach this day unto battle against your enemies: let not your hearts faint, fear not, and do not tremble, neither be ye terrified because of them; For the Lord, your God is he that goeth with you, to fight for you against your enemies, to save you.

There was a war coming—of that she was certain. Abigail wondered what the preacher knew that she didn't.

She turned back to watch Percy lower the door knocker for a third, loud time and the door opened. This would be the start of her own battle.

"I haven't seen him for two months," Rachel Sawyer insisted, and Abigail's feminine instincts told her the woman spoke the truth. She led them into the parlor, wringing a small monogrammed kerchief in her hands. "Won't you tell me why you arrive at my door at this early hour?"

Abigail turned to Percy faintly alarmed. What could they tell her? On the basis of a couple of sheets of paper discovered last night, her husband, among a handful of others, may be guilty of betraying England and complicit in the deaths of his brother spies?

"I will not tell you falsehoods, madam," he announced imperiously. "We learned overnight the situation in France has deteriorated and we are concerned for your husband's welfare. The Honorable Mr. Ridgeway is the only gentlemen who can find your husband and bring him home safely to you. But at present we can't locate him."

Rachel sat heavily in the seat behind her. A shaking hand covered her mouth and her wide brown eyes registered alarm. "I swear to you, I don't know. I don't."

Abigail crouched beside her and took her free hand, confident the other woman could see the fear in her own eyes. "Please, Mrs. Sawyer, is there anywhere Daniel and your husband favored, any place they talked about?"

She thought a moment with furrowed brow before answering. "It's been many years since we were there, but Jonathan and Daniel would always talk about the summers they spent at Hastings."

Abigail turned back to Sir Percy.

"Let us fly, my dear, we don't have any time to lose."

* * *

It was well after dark when the carriage reached Hastings, and Abigail was bone-weary. Despite the rhythmic roll of the carriage on the hundred mile journey from London, she could not sleep. Her driver, one of Sir Percy's own men by the name of Wheeler, was a taciturn lumpen she accepted under sufferance.

"Strike me! What kind of gentleman would I be if I were let a lady go off without an escort?" he had exclaimed. "Fear not, Wheeler will be on his way back to London once you're safely reunited with Ridgeway."

Abigail fingered the envelope sealed with red wax.

"What if I can't persuade him?" she had asked Percy. "Jonathan is his friend, his name on the list may not mean what you think it means. He maybe a target, not a contact. If he's been captured then…"

"Then the course of action will be Daniel's to decide, but I *need* know of his decision. Lives have already been lost. We can only help so many with the resources we have at our disposal and we can't afford to lose good men and women to traitors.

"Urgent business takes me back to Paris myself, but I will not be able to contact him. That would be too dangerous for the both of us. Tell him he has one month to uncover the truth, otherwise Jonathan Sawyer will be presumed dead. Or worse. There is a new moon three days hence. He has until the next new moon to return to Calais with or without Sawyer."

Abigail had listened to the instructions and committed them to memory.

A carriage, small and anonymous, rolled to the front of Percy's home, and Abigail prepared to embark. Before she reached the step, Sir Percy clasped her hand and kissed it.

The expression he gave her was filled with sympathy.

"'The course of true love does not run smooth,' the Bard advised, and it is something I well know myself." A wistful expression flitted across his face. "I trust your destination will bring you both joy."

Abigail squeezed his hand in return. "I hope I've been an adequate pupil, even though I've not always been a willing one."

Despite the tension, Sir Percy had smiled and kissed her wrist once more. "Dear Abigail, you have been exemplary."

* * *

The Hangman Inn lived up to its name. It was a cadaverous structure, windblown and bleached from the roaring gales and savage storms howling in from The Channel. Its shingle, a crudely painted figure of a man holding a noose, swung back and forth in the freshening wind.

Wheeler entered the inn first, his wide brimmed hat low over his eyes. Abigail waited in the carriage. Jane wouldn't recognize her now, dressed incognito. She wore no obvious displays of wealth. Her dress was one of her plainest—a sage green cotton. Her shoes were sturdy brown walking boots. She wore a bonnet low on her crown.

She passed anxious minutes waiting and, through a slit in the blind, watched not only the front door, but the sides of the building.

Hastings had only a fraction of the population of London, but a man who was good at hiding would not find disappearing here a challenge. Abigail hoped that habit proved stronger, and Rachel Sawyer's recollection was correct.

The carriage jostled as a gust of Channel wind hit it broadside. It was rapidly followed by needle sharp drops of rain. Abigail sat back in the carriage and wrapped her shawl around herself tightly. A flash of lightning split the air and was immediately followed by a loud peal of thunder.

It shouldn't take this long to determine whether Daniel was there or not, she thought impatiently. If he was not, there would not be enough time to search more than two other places before morning.

She leaned forward, reaching for the handle as lightning brightened the sky once more. Just as the answering crack of thunder filled the air, the carriage door was wrenched open by an external hand.

Abigail jumped and slapped both hands across her mouth to prevent a scream erupting in her throat.

"Get inside!" Daniel's face, wet from the torrential rain, looked as thunderous as the weather raging around him.

"I expected a warmer greeting. I've come a long way to speak with you," she told him.

Daniel reached into the carriage and pulled her by the arm toward the door.

"Don't test me, Abigail. You have no idea what I'm capable of right now. Move!"

With little gentleness, he pulled her to the ground. She followed him in a half stumbling run across the muddy forecourt. Daniel ducked beneath the low lintel, which Abigail herself only just cleared upright.

Despite the unpromising exterior, the inside of the Hangman was warm and cozy. They stood by the fire. His red-gold hair was dark as bloodwood as rain water dripped from strands at his brow. He shook his head and frigid droplets scattered in all directions.

He looked dark and dangerous, and something primal welled up in her. She was sure he had used his scowling glare to intimidating effect on others, but not yet her. But she would not be cowed. Not tonight. The message she carried was too important to him. To England.

"Once you've warmed up, get back on the carriage and get back London," he growled. "I mean it. Get out of here!"

"No."

Daniel reacted as though slapped. He stepped back and drew breath.

"The horses need spelling, there's a storm out, and it's night." Abigail crossed her arms resolutely. "I'm not going anywhere and certainly not before you hear what I have to say."

The tavern keeper approached, his beaming smile the only warm thing in the room apart from the fire. "My pardon, Mr. Smith. I didn't realize y'wife would be joining ye. My good lady is making up a nicer room with a lovely view out over the Harbor and your driver has brought in Mrs. Smith's bags. An' my girl will be bringing up a light supper and a warm posset."

Daniel looked down at the flagstoned floor, and Abigail fancied she could hear him grinding his teeth.

She offered the innkeeper a charming smile. "I do so thank you for your hospitality. I hope your wife hasn't gone to too much trouble. Whatever you have will suit my husband and I. You've been so very kind."

The middle-aged man's ruddy face flushed deeper at the sweetly spoken words. He nodded, then disappeared to see to the arrangements.

To Abigail's surprise, Daniel took a hold of her hand gently and curled his fingers around hers. "Well, come along, *wife*. I suppose I can't begrudge you food and a warm bed for the night, on the understanding you will be on your way back to London by morning."

Abigail held her tongue. It was an olive branch and she accepted it, but if he thought she was going to be dismissed like an errand boy, then he had another thought coming. She schooled her features into what she hoped was an adequate facsimile of wifely submissiveness. A slight curl of Daniel's upper lip suggested she might not have been wholly successful.

They climbed the half dozen well-trod steps to the upper floor—a maze of odd-shaped corridors and rooms, rising and falling on different levels, testament to a hundred years of ad hoc extensions—and followed the lamp light to the end of the hall. The innkeeper's wife and the daughter, aged about fourteen, emerged from the gloom.

"We've left the lamp lit, sir, so youse can be findin' your way. Just come downstairs if there be anything else ye need. We're not terribly busy this time o'year and your driver's comfy enough bunking with the grooms."

The mother nudged her daughter who was openly staring at them, Daniel in particular. Abigail suppressed a smile.

Daniel closed the door behind them. The room was as cozy as the Inn's hearth. A warm fire burned in the grate, and on a small table near the window sat a plate of cheese and a loaf of bread. A posset pot in blue and white sat on a trivet next to the plate along with two earthenware mugs. Behind a concertina screen was an oak cupboard with a mismatched tin glazed pottery ewer and washbowl. A relatively small, but comfortable-looking bed nestled in one corner in front of which sat Abigail's small deerskin-covered trunk.

Daniel poured Abigail a measure of the warm milk drink and handed it to her before reaching into his jacket pocket and pulling out a pewter hip flask. Abigail wasn't sure what was in it, but whatever it was Daniel drank a good measure of it.

She warmed her hands around the cup and waited for Daniel to speak.

"Wheeler tells me Sir Percy has gone back to Paris urgently and entrusted only you with the message," he began. "I should warn you, being a courier for him is hazardous to your health. One of our men was killed last week."

"It's about Jonathan," she said softly. "You may not want to hear this, but Sir Percy fears he may be a traitor."

Abigail waited, expecting an explosive outburst, an angry denunciation in defense of his friend. Instead Daniel quietly walked to the window and lifted the curtain where he watched the rain lash the window.

She licked her lips nervously. "It was in the document we discovered in Henry Witheren's study. There was a list of men whose names were crossed out in red with dates on them—"

"—they were Percy's agents or local supporters," Daniel said, his voice barely louder than a whisper. Abigail stepped nearer to hear. "I saw the names briefly."

Although he stood with his back to her, Abigail nodded and he continued. "There were other names grouped together along with the name of a Frenchman. Alexis Roux. Jonathan's was the only English name in the group." Abigail watched his hand clench at the mention of the name. "It seemed to suggest they are trusted members of the Committee of Public Safety. Those whose names were crossed out in red were also annotated with a date and initials. Many of the initials were J.S."

Abigail stepped forward to lay a gentle hand on Daniel's shoulder. "Sir Percy told me they proximate dates those people were killed."

"It's thin evidence to hang a man on," he answered.

"I know that, and Percy knows that. He's being cautious—he can't even trust his own wife. You must have heard the Marquis de St Cyr and his entire family were executed and Margeurite's name was on the warrant."

Daniel turned back to her, eyeing her thoughtfully. "Sir Percy sent you here instead of one of the other members of the League to talk me out of going to France in the belief I would be more likely to listen to you."

The accusation was made quietly and he shrugged off her hand as she reached to him.

Abigail shook her head.

"On the contrary, Percy wants you in France. You are to track down Alexis Roux and destroy his network before he destroys the League. Furthermore, if you find Jonathan and he proves to be a traitor, then your instructions are clear. You are to kill him."

Chapter Twenty-Five

Abigail waited for him watchfully. Silent moments passed, punctuated by the storm outside. Unlike the storm, Daniel's anger had dissipated.

"Percy must have given instructions," he said at last.

"No more than four weeks in France. Two weeks to get in, two weeks to get back to Calais. We're to rendezvous with Percy's men at a place called Le Chat Gris. He said you knew it."

"No."

Abigail frowned, confused. "You don't know this place?"

Daniel turned back from the window. The curtain dropped, hiding the tempest outside. "I know the place. But that's twice you've used the word 'we.' *You're* not going."

"By God, I am!" she swore.

Daniel shook his head and stepped toward her slowly. "Temper, temper my dear, your neck is far too pretty to be anywhere near a guillotine."

He caressed her with a gentle touch of his firm fingers. Her flash of temper sparked a desire that burned thoroughly. At his touch, her lips parted and eyes closed. She could feel him step closer.

Abigail reached for him and drew him nearer. This kiss was soft and sensuous. Then Daniel's lips brushed her ears. "France has become death itself. I see it in every face there. You are so full of life, Abigail. You invigorate me every time we meet. I just have to taste that, just once."

"Love me, Daniel," she asked, every fiber of her being aching with need. She pressed herself forward, molding herself to his hard-muscled form.

"My darling, don't you know? I already do."

His lips found hers once more and showed Abigail their mastery. His tongue plundered her mouth and hers dueled back. She felt the heat of desire between her legs and pressed against him where his need for her grew and hardened against the soft wool of his breeches. His warm hands touched the bare skin at her back.

Daniel had so skillfully unlaced her gown she hadn't noticed until that moment.

He kissed down the column of her neck and across her now bared shoulders. Her hands gripped the collar of his shirt. Her breasts ached, wanting his touch. Daniel loomed over her. Abigail took a step back to avoid losing her balance. He took advantage and stepped forward again and again until the bed touched the back of her thighs. He pressed forward once more.

She fell back onto the bed, her skirt hiking past her knees to reveal satin garters, the same color as her dress. Daniel helped the skirt rise further, pushing the fabric up to her waist and quickly loosening the drawstring of her pantalettes before his hands skimmed up to her torso outside the dress and he pulled down the neck of her gown, exposing her breasts to the cool air of the room.

Her rosy pink nipples puckered and stood erect, waiting for his touch. Abigail watched him through hooded lids. The blue of his eyes glittered, longing etched on his face as they swept over her. An answering look must have crossed her face because he swooped for another hard, demanding kiss.

Abigail yearned to touch him. She raised her hands to his shoulders and rubbed her hands over the crisp linen of his shirt. The feel of him clothed against her bared skin heightened her arousal and her legs restlessly sought his.

Daniel broke their kiss and rose from the bed. Abigail rested on her elbows and watched him strip off his clothes. She couldn't remember when she had wanted a man as much as she wanted this one.

And he wanted her too. The thought of it thrummed between her legs. She was so ready for him. His golden skin glowed in the firelight that flickered and touched his biceps, a substantial and well-defined boxer's upper body. The front flap of his breeches was open, the waist slipping from his hips.

"Daniel."

The rest of the words fled. Abigail sat up fully, then stood, allowing her own clothing to fall to the floor. They faced each other naked.

There was something in that moment which caused them to pause. Her eyes feasted, moving down his chest, sparse with hair, where thin, faint scars were apparent in some places. She gazed further down to where dark russet hair framed his erection, proud and unashamed.

Did Eve feel this way when she saw Adam for the first time? The same sense of wonder and anticipation? Did she feel a sureness he was made for her as she was made for him?

The past fell away like the clothes discarded on the floor. It was just them and it was new, honest, and right.

Abigail became dimly aware of the roll of thunder outside.

Daniel took her hand and kissed it. "This will be the first time for both of us," he whispered and her desire grew stronger.

"This is just the beginning," she whispered.

* * *

Daniel didn't reply; couldn't. Despite a near-overwhelming craving for the woman before him, he forced himself to go slow. It would be their first. But despite Abigail's optimism, it might be the only.

The new moon would be here the day after tomorrow, and he would sail to France—a nation that had declared war on him and his country. But he meant it when he'd told her she was life to him. With the future so uncertain, he wanted to drink of it deeply.

Abigail's hair, pure white and usually artfully arranged, hung in loose waves down her shoulders. The ends curled, caressing her breasts, full and round. She smiled up at him almost shyly, and his need for her surged. He guided her to the bed, onto the sheets. Abigail reached for him again and he captured her hands in one of his and pinned them above her head.

It lifted her breasts high on her chest, and he tasted them. Abigail groaned, and her legs shifted restlessly. Daniel positioned his own over and between them and felt the heat at her core. He teased her, rubbing his cock through the soft, silky curls between her legs and at her entrance.

Little mewling sounds of delight spurred him to extract louder sounds from her. Daniel released Abigail's hands, then reached down to softly stroke the sheathed swelling at the top of her cleft. The mewling became moans as her body writhed under his. Pure passion stoked his own.

He knew she reached her peak as she called his name and her hands gripped his shoulders, fingernails digging into his flesh. He started to enter and found her more than ready for him. Inch by inch he penetrated, gentle squeezes of her muscles drawing him further in until they were one. He stopped to look at her, cheeks flushed, lips full and wet. He dove in to taste them.

Abigail wrapped her legs over his hips and rocked. He almost lost it then. Daniel closed his eyes, the temptation to plunge in, to find his own release, almost overwhelming. She rocked her hips once more and squeezed. Daniel shot open his eyes to look straight into hers. A satisfied feline smile broke across her face, no doubt knowing she had his full attention. Abigail drew one hand down his arm, then slowly and deliberately touched her breasts, drawing his focus. His fingers trailed where hers led before they broke off to touch her flushed cheeks and those lips...

His self-control was near breaking point, and she knew it too. Minx.

Then she squeezed him once more and he was lost, plunging again and again into a whirlpool of sensation as they moved together. She urged him on with her body and with words which grew more fragmented and breathless as she reached a climax once more, a split second before he came.

"Abigail!"

CHAPTER TWENTY-SIX

The storm ended some time during the night, leaving the sun to rise to drizzling rain. Abigail turned into Daniel's embrace and was awakened with light butterfly kisses on her cheeks, her eyelids, and then her lips which opened to accept and encourage him.

At some point during the night, something had changed. A future, come what may, was to be cherished together, not endured alone. The lovemaking this morning was slow and languid, satisfying not only a physical need, but also a spiritual connection as they learned one another.

"You're not leaving without me," she whispered after a time. Her cheek rested against his which rose and fell in a heavy sigh.

"You have no idea what France is like now," he warned. "There's blood on the streets and more to come. Now she has declared war, anyone caught as spies will be shot, and if anyone were to become aware of your connection with the English Crown, no matter how indirectly, you will be guillotined."

Daniel drew a deep breath. He stroked her cheek gently and whispered, "Your life means more to me than my own."

"As your does to me," she argued. "I love you. I need to be with you, but it's not just that…you told me once you've not been to Paris. I have. I know the city. You need me."

Daniel heaved a sigh once more and was quiet. Abigail remained silent too, waiting for the inevitable objections. Perhaps he spoke them to himself, because he did not say them to her.

After a period of time Abigail wondered if he dozed. Then he spoke. "I imagine Percy has had something to say about this."

Abigail propped herself up on an elbow and tugged the blankets up to cover her breasts. "Indeed, he wrote instructions that explain everything. Every member of the Committee of Public Safety, every soldier is looking for the Scarlet Pimpernel. They are going to be on the lookout for any man traveling alone."

Abigail paused and watched Daniel digest the information. She continued.

"They will less likely suspect a man who is traveling with his wife. There are forged documents for two people—Rene and Suzanne Perret."

Again, Daniel was silent, thoughtful. Abigail waited long moments before he finally spoke.

"One last time, Abigail, are you sure? Being with me means giving up fine gowns and jewels and servants. We'll be most likely sleeping rough, and you will have to get your hands dirty. Furthermore, when it calls for it, you will have to obey me without question or second-guessing. You are going to have to trust me as I do you."

Abigail sat up and raised her chin. Daniel sat up also. His look turned dangerous, blue eyes glittered, and his upper lip curled.

"Do you trust me?"

Without hesitation Abigail answered, "I do."

* * *

The rest of the morning was spent examining the papers Percy had given them. The identity documents and traveling papers were accompanied by a personal note from Percy, a warning to be cautious.

Functionaries were just as likely to lose their heads as aristocrats. The Revolution's competing factions—the Jacobins and Girondists— were fighting among themselves for control of Republican France, and an authority who signed papers today might well be arrested under suspicion tomorrow. It was best to be cautious.

Daniel left soon after breakfast for provisions. While he was gone, he instructed Abigail to sew coins into pocketed strips of bias binding, then pick open the linings in their coats and jackets and hem the strips into them.

Then, when she had finished, to burn every single paper bearing the mark of the League.

By midday, the sky had cleared. To avoid prying eyes and curious ears at The Hangman, Abigail and Daniel walked up to the cliffs and wandered in and around the abandoned ruins of Hastings Castle, high over the historic township.

Daniel felt drawn to the edge of the cliff, leaving Abigail to explore on her own.

Alone but for the calling of the gulls, he stood staring at the horizon where the shores of France lay visible. Here, more than seven hundred years earlier, the Normans had invaded England. Now war threatened her shores once more.

After a time, despite the freshening wind, he could hear the sound of a woman's footfalls approaching. Abigail joined him in silence, somehow knowing he would speak when he was ready.

"Percy sent us to Vendee on news of the uprisings," he said, words ripped from his throat as the wind rose further. Daniel settled an arm around her and urged her back into the shelter of the ruined castle chapel.

"There were spot fires of resistance across the old provinces. We met with those who opposed the revolution and were anxious to see what support England could provide. In the north, Austria had the same intentions—after all, the Queen is one of their own."

Abigail wrapped her shawl around her shoulders and listened. Daniel picked up a pebble while poking through a tuft of grass and rubbed it with his thumb. His attention remained on it while he spoke.

"Anyway, Jonathan and I had been given names to approach. We were coming close to establishing a resistance network from Normandy to Poitou Charente and across to Paris—residents who would welcome anything up to English troops on their soil. For their safety and ours, Jonathan carried half the list. I carried the other.

"A very clever and ambitious officer by the name of Alexis Roux was appointed by Robespierre as representative of the National Assembly to the District of Vienne. To say Jonathan and I were thorns in his side would be no exaggeration. Perhaps we'd become too cocky, I don't know. Anyway, one of our meeting houses was raided. Everyone scattered in all directions. I managed to elude the soldiers for three days. I have no idea how many managed to escape or how many were caught.

"I felt certain Jonathan must have escaped. I waited at a pre-arranged rendezvous at La Rochelle for five days. One night I returned to my room at the inn and found it had been broken into and searched. They didn't bother to be careful. They tore the place apart and probably would have done the same to me if I'd been there."

"I don't know why they weren't waiting for me or how, except by Providence alone, my list, which I had hidden behind a skirting board, remained undiscovered," he continued. "I couldn't wait for Jonathan after that, not if Roux's men were so close. I returned to England and was assigned to Bath.

"One month later, I received a letter from him. He'd managed to escape to Paris. He sent coded details of troop movements between Paris and La Rochelle and up to Calais."

"How did you know the letter was from Jonathan?" Abigail asked. "You might have been tricked if Roux had captured him."

Daniel nodded his acknowledgement. "We have a signal known only to him and me. A private joke really, it looks like an idle scrawl. In the corner of the envelope, he drew a little primrose flower. When I saw that, I knew it was him and I gave the information to Percy. Do you see now why I have to get to Paris at all costs? Percy used the information in good faith and now good men and women have died because of it.

"If Jonathan is a traitor, then so am I."

"No!" cried Abigail. "I don't believe that and neither does Percy. Otherwise why would he send you back?"

"To right a wrong. One way or another."

* * *

The Church of All Saints stood one street back from the shore. Daniel stood outside the fence and gazed up at the square castellated tower before passing through the gate and into the church itself. Inside the sanctuary, quiet and deserted save for their booted footsteps, they walked down the aisle.

Daniel had been quiet all evening, and Abigail sensed a reflective mood in him she was loathe to break, so she remained as silent too as he took a seat on the front row pew. She sat beside him. Daniel looked up at the altar for a moment, then sat with his head bowed. She heard him whispering The Lord's Prayer under his breath.

She was reminded of soldiers and sailors. They sought prayers, absolutions, and benedictions before leaving for war. At that moment, the task seemed overwhelming, and for the first time fear seeped in like cold water through her veins.

Abigail closed her eyes and prayed too.

The evening clouded over once more, making the night of the new moon dark. A wind picked up and sounded eerily up the cliffs. Daniel wheeled a small handcart containing two small trunks, each two feet by three feet, and two leather hold-alls. Abigail would have had three times as much luggage for a weekend trip alone, but she kept the wry observation to herself.

They made their way down to the Jasmine, a single-masted clinker-built boat, just large enough for the two of them and their luggage, designed only for short journeys. Somewhere in the town a clock chimed the eleventh hour. The shore was surprisingly busy. Fishermen heading out to try for a night's catch aided by the new moon paid no heed to two walking toward the small vessel.

Daniel pushed off, unfurled and adjusted the sail, and the little boat was propelled along. He smiled at her and leaned in for a kiss.

"Get some sleep while you can," he said, nodding at the covered void at the bow. "We should arrive on the coast of France in a few hours time."

* * *

Curlews were the first to greet them, protesting their presence on the lonely stretch of beach south of Calais. Soft white dunes studded with spiky tufts of grass made unloading the boat slow going. Daniel lowered the sail and dragged the boat as far up the beach as he could manage.

"Wait here, I'll be gone a while. I want to see to our transportation."

Abigail hunkered down at the bow of the boat, and Daniel kissed her once more before covering her beneath the sail and she heard the sand break under his feet as he walked away.

She closed her eyes and considered how much her life had changed in such a short amount of time. Once it was devoid of purpose, empty despite the things and activities she used to fill it. Now she felt reborn. Born into a life that mattered to Daniel, a life that had proved its worth to Percy. The sacrifice of her old life had introduced her to love.

Desire she had experienced before, but this was different. Daniel's was a life she cared more for than her own. And he felt the same about her. He was not ashamed like some of her lovers who had professed love in clandestine trysts, then ignored her in the light of day. Or others who squired her around only as a trophy, an ornament to enhance their own worth.

Daniel loved her for who she was. How could she not love him in return?

At some point she must have slept, for when she next opened her eyes, dawn had broken with a rosy pink glow. Abigail shifted her position and took in the sky. Large clouds were red, edged with gold from the rising sun over the dunes. Seagulls in packs squawked as they were borne aloft by the breeze, seeming to argue over the best place to dive for fish.

A jangle of bridles attracted her attention. Down the beach on the hard-packed sand left by the receded tide was a man driving an ancient-looking horse and cart. The glare of the morning sun made it impossible to identify the traveler.

Abigail's heart began to pound and she considered her options. If she stayed where she was, he might drive past and be unaware of her presence as long as he did not stop to examine the boat. If she made a dash from her hiding place, she might be spotted and draw unwanted attention.

Where was Daniel?

The horse and cart drew closer, and Abigail drew a hand over her eyes. The man looked up before she could hide herself again, but much of his face was hidden beneath a wide-brimmed hat set low over his eyes. He was dressed in a plain shirt and pantalons, the trousers favored by peasants.

"Bonjour!" he called. "*Comment tu fais ce matin?*"

Abigail laughed and emerged from the cover of the sail as she recognized the voice.

"*Je fais très bien. Est-ce vieux cheval va nous faire à Paris?*" she called.

Daniel alighted and gave the gray horse an affectionate rub on its neck. "Be kind!" he admonished with a laugh. "Pierre de Lune is a fine old horse and he might get upset if you don't speak kindly to him."

Abigail examined the beast while Daniel loaded their possessions into the cart. Pierre de Lune was an odd name for a horse, but it seemed to fit him.

"Forgive me, *Moonstone*," she begged the animal in a stage whisper for Daniel's benefit. "You seem to be a very sturdy chap after all, and I'm sure you will get us to Paris in style."

Chapter Twenty-Seven

Daniel and Abigail—now Rene and his wife Suzanne in accordance with their false documents—traveled two full days without incident, telling those curious enough to ask that they were on their way to Paris to see Suzanne's sister because her husband had offered them both work after they had lost the farm following years of poor harvests.

At the end of their third day, they stopped at an inn and a stranger, a stooped old man, overheard their story, and he muttered his disapproval.

"Paris is not the best place to be, *mes amis*," he warned as he approached them. Abigail stepped closer to Daniel as the man stopped. Gray wispy hair fell across eyes of the same color.

Daniel immediately stepped forward to put himself in front of Abigail. He thrust his hand out.

"Citizen Rene at your service. I'd be indebted to know news of Paris. I've never been there and it's been what…? Ten years?" Daniel turned to Abigail, "since my wife was there. Not since her sister married Bernard."

The old man shook his head. "There are executions daily. They took Place Louis XV and renamed it Place de la Revolution. It is now awash with the blood of priests and aristocrats to appease the new god of the city."

The man looked around furtively as though he had said something indiscreet. He backed away and nodded to the innkeeper.

"Wait," Abigail called. "Won't you stay and tell us more about what is happening in Paris?"

The old man shook his head and turned to the door.

"Oh, don't you be payin' him any mind," a tavern girl told them, giving a contemptuous glare at the old man's retreating back before facing them. "I'm sure he's exaggerating. But it would be fun to see, right?"

At Abigail's puzzled frown, she continued. "I mean, a real execution by the guillotine contraption. A man just has to lie there and wait for the drum roll and then, one, two, three, plop! Off with his head! Quicker than killing a chicken."

Abigail grimaced and the girl shrugged her shoulders dismissively. "Oh, you're one of them sensitive types, them that don't like blood, eh? I wouldn't worry, *cherie,* it is only those worthless aristos."

Daniel steered Abigail away from the girl to sit at a quiet table. Over a warm meal, she spoke softly, still in French. "What do we do? Ask one of the other travelers?"

He shook his head and leaned in closer. "Curiosity will only arouse suspicion," Daniel whispered in her ear in English. "We'll hear more the closer we get to the city. Best be prepared now. When we get upstairs let's go through the Paris map once more. Three more days until we're there and I'd like to be prepared for whatever hell we're expected to face."

Hours later, when Daniel lay down and closed his eyes, the map of Paris seemed imprinted there. They would follow the road from Beauvais and cross the Seine several times before they entered into the city itself. He would see the Place de la Revolution for himself before crossing the Pont Neuf and venturing south to a town at the edge of the city—Bicetre, the location of Jonathan's last communiqué.

Abigail shifted beside him and with his eyes still closed, he reached out to touch her arm, then the curve of her waist clad in a soft cotton shift. She hummed softly. He was a contented man despite their circumstances. Despite his very justified misgivings, Abigail had proved herself an excellent companion. Her French was very good— much better than his—and she was quick-witted too. Partners as well as lovers.

And he did love her.

He hated to admit it, but he had felt the stirring of attraction from the moment he caught her cheating at Faro at the Ashford's. But it wasn't until the night of Templeton and Hamberley's misadventure, when she had proved herself so capable and resourceful, a woman he could rely on, that he realized he was coming to love her.

"Daniel?" Abigail's soft voice broke his thoughts. He rolled on his side and opened his eyes. Soft gray-green ones met his. He allowed his gaze to wander over her face, the fine soft white hair, the shape of her brows that framed those mesmerizing eyes, the over-generous lips that tasted of her.

His scrutiny of her was mirrored in her face and, although tired, stirrings of desire were awakened.

"Why did you leave Cambridge?"

The stirring withered and died, and his body expressed its disappointment.

"Bossy told me…" Abigail began.

"There's plenty Bossy doesn't know," he grumbled.

"Is what happened there the reason why you're estranged from your family?"

Daniel sighed and rolled onto his back, closing his eyes. A moment later Abigail rolled onto hers, apparently believing he wasn't going to give her answers. Under the blankets her hand tentatively reached out for his.

The memory of what happened pressed down like a weight on his chest, making it difficult to breathe. He could try to ignore it and wait for the pain of it to pass as he had always done or he could push back and dislodge it. He had demanded Abigail's honesty and trust; he could offer no less of himself.

After a moment more, Daniel opened his eyes and found his voice.

"I was seventeen, one of the youngest boys taking first class honors. I love mathematics. I had plans to become an engineer, much to my father's horror. That was too much like working with one's hands, despite the fact this coming century is going to be a great age of industry. Everyone can see that.

"Anyway, I'd made friends with a fellow by the name of Reggie Short. He was a special scholarship recipient, another thing my father disapproved of. His family came from a long line of blacksmiths, but his father had become a moderately successful boilermaker who had an interest in Mr. James Watt's inventions. I spent holidays working at his factory just to see boilers being made. One day Watt's engines will pull carriages."

Daniel fell silent a moment before continuing.

"One night Reggie and I had too much to drink at the tavern and on our way home we were set upon by footpads. We ran and they chased us to a stone bridge over the canal. We fooled them by slipping over the coping onto a narrow ledge and hiding there. It was wide enough to crawl on so I managed to get along it and drop onto the towpath.

"Reggie was halfway across when one of the thieves looked over and saw him. He made a grab, and Reggie fell into the water. I saw him surface and scramble for the bank, but the rest of the gang were nearly on me so I ran for my life. I thought Reggie was right behind me.

"He didn't return to our rooms that night and the next day I went looking for him.

"A carpenter found Reggie's body a few days later a mile up the canal. It must have been dragged by a working boat. I was arrested under suspicion for his death, but the coroner ruled it misadventure. He said Reggie mustn't have been able to climb the bank because he was drunk and he drowned.

"As you can imagine there was quite a scandal brewing. My father was as keen as the university to hush up the whole thing and, to be sure, my father made it worth their while. The old man was certain I would follow his career choice for me now and become a lawyer.

"He made me give up my place. I made him give up his youngest son."

A moment, then two, ticked by. Daniel brought himself back to awareness, tethered by Abigail's hand still in his.

"I left and lived hand-to-mouth for a while. Then things got worse with no income and no family support. I was caught stealing food from George and Bossy. I imagine Bossy has given you a full accounting from there."

Abigail squeezed his hand and said nothing. He was glad. His words had been spoken into the silent darkness and, little by little, the weight on his chest disappeared. It was the strangest feeling. Perhaps confession was good for the soul after all. Daniel made one last admission.

"I've told no one this but you."

He rolled onto his side once more and watched the woman beside him. Her eyes shimmered with unshed tears before she blinked them back and faced him. She kissed his hand where it joined with his.

"I love you," she whispered and, again, it felt as though another weight had been lifted.

* * *

As they traveled toward Paris, the traffic increased. Refugees traveled in all directions, some fleeing the cities, others drawn toward it. Some could afford carts, others carried their only worldly possessions on their backs. Every face was careworn.

At noon, Abigail and Daniel stopped at the side of the road, a little distance away from where another family had halted. Daniel built a small fire to cook small strips of mutton. A child about seven circled the edge of their camp, eyeing the sizzling meat with envy. Abigail watched the child for some time. The mother, thin and wearing much-mended clothing, nursed an infant to her breast. Two other children had wandered into the meadow to gather wildflowers.

The woman's husband pulled a small dark loaf from a cloth and laboriously cut five pieces. No other food emerged.

Abigail located the curious child once more, standing by a sapling. She moved to the fire and placed a hand on Daniel's shoulder.

"I know, I've been watching them too," he said, voice low.

"Is there anything we can do?"

"We can share only what we've provisioned for the day. Remember, we're supposed to be poor travelers too. It might be worth seeing what they know of the situation in Paris, but too generous shows of charity will only rouse suspicion."

Abigail nodded her understanding. "I'll approach the mother."

"Be careful."

"Bonjour, citoyenne! Will your family not join us? My husband and I are going to Paris to see my sister. Have you come from there?"

The woman did not reply, simply clutching her baby closer. She looked up at her husband who still had the knife in his hand. He too said nothing. Abigail turned back to the wife who shook her head vigorously.

The smell of cooked meat wafted across and the husband's stomach growled audibly. Clearly embarrassed, he grew angry.

"You're well dressed and look well-fed, why do you go where there is want and starvation? I've heard of the Committee sending spies along these roads looking for citizens not loyal enough to the Republic. You could be one of them."

He advanced with the knife, and Abigail took a step back to find Daniel at her shoulder.

"My wife means no offence, citoyen," he told the man, stepping in front of Abigail. "We've come from Normandy. We are concerned about my wife's widowed sister and her children in Paris."

Abigail marveled how at how quickly their cover story could change from moment-to-moment as they need arose.

"There's still plenty of food to be had up north if you are prepared to deal with English smugglers," said Daniel and he glanced about furtively, as if he feared being overheard. "Not that I would ever suggest anything of the like to loyal citizens of the Republic...it's just what I've heard said."

The man was a simple laborer whose expression was unartful. During Daniel's tale, his face changed from suspicious to calculating. The aimless travelers now had a destination and a reason for going. A level of trust had been established and the man allowed his family to join them.

The child Abigail had first seen approached and accepted a strip of meat before he retreated to sit under the tree to share it with his two sisters.

"There are executions every day," answered the man. His name was Gaston, and he was garrulous now his trust had been won and his belly warmed. "They had them in our arrondissement, but after a week they moved their contraption to another because the ground was too soaked in blood. The stench is so horrible even the horses shy away. Good citizens are expected to go to at least one of their wretched executions. Some treat it like a fete. My wife and I went once. Never again. They execute children because they are aristos… I don't care whose they are, you don't kill children."

Daniel kept a watchful eye on the advancing sun and when he and Abigail took their leave, Gaston's loose tongue had yielded, though he would never know it, a lot of useful information, including the location of some garrisons and the next checkpoint.

They only traveled a few miles more before the sun sank behind the hills. Streaks of gold, pink, and purple clouds added vivid color to a sky changing from blue to gray as the sun lowered. They would arrive at the gates too late. They would have to spend the night outside the town.

Chapter Twenty-Eight

Paris was not as Abigail remembered. It even *smelled* different. There was smoke as well as a strange metallic odor that lingered in the nostrils and settled in the throat. As she and Daniel approached the heart of the city, posing as one of many refugees from the country where a hardscrabble existence could no longer be sustained, she frowned at the observation and wondered what had changed.

They followed a procession of pedestrians across the Pont Neuf and along the riverbank past the front entrance to the Palace of Tuileries. She paused at the iron gates, unable to stop from staring. Six years earlier, as a lady in waiting to Princess Charlotte, she had been feted as a guest of the court of Louis XVI. Now behind its barred gates, Queen Marie-Antoinette, or Widow Capet as she was now called, remained in seclusion.

Calls for a trial grew stronger by the day. The beautiful, vivacious Queen charged with such outrageous libels as having affairs with both men and women, all utterly untrue. The worst of all, they accused her of an incestuous relationship with her own son; her own precious son!

Abigail pressed her fingernails in the palm of one hand in an attempt to calm her outrage. It was lies, all of it, and laughable on its face. But when the mob has decided on its enemy, it will tell any lie, repeat any slander, and further embellish it to justify its hatred.

How did these monsters sleep at night?

Daniel squeezed her hand.

"Say your goodbyes quickly, we shouldn't linger too long," he whispered urgently.

With one quick glance back, she walked with Daniel down the Rue St Honore.

A passerby glanced at her momentarily, and she drew down the plain cotton cap she wore now almost constantly to cover her white-blonde hair. Although natural, it might have her targeted as an aristocrat. Ludicrously, the Paris Commune had banned blond wigs for that very reason.

Daniel wore a red Phrygian cap to blend in with the rest of the sans-coulottes who roamed the streets. He looked the part, but for a moment or two Abigail was convinced anyone could tell who she *really* was just by looking.

She had not wanted to come to the place where Louis was executed, Place Louis XV—or Place de la Revolution she corrected—but Daniel insisted, unwilling to leave her on her own in one of Percy's safe houses on the Rive Gauche.

They had arrived in Paris yesterday and Daniel seemed determined to see all of it on foot. Their safe house was a room let by an elderly widow off one of the quiet side streets several blocks back from the river, close to the *Hospice de la Salpêtrière.*

Only six months ago, mobs rampaged through it, "liberating" prostitutes sheltered there and dragging unfortunate mad women out onto the street and slaying them. The hospital was reputed to be the largest in the world. Thousands of patients and inmates called it home, but now it was a madhouse without as well as within. It too bore scars—hastily erected new parapets, fresh roofing mostly complete, lines of smoke-stained walls where buildings had been torched.

Despite her reservations about this excursion, Abigail felt safer with Daniel than she would have been on her own in Fauborg Saint Marcel. The Rive Droit was a much more familiar part of the city to her, but landmarks had disappeared. The statue of Henry IV that sat overlooking the Pont Neuf for nearly two hundred years was gone. Now at the crowded Place de la Revolution, the statue of Louis XV had been smashed apart and the massive stone plinth on which it stood looked out of scale on the square.

As they moved past it, Abigail's eye was drawn to the superstructure of the guillotine standing fifteen feet high on an eight-foot-tall stage, designed to give the gathering crowds an unimpeded view. A tumbrel rolled across the face of the machine, blackened with the blood of the many who had felt its blade but briefly. Inside the tumbrel were a half a dozen souls, including women, their hands tied to the sides of the cart.

The crowd let out a mighty roar as the first of the victims, a scared-looking young man, aged about twenty, stumbled as he was pushed up the steps. He had his hands tied behind his back. He looked out over the crowd, but said nothing. The young aristocrat's clothes looked fine, but they were not clean, though his light brown hair, tied back with a ribbon, shone in the spring sunshine.

She was too far back to hear the charges being read, but the jeers of the crowd made their verdict plain. Two soldiers propelled the man forward and forced him to lie prone on a board. His head was locked into a stockade and the drumroll started.

Abigail let out an involuntary gasp and looked around for an escape from the crowd that pressed around them. Daniel held her close, standing behind her with both hands holding her arms.

"Make it quick," he muttered, and to Abigail it sounded like a prayer.

The drumroll stopped. Abigail closed her eyes and held her breath. On its downward travel, the metal blade sounded like a high-pitched scream. It stopped with a clang.

The crowd roared its approval in a sound so deafening that Abigail started. She opened her eyes to see the young man's head held aloft by the gathered hair, blood dripping down the arm of the soldier who raised it like an offering.

The dead man's jaw drooped open and seemed to let out a silent scream.

* * *

Despite the revulsion he felt, Daniel struggled to look away from the atrocity on the stage. It was revolting and undeniable. Finally, he shook himself and looked down at Abigail.

She turned to him, her face pale. Her beautiful eyes were wide and her mouth open in shock. For a half second, it was as if it were her head he could see presented to the crowd, and a shudder of dread went through him.

Daniel gathered her to him. "Let's go," he muttered, shouldering through the crowd.

Stupid. Thoughtless, he cursed himself. She should not be here. Not at the Place de la Revolution, not in Paris, hell, not even in France. He should have tied her to a chair back at the inn at Hastings. Then she would have followed, another voice answered, and Daniel knew this to be true.

They pressed through toward the Champs-Elysees. As two officers passed them, Daniel overheard a snatch of conversation.

"The Pimpernel has been reported in the city, and Robespierre is none-too-pleased. Chauvelin is due back in the city soon and he's even called Roux in from Poitou-Charente to try to root out the man and his followers."

A quick glance at Abigail's expression told him she had heard the conversation as well. He suddenly pressed forward, calling on the officer who had been speaking.

"*Pardonez moi*, Captain, forgive me for overhearing, but did you say that Colonel Roux is in Paris?"

The more senior of the two officers looked at him with suspicion, while the younger man eyed Abigail appreciatively.

"What is it to you, citoyen?"

"My cousin serves as an adjutant. If the Colonel is in town, so will he. I have family news he will want to take home to his mother."

The two officers looked at one another. One shrugged, the other turned back to Daniel.

"If your cousin is here, he'll be at the barracks on Rue de Tournon."

Daniel thanked them, then fell back as they walked on.

"Well, that confirms that Jonathan was right to leave Vienne," he said, more to himself than to Abigail.

"Then what do we do next?" asked Abigail urgently. "If Percy's playing heroics then it makes our job more difficult."

Daniel shook his head. "On the contrary, if soldiers are jumping from one side of the Seine to the other, it could give us the perfect cover. "Now that we know what we're dealing with, we need to find where Jonathan has been staying."

"It's been six months since you've heard from him, what if he's no longer here? Is there any way he could leave you a message if he wasn't able to get a courier out of Paris?"

Daniel smiled. Beautiful, practical Abigail. He kissed her.

"If anyone could, it would be Jonathan."

* * *

The next day they walked to Bicetre just outside the ancient borders of the city. Daniel shaded his eyes and looked out. Paris was not what he'd imagined it to be. From the slight elevation they could see the densely packed streets falling away to the river where Notre Dame Cathedral, now dedicated to the Culte de la Raison, dominated the view.

The little hamlet of Bicetre had nothing much to recommend it. The most significant feature was its grand hospital. Over a century old, it was a massive structure built on the grounds of what was Winchester Manor, the medieval home of John of Poitoise, Bishop of Winchester.

"Why on earth would Jonathan come here?" Abigail asked, brushing the dust from her skirts as they sat on a bench opposite the hospital. "I can't imagine this is the type of place Roux would come to entertain."

Daniel pondered the same thing himself. The walled complex was completely self sufficient with its own produce gardens. The sick, the infirm, and the insane all confined within its walls.

"True," he admitted. "But it is a good place to hold a large group of people without suspicion or going to the trouble of arresting them."

He drummed his fingers on the seat beside him, thinking. "Perhaps that's why he was here. It may also explain why he was connected with a large group of names. He may have discovered the hospital was being used to hold traitors to the Revolution."

Abigail stood, turning her back on the building, and gave him a look of distaste. "I hope you're not suggesting that we feign illness to have ourselves admitted?"

"If I were of such a mind, it would most certainly only be one of us. This is a men's hospital and insane asylum."

Daniel flashed her a smile, but was treated to a deliberate head to toe evaluation in return.

"You look healthy enough, so insanity it will have to be," was her verdict.

"Wench!" he called after her. And Abigail's response was a laugh as she walked toward their next stop, a tavern, the only other significant building in the village.

The inn was large and although it was far from the evening meal hour, it was well patronized. Daniel ordered a bottle of wine and when the innkeeper returned he asked if any letter waited for Simon Tolbert. The small and weedy man with sunken cheeks and a ruddy complexion started at hearing the name, then shrugged.

Abigail gave Daniel a slight frown before turning to address the innkeeper. "Oh please, won't you look? It may be from my brother. I haven't seen him in more than a year and maman worries so."

"You should be careful for what you wish for, citoyenne, a letter may bring bad news as well as good," he grumped before disappearing through the cellar door once again.

"What do you make of that?" she whispered.

Daniel shook his head, as much to forestall any questioning as it was an answer to her. He waited for the innkeeper to reappear, which he did a moment later with a dog-eared envelope.

It added to his unease—an old envelope meant no recent news. The innkeeper threw him a hostile glance and passed the envelope to Abigail who gave the man a tremulous smile.

"*Merci, merci beaucoup*, citoyen," she said. "Any news from my brother will be good news I'm sure."

Daniel steered her to a quiet table just inside in the door and he positioned his chair near hers, ensuring he had a view of all the comings and goings. Abigail poured the wine into two cups as he studied the front of the envelope and Abigail's expression. He watched her scrutinize the scrawled address, no doubt arriving with him at the conclusion that the letter had been written in haste. Her disturbed countenance also betrayed her discovery of the absence of the little flower drawing.

Abigail put a hand on his. Now her expression was filled with sympathy. He knew even better than her what its absence met.

Daniel opened the folded letter inside. The writing was rough.

I'm being followed. I'm sure of it. I barely sleep at night and wake at the slightest sound, and Rue Anne is a quiet street.

I believe R. has a connection with the hospital, although I don't know what. I've watched him and his men enter and then leave some days later.

I met a physician by the name of Pinel who has been just been appointed here. He thinks I have early signs of a mania. I let him think so. It would gain me access to the hospital.

Rachel fills my heart and my thoughts constantly.

Can I let you in on a secret now that I'm in a confessing mood? I know you love her. You always have. She has always loved you too.

I hold no resentment. How can a man resent a rose from blooming? It will do so regardless without his consent.

Have her declare me dead. Marry her on your return. Your mutual happiness will satisfy mine.

I'm not a superstitious man, but I believe I will never see home again. The mobs grow ever violent and if they raid here as they did Salpêtrière last month, there will be much more blood on the streets.

When did the world go mad? Is this liberty? The freedom to behave like rabid dogs because the mood strikes?

Daniel lay the paper on the table lest Abigail see his hands shake.

Hell and damnation.

He barely heard her leave the table and ask the innkeeper for directions to Rue Anne.

Daniel feared for his friend's state of mind. Perhaps the letter was written deliberately to deceive should it have fallen into the wrong hands. But then there was the state of the handwriting… And yet the absence of their mark, the primrose…

It could be anything or nothing.

Hell and damnation.

"Come on," Abigail whispered, placing a hand on his shoulder and giving it a squeeze. "I have the directions."

Daniel nodded. There was no time to burn the letter. He placed it in his pocket.

They left the inn as the afternoon sun cast lengthening shadows across the streets.

And he couldn't shake the feeling that in at least one of those shadows lurked whatever grim fate had befallen Jonathan, its malice now directed at them.

CHAPTER TWENTY-NINE

"*I know you love her. You always have. She has always loved you too.*" Abigail hadn't given Rachel Sawyer a moment's thought since she'd left London. Her sudden appearance—albeit in letter form—cast a shadow every bit as cold as the ones cast the by the trees on the boulevard.

Abigail gave Daniel a sidelong glance as they hurried down a narrow street.

His face wore a grim expression which added to her apprehension. His friend had given permission to court his wife on the full expectation tender feelings would be reciprocated. Jonathan Sawyer did not sound like a maniac. He sound tired and resigned.

There was no clue to be gained from the face of the man beside her.

Jonathan was alive. He had to be alive, not only for his family's sake, but for hers. There could be no other outcome.

Rue Anne was not a large street. In fact it was little more than a lane between two avenues. Densely packed houses clustered along each side of the cobblestone thoroughfare. There was very little to distinguish one domicile from another.

They walked from one end of the street to the other before stopping in front of a house that looked abandoned. The mullioned windows on the lower floor were smashed, and the front door sagged on its hinges.

A curious neighbor opened her door, and a cat scooted out from behind. The wizened-faced woman glared for a moment, then spat a foul smelling substance onto the pavement.

"You won't find anyone there, not since the Committee of Public Safety came for the Dubois'," she informed them. "Took them all away, the lodger, and even petite Marie."

"Do you know where?" Daniel asked.

The woman laughed and started singing:

Ah! ça ira, ça ira, ça ira
les aristocrates à la lanterne!

Abigail rapidly translated the words and shuddered.

Ah! It'll be fine, it'll be fine, it'll be fine
aristocrats to the lamp-post

"Can we look inside?" Daniel asked. "That damned lodger owed me money."

The woman shrugged. "It doesn't matter to me," she said. "But you're five months too late. There's not a sou left in the house, I can tell you."

The woman cackled once more and slapped her knee as if she had told the most amusing joke. Then she sobered up and eyed Abigail from head to toe. She nodded to Daniel.

"You should put this one to work, citoyen. She'll more than make up for your losses, I'm sure!"

Daniel forced a snarl into a grin at the hag and, with a powerful shove of a shoulder, forced the front door inward.

Dust motes danced in the light disturbed by the sudden stirring of air. Drag marks from furniture looted from the home scored the floorboards. Furniture too large to fit through the doors and windows had been simply smashed.

"Vandalism?" she asked. Daniel shook his head.

"I think they were looking for something."

"Then where should *we* look?"

"Skirting boards, cornices, and door frames. You take upstairs. I'll search down here."

Abigail looked at the dusty balustrades and the rickety newel posts with contempt and decided to walk up the centre of the stairs without their aid.

There were three bedrooms. She tried the smallest first on the basis that a lodger would be afforded the least amount of space. A wooden bed frame stood broken apart against the window. In the centre of the room, a low wardrobe with its hinges ripped off had been tipped on its side.

From below, Abigail could hear Daniel knocking and banging walls. The reality of their mission dawned and sat in her stomach leadenly. They had come all this way and it was too late.

Jonathan was dead.

Daniel and Jonathan. *David and Jonathan.* Two men who were closer than brothers…

The water filling her eyes was not all from the dust. She blinked it back.

Abigail inspected every inch of two upstairs rooms and grimaced as greasy dust coated her fingers. She found nothing. Only more broken furniture. She wiped her hands on a small kerchief and looked around the last room. A small object caught her attention. Measuring no more than three inches in length, it lay forgotten or ignored.

It was a wooden carved doll, dressed in a crudely made dress of patterned material that was much faded.

Abigail recalled the doll she had as a child, but hers had a hard paste porcelain head and beautifully painted vivid blue eyes and rosebud mouth. Her doll wore the most exquisitely embroidered satin dresses, miniatures of her mother's own gowns.

She smiled, discovering the peg-mounted head swiveled this way and that with the turn of her fingers. This doll was obviously homemade and much-loved, perhaps more so than hers, she considered. The thought of a terrified child being dragged into the streets to watch her family lynched, then possibly murdered herself, was beyond Abigail's comprehension.

Without really knowing why she did so, she picked up the doll and stuffed it in her pocket.

The afternoon sun had dipped below the houses opposite and the barest amount of light filtered through the filthy windows. Abigail shivered, but it was more than from just the chill of the early spring evening. As a line of gooseflesh rose up her spine, a feeling of unease grew.

Downstairs was quiet. Unnaturally quiet.

From the second pocket of her russet dress, she felt for the knife Daniel insisted she carry ever since they'd reached the outskirts of Paris. She wrapped her fingers around it and wondered whether she would have any chance against an assailant.

Tempted though she was to call out Daniel's name, Abigail considered surprise a more potent weapon than the one she now wielded in her right hand. She cautiously walked to the top of the stairs and looked down into the small parlor below. A man stood with his back to her, silhouetted against the remains of the daylight that poured through the ajar front door.

He shifted and the muzzle of a pistol was clearly visible in his hand.

Daniel!

Holding a baluster for support, Abigail leaned as far as she dared without overbalancing.

A second man held Daniel at sword point. His hands were raised and the matching knife to hers lay useless on the floor. A bruise and a small cut were visible on his cheek. Daniel's eyes flickered up to hers only briefly, but it was enough.

She would have to provide the advantage.

Abigail felt the post loosen and she pulled back to restore her balance. Her knife returned to her pocket once more.

One chance.

It was all she had. It had to be now.

A twist of the wrist and the baluster came free. She mustered every ounce of anger at her disposal and released a pent-up scream of rage as she ran down the stairs like a Valkyrie.

The man at the bottom turned. Abigail swung the post like a club and caught him across the temple. The pistol shot went wild, showering her with plaster from the ceiling.

He staggered to one knee. Abigail bludgeoned him once, twice, three times until he lay prone on the floor.

The second man had turned at her scream and, while she swung the first blow, Daniel used the distraction to kick the swordsman in the stomach, forcing him back against the staircase. Daniel rolled forward, picked up his knife from the floor, then thrust heavily up under the man's ribs.

The sword clattered to the floor. The man clutched at his abdomen.

Daniel dashed for the door, grabbing Abigail's wrist in a vise-like grip on his way past, forcing her to run to keep up with him. They sprinted down the street, taking several turnings without pause. Abigail was certain she heard pounding feet behind her until she realized it was her own pulse in her ears.

By the time they stopped at the checkpoint with the last of the day's stragglers looking to return back into the city itself, Abigail had a stitch in her side and every breath was an agony. Tears pricked her eyes, and she leaned heavily on Daniel for support.

He kissed her hair and stroked her head tenderly. "Just one more ordeal, my love," he whispered.

Abigail thought Daniel was being optimistic, but a half nod was the only answer she could muster in response.

"Papers," the gruff and portly sergeant demanded. Daniel furnished the document from his pocket. The soldier cast an eye over Abigail, then back at him, eyes narrowing as he observed the cut on his cheek.

"What's wrong with her?" he said.

"We've just been up to the hospital at Bicetre, she's found out her brother is dead."

The sergeant harrumphed, then waved them through the gate.

They walked on and on in silence, Daniel's pace barely slowing to accommodate her. His shoulders were tense and his expression was guarded, even from her.

Not only did her chest ache, so she did her heart. Jonathan couldn't truly be dead. How could he be? He was as brave and as resourceful as Daniel. He was one of Sir Percy's Blakeney's own men.

He had a wife and children.

She recalled his letter once again and a selfish part of her heart wondered what Jonathan's death meant for her.

Not the time! Not the place! She ruthlessly tamped the thought down, ashamed. Daniel had lost a dear friend, a brother, and she was sizing up the young widow as her competition? It was a good thing night was falling to hide the shame that flushed her cheeks.

As the first of the night stars appeared in the lightly clouded sky, lamplighters walked the city igniting the street lamps. Daniel and Abigail blended in with the other early evening strollers, but as they crossed back into the thirteenth arrondissement, Daniel paused.

"I don't know if it is safe to go back to Widow Boyer's home. We have to find alternative accommodation tonight."

He started walking again, toward the river, expecting her to follow. She refused.

"Stop."

Daniel walked a few yards further and then halted as he seemed to realize she was not behind him. "What?" he asked irritably.

At that moment, the gulf between them seemed vast. Daniel wore his defensiveness like a mantle. It was impenetrable. The torrent of words she wished to say rushed past her before she could pull enough of them together to articulate the full depth of her feeling.

"I'm sorry."

Those two words summed up everything, yet seemed wholly inadequate to the task.

Suddenly conscious of the fact that they had been conversing in English, Daniel hurried back to her and pulled her along.

"What for now?" he hissed. "Stop being so damned sorry for everything!"

"Jonathan was your friend—"

"—He's not dead!"

Daniel pulled up suddenly. Even in the semi-darkness lit only by lamplight she could see his face was dark with anger.

"He's not dead," Daniel averred with a sharp stab of his finger, then he hesitated, his shoulders sagging. "We don't know that he is. We only have that old crazy woman's word for it."

Abigail's heart ached for him. She wanted nothing more than to wrap her arms around him and hold him, offering him what little comfort she could.

So long fuelled by nothing more than adrenaline, Abigail's emotional resources had reached their nadir and tears sprang easily to her eyes. She turned away, determined not to let him see them fall, and brushed them away.

Daniel's hand on her shoulder seemed at once an apology and a gesture of conciliation. "Any ideas where we should go next?"

"We're close to Val-de-Grace," she whispered. "Perhaps we can find something to eat and shelter there for the night."

The dome of the church was silhouetted against the twilight sky, just two blocks away. Abigail took a deep breath. Her first few steps were stiff. Leg muscles ached from miles of walking.

Daniel fell into step with her.

When they arrived, access to the church and grounds were barred. A permanent sign had been erected by the gates:

Property of the people of France

By order of the National Assembly

Abigail looked enviously at the abbey kitchen gardens behind the iron fence. The hope of at least a warm meal and charitable hospitality thwarted.

A sharp whistle sounded in the distance and the sound of running footsteps approached them.

Arretez!

Two men appeared in view, one clasping a bundle to his chest. As they approached one of them yelled, "Follow us, otherwise they will arrest you too!"

The whistle sounded again followed by the sound of more booted feet that echoed along the narrow alleys and stone buildings, obscuring its direction. Abigail and Daniel hesitated before a muzzle flash could be seen just a block away. The report of the shot followed a split-second after.

They ran after the direction of the other two men.

Abigail and Daniel ran past the Observatory, using the shadow of its multi-story edifice to hide their location and pass down into a small glen. To Abigail's alarm, the sound of the soldiers grew nearer.

"Friends!" a voice called to them. "This way!" One of the men crouched by a bush and waved them over. "Come on!"

Out of the corner of her eye, Abigail saw Daniel reach into his pocket to where she knew he held his knife.

As they rounded the bush, the man who had waved to them ran to a sheet of iron propped up on the hill and disappeared behind it. Daniel glanced swiftly up to the other side of the hill where a line of torches was now coming into view. Abigail knew as well as he did that they had no choice but to follow.

CHAPTER THIRTY

A single candle lay inside a small adit, just wide enough for them to walk two abreast. Daniel picked it up and handed it to Abigail. His meaning was clear—if he had to defend them, he would need both hands.

The white chalky walls reflected the light down a tunnel which turned black as it pushed further into the hill.

"Do not fear, you are among friends," whispered a voice that echoed eerily down the passage ways.

"Who do we have the honor of calling friend?" asked Daniel.

"Come further inside to safety. The soldiers are superstitious; they won't come any further than this entrance."

Daniel placed his left hand on the small of Abigail's back to gently urge her forward. She glanced up at him and he gave a nod of confirmation making sure in the candlelight that she caught a glimpse of the knife he carried.

They rounded the corner and the passage continued for about fifteen yards to where a small lamp stood, indicating another corner. They rounded it and then another. Dotted at intervals of about ten yards, small lamps lit their way until they entered another passage. Abigail suppressed a scream. A skull in the wall eyed her sightlessly. She raised her candle higher and could see skulls, hundreds of them, twenty feet along and lining six feet up the walls.

Bones of other sorts too were neatly stacked in rows.

"There's no need to fear. Our sentries will keep a look out," the voice laughed, amused by his own jest.

They walked further and a vaguely smoky smell coalesced into actual smoke clinging to the ceiling. The smell of warm stew mingled with the smoke and beckoned them to continue. Around another corner, the passage opened up into a large chamber in which thirty adults along with half a dozen children were gathered.

At one end of the near-circular opening was a makeshift altar. One of the young men who had run past them on the street had unwrapped the bundle and was admiring a silver communion cup.

He looked at them and grinned. "It's not really stealing if we're taking back what used to be ours."

The voice which had encouraged them belonged to another man, aged about twenty-five. He wore small round glasses, but the eyes behind them were sharp. He stood by a three-legged cauldron above a compact fire, the source of the smoke.

"Welcome to *L'église sous terre*—the church underground," he said, holding out his hand. "I'm Jean-Baptiste."

Daniel pulled out an empty right hand and shook the younger man's hand.

"I'm Rene and this is Suzanne," he replied. Jean-Baptiste gave a formal nod to Abigail before addressing them both.

"I used to be a seminarian at Val-de-Grace before it was disestablished by the National Assembly. I suppose you know all the churches have been turned into public buildings, at least those not converted to temples to the 'culte de la raison.' Now we meet in the catacombs and the abandoned mines under the city to avoid arrest. "In midst of death, we are in life." Apparently a private jest. A wry smile touched his lips.

An old woman handed them both wooden bowls filled with the steaming hot food and gestured to them to sit on one of the pews that lined the walls. Abigail whispered a quiet *merci* and gingerly sat, muscles protesting.

"Yes, please eat," said Jean-Baptiste. He gave a little formal bow and excused himself, leaving the chamber.

They ate, as did the others around them, talking quietly in groups until the end of the meal when the one of the women gestured the sign of the cross before a silver gilt table crucifix and placed a bottle of wine and part of a loaf of bread on the altar.

That appeared to be the signal for the others to gather. Jean-Baptiste returned, now wearing a black soutane over his sans-culottes clothes.

A guitar was produced and notes from a strangely familiar tune plucked. The gathering began to sing:

C'est un rempart que notre Dieu,
Une invincible armure,
Un défenseur victorieux,
Une aide prompte et sûre.
L'Ennemi, contre nous,
Redouble de courroux:
Vaine colère!
Que pourrait l'Adversaire?
L'Eternel détourne ses coups

The hymn was familiar and Abigail vaguely recalled it as one written by Martin Luther. She struggled to remember the English version:

A mighty fortress is our God,
a bulwark never failing;
our helper he amid the flood
of mortal ills prevailing.
For still our ancient foe
doth seek to work us woe;
his craft and power are great,
and armed with cruel hate,
on earth is not his equal

At the conclusion of the mass, groups of two and three left. Some turned right to return down the passage, others to the left.

At Daniel's questioning glance, Jean-Baptiste, now having removed his soutane, offered an explanation. "I didn't think you were locals. The city is riddled with many such tunnels, so much so that special care is made when new buildings are erected. Entire structures have collapsed into subsiding holes before now. Many of the tunnels lead to various parts of the city, even close to the river itself, but it is dangerous to go that far."

He regarded them closely.

"Tell me," he continued, "as good citizens of our fine Republique, what reason do you have for running from the guard? You could have easily shown your papers and be sent off with a reminder to be home before the curfew."

Abigail shot Daniel a nervous glance, but said nothing.

Sensing reluctance, Jean-Baptiste shrugged, then stood. "I understand. I'm not your confessor and it's not for me to judge. I simply to invite you to go in peace."

"We'd like to stay here in peace," said Daniel. "I don't think we will be able to go home tonight."

The young priest gave them a considering gaze and asked, "You two are not married, are you?

Abigail stared at the floor. Daniel shook his head and answered gravely, "Not in any recognized jurisdiction."

Jean-Baptiste flashed them a conspiratorial grin.

"Well, according the National Assembly, I have no authority to perform marriage either, but I dare say that fact matters not to God. If you wish, I will wed you now and we'll all say to hell with the state's interference with things that don't concern them."

Abigail raised her head slowly. This was the stuff insanity was made of. It was on the tip of her tongue to refuse, until she looked at Daniel. His mouth wore a look of uncertain amusement, but his eyes told another tale; one of longing mingled with fear and a small portion of regret. She wondered what her face revealed to him.

"I have nothing to offer you," he said to Abigail. "Nothing a woman like you deserves or should expect." He took both of her hands into his. "I have no home and no great fortune. We have pasts that haunt us, a present that is uncertain, and a future which is unknown."

He raised her hands to his lips and kissed them.

"I know nothing at all but this: I love you. My life is yours if you'll have me on those terms."

Without hesitation, Abigail replied, "If you can come to love a stubborn, ill-tempered shrew like me, you're either a madman or a saint," she said, her voice hoarse with emotion. "But I love you like no other—"

Damn sentimentality! She cursed to herself once more as she actively fought against the tears that welled close to the surface. How could she not love this man, the only one who accepted her as who she was, who saw through the facade of the brittle-mannered coquette to see the woman underneath?

Abigail swallowed, realizing she had come close to saying his real name. "Whatever the future holds, we share it together. Until death and not even then."

The cleric clapped enthusiastically. "Hey, Patric and Simone, they sounded like marriage vows to you, right?"

The middle-aged couple tidying the chamber and extinguishing some of the lights looked at one another and then back to Jean-Baptiste.

The man grinned through his salt and pepper stubbled face. "We are witnesses to that."

"*Bon*! I'm sure the Holy Father in Rome will understand we do things a little differently in these trying times."

Jean-Baptiste brought them to the altar and opened The Bible and read:

The man said, "This is now bone of my bones, And flesh of my flesh; She shall be called Woman, Because she was taken out of Man." For this reason a man shall leave his father and his mother, and be joined to his wife; and they shall become one flesh. And the man and his wife were both naked and were not ashamed.

"The state cannot offer you marriage," he said. "It is a sacred union of two that binds body and soul and is made before God and earthly witnesses. After you are gone from here, only God will bear witness to the vows you made to one another. Do not dishonor Him or one another."

The young man paused and stepped back as though pleased with his handiwork. After a moment he looked at Daniel and prompted, "It's customary about now to kiss the bride."

Daniel laughed, and everyone joined in. He swept Abigail into his arms and kissed her thoroughly. She wrapped her arms around his and hugged him tightly. Perhaps it was the result of the long and harrowing day, the absurdity of a wedding without plans or a gown or orange blossoms, and yet it was a strangest thing—her spirits were lightened.

Daniel pulled a small gold signet ring from his little finger and placed it on her ring finger. "A token, albeit a very small token, of my devotion."

Abigail felt the weight of it and in the candlelight saw the Pemberley coat of arms, the only acknowledgement she had ever seen of his family connection. Now it was her family.

Patric approached. He shook Daniel's hand and kissed Abigail's cheek; his wife did likewise.

"We can't offer you a wedding feast, but we can offer you a bed for the night," he said.

Daniel shook the older man's hand once again. "My wife and I would be delighted to accept."

* * *

The attic room was small, containing a bed and a small washstand which only just fit under the dormer window.

They needed no more than that.

The remains of a candle stub used to light their way guttered and died in its holder unnoticed. Daniel moved over her, needing no light to find her curve of her breast with his lips while his hand skimmed the flare of her hips and the soft warmth of her thigh. She whispered encouragement in English. In her desire, the mastery of another tongue was lost as they explored the language of their love together.

Their lovemaking was unhurried. For them both, it was an affirmation of life and declaration of devotion to a life enjoined more than temporally.

Flesh of my flesh, bone of my bone…

Pleasure surged through Abigail at his touch, and yet her need was not yet sated. With her body and her tongue and her words, she encouraged him to join her on a peak of true joy.

Under her fingers, his back quivered. When she kissed him, she found a sensitive part of his earlobe that made him groan as she licked it.

He entered her slowly to prolong their pleasure.

…one flesh forever joined…

Suddenly tomorrow didn't matter. Not the next minute, nor next second. Now, only now as their mutual delight affirmed something more than sating a physical yearning.

They belonged.

They belonged to each other.

CHAPTER THIRTY-ONE

The banging on the door downstairs only half filtered into Abigail's consciousness. The pounding on the door outside their room woke her with a start. Daniel was already half dressed when the door swung open. Abigail grabbed her clothes from him and dressed under the bed covers as Simone entered, looking pale and grim. She bustled past and opened the window.

"Soldiers are searching house by house," she said harshly. "They cannot find you here. Your only way out is across the rooftop. We will delay them as much as possible. Godspeed."

There was no time to even put on shoes. Abigail carried hers in one hand as Daniel helped her out onto the roof. After them, the window shut and the curtains were drawn. Inside, they could hear the sound of the room being expunged of their presence.

Dawn had only just peaked over the hills to the east, and the orange rays of the sun made the morning look warmer than it was. Mist was beginning to evaporate off the slate roof from the dew that had condensed over night.

As Abigail exhaled, steam filled the air. Daniel took a few steps across and hoisted himself up to the roofline. She accepted his hands and scrambled to join him. Just three chimneys along at the end of the terraced row, a large elm tree spread its arms wide.

"Let's see if our luck holds as well as those branches," he whispered.

Abigail secured the buckle on her shoes and watched Daniel consider the descent.

"I'll go first," he said. "Then I'll help you across."

Daniel lowered himself off the edge of the roof onto a large branch which bowed slightly under his weight. He breathed a theatrical sigh of relief and reached his hand out to her.

Their fingertips grazed on the first pass and Abigail tried again; this time their hands held and he pulled her across to the bough. He aided her down each limb until they were six feet above the ground. Daniel nimbly dropped to the ground and reached up toward Abigail who was sitting on a branch.

"I'll catch you," he said. "Just let go."

Daniel was good as his word, securing her around the waist as he lowered her to the grass beneath the tree.

"Arretez vous!"

A soldier brandishing a sword came charging to their position.

Daniel shoved her away from him forcefully. "Run!"

The lone soldier was caught by surprise as Daniel ran toward him. The man swung wildly, but he was tackled low and thrown to the ground. The soldier lost his grip on his sword and it was swiftly in Daniel's possession.

He held the sword in a fighting stance as he saw another two soldiers, all regular infantry men judging by their uniforms, hurry toward them.

Daniel seemed to sense without seeing that Abigail hesitated. Without once looking her way, he yelled, "Go! Go now!" The first of the swordsmen reached him.

Abigail ran, although every inch of her screamed she should stay. For the first time in her life, she prayed as though her life depended on it.

* * *

Against two swordsmen, Daniel had a reasonable chance. He kept the two soldiers equally occupied for a minute before reinforcements arrived.

Unfortunately, the reinforcements were not for him.

Not even he would take odds of six-to-one under those circumstances.

Despite the cool morning, sweat poured down his face and his stomach took the inopportune time to remind him he had not eaten that day. Without being asked, he threw the steel to the ground at the feet of the soldier from whom he had liberated it, and raised his hands in the air for surrender. Two soldiers secured his arms while four others kept their swords pointed at his belly.

He prayed he had bought enough time for Abigail to escape. Oddly, he felt the absence of the signet ring he had forgotten he owned. It was now worn by Abigail. A paltry symbol of their unity, but hopefully enough to satisfy solicitors.

If he couldn't be a good husband to her in life, he rather thought he could be one after his death.

The half dozen soldiers didn't seem keen to take him into custody. They waited.

Minutes later, leaving by the front door of the house from which they had so recently escaped, came a large, powerfully built middle aged man dressed head-to-toe in black.

Although Daniel had only ever seen him from a distance he recognized him immediately.

Colonel Alexis Roux.

Nothing about the man was impulsive, from his crisp and finely tailored attire to his measured walk, Roux seemed to approach everything with an objective curiosity.

The detachment of soldiers parted to let him through.

"*Le rouquin Anglais,*" he greeted, making reference to the color of Daniel's hair. "*Le renard de Anglais.*"

Daniel showed teeth some might confuse for a grin. "The English Fox... I didn't realize I merited my own nickname. If I had, I wouldn't have stayed away so long."

Although well past middle age, his hair silver and slicked back from a high forehead, Roux was a sly fox himself. He circled Daniel as though examining his prey.

"I knew you'd be back," he said silkily. "I just didn't know when…or appreciate you would have such charming company."

He turned to the men. "Where is the woman?"

The most senior of them answered. "She made her escape while we were capturing this prisoner, sir."

"No matter, we'll have her soon enough, then we'll see how much bravado our 'perfidious albion' has. Send two men to look for her and tell the detachments to bring her to me *personally.*"

The sergeant nodded and appointed two men to the task.

Roux turned to Daniel. "Where is it?"

Daniel remained silent. He wasn't quite sure what "it" was and thought it against his better interests to ask. A punch to the gut, delivered by a gloved fist, was the next question. Pain radiated through him, and he let out a hoarse gasp.

Roux stepped closer. "Don't make me use force. I do so hate unnecessary violence. Tell me. Where is the list of traitors to the Republic?"

Daniel straightened, ignoring the pain in his mid-section. "I have no list."

Roux conceded the point with a shrug. "Perhaps not. But your friend did—the one you left behind."

"Then you'd better ask him."

"Ah, *je regret,* I cannot. Your friend is dead."

Daniel swallowed to hide the bitterness of having the news he feared confirmed to him. Once again he had failed a friend. Always going when he should have stayed.

God forgive me, Jonathan, he begged. Forgive me, Reggie, forgive me.

He mustered every ounce of bravado he possessed. "That was careless. You kill a man and an entire family and you cannot find a list." Daniel smirked. He tensed his muscles and waited for another blow. It didn't come.

"The list, Monsieur Ridgeway," Roux asked with exaggerated patience. "Your life is in a perilous state, and death awaits you around every corner. I won't bother appealing to a fictitious afterlife to give you succor, but there are many ways for men to die and not all of them pleasant. Being my guest for a while will make you long for Madame Guillotine as your lover."

Roux paused as though a thought had stuck him.

"Perhaps you tell the truth after all, *mon amis*."

He turned to the soldier who stood at Daniel's left shoulder. "Deliver this man to the lunatic asylum at *Bicetre Hopital*. Then join Armand. Find the woman."

* * *

Abigail hid in the shadows of an alley opposite Widow Boyer's home for most of the morning, waiting for Daniel to return. He did not. Fortunately neither did anyone else. After long hours watching, she was certain now the house was not watched.

She observed a dust cart make its way up the street and round the corner. It was the last of the traffic she could see.

A rap on the door and Abigail was swiftly admitted. The old lady asked no questions and Abigail furnished her with no explanations either. She opened the trunks and rummaged through every item of clothing they possessed, pulling out the strips of coins sewed into the linings.

The revolutionaries were brutal in their dealings with spies and traitors, but they were also corrupt. The weight of the coins still in their bindings was heavy in her hands. No price would be too much pay for Daniel's life.

Abigail pondered her options. She was friendless in Paris. Despite her confident words to Daniel back in Hastings, everyone she once knew here was either in exile or had lost their heads.

What to do? What to do?

She sat on the small bed and forced herself to steady her breathing. Oh God, oh God…

She had pleaded with God before this, even tried to bargain with Him on occasion, but now she realized those other times were petty and foolish acts of selfishness. Nothing compared to the urgency of this moment.

But no words of her own would come. Panic loomed again.

Then Abigail turned to those words she had committed to memory as a girl, ones she had not given much consideration to then or since then. She closed her eyes and found herself back in the church in Hastings where she heard Daniel speak softly under his breath.

Our Father, who art in Heaven,
Hallowed be thy name…

* * *

Three hours later, Abigail examined her appearance in the foxed old mirror in the bedroom. Over her plain dress, she wore borrowed widow's weeds and a heavy black cloak. A folded piece of old linen in a small drawstring bag fastened inside the cloak made a passable dowager's hump as she viewed herself in profile, and a wicker basket covered with a checkered cloth contained everything else she dared take.

Her white hair was darkened with soot from the fireplace and she pulled the hood of the cloak well up so it fell low on her brow. As she crossed the first street, she hoped it would be enough to fool the soldiers looking for her.

After walking awhile Abigail spotted the Dome of Val-de-Grace and made her way toward it. She had no idea if she could even find her way back to the hidden entrance to the catacombs, let alone whether Jean-Baptiste would be there.

Daniel's life was in her hands. She glanced at the engraving on the ring she now wore and committed it to memory—*virtus et fortitude*.

She would need both.

With her back stooped, Abigail crossed crowded streets at a measured pace, in keeping with her disguise. No one appeared to pay her any mind. Where she saw soldiers patrolling a street, she would walk down another avenue or remain in the shadows until they had passed.

She crossed into Rue St Germain and on into the market square, and now there was no avoiding them. Soldiers were everywhere, singly and in pairs. They strolled the stalls at their ease, paying little heed to the press of the crowds surrounding the trestle tables and carts.

Abigail shuffled in and examined the meager produce, moldy fruit, vegetables thin and wilted. She wouldn't give tuppence for a tableful back home; a farmer would be ashamed to feed his pigs such fare. And the prices! She couldn't believe how much people were willing to pay for poor offerings.

Yet pay they did, these gaunt-faced men and women who squabbled for rotten vegetables, knowing there was no meat to be had and what was in front of them was the best they could hope for.

"Hey you! Stop!"

Abigail froze at the barked command and waited for an arresting hand on her shoulder. It didn't come.

A small boy with something pressed to his chest rushed past her quickly and the sound of pounding boots followed behind and then passed as a man chased the child.

"Are you going to buy something or are you just going to stand there?" the stall holder demanded.

Abigail reluctantly picked the best of his impoverished display of apples and resentfully handed over enough coin to buy her a crateful back in England.

The walk back to the Val-de-Grace took three times as long as it needed to and by the time she had reached the grounds her back ached from stooping.

In daylight, the farmlands which spread out south of the church seemed different. The stone Observatory loomed large ahead of her. Should she go to the left or the right? Further along the road, the top of the Bicetre Hospital perched ominously in the distance.

"Old widow, you seem lost."

Abigail jumped at the voice which called out to her from the middle of a field. Dressed in a farmer's garb, his glasses glinting in the sunlight, stood Jean-Baptiste. Abigail could not believe her eyes and blinked, openmouthed. She hurried to him.

As she approached, she could see his eyes widen at the age-shrunken widow suddenly standing straight and running to him.

"Suzanne!" he exclaimed. "What are you doing here? Why are you dressed like that? Where is Rene?"

The questions came out in a rush as Abigail struggled to catch her breath. Then Jean-Baptiste, apparently deciding it was not safe to be standing in an open field talking to an unexpectedly agile "widow," grasped his hoe and urged her to follow him down into another field, unseen from the road.

"Soldiers came after us," she gasped. "Dan—I mean Rene told me to run, but he was arrested."

Jean-Baptiste's mouth tightened into a thin white line. "I have thirty families who rely on the safety of the catacombs, and you risk bringing the dragoons down on us?"

"I didn't know where to find help. I have no one else."

Abigail's statement sounded more like a plea to her own ears and so to Jean-Baptiste, for his shoulders slumped and he sighed.

"Come, I'll hide you, but you have to be honest and tell me the full story."

* * *

Abigail watched Jean-Baptiste's face as she told him as much of her story as she dared. It was the truth, just not all of it. That would be too risky for too many people, including those now with her.

"So you do not know what really happened to the Dubois family and the Englishman they housed?"

"No, only what the old woman told us—that the whole family had been hung."

Jean-Baptiste looked to a plain-faced woman in her fifties as though waiting for her verdict. The woman's short hair was iron gray and she was dressed in plain, practical clothing with little regard for their fitment.

It had been a frustrating wait for Abigail, cloistered in the catacombs until after dark where now a group of six men and women were gathered—her judge and jury. They each represented leaders of eglise sous terre groups across Paris.

"Colonel Roux is not a liked man even among the committee, but Robespierre finds him useful from what I understand," said the woman. "Even so, I cannot imagine he would execute young children. A girl you say?"

"Why not? They send young aristos to the guillotine, don't they?" protested Abigail. "But Roux doesn't have what he's looking for, I'm certain of that. Now he knows Daniel has been looking, he may turn his attention back to the girl again if she's not already dead. This…" Abigail fished the abandoned doll from her pocket. "It cannot belong to a girl any older than eight."

The woman eyed the toy, but her voice and expression were gruff. "There are so many orphans. How we find one among so many only God knows."

"God may be good enough to let us know too, Sister Carmella," soothed Jean-Baptiste at seeing a thunderous expression of anger cross Abigail's face. "I can make some pretext to search the records. If there's one thing the revolutionaries do well it's keeping tally of the people they kill."

"Then we have to find Daniel," said Abigail.

Both Jean-Baptiste and Sister Carmella glanced at one another, then turned to give her a pitying look.

"*Ma cherie,*" said Jean-Baptiste. He reached out to take her hand. "There is every chance your husband is already dead."

CHAPTER THIRTY-TWO

He heard a door being unlocked and it was the smell that assailed him first—a rank odor of vomit, sweat, and piss—but worst still was the over-arching stink of fear.

Daniel stood, blinded by the sack over his head and with his hands shackled behind him. He was given a short, sharp shove to the centre of his back and he stumbled forward.

"My dear Philippe, I have brought you a most interesting case," said Roux behind him.

The man to whom Roux spoke vocalized a thoughtful "uh hum" in response, also from behind.

"This man is not one of your usual patients; he is not an imbecile. On the contrary, he is very intelligent, but he is also clearly deluded. He thinks he is English and he knows enough to be dangerous on that account."

"Dangerous? How so, Colonel Roux?"

"He is violent. He killed one of my men and put another in this very hospital just a day ago. He should hang, but he may be of some use to the republic alive. I wish to leave him in your care while we carry out some investigations."

The sack was removed, and Daniel blinked. For the first time, he could see where he was.

The cell was three yards square and it appeared it was to be his alone. A small transom window, a little sliver of dirty glass, allowed a meager amount of light to struggle into the stone walled room.

"He seems to be in good physical shape…" The speaker loomed into view, walking around Daniel, inspecting him. Philippe was an earnest looking, gray-haired man in his mid-forties with a high forehead and hawk-like features. He looked over Daniel's shoulder to Roux. "Is it necessary to keep him in chains, my dear Roux? You know how I detest these things."

"Keep him as you see fit," Roux answered, "but I must have access to him day and night as the investigation continues. After all, this is for the security of France."

"Yes, well, he seems compliant enough now. We'll fit him with one of Citizen Guilleret's chemises though, just to be sure."

Not once was Daniel addressed. He remained in the centre of the room as both men departed. When the door closed, the room turned nearly black apart from the shard of gray light that came from the window above.

In the distance, he could hear the sounds of weak screams and he allowed himself a swallow of dismay.

Daniel bent his arms at the elbow and gave his bonds an experimental tug. Conscious that he might be observed, he walked the perimeter of his cell cautiously. It was made of stone, quite possibly from the thirteenth century manor on which Bicetre Hospital now sat.

Daniel sank to the floor. He breathed in deeply, then exhaled. He then breathed in again. The voice of Bossy filled his ears. *"David used what he had an' trusted in the Lord. You do the same. Pray to God first."*

Our Father, who art in heaven,
Hallowed be thy name…

A period of time passed. Daniel couldn't say how much. He pulled himself out of his meditative state as he heard the sound of keys being jangled, then inserted into the lock.

He raised himself to his feet and waited for what was to come. Abigail filled his thoughts. In his mind's eye, he found her face and kissed it. He breathed in deep and instead of the stench of the asylum, he could smell her scent, rose and jasmine, and the warmth of a summer evening they were yet to share.

Two burly men entered, one carrying a rough, heavy canvas shirt with overlong sleeves. Was that the chemise the man called Philippe had mentioned? One of the men grasped Daniel in a tight headlock while the other removed his shackles. Then they quickly manhandled him into the shirt, but in reverse, with the opening at his back.

As he resisted the urge to struggle—he knew it would be useless—he realized the too-long sleeves were sewn closed at the ends where they were reinforced with leather and there were leather straps and buckles. The men drew the straps behind his back, causing him to wrap his arms involuntarily around his own chest, and as they buckled them he understood the purpose of the garment.

Released by the men, but constrained by the chemise, Daniel sank to his knees. He shrugged and twisted against the canvas, but it restrained him as effectively as any iron shackles. Daniel spied movement in a dark corner of the cell near the door. The man Philippe stepped forward.

"There, there, my friend, you will find this more comfortable than being chained to a wall, let me assure you. It is for your benefit until we can find the thing that will make you well."

He turned to one of his orderlies. "Get him a half draught of laudanum. Not too much though, Colonel Roux will want to question him shortly."

As the man left the room, Philippe turned back to Daniel and looked at him thoughtfully for a few moments.

"Dr. Pinel?" said the remaining orderly, interrupting his cogitations. "You will be wanted in the wards shortly."

"Yes, yes," he replied, brusquely. "I want to first make sure our newest patient is comfortable."

He smiled at Daniel, then, after another moment's consideration, turned away. "Be sure he is fed." He reminded the orderly and left.

The orderly stared blankly at Daniel. Daniel tried to return an equally neutral gaze, his eyes flicking to the open cell door as the other orderly returned holding a wooden cup.

The first man crossed to Daniel and, without a word, pulled his head roughly back by his hair. The man with the cup poured a bitter liquid into his mouth, and he had no choice but to swallow. A few seconds later, the door was locked again, and Daniel was alone once more.

Again, time seemed to stand still. Daniel thought of Abigail. In his minds' eye, he could see her lovely face in front on him, those cat-like green eyes and those lips. In his imagination, he kissed her once again and she responded.

He was unaware of growing arousal until it pressed against the confines of his breeches and he suddenly realized he was lying on his side and half dreaming, sedated by the laudanum. He struggled to his feet.

The cursed backward jacket allowed him to walk, but provided no free movement for his arms at all. A primal panic—the fear of being trapped—quickened his breath, but he fought it. Daniel called Abigail to mind once more, trying to bring his cognition into focus. He recalled telling her about his youthful ambition to become an engineer.

What he hadn't mentioned was that, through an intermediary, he had now invested everything he had into the engineering works owned by Reggie's father. Daniel had deprived him of his son when he'd fled to save his own skin; the very least he could do was ensure he wasn't deprived of his livelihood as well.

Daniel's mind began to wander again, another side effect of being drugged. Would he get out of here? Would he ever return to England? If he did, he would resign. Yes, tell Sir Percy no more spying. He would retire to Cornwall and be an engineer. He would perfect a steam system to drive the horseless carriages he and Reggie had spoken of. It would be larger than a normal carriage, but they'd heard of one in America that had been built to run on rails. Daniel had told Jonathan about it once, but he'd just laughed; his friend didn't share the vision.

Jonathan.

A million regrets would ever be associated with that name. Then thoughts of Rachel briefly came to mind and…

Concentrate!

The cell door opened, the hinges groaning against the weight of the door. Daniel could see the silhouette of a man filling the frame. Roux entered the room.

Daniel watched two men follow behind and he prepared himself for a beating. It was inevitable and, in this abominable jacket, would be a terribly one-sided affair.

But the men stayed to either side of the doorway. Daniel struggled to his knees.

"Let me properly welcome you to the new France," Roux intoned. "We are a civilized country based on reason, science, and progress."

Daniel sniggered. "If your mark of civilization is beheading women and children, then you can keep it."

"Now, now, that is no way to talk to your host. We're going to have a little game, you and I. It's so simple a child can play. You ask me a question and I shall answer. Then I'll ask you a question and you shall answer."

"Who wins?"

"The one who answers the most questions, of course. The prize is deciding how you will be executed—guillotine, hanging, firing squad, or the rack. Because I am a fair man, I'll let you ask first. Anything you like. I shall answer honestly and I shall expect you to do the same."

Daniel considered his options. He could not escape from here without assistance, and it would take time for Percy to mount a rescue, if he was in a position, and inclination, to do so. He would play Roux's game for as long as he could and satisfy his own curiosity at the same time.

"What happened to Jonathan Sawyer?"

Roux's eyes lit up as he realized the game had started.

"Ah, we begin! *Bon.* Jonathan Sawyer was killed by a mob. Strung up on a lamppost. I was none too happy, let me assure you. He had information I wanted and I never got to speak to him.

"Now, my question to you. Did you find his half of the list of traitors? I am presuming it is the reason you returned."

"I returned because Sawyer was a friend."

"You haven't answered my question," Roux warned.

"No. I didn't find any list. Your men interrupted the search."

"Very well. Your question…"

Daniel licked his lips, his throat thick with dust and sour with the aftertaste of laudanum.

"May I have some water?"

Roux nodded to a man behind him who left the cell and returned momentarily with another wooden cup. Roux held it to his lips, and Daniel took long quenching sips.

As Roux pulled the cup away, he learned in to Daniel and whispered. "Where's the woman?"

Revived by the drink and buoyed by the thought that if he was asking after Abigail, then she had not been caught, Daniel laughed.

"If she has any sense, she'll be half way back to England by now."

"Does she have the list?"

"Uh-uh. That's two questions for you."

Roux nodded his head to concede the point.

"What happened to the family?" Daniel asked.

"The family of traitors? The parents and eldest son were strung up by the same mob. The girl child was saved. She was sent to *Hospice de la Salpêtrière.*"

She wasn't saved, Daniel thought. She was condemned. *Salpêtrière*, where ten thousand prostitutes and mad women live alongside the sick and infirm. He said a brief prayer for the child.

"Who is the Scarlet Pimpernel?" asked Roux, getting to the point.

"The most unlikely man in England."

Daniel's answer earned him a cuff across the side of the head and his ear rang with the violence of it.

"That was not a truthful answer."

"Then I am the Scarlet Pimpernel."

Roux raised his arm again, but stopped. Daniel could see him considering the answer.

Then the blow struck once more. Daniel laughed which served to anger Roux.

"You ask for the truth and when it doesn't suit your purpose you resort to violence. Is this the reason France offers the world?"

Roux's response was a hard punch to the jaw. Unable to fend off the blow, Daniel fell painfully onto his back. More blows rained down and in, not only from Roux, but also from the two thugs who accompanied him.

Daniel curled up, unable even to protect his head, but used to taking blows and, though frustrated at his inability to return them, was able to force himself to remain calm. He would not give Roux the satisfaction of crying out and pushed through the pain by gasping out words.

"The Lord is my shepherd; I shall not want..."

The blows stopped, and Daniel felt the agony ebb away as he continued softly: "Yea, though I walk through the valley of the shadow of death, I will fear no evil: for thou art with me; thy rod and thy staff they comfort me..."

Roux leaned in to listen. Daniel's speech was muffled and indistinct, so the man brought his ear closer to Daniel's mouth.

Daniel drew in a ragged breath, then enunciated four words clearly in English.

"God save the King!"

It took Roux a moment to stand. Then he kicked Daniel's head. Daniel's vision swam and he blacked out.

* * *

For once Abigail was glad not to have a mirror. The dress she wore might have been green once, but now it was faded to an indistinct color. It hung on her like a sack, fitting only where it needed to for practicality rather than aesthetics. It might as well have been a nun's habit, except the National Assembly had banned ecclesiastical dress.

On the subject of personal vanity, most of her lustrous blonde hair lay on the catacomb floor and she was only now getting used to it. Abigail wondered whether Sister Carmella had taken perverse pleasure in wielding the shears.

Her fingers were sore from sewing. She pushed a needle through the small piece of fabric in her hands and narrowly missed her finger as she recalled the conversation.

"Have you raised children?" Sister Carmella had asked her. Abigail answered in the negative.

"Can you cook?"

Abigail answered no.

"Please tell me you can do something of use," the frustrated nun had demanded.

"I read and write English, French, and German. I play the pianoforte, the harpsichord, and the guitar. And I paint. I can also run a large household and throw outstanding parties."

"Parties and balls are in no demand at *Salpêtrière*. Neither are concert recitals. Can you at least sew?"

"Oh yes, I can do that too," Abigail had replied, and the older woman's face calmed.

"Then I can use you. The children's garments are always in need of repair. You will at least pretend to be a nun even though you do not look or behave like one."

Today was Abigail's fourth day at *Salpêtrière*. She boarded with the nuns who nursed the children in a complex as large as a town.

The nuns did their best to keep the children away from the insane, or the bad influence of the diseased and drunken prostitutes, but they weren't entirely successful. Some days the violence inside was worse than that outside on the Parisian streets.

On her first morning, Abigail had had to bodily block a drunkard from grabbing a child. On the second day, she had apprehended a prostitute instructing a ten-year-old how to pick a client's pocket.

The new regime resented the clergy, but grudgingly accepted no one worked harder and more diligently with the poor, infirm, and insane than they. The regime had stripped the Benedictine nuns of their habits, but not of their faith and mission.

Abigail rose with them for prayers early each morning, ignoring the looks of contempt cast their way by some of the ardent revolutionaries, and went to bed straight after evening prayers, her fingers and back aching.

Each new person she met, she asked the same question. "Do you know Marie Dubois?"

Each time the answer was a shake of the head.

This morning, she was assigned to the laundry, a long narrow room, open at each end. In the wall halfway along were two large fireplaces on which cauldrons of water were boiled for washing. Overhead, suspended on timber frames, were garments of various shapes and sizes, steaming as they dried by the sweltering heat of the fires.

Abigail sat on a bench at the far end of the room with a pile of dried and folded clothes beside her, repairing them the best she could. A squeal and the sound of a child bursting into tears came from the entrance to the laundry. Abigail paid it no heed until one of the nuns with a girl in tow stopped in front of her.

"Do you have anything for this child to wear, Sister? She was in a fight and you can see the neck of her tunic is ripped right down to the sleeve." The nun looked at the girl and shook her arm. "You're naughty and stubborn!" She looked back to Abigail. "She won't let me help her at all."

"What's her name?"

"Marie."

Hope stirred. Although it was a common enough name, Abigail judged the girl to be about the right age. She nodded and smiled at the child. The girl stared back with wide brown eyes.

"Leave her with me, Sister. We'll have her looking her best in no time, won't we?"

Both the nun and child returned expressions of disbelief.

When the nun was gone, Abigail smiled at the girl and put her sewing down. She sorted through the pile of repaired clothing and drew out a tunic, holding it up to the girl to judge its size.

It would be a little too large, like the dark blue cloak the child wore over her damaged dress, but it would meet the temporary need, something to wear while she quickly stitched the ripped garment. Abigail put her hand on the cloak collar to remove it and the girl shied away.

"I promise you can have your cloak and dress back, Marie, but I need to put something on you while I fix yours."

The girl shook her head vigorously and nut brown strands of hair escaped from her pony tail.

"Oh," Abigail said with a comical frown, "my friend will be very disappointed."

The girl tilted her head, curious as Abigail fished in the pocket of her dress. She pulled out the wooden doll.

"Poupette!" the child cried and reached out for it before suddenly remembering something and lowering her arms.

Abigail had seen similar reactions in children apparently favored over others. Being given a doll, even a crude one like "Poupette" would certainly mark Marie for jealous bullying. Children could be savage little beasts who taunted with fists as well as words. Her heart ached for this little girl who'd had everything taken away from her.

But she needed to be sure this was the little girl she had been searching for.

Abigail looked about at the two other nuns at the washbasins. They sang softly to themselves as they worked and paid her and the child no mind.

"This doll belongs to a special little girl," said Abigail.

"Her name is Marie," the girl responded.

"The doll or the little girl?"

"Yes."

Abigail swallowed a measure of frustration and forced a pleasant smile on her face. "If you give me your cloak and dress, you can hold poupette while I see to yours."

Marie considered the bargain and her gaze fell back to the doll. She nodded.

Abigail struggled to hide a smile, feeling elation at the win. She tugged the cloak and damaged tunic off the girl, slipped the replacement tunic over her head, and directed her to stand near the fire to stay warm.

The girl cradled the doll as Abigail considered how on earth she could confirm the child's identity without arousing suspicion. Moreover, how would she get the girl out of this place even if it *was* her?

Abigail examined the dress. Another tear at the back had been hidden by the coat. It was beyond repair, good for nothing but rags.

She called the child over and held up the tunic. "I'm sorry, I can't fix it," she said. "You'll have to keep the one you're wearing."

Hugging the doll, the child shrugged. "It wasn't mine anyway."

Abigail picked up the cloak to slip it back on the girl. As she did so, the hem swung out and she heard the sound of something solid hit the edge of the wooden bench.

The girl put a thumb in her mouth and watched as Abigail examined the garment. She felt something the size of a coin sewn into the fabric folds.

She sat and unpicked it quickly.

"Are you Marie Dubois?" she asked as casually as she could while concentrating on the task.

The girl did not answer the question.

"Jean bought that cloak for me. It's mine," she said instead, a note of apprehension in her voice.

Jean… John? Jonathan? Abigail pulled out the object. It wasn't a coin.

It was an eye-miniature—one of very fine quality, but it wasn't that which made Abigail's heart pound in her chest. It was that she recognized the subject.

It was Rachel Sawyer.

CHAPTER THIRTY-THREE

At the sound of someone else entering the laundry, Abigail started and dropped the miniature in her pocket. She looked up. Someone was talking to one of the nuns at the basins, then they turned and left.

Marie Dubois continued to stare at Abigail in silent accusation, suspecting her of wanting to steal her cloak. Abigail examined the garment further, inserting two fingers between the outer and the lining to see if anything else was secreted there.

She fished out a gentleman's white silk kerchief, out of place not only in the garment, but also in what the Dubois family might have owned. Abigail turned it over. It was covered in random letters of the alphabet written in pencil, utterly indecipherable. More telling, in the corner of the kerchief, were the embroidered initials JS.

"You said John bought this cloak for you?"

Marie nodded.

"I'm a friend of John's," Abigail told her as she stuffed the kerchief into her pocket alongside the miniature. "He asked me to look for you."

"He did? He made poupette for me too."

"Really? I'm here with another friend of John's."

"Rouquin?" she enquired, eyes lighting up.

Abigail laughed. She suspected Daniel had been teased aplenty about the color of his hair.

"He said a man with red hair was his friend," the girl continued, encouraged by having made an adult laugh.

"Well, he's my friend too."

Marie was a pretty little child when her features were animated in a smile. It occurred suddenly to Abigail that she had not seen any child smiling since she'd arrived in Paris, only eyeing strangers warily or, worse, just staring, gaze hollow and vacant.

Abigail retacked the hem of the cloak and secured it around Marie's shoulders. She considered her options. If Roux suspected Jonathan had smuggled a message, then the girl's life was in danger too. She had to get herself and Marie out immediately. But how? Rapidly Abigail measured, then discarded a number of options before deciding on one.

She grabbed a faded red dress from the clean laundry pile and another child's dress. "Marie, will you listen to me carefully?"

The child nodded gravely.

"We're going to play a game, and I will need you to copy everything I do. Will you do that?"

She nodded enthusiastically at the thought of a game. Abigail responded with a smile.

"Follow me!"

Marie slipped her hand into Abigail's. She was touched by the girl's trust and folded her much larger hand over hers. They left the laundry together and avoided some of the most populated sectors of the hospital. The bell for the noon meal rang and those who were ambulatory made their way to the refectory. The courtyard closest to the gate was largely empty when a voice called out.

A harried looking man in his forties confronted them.

"Sister, where are you taking this child?"

"She has scabies, doctor."

"I have scabies," Marie dutifully repeated.

Abigail shifted the bundle of clothes under her arm and started scratching her forearm. Marie copied and the doctor stepped back.

"These clothes have to be burned and the girl needs a disinfectant bath."

Marie tugged on her arm. "I don't need a bath."

Abigail turned to her and raised an eyebrow in admonishment, then started scratching the other arm. Marie remembered the game and copied the action.

"I have scabies," she told the doctor gravely.

The man looked back to Abigail who tried her best to look like a nun.

"Then what are you waiting here for? Get that girl seen to before she infects the entire block!"

Abigail bowed and hurried Marie along with her, the child trying to bow too as she ran along.

Between two buildings, Abigail took off her plain dress and cap, and put on the purloined dress. It was slightly too small. Her bust strained the fabric and it was a tight fit to the waist. What's more, the hem fell some inches above the ankle.

From a nun to a prostitute. If their situation wasn't so serious, Abigail would have laughed.

* * *

"What day is it today?" Daniel asked hoarsely,

The orderly who'd brought in his meal for the day—a weak, almost flavorless broth—answered, "Primevere."

"Pardon?"

The young man looked at him. "Primevere, the first day of Germinal."

"Germinating Primrose"—what? Daniel shook his head and regretted the move. Blood pounded in his temples, and his neck hurt. He tried again. "When's the new moon?"

"Ah…ten days time, citizen. That would be…" the man concentrated hard, obviously reciting something under his breath, trying to remember how to get to the name of the day. "Couvoir."

"Right, I'll remember," Daniel said with a sigh. "Ten days after *primrose* is *hatchery*."

The orderly nodded.

Of all the idiotic things the republicans had done, establishing a ten day week and giving every day of the year its own name had to be top of the list, Daniel concluded.

Five days had passed since he had been placed in this cell. He was relatively sure of that, although sometimes, for hours at a time, his mind had wandered aimlessly during which he was filled with an overwhelming ennui that seemed to run counter to the urgency of his situation.

The daily laudanum doses had continued and, to an extent, he was grateful for it. The bitter drug eased the pain from the first day's beating and from the spasming cramps caused by being bound within the chemise de force. But he itched all over and couldn't scratch. It was driving him crazy.

At least he hadn't been beaten again, at least not seriously, and Daniel took his blessings where he could. One of the orderlies liked to punctuate delivery of the meal with a slap across the side of his head, but that was nothing, and the young orderly who had brought today's broth was fairly pleasant.

The man stood back and looked on as Daniel got down on his knees and leaned over to consume the broth from the bowl like a dog at its dish. As the warmth filled his stomach, Daniel wondered, not for the first time, how much longer Roux would keep him here before his usefulness was deemed over.

The light from the open door dimmed again and Daniel, looking up, identified the shadow. He struggled to his feet, soup dripping from his stubbled chin.

"'Speak of the devil and he shall appear.'"

"This is the Republic, Ridgeway, we don't believe in superstitious nonsense," Roux drawled as he stepped into the cell. He swept a rather fine cloak in front of him and sat on a stool which had appeared in the cell on the second day. "But it is you who rather bedevils me, if you may allow me to say."

Daniel closed his eyes for a moment, mustering his concentration. "How so?"

"You ask me of the fate of the Dubois family and then, just one day ago—poof!" The man waved his hands like a magician. "The little girl disappears from *Salpêtrière*."

Daniel hid his surprise behind a jest. "You must really believe me the devil if you think I can leave this cell, travel five miles to take a child, and return to my nice cozy jacket without detection."

Within the confines of the garment, Daniel flexed and unflexed his fists. He lamented, oh dear God, Abigail, what the hell do you think you're doing?

As though he could read Daniel's mind, Roux continued, though his reference was to Daniel's spoken words.

"I thought the same thing." Roux smiled. "'How would I do it?' I asked myself. Then an answer came. An accomplice. A beautiful blonde accomplice."

Daniel said nothing. His shoulders ached from the tension and the confines of the jacket, but he worked the muscles the best he could.

"I think I'm through with playing the gentleman," stated Roux. He stood and stretched. "My men are looking all over Paris for her. I've made it clear they can have their amusement with her as long as she's still alive when they bring her to me."

Roux stepped closer. "I may extend an act of kindness and let you see her one more time before you watch that pretty little head severed from her shoulders. I guarantee it will be the last memory you have before you meet the same fate."

Daniel fought the words from taking root in his mind and painting pictures of a barbaric fate for Abigail. His every instinct wanted him to launch himself at the man. He dropped his chin and forced air into his lungs in one huge effort to calm himself.

Roux had paused, watching the reactions of his captive carefully. He continued, "I could change that arrangement, of course. Not for you—your fate, I'm afraid to say, is sealed, but I could let the woman live. As long as I am the one to reach her first and not my men. Just tell me where she is and I will spare her."

Daniel muttered under his breath, and Roux stepped forward to hear.

"What did you say?"

Daniel raised his head and muttered indistinctly once more. Roux moved even closer.

"Speak up man!" he demanded, thrusting his face at Daniel's.

Daniel grinned, then slammed his forehead into the Frenchman's nose.

"I said, 'go to hell,'" Daniel told him as Roux staggered back and his two guards rushed in.

The men laid into him, but, through the pain of the savage beating, shortly before he lost consciousness, Daniel felt the warm satisfaction of seeing Roux clutching his face, blood streaming from behind his hand and dripping on his fancy cloak.

* * *

"It has to be tomorrow," Abigail avowed. "Once they discover the child is missing, they will look for her and have no reason to keep Daniel alive."

She glanced over to where young Marie Dubois slept peacefully on a thin pallet by the fireplace in the catacombs.

Then she looked down at her hand where Daniel's signet ring sat on her third finger. She closed her eyes and said a quick prayer. She would fight heaven and earth to save him, but even she was forced to admit it would take nothing short of a miracle to do so.

Jean-Baptiste and Sister Carmella were among the small group in the chamber. One of the men had just confirmed Daniel was being held in the asylum at Bicetre. Abigail rose and tore open the hems of the cloaks she had brought with her, extracting the belt of coins. She held it up.

"How much will it take to bribe the guards?"

"Abigail, you're asking us to risk too much," Jean-Baptiste warned.

She looked at him sharply, then looked away and swallowed, forcing sharp words back down. She tried humility instead. "You're right. I apologize. I've asked too much already. You are aiding foreign spies and just what you have done so far puts you under sentence of death."

She folded the belt of coins into her pocket and dusted down her skirt.

"But I will not abandon Daniel," she added, blinking back tears. "I will go and get him myself…"

In the awkward silence that followed her declaration, Abigail watched the grim faces before her flicker in their resolve and heads drop. She felt ill to the pit of her stomach and a chill ran through her veins. She would ask no more from these generous people. They were right—to risk the lives of hundreds, possibly thousands of men, women, and children in the eglise sous terre was too high a price to effect what was likely a doomed rescue attempt.

The silence lasted but a moment. "I'll go to Bicetre with you, madame."

Abigail turned and a young man stood beside her. She recognized him as the one who had "liberated" the communion cup a week earlier.

"Are you certain, Georges?" asked Jean-Baptiste.

"Yes, I am. Why not? I know Bicetre after all, I work there. I know where the cells are and I am not afraid to die. I'll be a martyr like Saint Stephen."

Abigail hugged George and he blushed at her profuse thanks.

"Then that is settled," agreed Sister Carmella. "If you are successful, we can get you as far as the River. Then you can leave at nightfall and drift downstream until you're in the countryside."

* * *

They had had to crawl the last hundred yards before emerging from the partly collapsed adit, but it had been necessary to leave the city that way without a pass or useable identity papers for Abigail.

"Where are we?" she asked.

"Ivry. Bicetre's this way," he replied and led on.

What remained of Abigail's shorn blonde hair was hidden beneath a red Phrygian cap. She was dressed as a young revolutionary patriot and accompanied Georges, dressed in exactly the same garb, to the gate of the large facility in the late afternoon sunshine. She followed him through to the left wing of the structure.

"This is one of the oldest sections; it was built on top of the Bishop's manor," he told her as they walked through the rabbit warren of corridors. "I know of a disused passageway. I think it used to be part of the sewer system, but it hasn't been used in over a century."

Abigail wrinkled her nose at the prospect. Oh, if only Lady Jane Ashford could see her now...

"Then, as agreed," she said, "I keep watch on the superintendant on that floor while you find which cell Daniel is being held in. You let me know and then you leave."

George scuffed his boots in silent disapproval.

"I mean it," she warned, "you leave. It's all our heads if this goes badly."

The young man grumbled his assent.

They made their way to the second floor without difficulty. Abigail wielded a broom while Georges carried a bucket of water and a mop. He called her to a halt outside a small, doorless room, little more than an alcove off the main passageway. Crowded into the space was a small desk and a large man.

"Hallo, Citizen Albert," said Georges, stepping forward.

"Huh?" the florid-faced old supervisor grunted, looking up. "What are you doing here?"

"This is my cousin," Georges replied, nodding back at Abigail. "He came in from the country. I spoke to Russert and he said it was all right for him to follow me around so I can show him how to do things."

The man squinted at Abigail through his thick glasses. She kept her head down.

"Looks like a strong breeze could knock him over," Albert said to Georges, letting out a large belch.

"He's stronger than he looks," Georges assured him.

Abigail nodded in agreement, and Georges stepped back and put down the mop and bucket.

"Mop here and up along there," Georges instructed her loudly for the supervisor's benefit, then added in whisper, "Told you he was blind as bat."

He took the broom and walked off down the passageway, disappearing down the steps where it turned left. Abigail started mopping the floor outside the alcove. The man watched for a moment and lost interest. He sat back in his chair and almost immediately started to nod off.

The mopping took Abigail further and further down the passageway. As she went, she glanced back every now and then to see if the supervisor had emerged. He didn't.

She was nearly two-thirds of the way along to the turn when Georges returned.

"I've found him in the third cell down. I think it's him anyway, I went all the way along and he's the only one with red hair," he whispered. "I only looked through the hatch. The door is locked. Albert has the keys on his desk."

"Will anyone miss him if he went missing from his post?"

Georges shrugged.

Abigail pulled out her knife. The lad's eyes widened.

"Get out of here," she hissed.

"No. I will not."

"I don't have time to argue with you."

"You kill him and no one gets out of here alive."

Abigail closed her eyes, sighing with impatience. She opened them to find Georges nervous, but resolute, brandishing the broom across his chest like a soldier carrying a musket into battle.

"Then how do we get the keys?"

Georges grinned and drew Abigail back down to the supervisor's tiny room, peering around the corner.

"He sleeps very soundly," whispered Georges, "especially after his lunchtime meal. See the bottle of brandy?"

Visible beneath the desk, it sat by his feet, three-quarters empty. Abigail nodded and George stealthily moved forward and lifted the keys from the desk without a sound while the superintendent slumbered on. He and Abigail hurried back along the passage and down to the third cell.

Abigail looked at the heavy timber door.

"Keep watch at the stairs," Abigail instructed as she unlocked the door and handed the keys back to Georges. He went and stood at the steps.

Abigail pushed the door slowly to avoid making a sound. The stench is the room assaulted her as she stepped inside.

The muscular figure of a man lay on his side facing away from the door in the middle of the room. He had red hair and appeared to be trussed up in some assortment of canvas and leather straps.

"Daniel?" she whispered.

The man scrambled awkwardly to his knees and faced her.

She was unable to hide her dismay at his battered face, but it was Daniel and, after a moment's expression of surprise, he grinned widely.

"It's a good job my arms are restrained, Abigail, because I don't know whether to hug you or throttle you."

Chapter Thirty-Four

Abigail examined the odd garment which bound Daniel's arms across his chest. He turned around. "Get the straps undone quickly, Abigail. Roux's an unpredictable visitor."

Daniel grunted as she tugged at the straps and buckles, and groaned out loud when his arms were finally released and he worked his cramped shoulders, shaking the chemise de force off onto the floor. He stank, but, even so, nothing could smell sweeter to Abigail. They embraced for a brief but intense kiss before emerging from the cell.

Georges waved them along to the steps. Daniel shuffled painfully and accepted Abigail's support. Georges went ahead and poked his head around the corner of the alcove where Albert lolled back in his chair, snoring violently. They slipped past and began to hurry. The light through the windows cast deep purple shadows.

They rounded a corner and hastened down another passage, then Georges came to an abrupt halt, pointing to a small cupboard door in the wall, just large enough for a man to squeeze through. He opened it and there was nothing but darkness within.

"We're over the old manor. There is a six-foot drop down to a passage about three feet inside here. The passage zigzags to a small opening outside the wall."

Daniel squeezed in first, found the ledge and dropped down, groaning softly. It was almost pitch dark. Abigail could barely make out Daniel lifting up his arms to help her down. When Georges clambered in and pulled the cupboard door closed behind him, the darkness was complete.

Together, they felt their way along the rough stone walls. By the time they reached the outside, pushing through grass that overgrew the exit, the last of the daylight was vanishing.

Georges led them back to the adit from which he and Abigail had emerged earlier and shoved a small satchel at them. "Here, it's clothing and some food. You remember where the fallen ceiling began? Someone will be waiting near there to guide you back through the tunnels. Bon chance, *mes amis*, you give every decent Frenchmen hope we can be truly free of tyranny."

Daniel shook the young man's hand and thanked him.

"What about you?" Abigail asked. "When they find Daniel gone, the old drunk will point the finger at you."

"I'm not going back," he replied. "Two nights ago, the population of Vendee started fighting back against these godless Republicans. I'm going to fight the revolutionaries with our Catholic brothers there. We're going to take back our country for *Dieu et Le Roi*."

"Does Jean-Baptiste know?"

"I didn't tell him. He wouldn't approve. But he is a priest or nearly so—it's not for him to sanction war. *Bon chance* and Godspeed, my friends!"

Georges slipped away into the increasing gloom and Daniel and Abigail crawled into the adit. It was so cramped, Abigail feared at first that Daniel would not fit, but he squeezed through.

It was black inside and difficult to crawl over the rubble that had apparently fallen from the roof. When it widened out, there was no sign of an escort, just blackness and the sound of dripping water.

"Daniel?" she asked softly, knowing he was near because she could also hear him breathing. Before he had time to answer, Abigail suddenly sensed rather than saw a diffuse grayness relieving the inky black beside her and was unable to stifle a gasp as a pale face loomed out of it. The ghostly appearance of the youth's visage was heightened by the fact he held his shuttered lamp below his face.

"Follow me."

* * *

Their taciturn escort took them as far as the catacomb chamber and disappeared silently the way he had come. A nervous Jean Baptiste awaited them in the centre of the chamber. He sat upon a three-legged stool with a lantern beside it.

"Where's Georges?" he asked immediately, getting to his feet.

Abigail relayed the young man's message, and the seminarian grimaced.

"I fear for that young man," he said, shaking his head. "'He who lives by the sword will die by the sword.'"

He looked at Daniel who had already collapsed onto the vacated stool, exhausted. One eye showed evidence of being blackened and there was an ugly cut on his cheekbone. Under the stubble of nearly a week's growth, his chin sported an angry bruise and several grazes.

"It's clear you are in no condition to go anywhere tonight, and there is rain expected," said Jean Baptiste. "You will need to stay here for at least another day. Our eglise sous terre committee has decided to move you further underground. It is no longer safe to be using this section."

Jean-Baptiste picked up the lantern, the only source of light. Abigail glanced quickly into the chamber where they were wed. It was empty. Even the coal and ash of fires past had been cleared away.

"Bring the stool," he called back as he headed for a passage. Daniel did not object to Abigail helping him to his feet and picking up the seat. They followed Jean-Baptiste.

Their refuge was foreboding now that it was no longer lit by regular lanterns, and the narrow twisting passageways added to the claustrophobia. They passed through one section and into an open chamber. Four men waited beside a pile of limestone blocks and, immediately as the three passed, they began hefting the blocks.

"They're walling off that section. They will make it two layers thick, just be sure," Jean-Baptiste informed them.

After nearly a mile further on foot, the passage opened out into another chamber which glowed with flickering light. The altar had been set up; the white tablecloth and silver gilt table crucifix glittered in the torch light. A candelabra filled with votive candles burned in one corner.

In a rare show of emotion, Sister Carmella rushed up to Abigail and kissed her on both cheeks.

"Marie? Is she safe?" Abigail asked.

"She is," Sister Carmella confirmed. "She went to sleep an hour ago, clutching her doll. She would not let it out of her sight. She kept asking after you and rouquin."

She looked at Daniel's hair, but was unaffected by the evidence of his beatings; perhaps she had seen worse. "When Marie wakes, I will tell her you've both returned safe."

Abigail turned to Daniel. The poor man looked dead on his feet. He needed a wash and a decent sleep. He wore a questioning expression, but the answers to anything he wanted to know could wait.

Abigail stroked his face to reassure herself he was real, then dropped her hand to take his.

"I found the girl from where Jonathan stayed. He hid some kind of cipher in the lining of her coat."

Daniel closed his eyes, nodded, and then swayed, remaining upright only with the aid of Abigail and Jean-Baptiste.

"We've prepared somewhere for you to sleep. It's not much, but it is private," said Jean-Baptiste.

He helped walk Daniel up a flight of roughly hewn stone steps and through a door. They were in a basement.

"Some good friends of ours own a shop above, but tomorrow is *decadi* so it will be closed. The Good Lord decreed men must work six days before they may rest. The Secularists and the new calendar demand we toil for an extra three days before our respite." Jena-Baptiste shook his head ruefully. "Someone will be back in the morning to give you some breakfast. You will need to decide what to do with Marie. Sleep well my friends."

Jean-Baptiste left through the door that led back into the catacombs.

A bedroom of a fashion had been made in one corner of the room—a straw-filled mattress on an old bedstead, with wooden crates stacked around forming makeshift walls.

The wooden floor and paneled walls reflected warmth and comfort in the yellow glow from the lamplight. At the other end of the room was a coal-burning stove radiating heat. On it, a large kettle released tendrils of steam.

Food and a bottle of wine stood on a small table set with a pair of mismatched chairs, and Abigail was surprised to look behind a three-panel screen and find a stone sink set in the wall and a beaten copper hip bath.

"Eat, bathe, or sleep?" she asked as she surveyed their accommodation.

"Yes," Daniel replied from the table where he slumped with his head in his hands.

"That's not very helpful."

Daniel forced his eyelids open slightly and grinned tiredly at her.

"Kiss first?" he suggested.

"Hmm," she said, wrinkling her nose. "Considering the way you smell, perhaps a bath first, and I can check on your injuries. Or perhaps you'd like to sleep first, but—"

"Stop."

"—if you bathe I can also prepare our supper, then I can tell you about the cipher and perhaps we can work out how…"

The end of the sentence trailed away as Daniel rose and took hold of her arms firmly.

"Stop for a moment," he said. "You've probably been existing on little more than fear and excitement for the past five days and you need to stop. Catch a breath, otherwise this is all going to come crashing down on you like a landslide and we're not out of the woods yet."

Abigail blinked at him, then frowned. There was too much left to do and not enough time to do it.

"Remember in Bath, the night I approached you with your assignment?"

Abigail frowned deeper.

"I told you in our business, we take opportunities where we find them. That also includes the opportunity for rest. I'm here and I'm safe. You are here and you are safe. At this moment in time, nothing else matters. Don't worry about tomorrow. Don't even worry about the next hour."

Then his voice became low and husky. "Just be here *now*, with me."

"But your injuries—"

"—are just bumps and bruises in the scheme of things."

"I worry about you," she said softly, emotion close to the surface.

His hand left her arm and he stroked her hair tenderly and then rubbed gentle circles on her left temple. Abigail closed her eyes. His other hand found the other temple and treated it the same.

Abigail sighed and closed her eyes.

"I worry about you too, my love," he whispered. "I worry about what is going on up there on the streets. I worry about what is going on in that lovely head of yours. You are brave and fearless, but I know there is a limit; there is one in all of us. I know what it is like to go to that limit. And I've seen men go beyond, and come back broken in spirit. I never want that for you."

Tears leaked from her closed lids. He kissed one, then the other.

"There are things in our lives we cannot control, but if my life has taught me anything, we find control when we finally let go."

It seemed an age before Abigail finally opened her eyes. She lay her head against Daniel's chest. Daniel's arms around her were not there to hem her in, but to protect her, to make her feel safe.

And they did.

The tears that she shed had seemed to have lightened the load of years. A peace had settled, quiet and contemplative. Abigail looked up into his eyes, bright and shining despite the dark shadow around one of them. She saw the remains of tears no longer held back. He gave her a small smile before glancing at the stove where the steel kettle steamed vigorously.

They broke their embrace and, with quiet efficiency, Daniel bucketed several gallons of water from a barrel into the hip bath. Abigail added the contents of the kettle and alluring curls of steam beckoned them both.

"It's a pity it's too small for the both of us," he suggested.

"You bathe first. Jean-Baptiste left a razor and some other things over here. I'll wash while you shave," she said.

Abigail watched Daniel undress. Perhaps it was leisurely, or perhaps his arm and back muscles, confined too long in one position, made the act of disrobing difficult. He did not ask for help and she did not offer it this time.

Even by lamplight, the bruises on his back were livid and prominent, but she no longer saw them, rather noting the strength of his muscles along his shoulders, his back, then lower, to his buttocks, his thighs, his calves as he climbed into the tub.

He sluiced water down his down his back, and she studied him once more. She prepared his shave, using the brush to foam up the soap. When she turned to him, he was seated in the tub, watching her.

"Lie back," she whispered. "Let me shave you."

Daniel did so, baring his neck for her. She could see his pulse beat steadily and Abigail felt an answering call of her own. The draw of the straight blade razor was like a caress as she scraped away his week-old beard. The skin beneath it was smooth. The bruises were less severe than she feared.

She finished the task, and Daniel stood once more and faced her. He took the soap from her hand and washed himself, across his chest, along and under his arms, then down to where evidence of desire for her was beginning to stir to life.

Abigail understood what he was telling her without words. He was showing her he was real and whole, solid and strong, and *hers*. She reached out to touch him, but he intercepted her hand and kissed it.

"You next."

She undressed as he did, removing the tunic and breeches she wore as her disguise. She removed her red cap.

"Your hair..." he said.

"...will grow back," she assured him.

Daniel offered his hand as Abigail stepped over the side of the tub. He changed places with her.

She stood nude in the still warm water, enjoying its feel around her calves. Daniel scooped a bowl of water and drizzled it over her shoulders and her breasts. One side, then the other. Rosy pink nipples puckered under the sensation. She accepted the soap from him and ran it over her limbs, across her breasts, down the junction of her thighs.

Even the cloth wrapped around his waist could not disguise his desire for her and it caused hers to ignite. She enjoyed the longing she saw in his warm blue eyes and the desire that increased as she touched herself. Then it became less about bathing and more about the sensuous feeling it aroused in herself as well as him.

Daniel took her hand, this time kissing each finger in turn, running his tongue up and down each length. She needed him. Abigail needed to feel him in her and the thought of it stirred her more.

The need was vocalized in a groan and an answering chuckle was returned.

Daniel moved behind her and pulled her back to his chest. As one hand caressed and stroked her breasts, another hand moved lower and began stroking the silky curls between her legs. She rubbed restlessly against him where his erection nestled between her buttocks.

Daniel's fingers found her core and he circled it with his thumb. She bloomed under his hand. Abigail pressed her weight into his chest, to help her stay upright as his fingers played with her folds.

Arousal surged though her restlessly and she could feel the peak of her desire approaching. The beginning of a keening wail started in her throat as he brought her to the summit.

"Shhhh," Daniel advised as he placed one hand over her mouth even while he continued touching her, his actions faster in response to her own.

He kissed her neck, nipping slightly, then soothing with his tongue. Abigail was grateful for his hand over her mouth as her orgasm came crashing over her in waves.

Daniel released her, taking care she could stand without aid before wrapping her in another cloth, tucking it in around her breasts, and lifting her from the tub. She rubbed against him restlessly as he swept his arms up her back, her neck, and through her hair as he kissed her. Abigail's mouth received him eagerly, their tongues touching and tasting each other.

Her fingers left his hair and flirted with the edge of his towel and loosened it. "Now," she informed him. She steered him to the bed and shoved his shoulders. He acquiesced by falling onto the bed. He threaded his fingers and placed them behind his head.

Oh dear Lord, he was magnificent! Abigail no longer saw his injuries. Her eyes feasted on him as she removed her own towel. She straddled him and reached to kiss him on the lips. She stretched herself over him, so they touched skin to skin.

Her legs slipped to either side of him, and she positioned herself over him, then lowered herself inch by inch until she had covered him completely.

Daniel groaned. He pulled himself up just far enough to cup the back of her head and bring her down for another kiss. He thrust up as she squeezed, and the sound of their moans were captured in the seal of their lips.

Abigail moved up along his length and then back down, savoring the feel of his hands as they now cupped her breasts. Then the urgency came and she moved rapidly. Daniel's hands slid up her thighs to the junction of her legs. Deft fingers brought her to her peak once more. Then he stilled her hips with his hands and she savored the sensation of him moving in her with thrusts increasingly erratic as his own pleasure overtook him.

Later, they sated their hunger for food as they had sated their hunger for one another. They lay in bed, his arms around her. Daniel's arms slid down hers, his fingers caressed her fingers then played with the ring she wore on her left hand.

He kissed her hair and she responded sleepily.

"I'm looking forward to going home with my wife," he whispered.

CHAPTER THIRTY-FIVE

The next morning Daniel and Abigail were down in the catacombs again. No sooner had they walked into the chamber than Marie rushed up and threw her arms around her, hugging tightly.

"You're back! You didn't leave me like maman!"

Abigail responded with a kiss to the top of the child's head and a gentle hug.

Abigail looked at Sister Carmella whose expression was tight. She thought she understood the woman better now. How could one go on hearing the same story again and again from so many children and not create an emotional bulwark against the pain?

Abigail stroked the girl's hair softly. "I promise I will never leave you, Marie," she said, not knowing if the promise was hers to make. With an arm around the child's shoulder, Abigail turned Marie to face Daniel who stood beside them.

As the little girl's eyes rose higher, she saw the color of his hair and clapped.

"Rouquin! What Jean said was true, you do have red hair!"

"Marie," Abigail began gravely. "This is Daniel. He was John's very good friend and has been very sad that he went away."

The little girl pushed forward and hugged Daniel around his legs.

"He was my friend too," she told him.

"Can we talk about John?" he asked.

Marie nodded. "He gave me poupette." She held out the doll for him to inspect which Daniel dutifully did before handing it back to her.

Gently, they asked her about Jonathan. When he had given her the cloak? Did she know he had put something special inside it?

"He put in a picture of a pretty lady for good luck," she said.

Abigail had left the miniature with Sister Carmella for safekeeping. She passed it to Abigail now, and Abigail in turn passed it to Daniel. He looked at it for a moment before putting it in his pocket.

"Jonathan must have known he wouldn't be returning," he said softly.

"Marie, shall we make a new dress for your poupette?" invited Sister Carmella, holding out her hand. Marie allowed herself to be drawn away to a corner of the chamber where another plainly dressed young woman, clearly another nun, was entertaining some of the other children. But as she went, she looked back, unwilling to take her eyes off Abigail and Daniel.

They sat and laid out the silk kerchief with its indecipherable series of letters.

"Can you make anything of them?"

Daniel studied them closely and was silent for several minutes, looking at the lines several times over.

"They are words, that much is certain, you can see how these symbols repeat," he said after some time. "It's not a code I recognize though. We used several, but this isn't one of them."

"Do you mean this is of no use at all?"

Daniel flashed her a smile. "If it's no good to us, it is no good to Roux and the Republicans either. But I can't imagine Jonathan wouldn't have left a break code clue. Are you sure there was nothing else in her cloak?"

"I looked thoroughly."

"What about the dress she was wearing?"

Abigail's stomach fell. "It was threadbare and torn; I didn't think to keep it. I'm sorry."

"No, you're probably right," he agreed. "It could be Jonathan had it on him when he was taken or Roux has it and doesn't know what he possesses."

Abigail tugged at Daniel's arm and nodded to Marie who was dressing her doll in a new dress quickly fashioned from a small square of cloth by the young nun.

"We can't leave Marie here," Abigail whispered. "Roux may be looking for her as well."

"He is. He told me—"

"—And that orphanage, Daniel. It's no place for a child. France is at war with itself and that's bad enough. How long before there's a wider war, maybe an occupying army right here in Paris—the Spanish, the Austrians—even our forces?" she continued urgently. "It will only be worse. We have to take her with us."

Daniel looked at the child for a long moment and bowed his head. Abigail waited expectantly, uncurling her fingers from her skirts.

"Do you appreciate how much additional danger taking her with us brings?" he eventually said. "Her presence adds an extra day to our journey at a minimum. On top of which, we don't have papers for her. It's all over the first time we're stopped at a checkpoint. And have you given any thought to what happens if we make it back to England? Do you want to put her in an orphanage there?"

"No..."

"Then what? Keep her? You'll be that child's mother. Are you ready for that responsibility?"

Abigail swallowed bitterly. Daniel was right. She had allowed sentiment to rule her head. She hadn't thought it through, hadn't considered anything beyond her pity for Marie who had lost her mother and father...

"You'll be that child's mother."

She looked at the girl as the full weight of the thought occurred to her.

A child's mother.

"Your answer, Abigail," Daniel pressed, "because we only have a few hours to prepare."

There was something in his tone of voice that made her look up. His expression was unreadable. Hers apparently was not.

He cupped her cheek. "If you're prepared to take the risk, then so am I."

Abigail threw herself into Daniel's arms and hugged him.

"Jean-Baptiste!" he called, his arms still around Abigail. "We need to forge marriage and birth certificates for the Perret family. Mother, father, and daughter."

The seminarian grinned, then crossed himself.

"I'm going to pretend I didn't hear anything about forgery, *mon ami*," he said, "but it just happens to have crossed my mind that I should introduce you to a friend of mine. That is if you can tear yourself away from your wife and daughter."

Daniel kissed Abigail on the cheek, then approached Marie who played with the other children.

He knelt down, catching her eye. The girl sat up from her play and touched his hair.

"It's soft," she said in quiet surprise.

Abigail saw Daniel's tender smile and her heart melted also. He glanced up and beckoned her to join him.

"Marie, Abigail and I would like to you come on an adventure with us," he said. "We'll go for a ride on a horse and cart and then we'll go for a ride on a boat!"

The child's eyes lit up momentarily, then the spark disappeared.

"Won't maman and papa be worried? They've been gone so long, they won't know where I am."

Abigail drew in a deep breath to quell the painful response that stirred in her breast. Did Marie not know her parents were dead?

It was highly unlikely she had never seen a dead person. Abigail herself had been only a few years younger than Marie when her mother died and she had seen her laid out in the drawing room as though asleep while mourners called to pay their respects. Still, a death from pneumonia was hardly the same as death by hanging…

Had Marie witnessed that atrocity too? Abigail prayed it was not so.

"You parents know where you are…" Abigail began.

"How?" the girl asked plaintively. "Why don't they come for me?"

The young nun answered. "They're with the angels in heaven. Remember when you asked Sister Carmella yesterday?"

The girl cocked her head, recalled, and nodded.

"They're with Jesus and they're looking down on me always," she said, obviously repeating the sister's words.

"Well, John sent us to look after you," said Daniel.

"Is he in heaven too?" Marie asked gravely.

Abigail watched Daniel swallow the response, "Yes, Marie, he is."

* * *

Daniel departed with Jean-Baptiste, taking most of their money. The forged documents would not be cheap. Abigail, at risk of losing track of time in the constant lamp-lit world of the catacombs, busied herself preparing only essentials to take with them.

It would be only as much as she and Daniel could carry, and Marie too would need to share the load. Three satchels would be required for their clothes and cooking equipment. They would need two canteens and a bag with flints and a small amount of kindling, plus another small bag with whatever provisions they could carry on foot. Marie also needed sturdy shoes.

Sister Carmella arranged the goods, mostly from their stockpile, and shoes by swapping Marie's with those worn by another child.

If they had to venture into a town or village en route, the few coins that remained would be needed for bribery as well as bargaining for food. Abigail was under no illusion that their escape from France would be as easy as their entry.

Later, Abigail and young Sister Josephine made a game with Marie. A big game of pretend for their grand adventure. Marie would make believe Daniel and Abigail were her maman and papa. If anyone asked where they were going, she would say they were visiting her cousins in Boulogne. The girl was quick-witted and had already proved herself with the mimic game at *Salpêtrière*. It didn't take much practice for her to be perfect.

Daniel returned some hours later. He urged Abigail away from Marie who, having earlier complained of tiredness, had fallen into a deep sleep.

"The streets are teeming with soldiers," Daniel told her.

Jean-Baptiste and a gruff, bewhiskered older man, introduced to her as Louis, confirmed the report with a nod.

"Is the whole city is looking for us?" Abigail asked with alarm.

"Don't flatter yourself," said the older man with a sardonic laugh. "The National Assembly is sending more troops to the north to fight the Austrians, that's why. There are rumors they will call a mass conscription within months. I'm not looking forward to army life at my age.

"Still, all the soldiers on the streets may be good for our purposes tonight. Colonel Roux will only have a limited number of men at his disposal, and with the troops leaving the city, there will be a lot of other people out as well."

He spread a map across the table and placed a lamp beside it. "They are likely to take the main road north through Beauvais," he said, tracing the route with his finger. "There are also troops heading south to stop the rebellion in Vendee…"

At mention of the province, Abigail thought of Georges and silently prayed he would be safe.

"…so the best and fastest way for you to travel," continued Louis, "is west, down the Seine by boat." He looked up at Daniel. "I would not risk going as far as Rouen. The navy is there. Get off at Bonierres-sur-Seine or maybe Les Andelys or La Roquette. Then you must find your own way north to Calais."

Daniel stared at the map for some time as though committing it to memory. "When do we depart?" he asked.

"There will be a disruption to the changing of the guard because of the troops leaving the city," said Louis. "We'll take advantage of it. That leaves us eight hours. I suggest your family gets some sleep, you will have a long night ahead.

* * *

As Abigail lay down next to Marie and pulled a blanket up over them both, she wondered how she would be able to sleep, but in the darkness of the catacombs, listening to Daniel in discussion with the two Frenchmen, she closed her eyes.

Then she found herself being gently shaken awake.

"It's time?" she asked.

Daniel nodded.

By the glow of the lamplight, she could see he had shaved and was dressed as a sans-coulette fisherman. His cap was black wool.

"Have you slept?" she enquired.

Daniel nodded. Abigail frowned. Then he shrugged. "Some. Marie woke an hour ago. I told her to let you rest."

Abigail dressed as a peasant woman and hid her hair once more beneath a bonnet. Marie was dressed in plain but warm clothes with poupette in her hand.

Jean-Baptiste greeted them in the large chamber, along with Sisters Carmella and Josephine. Louis stood aside with their packs.

"May God bless and keep you safe," said Jean-Baptiste.

The two nuns hugged Abigail and Marie for the last time, and Josephine presented the child with a gift, a new dress for poupette made from soft pink silk that had probably been a kerchief before the Revolution.

The travelers donned their satchels and went out into the Paris night through the rear door of the shop where Abigail and Daniel had spent the previous night.

Although midnight, the streets were crowded. They followed a group of civilians down the avenue toward the sound of martial music.

Marie clung to Abigail's legs before Daniel picked her up in his arms. The girl buried her head in his shoulder, demonstrably afraid of the crowds.

Who knew what meaning they had for her, wondered Abigail.

The old man took turnings left and right, and the crowds thinned out. Soon, they approached the banks of the Seine. A river-going galiote stood at a mooring. It was a much bigger boat than Abigail had expected, but on closer inspection, it appeared barely seaworthy.

"Do you know how to sail one of these things, boy?" Louis half-grunted at Daniel.

Daniel nodded.

"Good, because I don't have time to show you. Don't raise the sail until you're well out of the city. Let the current take you, and beware of the sand banks. If you are challenged, you're carrying cases of burgundy to sell. There are three crates."

"That's very generous of you, Louis," said Abigail.

"Not my wine, not my boat. You paid for it."

He gave Abigail a glance and spat forcefully to the ground.

"Never did I think I'd live to see the day I'd be helping *les goddams*." He spat again. "Then again, I never thought I'd see Frenchmen fighting one another."

CHAPTER THIRTY-SIX

"**D**id you know goats can stare for ages and ages?" Marie asked Abigail. Abigail took the challenge and stared back at the animal.

She was as surprised as anyone when, on the second morning after leaving Paris, the goat appeared. It stood on its hind legs and shoved its nose into the boat as they sat at anchor on the riverbank where they decided to spend the night.

It was a good two minutes before the goat bleated and trotted a few yards away.

"I won, it lost!" said Abigail triumphantly.

"Not it—*she!*" laughed Marie, helpfully pointed out the animal's udder as it swayed, full and pendulous. "And she only gave up because she needs milking."

Abigail had done many things in her life—danced with Continental royalty, joined the hunt with the Prince of Wales, cheated at cards, romanced the best of the Beau Monde and, now, spied for England.

One thing she had never done was milk a goat.

"Cafe au lait for breakfast?" Daniel had enthused.

And not unreasonably too. Their provisions needed carefully rationing and there was no other fresh milk today. Nonetheless, they had made good time on their first day of travel downstream. The weather had been kind, and encountering the goat this morning was another piece of good fortune. Apparently.

"The nearest farm has to be nearly half a mile back upstream," Daniel supposed. "She must have slipped away from the herd. We can have her milked and on her way back to her owner before he ever knows she's gone."

Abigail began to stalk the goat while Daniel rekindled last night's fire. The little creature seemed to laugh at her once more and eyed the bailing bucket in her hand.

She had only ever encountered a goat once and that was as a child when the animal had run at cousin Geoffrey, ramming his shins and sending him flailing into a freshly dug garden bed.

Abigail approached cautiously. She placed the bucket under the goat's hindquarters and, kneeling, hesitated at touching the dangling protuberance.

Sensing someone at her shoulder, Abigail turned to find Marie looking at her quizzically.

"What?" Abigail said, fighting to keep her irritation under control. "Am I doing it wrong?"

Marie merely nodded and stepped forward. The goat let out one last single bleat and remained still as the girl coaxed warm milk into the pail.

Once relieved of her burden, the goat skipped away a few yards and munched on some grass.

"Didn't your mama ever teach you how to milk goats?" Marie asked with artless curiosity.

"No, she did not."

Abigail laughed at the very idea of her mother coming within twenty yards of such a beast. She didn't even like horses, although the family fortune had been made breeding thoroughbreds.

"Didn't she teach you anything useful at all?" the girl asked, her pretty brown eyes wide.

Let's see, Abigail mused to herself. There was dancing…flirting… cards… There was embroidery, no, that was her governess. Coming to the end of her very short list, Abigail shook her head. "No, I don't suppose she did."

When they approached to the fire, the smell of omelet beckoned them forward.

"Don't tell me that you just happened to find a few wayward hens too?" Abigail asked.

Daniel glanced up, winked, and slid the meal onto a tin plate. "The less you know the better," he told her.

Abigail thought better about pursuing the topic. The eggs were delicious and she ate them without comment, but she was pretty sure they weren't chicken or duck.

Soon, they were back in the boat as light drizzle turned to rain.

"Much farther?" asked Abigail, sliding across the bench to give Daniel room as he climbed in. He pulled at the anchor embedded in the soft mud and the vessel shifted, pulled by the current.

"Tired?"

"Mmm hmmm," she agreed.

"Home soon," he promised.

Abigail smiled wanly. It wouldn't do for him to know how tired she was.

She stood and started packing the requirement for their walk and the evening stop. The thought of spending the night sheltered from the elements spurred her on, heedless of dripping hair and mud clinging to the hem of her skirts.

She would have cared before. She would never have left home looking anything other than resplendent and would have been furious to get in such a mess on her travels.

Home was, however, now a place she could barely conceive of. England seemed like a distant memory, although they had only been gone three weeks; Italy was just something she simply once dreamed about.

Home was now an inn, a tunnel, a boat, a riverbank—impermanent and interchangeable.

Home was where Daniel was.

He ran up the sail and, with a sharp snap as it caught the light breeze, the boat moved on.

* * *

The day drew to a close quickly, a weak sunset obscured by clouds that released fits of miserable rain. Daniel had spotted a windmill on a rise a few hundred yards ahead and one look at Abigail and Marie huddled against the drizzle in the bow of the rotting boat was enough to make up his mind to seek better shelter for the night.

The mill was more dilapidated than it first looked, but Daniel knew the crumbling structure would buoy the intrepid group's spirits more than the improvised shelter. The vanes would have been covered in canvas at one time to catch the breeze, now only thin, dirty strips of it wafted in the breeze, rotting on the timber frames. The building itself was in fair condition though. At least the roof was whole.

Inside, each time the wind blew harder, the mill's still-intact gears creaked and groaned at the half-hearted spasms of the vanes. The sounds gave the building a haunted air.

Daniel set a new fire on the dirt floor, and the smoke climbed into the building and escaped in fitful billows through paneless windows. They dressed in the least wet of their clothes and hung everything else up to dry and air.

Hours later, he stood under the lintel of the north-facing mill door. The rain had cleared and the night was clear. The long spray of stars of the Milky Way stretched out like a luminous hand across the sky.

He felt Abigail's presence and turned. She pressed a warm cup into his hand and pulled a shawl over her shoulders.

Daniel thanked her for the warm drink and they looked out at the night together.

"I lost my bearings yesterday, are we facing east?" she asked.

"No. See the large star up there?" he said, pointing to the one at the end of an arc of stars. "It's that one there, the tip of the Ursa Minor."

Abigail wrapped her arms around him and watched him point out the constellations, explaining how it was possible to navigate by the stars.

"So that's not the moon rising over there?" she asked, pointing to a hill about four hundred yards away. It was silhouetted in darkness, but an unmistakable corona rose over it.

Daniel frowned and stepped forward out of Abigail's embrace, away from the building. He looked up at a crescent moon suspended midway up the eastern sky. He looked back to the north. The distinctive glow remained.

The nearest town was miles away so…

He turned back to Abigail.

"Pack up."

"What? Marie's only just gone to sleep."

"Only what you can put in the knapsacks."

Daniel watched to see she had understood the urgency in his voice and, as she turned back into the mill, he strode off toward the hill.

"When you're done, don't wait for me," he called back. "Go straight to the boat and cast off."

Despite the unfamiliar ground and the weak moonlight, Daniel climbed the hill unerringly and, close to its peak, dropped to the ground and hugged the terrain as he scrambled to the very top. He felt the breeze across his back reminding him of his exposed position and lifted himself to his elbows to look out.

Constellations of silver stars above and a constellation of warm yellow lights below, dozens of them dotting the plain before him, confirming his worst fears. They were less than a mile away from a French Republican Army encampment.

Daniel watched them for several minutes, determining how many they were. He assumed they would be headed to Vernon, which meant they would meet head-on as they crossed the river.

He cursed quietly and then considered his options. He had told Abigail to pack and leave. She and the girl would be sailing right past them. Would it be enough? He could draw attention to himself to buy them time, but then it might rouse the French enough to conduct a thorough search.

A twig snapped behind him. Daniel rolled over and onto his feet, pulling out his knife ready for an attack.

Marie rushed forward and into his arms.

A rush of unfamiliar paternal feelings warred with his soldier's instincts for several moments before he enfolded the girl into his embrace.

"What are you doing here?" he asked. "Why aren't you helping Mama-Suzanne to pack?"

The girl looked up at him, her large brown eyes frightened. "There's a bad man."

It took another moment for the words to make sense. His legs reacted before his mind could. He sprinted down the hill and toward the mill.

He heard the man's laughter inside carry over the increased clatter of the gears from the freshening evening breeze and added more speed. The mill's noises masked his arrival at the doorway.

Abigail was backed into a corner by a man twice her size. She held out her knife and had obviously succeeded in fending him off so far, but Daniel knew such a confrontation between mismatched combatants was doomed to be short-lived.

An abandoned tricorn hat with its limp and dirty cockade lay on the floor; beside it a blue jacket removed any doubt the man was a soldier.

The assailant lunged forward with another gale of laughter and grabbed Abigail's wrist, knocking the blade from her hand to the floor.

Fury burned through Daniel as he measured each step separating him from the man he was going to kill.

He moved before Abigail could react and give him away, pulling the attacker back with a left hand around his forehead; his right hand went to the man's chin. He had just enough time to grunt in surprise and stumble back a half-step before Daniel jerked his hands violently left and right. There was a loud crack and the man sagged back against him, gurgling softly. The soldier's dead weight slipped to the floor and his body jerked convulsively for a moment, then stopped moving.

Daniel pulled Abigail away from the wall and her assailant's body. Her vivid gray-green eyes were wide in shock, and he held her firmly in his arms, waiting for her tremors to still. Only when they had ceased did he pull away slightly.

"Are you all right?" he asked. Abigail gave a tremulous nod, then stopped for a large intake of breath. When she next looked up at him, he saw all of her strength and determination in those eyes. His heart swelled and he kissed her.

"Where's Marie?" she asked, and at that moment the girl ran in and rushed to them, throwing her arms around them.

Daniel immediately stood back and looked up at the dilapidated timber stairs rising to the second and third levels of the windmill.

"That man was a forager," he said, cautiously climbing to the mezzanine that housed the gears, "and the glow over the hill is a French army encampment. They're only a mile from here."

Daniel grasped a thin timber railing on the mezzanine, worrying and tugging at it until it broke loose. He dropped it to the floor below where it clattered on the stone.

In answer to Abigail's puzzled face looking up at him, he gave her an explanation as he descended. "When our friend here doesn't return, someone will come looking for him. If it looks like his death was an accident, they may not come looking for us."

"What do you want me to do?"

God, he loved this woman.

"Grab everything—like we were never here," he said and she immediately began gathering their belongings.

"You too, Marie," said Abigail. "We're going back to the boat. Come on, get your things."

Daniel went back to the corpse and dragged it beneath the edge of the mezzanine, then repositioned the broken railing nearby.

He was slinging a full pack on his shoulders when he turned to see the little girl staring at the body on the floor. He scooped her up in his arms and marched toward the door.

"Papa-Rene, is the bad man sleeping?"

"Shhhh," he soothed. "He won't wake up. Everything's going to be all right."

CHAPTER THIRTY-SEVEN

He lied. Daniel stood at the back of the boat with his hand on the tiller. He scanned the river ahead, watching for shallows, then looked down to where Abigail and Marie were huddled asleep in the bow.

He lied about sleeping, he lied about everything being all right, and he lied about being happy having Marie accompany them.

How could he be? This deception would only hold for a small amount of time.

Invading armies or not, Roux would be able to bluster in the right ears at the Assembly and raise enough men to hunt them down. After all, stopping English spies was important for national security. Roux knew of Abigail, he knew she had taken Marie from *Salpêtrière*, and he surely now appreciated the child had some importance in his quest to find Jonathan's missing list. The Frenchman would expect them to take the shortest route to the coast, but was probably buoyed with the knowledge the child was slowing them down and making them obvious.

Now there was a dead man who could still point a finger at them when that weak little "accident" set-up was recognized for what it was.

Daniel wondered who he was trying to fool. They may as well paint targets on themselves. He imagined the days ahead, waiting for the inevitable challenge and arrest. Worse still would be the grinding tension of waiting for the girl, no matter how biddable and bright, to inadvertently give them away.

Daniel sighed. A sham marriage and a sham family. Perhaps his father was right—he was a useless failure, offering less than a man should as husband and father.

He realized he was clenching his jaw and forced himself to relax. He hurt all over. He hadn't mentioned it to anyone, but he thought a rib was cracked under the violet bruise on his side. He'd lied about that little souvenir from his Bicetre beatings too, hiding it from Abigail even through their lovemaking.

He momentarily let go of the tiller to stretch the tired and aching muscles across his back and shoulders. The pain throughout his body added to his mental discomfort, as well as the physical.

Retaking the tiller of the shallow draft vessel, he returned to his musings.

They would reach the town of Vernon by mid-morning. He almost laughed recalling the original plan for extraction.

Five days. Just five days to arrange transportation and journey the one hundred and seventy miles from Vernon to Calais. That is, if they could slip through Rouen, home of the French navy.

Leaving one hand on the tiller, Daniel scrubbed his stubbled chin with the other. The more he pondered the options, the more he could see Percy's rendezvous slip out of reach.

He'd failed. A failure. Everything he touched ended in death. He shuddered in a deep breath.

One step, he reminded himself. Just one step at a time. And the next step was Vernon.

A contact of Blakeney's might still be there. He could be persuaded to take in two extra lodgers while Daniel left to find a safer way out. Perhaps there might be time to find Marie Dubois's relatives.

Then Daniel was struck by inspiration.

He would send Abigail and Marie south.

The more the night wore on and the immediate danger of encountering the French army receded, the more Daniel devoted his mental energy to the plan.

Abigail and Marie could be safely on their way to Marseilles while he lay a false trail to the north. Sailing from Marseilles, they could be in Naples within a couple of days. Safe. And with a new life bought with Abigail's misbegotten fortune.

She could spin any tale she wished about how she became guardian of the child. Yes. That was it!

Alone he had half a chance of making the rendezvous, traveling with Marie and Abigail there was none. So, within twenty-four hours he would be gone, leading Roux a merry dance all the way up to Calais.

And he would never see them again.

He would be walking away from a woman he loved.

The warm satisfaction the plan had given him started to cool. Then it settled in a hard cold lump in his gut.

Marie stirred in her sleep, then opened her eyes and watched him silently.

Daniel ignored her, pretending to concentrate on the rigging as the sail flapped in a stiffening breeze. An involuntary shiver ran through him as the wind cut through his damp clothing.

He was aware of his repeating patterns of behavior. He had walked away from his family when he might have still been able to come to some accommodation with his father. He had walked away from Rachel when he knew his marriage proposal would be accepted. And now he was preparing to walk away from Abigail, a woman he loved with more passion and more depth than he ever could conceive possible.

But this was different, he told himself. He wasn't just sparing their feelings, he was hoping to spare their lives.

Suddenly, Daniel felt a pair of small arms wrap around his hips and the warmth of Marie's body as she hugged herself close to him.

"It's all right. Don't be sad."

"What are you doing awake?" Daniel asked, his voice gruff from a sudden surge of emotion he was trying to tamp down. He brushed a lock of hair from Marie's face and settled a hand on her shoulder.

Marie lifted a hand skywards and pointed to the North Star.

"I spoke to maman and papa in heaven. They are very sad they're not here."

What could he say to the girl? Daniel choked down his own fears at the days ahead.

At the front of the boat, Abigail stirred and sat up. She wrapped a blanket around herself, watching them both.

"I know," he told the child, knowing his words offered woefully inadequate comfort.

"But it's all right," Marie continued, "Jean spoke to them too and said you would take care of us."

Daniel closed his eyes. Dammit, why wouldn't that lump in his throat disappear?

"That's right, Marie," said Abigail softly. The boat rocked slightly as she joined them at the stern. "The three of us are going to be a family. And we'll take care of one another."

The sound of Abigail's warm voice, husky and raw, and the feel of her hand as it slid across his back, eased the ache in Daniel's shoulders as well as his heart. He met her eyes and, even by the insubstantial light of the moon, he could see them shine.

"Don't do this all alone," she whispered to him, easing closer until the hand which had touched his back followed the length of his arm and covered his hand where he held the tiller.

"Let me help. Let *us* help."

The warmth of Abigail and Marie made him realize how damnably cold and exhausted he was.

Suddenly, the sounds of the night surrounded him—the plaintive call of an owl, the rhythmic croaking of frogs and the occasional rustling sounds of water rats foraging on the riverbank or the soft splash of an otter slipping into the water in search of fish.

Daniel found himself swaying on his feet and placed a foot behind to steady himself.

"Marie, make up a comfy bed for Papa-Rene," he heard Abigail instruct.

He opened his eyes once again and saw Marie straightening the blankets that were their bedding.

"Let me take the tiller," Abigail said, squeezing his hand in encouragement.

Letting go was difficult.

"Keep the boat pointed down river and the sail taut," he instructed softly, stepping away from the stern. Abigail furrowed her brow as she took full control of the boat, then nodded, apparently getting a feel for the task.

"Get some sleep," she whispered. "It won't be long until dawn."

Daniel shuffled his way to the bow and settled into the nest of blankets, vaguely aware of Abigail's scent still on them. He closed his eyes and unsuccessfully stifled a yawn. He felt small hands cover his shoulders with the blanket and the child snuggle in beside him.

Tomorrow…tomorrow he would do it.

He would send Abigail and Marie safely on their way south toward Marseilles. He would leave and buy them as much time as he could.

The sound of the water slipping around the hull pulled him toward sleep and he fought it for a moment—a drowning man gasping for the air of conscious thought. It would be easy to let Abigail go, he reasoned with himself. He could be halfway to Amiens before Abigail knew he was even gone.

Let go, he breathed as the call of Morpheus pulled him under.

It would be easy to let them go.

He lied.

* * *

The town of Vernon sat on the banks of the Seine and was busy. Market day brought in farmers from neighboring districts to sell whatever produce they could spare. More commonly these days however, people were selling possessions.

They were among them. Daniel had managed to sell the boat and two of the cases of burgundy by late morning and now he led the way up the slight rise to the inn with the last case on his shoulder and Abigail and Marie trailing behind him.

Across the river, traversed by a medieval stone and wooden bridge, stood the Chateau de Tourelles. The simple square keep buttressed by four cylindrical towers had not been used for defense for more than one hundred and fifty years.

The residents of Vernon ignored the encamped army on the opposite bank and so did Daniel as he haggled a decent price from the innkeeper for the wine. Marie paused to put poupette in her pocket, then stood on a chair, fascinated by the activity she could see through the window.

Abigail joined her, sitting at a table, to watch the view and half listen in on Daniel's conversation with the innkeeper. It had now turned to making inquiries about staying for a couple of nights and where one might purchase a horse.

Abigail was hungry and tired. After nearly four weeks, she missed clean clothes and clean hair, not to mention decent food. She listlessly traced with a finger a groove on the table closest to the windowsill while she watched Marie peer through the window out into the market place.

Tired? No, she was drained. A small voice told her if she had just minded her own business, she could by now be wearing silks and satins, sipping a chilled bianco while she warmed in the Neapolitan sun.

She couldn't resist allowing the thought to play itself out. Then the smell of freshly baked bread, the sharp tang of yellowed cheese followed by a dark fruity aroma of burgundy, brought her back to the present.

Abigail opened her eyes to see the platter of food that had been placed in front of her. She eased Marie down from the bench and had the girl sit beside her.

Light from the window spilled across the table and she could see the carving properly for the first time. It was a series of small five-petalled flowers.

They looked a lot like pimpernels.

When she lifted her head, she found Daniel watching her intently.

"Do you understand the significance?" his eyes seemed to be asking.

Abigail gave him a slight nod, then she turned to cut a piece of bread for Marie.

Despite the realization they might have a moment's rest among friends, there was something amiss.

There had been an edge to Daniel all day. She had put his curtness down to a role he was playing—a disaffected merchant selling the last of his possessions, but still Abigail was glad to have kept Marie occupied during the morning.

Her unasked questions remained so as the inn slowly filled with other diners, and their meal was consumed without a further word being spoken.

Afterwards, Abigail watched Marie playing quietly with her doll. A salt cellar had been adopted as another character in a fantasy conversation between the two inanimate objects.

"Come on," Daniel urged suddenly, picking up Marie and redepositing the salt on the table. Abigail shot him a questioning glance and then saw for herself what concerned him.

Soldiers from the chateau, one of them with a paper in his hand, had entered and were looking about the room.

Abigail saw the innkeeper and Daniel exchange an urgent glance before the innkeeper attracted the attention of the soldiers. A barmaid, aged not more than fifteen, slightly chubby, with a head of riotously curly red hair, placed a hand on Daniel's elbow.

"This way, while Thierry occupies *les militaries*," she whispered.

They eased their way around the room, unobserved in the throng of people who now crowded it. The girl took them into the family quarters. At the end of a passageway, she opened a small storeroom. A shelf in front of them was filled with folded linens.

Their escort eased her hand around one stack and fiddled with something. The intent was clear as a snap of a catch sounded. The shelves swung to the left to reveal another space, a narrow staircase leading up to a clean and comfortable attic bedroom.

"You'll be safe here," the barmaid told Daniel. "I'll come back later with an evening meal, and Thierry will let you know when everything is in place."

"Thank you, Michelle," he murmured as the girl left.

Marie pulled her hand from Abigail's, clapping her hands gleefully as she found a wooden rocking horse. She ran over to it and stroked its mane, then clambered onto its back, setting it in motion.

Abigail looked around the white-washed room, lit by windows angled in from the roof. The bedstead was cast iron, painted white. A sun-faded patchwork quilt rested on top. A small wardrobe and a dressing table, plain but sturdy, and a small drop front desk completed the furnishings.

"Much better than being trapped underground," she said.

Daniel responded with a meager smile. "That's good because you'll be here for a few days at least."

Abigail frowned at his use of the pronoun and was about question him until she heard the sound of footsteps climbing the stairs.

Thierry the innkeeper appeared.

"You are safe, *mes amis*, the soldiers were only placing orders for more provisions," he said with a grin. He carried two large pitchers filled with steaming water and placed them on the dressing table. Water stains on the timber indicated it had doubled as a washstand many times before now.

Behind Thierry another housemaid entered, arms filled with what appeared to be clothes and linens. She placed them on the bed.

"Your arrival was most unexpected," he continued. "We did not have a lot of time to prepare, but with The Pimpernel one learns to deal with the unexpected. This," he said, pointing to the clothes and hot water, "this is easy. The other things you asked for will take a few days to arrange."

"You have our eternal thanks, Thierry," said Daniel, his voice reflecting the tiredness etched clearly on his face.

Thierry shrugged off his expression of gratitude. "We are all in this together, we all play our part."

* * *

Abigail felt clean for the first time since arriving in Paris. She wore a dress and, while it was not one of her own elaborate day dresses, the pretty apple green gown was much better than the peasant frocks she had donned during the past month. The food which had been brought up to them was tasty and filling; the wine, excellent.

And yet despite these comforts, Abigail remained unsettled. Something wasn't right. Daniel was distant and withdrawn. Worse, she was convinced he was keeping secrets from her.

She waited for him to tell her; waited after their host had left; waited until Marie was bathed and dressed, now occupied playing with a spinning top.

Abigail decided she had waited long enough, but experience told her when to hold her tongue and pick her time. She brushed her short hair, wishing not for the first time she hadn't had to cut it, and watched Daniel shave. He was stripped to the waist with a straight razor in his hand and raised to his face.

Now was the time.

"So when were you planning on leaving us?" she asked, setting down the brush.

Daniel's grip on the razor tightened, but he said nothing. Recovering, he drew the blade across his chin.

The satisfaction of guessing correctly lit a spark of anger in Abigail. "Perhaps the middle of the night?"

The dig was enough for him to drop the razor in the bowl, turn, and glare at Abigail.

She matched the look. "I do hope you leave a note. For Marie's sake, if not for mine."

At the sound of her name Marie looked up from her play.

"Papa-Rene is leaving?"

"I don't know," said Abigail. Looking at Daniel, she raised an eyebrow provocatively.

"Is he?"

CHAPTER THIRTY-EIGHT

Marie ran to Daniel and hugged him tightly. "You're going to leave?" she asked again. "But you promised!" Daniel did not respond, instead throwing an irritated look Abigail's way.

The unanswered pause was long enough for Marie to burst into tears. "Maman, Papa, and now you!" she wailed. "Then Mama-Suzanne will leave me and I shall be all alone!"

The child's tears flowed and Abigail felt a pang of regret at her anguish. She approached to stroke Marie's hair. The girl swung away from Daniel and accepted a new comforter, leaving Abigail and Daniel to face each other with only Marie between them.

"You're beneath contempt," Daniel whispered harshly, his face reddening with restrained fury.

"Tell me I'm wrong!" she demanded, but, to her dismay, her voice cracked.

Daniel's incensed expression wavered. He looked down at the sobbing child and back at Abigail.

"Don't you understand? I want you both to be safe," he pleaded, his voice so soft it barely reached her.

Abigail glared at him. "We started this together and we'll finish it together."

The words he had spoken in Bath all those months ago were not forgotten. On hearing them, he closed his eyes.

"What about Naples?" he asked.

"What on earth are you talking about?"

"Your grand plans, Abigail!" At Daniel's explosive exclamation, Marie jumped and Abigail held her even closer. "You told me once nothing else mattered."

His anger was gone. His shoulders slumped and his hands dropped to his side, though his fists clenched and unclenched.

"We have less than four days to get to Le Chat Gris in Calais," he said flatly. She could not hide the look of surprise in her eyes that told him that she had forgotten. "Four days to get the three of us more than one hundred and fifty miles. It's taken us two days so far to get fifty miles out of Paris."

He swallowed, Adam's apple bobbing. "If I head north to Calais and lay a false trail for Roux, you can get yourself and Marie down to Marseille then on the first boat to Naples."

Despite her moment of exhausted weakness only a few hours ago, Abigail hadn't thought seriously of Italy in months. Her furniture was in storage in London and had been ever since she had heard the news of King Louis's arrest. Her head spun with confusion for a moment.

Then it dawned on her what Daniel's plans entailed. She met his searching gaze with one of her own. "What about you? What if Roux captures you again?"

She watched his shoulders sag, his eyes pleading with her.

"What about us?" she asked softly, raising her left hand where his signet ring shone in the light that streamed through the dormer windows. "What about you and me? Or were you just caught up in the moment?"

Daniel stared at the ring on her finger and his eyes brimmed with tears for a moment before he mastered his emotions once more.

In that moment, Abigail's bitterness vanished. Her heart broke at seeing him standing there—no family, filled with fear for those he loved.

"I love *you*, Daniel. Not Naples, not the Beau Monde. Just you."

She reached out and stroked his cheek, surprised he allowed the intimacy of her touch, then wrapped her arms around him. She felt

Marie shift from between them and glanced down as the little girl held them both.

"*You* are the only thing in the world that matters to me, Daniel. Please don't give up on us."

She paused, waiting for him to speak. He did not. Instead, she felt the power of his embrace, his arms around her, and the bare skin of his back under her fingers, warm and real.

* * *

It was agreed. They would leave tomorrow and they would leave *together*. Just four days to reach Calais, Abigail mulled on the matter. Even with the horse and cart that Thierry was obtaining for them, the odds were still tremendous.

Lying on the bed with eyes half closed, Abigail struggled against asleep, instead watching Daniel pore over Jonathan's silk kerchief and its indecipherable hieroglyphics. Even with his own exhaustion apparent in eyes ringed black with lack of sleep, Daniel refused her invitation to join her in bed.

"If we miss the rendezvous, we need an incentive for Percy to come back for us," he told her. He didn't need to tell her how much more dangerous it would be if they were forced to fend for themselves.

How much later she did not know, but the sound of whispered conversation woke her. She kept her eyes closed and listened.

"But *why*? That's a three and that's a four, so they go together like this and this."

"That's not the way the game is played," Daniel explained patiently. "You have to have a red card and then a black card."

"That's a stupid rule. I don't want to play *anymore*."

Abigail opened her eyes and rolled on her side to see Marie throw the playing card to the floor. The child went to the corner of the room where she picked up her doll and started changing its dress, her back to Daniel.

"That's what you get for trying to teach your daughter to gamble," Abigail chided.

"Patience is a perfectly respectable game," Daniel replied, and she softened the admonishment with a smile as she sat up on the bed.

"Did you get any further with decoding Jonathan's message?"

Daniel huffed a sigh of frustration and glanced at the desk where the silk was spread out. "I've tried every combination I can think of and still nothing," he said. "There are some obscure mathematical angles I haven't tried yet…what?"

"Mathematics?"

"Yes. All codes have a numerical or symbolic basis," he explained. "It's all about finding the key. But if you don't know where to begin, you're just stumbling 'round in the dark."

Abigail felt the deep frustration in his voice. If the code could not be broken, even if they made it safely to Calais and away to England, they would go having risked their lives and endured so much, but failed.

There was a sudden clatter of wood-on-wood and a rolling sound.

"Oh!" said Marie in dismay.

Abigail and Daniel looked at her. She held up poupette.

"Her head came off…"

Indeed, Marie's doll was without its head.

Abigail spotted it first. It had rolled eccentrically across the floorboards and under the rocking horse. She picked it up and examined its hand-carved features.

"Fix her for me," Marie pleaded. When Abigail turned around, the doll's body was in Daniel's hands. He stared at it silently.

"I've got the head here," said Abigail. "It should just push back on."

She held it out to Daniel, but his attention remained on the decapitated doll. His expression was odd.

Did he think of Jonathan when he looked at it, of his lost friend who had made it? Or of the executions he had witnessed in the past? Perhaps it was the soldier he killed to save her life?

She watched his brow furrow even more deeply. Was that somehow tied up with the reason he had wanted to leave her, that for her he had been forced to take another human being's life with his bare hands?

"Abigail…"

There was an edge to his voice, and he didn't look at her.

"Yes?" she replied uncertainly.

"Can you get me a needle?"

He rose as she did, but he drew his chair over by the writing desk where the light was stronger and sat down, still examining poupette.

A needle? He didn't need a needle to fix the doll—just pop the head back on. Abigail was beginning to think it would be quicker if she just did it herself. Nevertheless, she rummaged around until she found her etui, extracted a needle, and handed it to him.

Daniel plied the needle down the hole in the centre of the doll's torso, pressing the point in, then pulling it back. After several attempts he brought out the needle with what appeared to be matchstick stuck on the end. Something was wound around it.

"Is that…?"

Daniel gently unwound a strip of fine onionskin paper from around the sliver of wood, smoothing it across the writing slope where it tried to curl back up. He held it down at each end.

When he turned to her, his eyes were wide, brighter, and more alive than they had been in the two weeks since learning of Jonathan's death.

"His final message to us, Abigail. The key. It's been with us all along."

He let go of the strip and it coiled again on the desktop like a spring, unable to forget its shape. As he stood, Abigail threw her arms around him.

Daniel rained kisses down on her head and cheeks. His lips were about to descend on hers when she felt a tug at her waist. A little face peered up at her and one hand clutched a fistful of her skirt and another a handful of Daniel's jacket.

"Can I have poupette back, *please*?"

* * *

The onion skin scroll was a mere three inches long and perhaps less than a half inch wide. It was so finely inscribed that Daniel spent an hour laboriously copying its contents so he could read it without straining. The day had all but disappeared, and he now worked by lamplight, dressed in a linen nightshirt.

Marie lay fast asleep on a cot, holding her restored doll to her chest.

Abigail herself was dressed for bed in a simple linen nightdress. She suppressed a yawn and leaned over Daniel's shoulder, trying to make sense of the writing in front of him.

It looked like a mathematical formula and she commented as much. Daniel took her hand from his shoulder and kissed it.

"It is," he told her, "but it makes no sense without the key."

"How do you know which letters hold the key?"

"That was the genius of what he did. Instead of just relying on encrypting an alphabet, Jonathan hid it further by using another code. It's a very clever variation of the Vigenere cipher. It's not just one code. It's six."

He pulled out another sheet of paper, which at first appearance seemed to be an exact copy of the letters on the silk, but instead of many continuous lines of letters, Daniel had broken it down into many dozens more, all starting with the same six letter combination.

"That's the cipher key."

"So does that mean you've cracked the code if you know what symbol corresponds to what letter?"

"Not quite…" Daniel tapped on the algebraic formula in front of him. "Each time you see the code pattern—the key—the alphabet shifts again. Each row starts with a key letter. In this case the first letter is 'I.'"

"How do you know?"

"Ah," he grinned. "I'm getting to that. For successive letters of the message, we take successive letters of the key string, and decipher each message letter using its corresponding key row."

Abigail blinked rapidly, trying to make sense of what he was telling her and feeling sure she was only grasping the rudiments. Another yawn came upon her and this one she didn't try to hide.

"I suppose it makes sense, but I still don't understand how you've worked it out."

"Jonathan put a third code on top, one that relied on something only he and I knew."

Abigail tapped her feet, her patience coming to the end. "Get on with it will you? I swear you're worse than Blakeney with all of his theatrics."

Daniel rose from his seat with a grin and took Abigail's hands one at a time, kissing them and placing them around his shoulders, before kissing her on the side of her mouth.

"Before I could understand the Vigenere code, I had to break a second one, the Baconian code," he said.

"Bacon as in Sir Francis Bacon?"

"You're a clever woman. That's why I love you." This time his lips met hers, soft and warm. Abigail savored the lingering taste of bitter coffee on them.

"Knowing it was a Baconian code reminded me of a conversation Jonathan, Rachel, and I had over supper one night after going to see the Boydell Shakespeare Gallery."

"About Bacon being the author of Shakespeare's plays?"

"Umm-hmm," Daniel affirmed, nuzzling her hair and running his hands seductively across her back. "There was one of Shakespeare's lesser known plays in which, it has been said, Bacon inserted an anagram of his name. The play was Cymbeline."

"I don't know that one," Abigail said, reveling in Daniel's touch as she dropped light kisses across his freshly stubbled chin.

"Few people do. We prided ourselves on our arcane knowledge and thought we were very clever. At any rate, that was the clue. The six letter name of the heroine was the six Vigenere cipher key—Imogen."

Daniel planted openmouthed kisses over her hair, her face, her neck. "Remind me to tell you the story of Imogen. I think you'll like her. She reminds me of you."

Abigail pressed herself closer, feeling the need to touch him. She felt him stir to life as they continued to kiss. Cool air caressed her calf, then her knee as she realized that the hem of her nightdress was being raised inch-by-inch.

"Shouldn't you, ah, finish?" she breathed, but the remainder of her thought vanished like the ether as Daniel reached a sensitive spot on her neck, just below her earlobe.

"I haven't even started yet," his answer rumbled in her ear.

As though they danced, Daniel advanced and Abigail retreated until they stood as one at the bed. Daniel pulled back the covers. Soon they were cocooned in soft cotton sheets, her back to his chest, and Abigail's nightdress crept higher up her legs.

Soon Daniel was touching her skin to skin. One of his hands roamed freely along her thighs, across her belly, and higher where his fingers played and caressed the underside of her breasts.

His other arm held her to his chest while he freely kissed her, touching her, bringing such pleasure and yet how she was positioned against him she couldn't reach, couldn't touch—only feel. Her fingers clutched the sheets.

Daniel seemed to sense her unease and he whispered seductively into her ear. "Shhhh, let me touch you." And he did, but his caress added to her restlessness. She rubbed her bottom against him. Daniel was satisfyingly hard against her cheeks.

His hand fell between her legs and they parted, warm and ready to receive him.

"Daniel, please," she begged as his fingers stirred up the urgency within her, the blossoming of a deep pleasure beginning to radiate from her core.

She guided him into her, rocking her hips to draw him ever closer.

"Abigail, my love," Daniel whispered. They held each other like that for what to Abigail seemed like an eternity of anticipation, then he stroked her as he rocked and they fell into a rhythm that brought pleasure crashing over her in waves.

Suddenly his hand clamped over her mouth, and Abigail cried into it again and again as the hard length of him filled her, plunging again and again until his own release came with a hoarse cry.

CHAPTER THIRTY-NINE

I t was a little before dawn when Thierry knocked urgently on the door. Daniel was instantly awake, so too was Abigail, unlike that night in Paris where she had been slower to recognize their danger.

He heard her slip behind a screen to rapidly dress. When she emerged he was alone.

"News from the garrison," he told her. "They're expecting the arrival of Colonel Roux this morning."

Guided by Thierry by low lamplight, they stayed on their side of the river, avoiding the garrison, and walked a mile before they encountered another man holding the bridle of a sturdy horse, already in harness to a wagon.

The pre-dawn gray lightened as long thin rays from the morning sun pushed their way over the hill. Abigail tucked a still sleeping Marie into blankets in a corner of the wagon, steadying herself when the vehicle tilted as Daniel climbed aboard.

"I refuse to say au revoir, my friend," Thierry told him, accepting an outstretched hand and pumping it firmly. "We will see you and your lovely family again under better circumstances, God willing. Go, put many miles away from here as you can!"

Daniel counted it fortunate to make Rouen by nightfall, a journey of nearly fifty miles.

The following day, starting before dawn, they had made equally good distance, which by his reckoning put them a few miles short of Abbeville by the time he decided it was too dark and too dangerous to continue.

As he unharnessed the cart, he watched Abigail deftly set and light a small compact fire, a new skill to add to her repertoire. Marie too aided in setting up camp, and a strange feeling washed over him. As he brushed the horse's coat, he pondered it until finally he knew its name.

It was belonging.

...And all the responsibilities that went with it, the small demons of doubt started to whisper, but he quelled them when Abigail looked up at him and smiled. Marie too noticed, and gave him a grin.

Daniel returned it fully, and joined *his family* by the fire.

Later into the evening, after they had eaten and prepared for the next morning's journey, he and Abigail sat by the flames. Marie slept with her head on his lap and he found himself absently stroking the girl's hair. He was content and allowed himself the luxury of thinking of the future. There were the engineering works in Cornwall and work to do to make a working locomotive engine.

"Penny for your thoughts," Abigail whispered.

He chuffed, remembering he had said the same thing to her what seemed a lifetime ago back in Bath.

"Just thinking about what waits us in England," he said.

Daniel waited for a follow up question, but there was none. The silence stretched out so he turned. Although the fire burned brightly, she nonetheless prodded it absently with a stick; a beautiful face, without artifice, needed no jewels, just the gold from the firelight that now painted her skin.

He closed his eyes once more and in his mind he started calculations on steam pressure, valve size, and piston length.

Abigail seemed unusually quiet the next day, but Daniel couldn't really fault her. Tomorrow night was the new moon. This was the final day, the last roll of the dice. He was gambling with their future and possibly their lives.

They encountered many more travelers on road toward Calais and he noted that Marie shied away from the increasing crowds. Worse, there had been soldiers in the towns and villages they passed and they made *him* nervous. Every one of those blue-jacketed crapauds, a reminder Roux closing in on them.

Pressing on through the afternoon through less populated country byways was difficult enough without the pace slowed further by the harsh afternoon sun right in his eyes. He sweated profusely and pushed his cap lower to soak up the damp that threatened leak over his brow.

Blessed relief came from a thicket alongside the road that blocked the sun.

"Daniel?"

Abigail's breathy appeal pulled him out of his solo ruminations. He glanced at her, then followed her gaze back to the road.

Four soldiers waited.

"As we agreed," he whispered between his teeth. He didn't need to look to know Abigail was ready.

Daniel stood and raised his hands in the air and dropped down from the cart and approached. Abigail had the decoded lists sewn into her dress. Her cloak contained the last of their coins and, for what it was worth, a small single-shot pistol. At the first sign of trouble he would do everything in his power to buy them time. She was to run with Marie and never look back.

He continued closer, looking at each man in turn, deciding who he would take on first. Odd, he frowned, that the soldiers remained at ease. The one in the middle even grinned.

"I made Percy a bet you'd be in Calais by morning," said Sir Phillip Glynde, removing his hat and sketching a bow, not to him, but to Abigail who stood at his side. "And I don't like to lose a bet."

Daniel watched the way the strong, fast yacht, Sir Percy Blakeney's *Daydream*, plowed through the choppy Channel waters churned white by stiff south-westerly winds. Salt-laden air billowed around him and his lungs were filled with the tang of it.

He had been out here for more than an hour since they had left the shores of France, watching the beach recede. He needed solitude, a chance to say a final good-bye to Jonathan, who had been like a brother to him.

Daniel bowed his head, letting it rest on the railing, and the Lament of King David filled his thoughts.

How are the mighty fallen in the midst of the battle! O Jonathan, thou wast slain in thine high places.

I am distressed for thee, my brother Jonathan: very pleasant hast thou been unto me: thy love to me was wonderful, passing the love of women.

How are the mighty fallen, and the weapons of war perished!

Daniel wondered how he was going to tell Rachel.

Sir Percy had offered to break the news, but Daniel could not allow that, even knowing how difficult it would be. He owed it to Jonathan.

He imagined the look in Rachel's eyes, filled with sorrow and genuine grief because, no matter what, she had loved Jonathan dearly. But afterwards he knew he would see something else in those eyes. Oh, she would mourn Jonathan as a good widow should, behind a black veil and with all propriety observed, but in her gaze would be an expectant hope, never voiced—oh no, Rachel would never be so forward—but there nonetheless, a silent invitation to recapture the promise of their past and raise Jonathan's son together.

Blakeney had accepted the decoded names of French resistance fighters with great interest in the tap room of Le Chat Gris at Calais. In the hours before the tide changed, they had discussed how best to aid the loyalists.

And Sir Percy had something for him. Daniel found pressed in his hand a letter from his brother, now the Viscount Pemberley, asking for a family reconciliation.

Daniel hadn't been to the family pile for what seemed like an eternity. To go back now would smack of victory for the old man, but then, on the other hand, a reconciliation with his brothers at this point would have his father spinning in his grave.

The thought of that made Daniel smile wryly.

Behind him there was a small cough—enough to alert Daniel to Abigail's presence.

He turned and watched her approach him tentatively. She stopped six feet away and it seemed like a mile.

Daniel's eyes flickered across her form. The peasant dresses were gone; she was now dressed befitting a lady, wrapped in a warm cloak. Even so, face free from powders, her blonde hair clean again, her form free of restrictive stays, no one could be more lovely than the woman who had accompanied him on the mad dash across France.

Beautiful, brave Abigail, a woman who had risked her very life for him. He would look forward to seeing that beaming smile on her face, dazzling the room with her beauty and grace, instead of the pensive expression with which she currently surveyed him.

Over her arm was a cloak for him.

"You've been out here for a while, I thought you might be cold."

He might have been, until her warm, rich voice thawed the ice that had started to freeze around his heart. Abigail had changed him, made him feel things he hadn't expected to feel—real love, acceptance, peace.

Did she feel the same now they were safe? They had until the end of the voyage to find out. Blakeney had made it clear Daniel would be welcome to stay in his current "employment." The decision rested on the woman in front of him.

He reached out to her and Abigail extended her hand in turn without drawing any closer. Their fingertips touched briefly as he took the coat from her. He shoved his arms though the sleeves, but didn't feel any warmer as she kept her distance.

* * *

Daniel may as well have been standing on the far retreating shore as only across the few feet of decking that separated them.

Blakeney's arrival had cast a pall between them. Perhaps it was the letter Sir Percy brought with him. Was it from the newly widowed Rachel Sawyer?

"We need to talk about what happens when we get to England," she said, rotating over and over the signet ring she wore on her left hand.

Men didn't marry women like her—not really. They preferred good-natured, easy-going, *biddable* wives. Women like Rachel Sawyer. In a year's time, after the period of mourning, Abigail would be reading their engagement notice.

She would fight for Daniel's very life, but she wouldn't fight for his heart if it wasn't hers.

She caught him watching her fidgeting and stopped hiding the hand beneath the folds of her cloak.

She looked down at the ring, then back up at Daniel. "Should I return it?" she inquired.

"It depends."

Her brows furrowed in annoyance. "On what?"

"On whether you would do the whole thing over again," he said, glancing back out to sea where the last of the French coast was disappearing from view. Abigail wasn't sure whether he expected an answer so she remained silent.

"You have a choice ahead of you," Daniel continued. "This could be the beginning of your grand adventure in Europe. Just think—Lady Abigail Houghall, the most famous expatriate hostess of the entire Continent with exciting stories to tell enraptured and enamored guests."

He moved away from the railing to stand by a cabin wall in the lee of the wind and ran a hand through his hair to smooth it. Abigail followed him.

"I'm not the only one with a choice," said Abigail, and she jumped at the sound of her own voice now it was not being blown away by the wind. "There is a perfectly lovely, respectable young widow waiting for you back in London. A woman who should have been your wife from the start. You could be raising a son you might have had together."

Daniel took half a step back as though he had suffered a blow. His lips, normally quick to a wry smile, were now bloodless and thin.

"You reminded me in Vernon that I had a wife and a daughter," he answered, his voice hard-edged and sharp like shingle on a beach. He leaned in so his eyes were level with hers. "Did you change your mind?"

"That was different and you know it!"

She forced her hands to unclench the dark blue wool of her cloak. The gold ring felt loose and heavy on her frigid fingers. Abigail turned her head to compose herself and allowed the wind to tug the hair from her face.

"I learned my lesson three years ago, Daniel. I'm not going to fight for a man who doesn't want to stay. A man who has had foisted upon him obligations not of his choosing..."

"No."

"Was that supposed to be an answer?" Abigail snapped. "Forgive me if I've forgotten the question."

Daniel sighed and folded his arms.

"Enough of this," he said at length. "Do you love me? Do you love me enough to keep the vows we made three weeks ago? Because as far as I'm concerned we're already married. We married that day beneath Paris, and it was a moment more sacred to me than a ceremony in Westminster Cathedral itself. I'm asking you the question: Do you love me enough to stay?"

Abigail blinked away the salt-laden wind that blurred her vision and made her eyes water.

"Yes," she whispered, "and I will love you always."

Daniel stepped forward and enfolded her in his arms. Relief crashed over her like the waves against the side of the yacht.

"Where we make a life together is our home," said Abigail. "That is enough for me. That is more than enough."

THE END

About The Author

Elizabeth Ellen Carter's first novel, *Moonstone Obsession*, was shortlisted for the Romance Writers' of Australia Emerald Award for Best Unpublished Manuscript prior to its publication in 2013.

Her next novel, *Warrior's Surrender* (2014), won the Readers and Writers Down Under 2015 Readers' Choice Award for Favourite Historical Fiction.

Carter has subsequently won praise and a wide readership for her highly researched historical romance adventures including a number of series and standalone novels.

Her titles *Dark Heart*, *Revenge of the Corsairs*, and *Live And Let Spy* were nominees for InD'tale Magazine's RONE Awards. The novella *Nocturne* was named one of the most anticipated titles of 2016 by Australian Romance Today.

Carter can be found online at www.eecarter.com

Captive of the Corsairs
by Elizabeth Ellen Carter

Book One in The Heart of the Corsairs Trilogy

Bluestocking Sophia Green's future is uncertain. Orphaned as a child and raised by the wealthy Cappleman family, she has become the companion to her attractive younger cousin, Laura, while harboring to her breast an unrequited love for Laura's diffident brother.

Sea captain Kit Hardacre's past is a mystery – even to him. Kidnapped by Barbary Coast pirates at the age of 10, he does not remember his parents or even his real name. All he recalls are things he would rather forget.

When Laura's reputation is threatened by a scandal, Sophia suggests weathering the storm in Sicily with their elderly uncle, a prominent archaeologist. Their passage to Palermo is aboard Hardacre's ship, but the Calliope, like its captain, is not all it seems. Both have only one mission – to rid the world of the evil pirate slaver Kaddouri or die in the attempt.

Initially disdainful of the captain's devil-may-care attitude, Sophia can't deny a growing attraction. And Kit begins to see in her a woman who could help him forget the horrors of his past.

Sophia allows herself to be drawn into the shallows of Kit's world, but when the naive misjudgment of her cousins sees Laura abducted, Sophia is dragged into dangerous depths that could cost her life or her sanity in a living hell.

"A thrill-packed read!" – *Romance Reviews Magazine*

"Elizabeth Ellen Carter knows how to write very believable characters and situations that keeps you wanting more." – *Marianne Bair*

Also in this series:
Revenge of the Corsairs (Heart of the Corsairs Book Two)
Shadow of the Corsairs (Heart of the Corsairs Book Three)

Available exclusively on Amazon from Dragonblade Publishing

DARK HEART
BY ELIZABETH ELLEN CARTER

Can love survive a dark heart?

Rome, 235 A.D. A series of ritual murders of young boys recalls memories of Rome's most wicked emperor. Magistrate Marcus Cornelius Drusus has discovered the cult extends to the very heart of Roman society.

Despite his personal wealth and authority, Marcus is a slave to his past – conflicted by his status as an adopted son, bitterly betrayed by his wife and forced to give up his child.

Kyna knows all about betrayal. Sold into slavery by her husband to pay a gambling debt, she found herself in Rome, far from her home in Britannia. Bought by a doctor, she is taught his trade and is about to gain her freedom when her mentor is murdered by the cult.

When the same group makes an attempt on her life, Kyna is forced to give up her freedom and accept Marcus' protection. With no one to trust but each other, mutual attraction ignites into passion. But how far will Marcus go for vengeance when he learns the cult's next victim is his son?

Can the woman who is free in her heart heal the man who is a slave in his?

Live and Let Spy
by Elizabeth Ellen Carter

The King's Rogues Book One

England, 1804: Refused his rightful promotion, Adam Hardacre quits the Royal Navy in disgust and is quickly approached with an intriguing proposition to serve his country undercover.

His first assignment takes him home to Cornwall to expose traitors plotting a French invasion of England. There, he meets newly unemployed governess Olivia Collins, who has stumbled upon a hidden secret from Adam's past – his youthful summer love affair with the local squire's daughter. It is a tragic history that brings Adam and Olivia closer than is wise.

However, with the attraction deepening to something more, neither realize that Olivia unwittingly holds the key to his mission.

As Adam infiltrates the plot, Olivia finds out the shocking truth behind his lost love's death many years ago, and both their lives are in danger. But their growing relationship is clouded by suspicion. Who can and cannot be trusted – anyone or no one?

Or... even each other?

"Exciting and romantic. I couldn't put it down!" – *Kristin Nielsen*

"A lively account of mystery, hidden secrets, wonderful characters, romance, and, of course, spies. This is one you do not want to miss." – *Barbara Michael*

"Adventure and mystery and a love that overcomes tragedy." – *Beth Meador*

Also in this series:
Spyfall (The King's Rogues Book Two)
Spy Another Day (The King's Rogues Book Three)
Father's Day

Available exclusively on Amazon from Dragonblade Publishing

WARRIOR'S SURRENDER
BY ELIZABETH ELLEN CARTER

A shared secret from their past could destroy their future...

Northumbria, 1077. In the years following William the Conqueror's harrying of the North, Lady Alfreya of Tyrswick returns to her family home after seven years in exile. But instead of returning victorious as her dead father had promised, she returns defeated by Baron Sebastian de la Croix, the Norman who rules her lands. To save her gravely ill brother's life, Alfreya offers herself hostage to her enemy.

When Alfreya gets to know her new husband, she finds he's not the monster she feared, and their marriage of convenience soon becomes a bond of passion. But Sebastian is a man with a secret – one that could destroy him.

As a series of brutal murders haunt their nights, the man who betrayed Alfreya's father returns, claiming to be her betrothed. He has learned Sebastian's secret and will use it and Sebastian's own family to further his own ambition – to destroy Sebastian, mark him a traitor, and plunge an unprepared England into war with the Scots...

"Plenty of action and even a touch of the supernatural which adds an interesting layer to the story. Ms Carter gathers together an interesting cast of secondary characters but the one who really stands out is the villainous, cunning and truly diabolical Drefan...a formidable enemy." – *Rakes & Rascals*

"Warrior's Surrender surpassed my expectations. The research and authenticity of settings, events, and characters was superb." – *Wordfrenzy*

"A complex, page-turning thriller that is also a story of resilience, rebuilding, and finding love. Without using any modern psycho-babble, Carter creates a terrifying villain who is quite obviously a psychopath." – *Lolly Russell*

"For those who like a generous but tasteful splash of hot and spicy in their romance, but also value a well-researched, historically accurate setting and an engaging story, Warrior's Surrender is a great find. Ms Carter's writing reminds me of Georgette Heyer." – *Story Enthusiast*

Available in ebook and print at your favourite online book retailer.